ONE COG TURNING

To Sue   *7th Signing!*

All the Best

AJ LAKEN

Text Copyright © 2017 AJ Laken
Cover Design 2017 Mark Hanley

First published by Luna Press Publishing, Edinburgh, 2017

One Cog Turning ©2017. All rights reserved. No part of this publication may be reproduced, stored in a retrieval system, or transmitted in any form or by any means, electronic, mechanical, photocopy, recording or otherwise, without prior written permission of the copyright owners. Nor can it be circulated in any form of binding or cover other than that in which it is published and without similar condition including this condition being imposed on a subsequent purchaser.

www.lunapresspublishing.com

ISBN-13: 978-1-911143-22-2

ACKNOWLEDGMENT

Many thanks to the Luna team for turning my dream of being published into a reality. Also Kat Harvey for her amazing editorial skills. Thanks also to my friends and family for their support; in particular Sarah who read the story first and stopped it going down a wrong path, Adam and Keith for listening to the germ of this story and encouraging me to continue, and finally Mark for creating an awesome cover. Hopefully I haven't missed anyone!

To Sarah and Reid

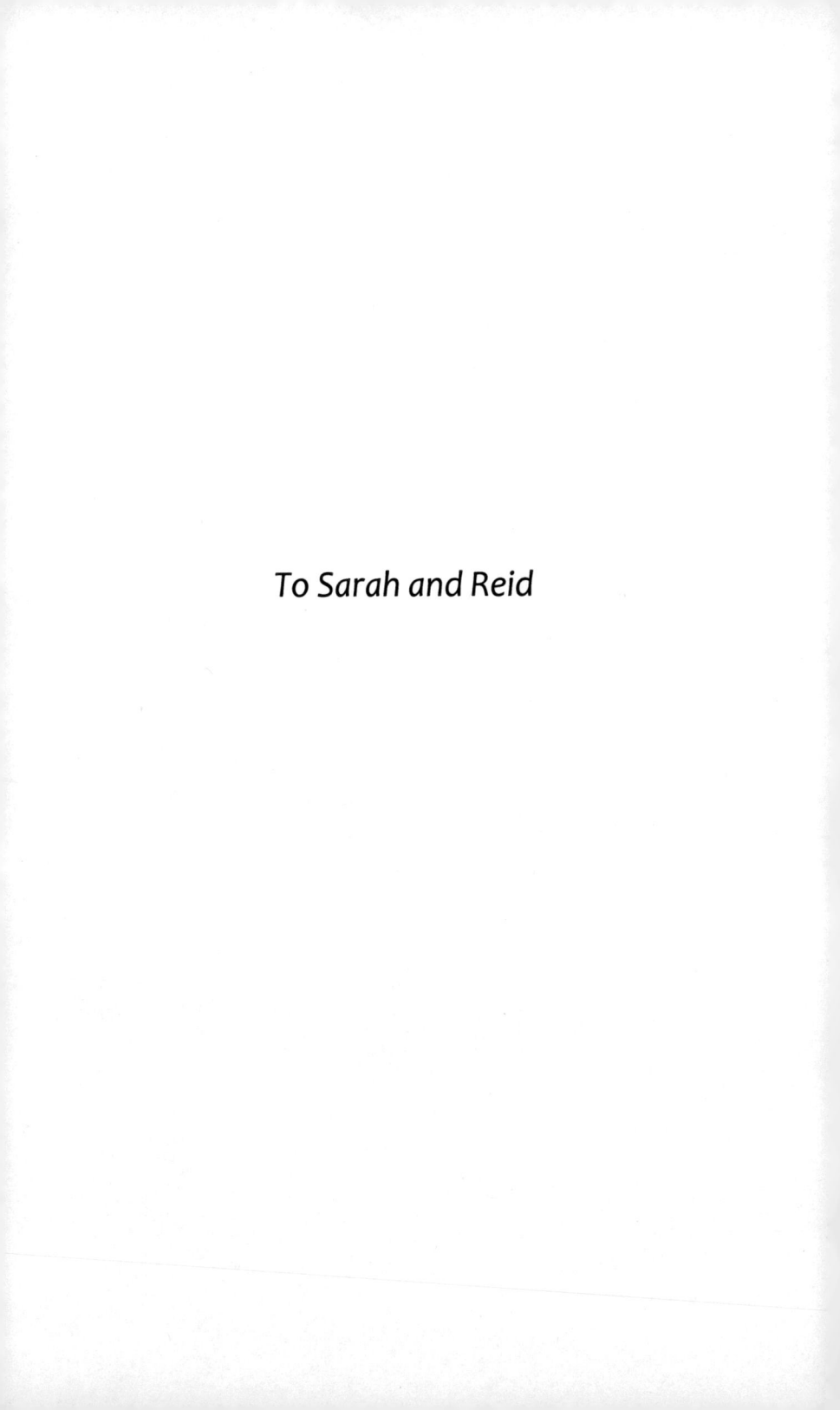

1

The stifling heat of the jungle made the young girl's tunic cling to her body like a drowning man to a rock. Beads of sweat ran down her face and back, mimicking the droplets of moisture dripping from the impossibly large foliage. The beach wasn't much further now but she was already anticipating what was coming next. With well-practised ease she sidestepped a hidden floor net. She heard a faint click when her foot touched the ground and ducked as a blade barely missed her head, taking with it a few strands of her raven black hair. *Well played old man*, she thought. *You have made improvements.*

She crept forward five more cautious feet. Then she heard it. A slithering sound, grotesque and unnerving accompanied by branches snapping. The hydrabasilisk appeared before her. Ten eyes peered down from five heads connected to a body fifteen feet in length. The serpent was twice the circumference of a twilight oak, covered in scales as hard as diamonds.

A spear appeared in her hand instantaneously; the jet black of the onyx blade glinting in the few rays of sun that could penetrate the jungle's canopy. Knowing the scene would look ludicrous to any observer, the girl let a smile cross her face. Slight, of average height, barely eighteen years of age, she crouched before one of the most fearsome creatures in the world. The advantage was hers though; she had fought this beast before and knew where to strike.

Lightning quick, she feinted left and spun round to the right, one of the heads snapping ferociously into the space she had vacated. She dodged sideways as the beast's left head curved towards her. From the corner of her eye she saw the middle head make a vicious dart forward. She crouched low and rolled, hearing the satisfying crack when the two skulls collided together. This was not enough though. Until dead, the beast would pursue her relentlessly. Mercy had been her undoing last time.

She swung herself onto the back of the creature and stabbed the blade into one of the hydrabasilisk's poison sacks at the base of its necks. The creature ululated in pain as the greyish green liquid poured out. Its poison was more erosive than acid and dissolved anything on contact — well, almost anything; there was a reason she had chosen the onyx spear. She slid down the monster's back, struggling for footing whilst it writhed in agony. With the poison coating the tip of her weapon she plunged the spear into her adversary's spine. The serpent unleashed one last burst of energy and she was flung from its back, skittering to a halt at the base of a nearby tree. She watched with a mixture of fascination and horror as the monster's flesh bubbled and fell from its bones. After contemplating her victory for a few seconds, she turned and carried on down the jungle path.

Before long she stepped from the end of the path onto the pulsating silver of a beach. It was only the second time she had made it this far after almost a year of effort. The cool breeze from the ocean felt exquisite after the oppressive humidity of the jungle. She allowed herself a moment to breathe deeply and enjoy the sensation of the wind blowing through her hair. Then she turned to face the castle.

It rose up at the end of the crescent-shaped bay, nestled at the feet of the dark mountains, its flying buttresses and gothic spires reminiscent of an eagle guarding its nest. It was a dramatic sight, like the castles in many of the tawdry romance novels so popular in the Estrian Empire. *The old man does have a flair for that sort of thing.*

She crossed the beach quickly, the fortress growing ever bigger in her vision, until she stood but sixty paces from its doors. In half a heartbeat, they swung open and fifty armoured knights poured out. The knights assumed battle formation. Shield bearers and spear carriers lined up first, behind them the swordsmen. They began to steadily advance towards her. When they had covered a distance of twenty feet she called forth her own forces. A hundred knights of sand rose from the ground, the shield bearers forming a tight square around her.

When she moved forward, the castle knights attacked savagely but their efforts were futile. For every stab, thrust and slash that found its mark the sand soldiers merely reformed themselves and continued their remorseless assault until all the defenders were strewn at their feet. She covered the last few steps to the castle and let her warriors dissolve back into their rightful home.

No sooner were they gone, the old man appeared before her. He was tall, rangy and in his mid-fifties. Close-cropped grey hair covered his scalp, atop a head criss-crossed with scars. His dark blue, military uniform was impeccably smooth.

'Well met, Lady Bellina.'
'Well met indeed, Master Alcastus.'
'Shall we retire then?' He enquired.
'Yes, let's.'

*

Bellina's eyes flew open and she felt the familiar ringing in her ears that followed a cognopathic disconnection. As the room in the real world came back into focus she noticed the immaculate tea service that lay before her — the silver teapot from Narvale, the fine bone china cups from Chenta and dark lumps of crystallised sugar, that and the tea both from far flung Mandira — all the luxuries that the privileged of Estria had come to expect thanks to the domination of their merchants and traders. She pressed the back of her hand lightly against the pot and felt the sharp sting of its heat, reminding her that her psychic journeys, though they felt like hours, only lasted a few minutes.

Bellina looked across the table and her dark green eyes met the misty blue of the master's. *Let's return to a more mundane form of communication*, his voice echoed in her head. With the press of a button on the palm of his glove, the glowing ruby and emerald on the gold choker around his neck began to dim showing that his cognopathic and thought-projection powers were now shut off. She looked down at the ornate platinum bracelet on her left arm. An eagle sat at the heart of it, she watched the ruby on its forehead and the emerald in its left talons dim in synchronicity. The sapphire in its other claw remained aglow, allowing her to retain access to her cognokinetic powers; she noticed Alcastus had left his active as well.

Throughout Estrian history, only a handful of cognopaths had been allowed access to their power restraint controls. It was another reminder of the power and rank Alcastus held as Head of Cognopathic Development. Although he could never remove the magically bonded restraint, something only the Emperor in his role as Holder of the Keys was empowered to do, it was still a privilege — one that did not extend to Bellina, even as the daughter of the Lord Chancellor.

'Shall I be mother?' Alcastus asked politely.
'Certainly, Master, the break would be most welcome.'
The silver pot levitated from the table and poured a stream of pale

brown liquid into Bellina's cup.

'Would two lumps suit, my lady?'

She smiled sweetly and nodded. *It would suit this lady to boil the eyeballs from your skull, you stinking goatherd.* Bellina savoured the thrill and relief of an unguarded thought. The cups levitated in front of both of their faces and Bellina took hers delicately with the correct extension of her little finger, as Madame Matresca had instructed her. She took a dainty sip of tea and sat her cup down while Alcastus swirled the fluid around his mouth in well-practised fashion before smacking his lips with contentment.

'Ah, hints of lemon, Varashi tobacco and blue teak. If I'm not mistaken this could only have been grown on the slopes of Mount Lindris, in the southern part of Mandira. A rare blend made even rarer by the growing animosity from Burkesh.'

'It is one of my father's personal favourites, Master.' *Will your blathering ever cease, you old twit.* She knew the lesson would not be concluded until Alcastus had reviewed and graded her performance, and his prattling could go on for hours.

'Well then! He is a man of excellent taste as well as wise judgement. Will you set us down, my lady, so we can conduct your review?'

The table and chairs, which had been levitating ten feet in the air under Bellina's power, glided smoothly to the floor. As always, Alcastus cleared his throat before delivering his verdict. 'Your navigation of the swamp was masterful, as was the traverse of the jungle. You avoided all my traps, even the new additions!' At this he gave a small chuckle.

'One was almost my undoing.'

'Almost is not success, but you remained alert enough to bypass it. Your defeat of the hydrabasilisk was thorough, though a little crude for my taste. But your use of the sand warriors to counter my knights was inspired and difficult to pull off. You must have an exceptional teacher!' Another laugh.

'I have been incredibly lucky to have been instructed by a cognopath of some renown,' Bellina replied, inwardly screaming in exasperation.

'All of this accomplished while keeping us levitated and fending off my own attempts at reaching your psychic centre — the maze was an exquisite addition by the way. It meant I could only spare the energy for fifty soldiers.' He paused dramatically. 'You are the first student to reach the gates of my castle for many years and, I have to say, it was truly a bravura performance!'

'You are too kind, Master.' Bellina cast her eyes down in deference. Inside she took scant satisfaction from his praise. *Very different from your judgement when we first met,* she thought, the resentment from the early years of her training bubbling up inside her.

'Do not get too carried away though: large heads topple quickly. There are still improvements to be made so let us examine some of the finer points.'

There was a hesitant knock at the door. *Praise the Gods.*

'Come in,' bellowed Alcastus.

The door opened, a young maid of an age with Bellina stood in the doorway. 'Begging your pardon, Master Alcastus, but the Lord Chancellor has requested the presence of Lady Bellina.'

'Ah well, it seems our lesson is at an end. Until next time, my lady.'

'I shall look forward to it, Master. Perhaps next time we can lower the power restraints further?'

'Perhaps we shall. It's been years since I last felt the thrill of a real challenge!'

He bowed theatrically which Bellina returned with a curtsy. *Oh you'll get a challenge you self-satisfied pool of vomit. You'll get a challenge indeed.*

*

Bellina stood outside the large, dark, night ash door to her father's study. She reached out and gave three sharp raps on the wood.

'Enter,' came the commanding response, exuding forcefulness despite the ten inches of wood it had to project through.

As she entered she saw a small, young man with mousey hair, hurriedly trying to stuff a multitude of maps and charts back into a weather-beaten satchel.

'Am I interrupting, Father?' Bellina enquired.

'No, no, Sholar Fontaine here was just leaving. He gifted me this fine vase which predates the Mage Wars by some two hundred years. An excellent find,' said the Lord Chancellor.

'I am glad it is to your liking my lord. This dig site promises to yield some important discoveries,' said the scholar, his voice squeaking with excitement.

'Excellent. I shall look forward to your next report with great anticipation. You are dismissed.'

The scholar gathered up the last few items on the table, bowed awkwardly to Bellina and her father, then scuttled off through the door.

Bellina sat in the chair recently vacated by the scholar.

'By all means my dear, *do* have a seat.'

'Grand and mighty lord, please forgive this humble girl the impropriety of taking a seat without command. I prostrate myself at your feet and beg for mercy!' Bellina retorted, throwing her arm to her head and pretending to swoon.

'Yes, yes, that's quite enough of your theatrics. Too much time with Alcastus, I fear. How was your lesson today?'

'Rewarding, I managed to reach the centre of his psychic core.'

The Lord Chancellor lowered himself wearily into his seat, putting a large mahogany table between them. 'Excellent!'

Bellina eyed the ancient vase on the table. Roughly two handspans tall and half that in circumference, it was jet black, decorated with elaborate intersecting circles of silvery blue that seemed to pulse before her eyes. 'How many more of these trinkets do you really need?' she asked sweeping her arms around the large room. It was filled with bookshelves containing ancient manuscripts and plinths exhibiting artefacts from the beginning of civilisation.

'The only way to navigate from the present and into the future, is through understanding the oceans of the past. If only a few more people over the years had held to this idiom, who knows what advanced state we may be in now!'

'I suppose,' she replied sceptically. Bellina, like the rest of Estrian society, considered the Lord Chancellor's excavations to be the old man's sole eccentricity. Something that made him at least a touch more human.

The scribograph on the edge of the table sprang into life, the mechanical hand scratching out a private message for the Lord Chancellor. He tore off the strip of parchment and read the message with furrowed brows. He sighed heavily and inserted his hand into the contraption to pen his response.

Bellina observed her father throughout, his broad shoulders drawn tight, his brow covered in ever deepening lines. She noticed that the stubble encircling his bald crown was rapidly turning from dark grey to white — the strain of the Burkeshi affair and twenty years as Lord Chancellor were visibly taking their toll.

'Ah, the joys of power,' he murmured.

'Father, perhaps it's time to start training up your successor?' Bellina asked, her voice full of concern.

'There's still life in this old hound, my love!' he replied flashing a rare smile. 'Anyway, time is pressing and we should get to the reason I summoned you here before your lesson's end. You are of an age now when a lady of your standing is expected to be betrothed and beginning a proper courtship with a man of equal social status. Since you have done everything in your power to scorn and ridicule the nobility—'

'Those witless bores deserve it!' Bellina cried, unable to restrain herself. 'With their endless twittering about the cost of their shoes and who has sculpted their hair to the most ridiculous height. If one of them had a single original thought in their whole lives, the shock would probably cause them to combust!'

'Nevertheless,' he pressed on, 'it is another problem that I do not need, so I am taking the trouble to arrange a partnership for you.'

'You'll be wasting your time; I'll refuse outright. If and when I become betrothed is for me to choose!'

'Bellina, must you constantly cause problems for me? The running of the Empire is a stroll through the ornamental gardens compared to you. You know how much placating I had to do after knowledge of your cognopathic powers got out. The nobles wanted you sent to the compound and I had to fight long and hard to stop them, convinced as they were that I was going to use you to pry into their minds.'

'As if there'd be anything there to pry into,' she said with a snort.

That was one of the main misconceptions about cognopaths. People thought that she and others like her would want to infiltrate their minds and listen to their thoughts when, in reality, the first thing a cognopath learned to do was block out the inane babble that passed for most individuals' internal dialogue. As such, the power restraints and constant supervision of her kind were required to put people at ease.

'You know you are the only cognopath allowed to live inside the city walls, scant privilege I know,' he said, leaning across the table and taking her hands in his. 'These past thirteen years have been a constant exercise in showing the world you and the other cognopaths are not monsters. Think of your betrothal as just the next step. If not for your sake, Bellina, then mine. Do not turn this into another one of your battles.'

Bellina looked deep into his eyes noticing the dark circles. *Gods, when was the last time he slept.* Shame rose up inside her. He'd fought hard to keep her by his side rather than being interred in the quasi-military School of Cognometry. She knew she was the figurehead for her kind, the key to persuading the public that cognopaths were equals and not second-class citizens like the enslaved mages who fuelled the Empire.

'I'm sorry, Father. I will do as you wish,' she finally replied with eyes cast down.

'Thank you, my love. I will start the arrangements this afternoon. Now give your father a kiss and be off, it has been a long and trying morning.'

Bellina rose, crossed the room and placed a heartfelt kiss on his forehead. She walked to the door. As she pulled it shut, she caught one last glimpse of him with his head reclined and his eyes closed. He looked so old.

'I love you, Father,' she whispered, before the door closed completely.

2

The young man checked himself in the mirror for a fifth time and, as always, he liked what he saw. A lean, muscled figure reflected back into his pale blue eyes, a nice match for the almost identical hue of his uniform. The gold of his buttons and the eagles on his lapels shone like miniature suns. The darker blue sash round his middle and expert tailoring helped to enhance his physique. The uniform was non-standard and created at great cost by the finest tailors in Tremore. He patted his blonde hair and replaced a few loose strands. 'How do I look, Benkins?'

'The very picture of Estrian nobility and honour, Lord Elvgren.'

'There are a few ladies from the Coldbridge district who might argue with you there!' Elvgren Lovitz clapped his manservant on the shoulder with familiarity before surveying the man fondly. A jowly face, in permanent danger of slipping free from its skull, topped a man of medium height. He wore a well-pressed suit of velvet, trimmed with genuine platinum thread. His hair receded in a sharps widow's peak, jet black despite Benkins advanced years. 'You must stop using that nortle squid ink to dye your hair, Benkins Don't you know it will make what little is left fall out, old boy?' Elvgren said giving a loud laugh.

'Your concern for the well-being of my tresses is most heart-warming, my lord.'

'That cheek will get you fired one of these days, Benkins. It's a good job I'm the affectionate sort. Now then, I had best get off to it!' Lord Elvgren turned smartly on the heel of his Escambrian leather boots and strode purposefully towards the door.

'Sir? Might you be requiring your training sabres?' Benkins enquired politely.

'And in a heartbeat, Benkins, you remind me how utterly indispensable you are! What would I do without you?' Elvgren said, letting out a long, theatrical sigh.

'Oh, I'm sure you would muddle through a whole half morning before collapsing in a heap, my lord,' he replied, passing him his weapons.

Elvgren secured the sabres in his sash, flashed one last grin at Benkins and stepped through the door to the training ground.

*

The crushed gravel crunched under Lord Elvgren's boots. Despite an overcast day and the threat of rain, he was pleased to see that the high-tiered stands which rose from the four walls of the training ground were filling up nicely. As always, the final Corrin day of the month meant that the great and the good, the high-born and the low-born, were permitted to watch the cream of the Estrian Imperial Army training. Entry was free but admittance was first come, first served and, despite the seating accommodating five thousand, crowds of people would be turned away.

The rank and file were just finishing their battle formations. Elvgren watched in appreciation as the multitude of men formed and reformed at the blast of Arms Master Greelix's whistle, a fluid and seamless motion like the ebb and flow of the tide. *This is why Estria's military force is the envy of the world*, he thought, *discipline and a dash of flair*.

Three short blasts of the whistle signalled the end of the exercise. Polite applause rippled from the lower tiers while raucous whoops and cheers exploded from the low-born seats at the top.

Elvgren stood aside and let the general infantry file past, casually acknowledging the sharp salutes his captain's rank demanded.

'Halt!' Elvgren called. 'About face and stand to attention.' The men paused and wheeled round to face him with the precision of a Gortrix timepiece. 'You man, come here!' Elvgren pointed at a young soldier who stepped forward. With an audible slap, he sharply backhanded the man round the face.

'Are you a major?' the young lord asked.

'No, sir,' the soldier stammered, the bruise already starting to show on his square jaw.

'Are you then, perhaps, a general?' he continued calmly.

'No, sir.'

'Then why the fuck do you think yourself important enough not to salute your superior officer?' Elvgren screamed into the soldier's face.

The man flinched but managed to maintain some sliver of composure.

'Begging your pardon sir, but my mind was elsewhere. I'm a new recruit see, wasn't even part of the battle formation. I was just told to hold the flag. I meant ye no dishonour, sir!'

'Why, pray tell, did you join the army, other than to insult your betters in rank and birth?'

'It's me mum, sir, she's been struck with an awful malady. I need the coin for the medificer and—'

'Enough!' Elvgren interrupted. 'I should dismiss you immediately from the service of our esteemed Emperor Isembert'—at this the young man fell to his knees and sobbed openly—'but I shall show leniency in light of your familial predicament.' A smile spread across the soldier's face. 'Stand man, what is your name?'

'Hubert Tesslet, sir.'

'Well, Recruit Tesslet, as I am feeling generous, the punishment shall be fifty lashes and a month's worth of half rations for you and your squadron. Now get out of my sight.'

The smile fell from Hubert's face. He cast a furtive glance at his comrades who stared back with barely concealed venom.

Satisfied with his display of command Elvgren turned away and walked past the crowd. Cries of 'Good show!' and 'Half a sight fairer than he deserved!' came from the bottom stands, while jeers and catcalls followed the hapless recruit from the upper levels. Some of the low-born tried to throng forward but were shoved back by the stern hands of the City Watch who were always out in force at training displays.

In the few minutes it took Elvgren to cross the yard to Greelix, the stands became filled to capacity. The two men bowed to each other, Lovitz descending just a little bit lower in deference to the Arms Master's fearsome reputation. Greelix rose to his full height — a few inches above the young lord, though, at the age of nineteen, there was still time to grow.

'An excellent show of discipline, Captain. If we'd had your sort at the walls of Stomsgrod we'd have tamed the barbarians in half the time!' Greelix growled, through a jaw set so tight it looked like his teeth might crack.

'You flatter me, Sir. But it is good for the masses to see that order is maintained in the Imperial Army. Appearances are everything, after all.' A sentiment that he clearly took to heart. 'Who pray tell is my opponent today, Master Greelix?'

'Does it even matter, Captain? You are the finest pupil I've taught from all the noble families for a thousand miles. The match is a formality played out for the enjoyment of those we are sworn to protect.'

Elvgren couldn't stop the smile spreading across his face, he let the warm feeling of self-satisfaction trickle through him like a fine brandy.

'As a matter of fact, Captain, here comes your opponent now.'

Elvgren lazily cast his eye to the training circle and took in his latest victim. A large brute of a man stepped forward with dark eyes and hair betraying a Tremoran heritage. His uniform was strictly regulation, showing he was not nobility, although his insignia marked him out as a captain.

'I suppose it would be rude to keep him waiting eh, Arms Master?' Elvgren smirked to his teacher. And with that they crossed over to the sword circle. Cheers, whoops and hollers followed in Lovitz's wake to which he responded with a regal wave. He stopped at his designated side of the circle.

With a raised hand from the Arms Master the crowd fell to silence. 'At my next signal the contest shall begin. As always, the demonstration shall continue until five points are scored on the opponent or they yield. Points are scored for touching the opponent's person with the point of your blade or driving them from the circle. Are we clear?' Both captains nodded. At this Greelix dropped his hand in a slashing motion and blasted his whistle.

Elvgren casually stepped into the circle and watched his fellow captain stride in purposefully before stopping ten feet across from him.

'I am, Trivani Costanza of—'

'I'm afraid I really don't care, my good man,' he replied, casually inspecting his nails and yawning theatrically. The performance was met with howls of laughter and cheers.

Costanza's face reddened. 'I have never been so insulted in my... Assume a fighting stance!'

'That would presume that I was about to engage in any kind of fight,' Elvgren retorted, flashing a smile and cheekily winking to the crowd, earning him more laughter.

Trivani's face turned a delightful shade of puce, then he charged.

Quick, thought Elvgren, *but not quick enough*. He sidestepped the charge and tapped Costanza on the backside. Trivani whirled round, his sabre tracing a wide arc which the young lord calmly avoided. Slash followed vicious slash as Lovitz danced round his opponent with the grace and speed of a skitterling in flight.

'Raise your sword and fight, you bastard!' spat Costanza, already flushed with exertion.

'I'm afraid if I did that, old chap, this little exercise wouldn't last too long and these people came for a sho—' Elvgren was cut short when an upwards swing barely missed his nose. He stepped back but was well within the range of the downward trail of the blade. Steel rang out against steel and he felt the vibration of the impact spasm through his arm. *That was a hard one*, he thought. *Time to get serious.* Elvgren ducked under Costanza's outstretched arm and used his opponent's lurch forward to whack him in the back with the weighted butt of his sabre. Trivani, to his credit, managed to turn the fall into a shoulder roll and just had time to return to his feet as Elvgren pressed his assault.

If Elvgren was quick in evasion he was a human blur in attack. His sabre danced in front of him like a silver snake and Costanza barely managed to fend it off. The young lord could see his opponent was tiring and he was getting bored. Elvgren pirouetted on his heel and smacked Costanza audibly on the jaw with the hilt of his sword, sensing the crunch as the blow shattered his opponent's lower jaw. Without pausing, he swept Trivani's legs from under him and placed his foot on his opponent's chest, sabre to the throat. 'Do you yield, Sir?' he said, pressing down hard on Trivani's sternum. Costanza looked up at him with hatred and shame in his eyes. 'I yearl,' he garbled from his pulverised mouth.

'The winner: Captain Elvgren Lovitz!' bellowed Greelix, and an explosion of cheers rained down on the young lord.

Elvgren drank in the scene. The rapturous applause, the adulation of the masses and an opponent of equal rank crushed beneath his heel. He breathed deep, loving every second of it.

*

Later that afternoon, after a few celebratory drinks and much backslapping with his fellow officers, Elvgren stepped back into the vestibule of his family home. Two servants rushed across the marble floor to take his coat and hat. They disappeared as fast as they had come, with only the clicking of their heels to remind him they weren't merely apparitions with a taste for fine clothes. Elvgren looked up at the sound of new footsteps descending the elegant winding staircase. 'Ah, Benkins, there you are! Be a dear and draw me a bath.'

'I'm afraid there is not the time for your lengthy bathing habits, my lord. We have a very important guest.'

After a hurried change of clothes Elvgren arrived at the door to his father's arboretum. Two servants swept open the double doors, bowing in the same motion. He strode down the gravel path, past the towering Pevontess dragon birches, their upper limbs touching the glass domed ceiling. He inwardly prayed that his father hadn't taken the opportunity to show off his jungle partition and that the meeting would not be conducted under the life-sapping heat of the magically fuelled lamps. Thankfully, his father's sense had prevailed over his innate showmanship, evidenced by the three figures he saw seated under the circular stone gazebo.

His father and mother sat side by side in ornate, wrought iron chairs. Across the serving table sat a man Elvgren had only seen from afar at social functions and peering out from the multitude of public bills that bore his visage. 'Lord Chancellor,' Elvgren spoke bowing lower than he'd ever had need to in his life. 'If I had known such an esteemed guest had done us the honour of visiting I would have come straight home!'

'Lord Elvgren,' the Lord Chancellor said, making the barest inclination of his head in recognition of Lovitz's bow. 'Do not worry yourself. It has allowed me the time to study the magnificent sculptures your father has recently acquired from his excavation site. It would seem we share a similar fascination with the first flowering of civilisation that came with the banishment of the Old Terrors.' The Lord Chancellor swept his hand around the gazebo at the statues and busts which inhabited the spaces between the columns.

Elvgren took them in. Faces of nameless emperors stared back at him. A few of the marble heads still had their mother-of-pearl and azurite eyes. They seemed to throb with life. Elvgren gave an inward shiver under their withering gaze.

'Please be seated,' said the Lord Chancellor.

Elvgren's chair was drawn up by a servant who melted out of the shadows and he sat, with his parents on his left and the Lord Chancellor on his right. He cast a glance at his parents. He could have been a clone of his father excepting the lines round the old man's forehead and the slightly receding hairline. His mother's dark hair was pulled back and kept in place with a platinum hair clasp studded with diamonds, allowing her to expose the full beauty of her heart-shaped face. Only the emergence of crow's feet betrayed her age, a physical development that none of the expensive imported creams and concoctions she acquired could halt. Both of them were dressed in their finest clothes, an expectant hunger in their eyes, like starving dogs waiting at a butcher's bin.

'Well then, since all the relevant parties are here, let's get to the bones of my visit.' The Lord Chancellor clapped his hands together and cast a steely stare at the Lovitz family. 'As you may be aware, my daughter, the Lady Bellina, has come of age. I feel it is time for her to start courting. I believe young Elvgren would be a good match.'

Elvgren's heart sank like a stone. The few sights he'd had of Bellina Ressa had been at parties where she had left a trail of red-faced and affronted nobility in her wake. How on earth could they wheedle their way out of this? The Lord Chancellor was not a man to be denied and the few who tried had a tendency to turn up in various states of decomposition.

'Lord Chancellor,' his father hesitantly began, 'this is indeed a great honour ... but we have already arranged a courtship for Elvgren, with the Lady Hortense.'

Well played father, thought Elvgren. Hortense was a much better fit for him, being ravishingly beautiful and unremittingly dim. He watched the Lord Chancellor's eyebrows rise a fraction.

'Then I would expect you to call it off with much haste. Now, with respect to a dowry and a sign of good faith, I would like all the lands you own in the Valdring Vale to be passed into my portfolio.'

Elvgren's father's eyes had lost their hunger and developed the look of a dog that had just seen a *bigger* dog eyeing up the butcher's bin. 'My lord, with all due respect, that's half my estate. It's a valuable source of income from wheat, not to mention its archaeological value.'

'I know. But I have only one daughter, the last ray of light in my life since the departure of my beloved Tabatha,' the Lord Chancellor said, taking a sip of tea. 'I am aware, though, of my daughter's faults: she's spirited, challenging and then there's her cognopathic abilities...'

'My dear Lord Chancellor,' Elvgren's mother chimed in, 'we never for an instant would consider the Lady Bellina's ... ah ... specialness to be an obstacle but—'

'Please, Lady Lovitz, spare me the horseshit. It *is* a problem, even after all these years and Bellina proving herself to be an exemplary example of her kind. I know her abilities are still a bone of contention with the nobility. As such, I am willing to offer a substantial incentive, one which a minor branch family to the Imperial Throne as you are, might see the value of.' The Chancellor turned his gaze upon Elvgren.

The young lord felt his insides shrivel like a sun-baked worm.

'How would you like to be Lord Chancellor, my boy?'

3

Cirona Bouchard sat with her large frame hunched over the morning newsprint in the Imperial Guards' dining room. The space was big enough for a hundred men, though it was currently occupied by a mere twelve. She ran her hand through the brown stubble of her hair and took a moment to digest the information she had just read. Reading — now that was a lofty ambition for a former Barrow Bottom orphan, let alone rising to the position of Master Guardsman at the palace. But learning her letters had been one of the privileges resulting from being taken into the army's academy at such a young age.

The main story was the continued blockade of Estrian ships by the Burkeshi fleet on the Strait of Hareef. Both sides were making bold claims and thinly veiled threats of retribution, the kind made by men who knew they'd never have to stand on the field of battle and smell the blood of their brothers in arms. The Burkeshis claimed that Estria was directly involved in the capture and enslavement of kaffars, the last free people of magical capabilities in the world. Estria responded that this was the work of pirates, operating well outside the government's purview. Moreover, Estria counter-claimed, trading outposts as far as the free state of Chenta had been ransacked and the merchants slain. The Burkeshis stated that these were the acts of bandits and roaming tribes of nomads.

Usually Cirona would have taken anything printed in the Estrian Messenger, or as the guards called it "the arse smudger", after its secondary use, with a large dose of salt; but the fevered comings and goings of the government bureaucrats *and* the Lord Chancellor himself, had her thinking. In the ten years of her service at the Imperial Palace she'd never seen the decision makers of Estrian politics look so flustered.

The last flare up with Burkesh had been twenty years ago. Fresh from the academy, she had won her first commendation for bravery. Back then Burkesh had not even been a centralised state, but a collection of ragtag multanates with no standing army or navy. The Burkeshis certainly knew how to fight, she had the scars to prove that, but against the sustained, monotonous precision of the Estrian Imperial Army, their resistance was quickly crushed. Trade had been the issue then too. Thousands dead just so Lord and Lady Fart-Arse could sip their infused teas. With the blood of good men and women spilt for such a noble cause, the trading outposts had been established and certain privileges granted to Estria to conduct its business on the eastern continent.

All that changed when Kurkeshi and his Arch Vizier, Marmossa, smashed the other multans before proclaiming the former the Grand Multan of Burkesh. In the ten years since, they had worked quickly, swallowing up the kingdoms around the tiny Burkesh, denying the former multanates their autonomy and summarily executing all other royal families. A very different method of governance to the Estrian Empire.

Cirona sighed and looked at the ornate Gortrix timepiece which occupied much of the far wall. Ten more minutes till the morning shift finished and she would have to take her post as glorified nurse-mother to the elderly Emperor. *How has it come to this?* she thought. The first person through the wall of Stomsgrad, the woman whose expert manoeuvring of troops had crushed the Mandira uprising, the countless assaults and attacks she had personally led that had earned her the rank of major and a wall full of medals; all of that gone so she could lead raids against the imaginary assassins and monsters that lived in the Emperor's closet or down his privy. In her ten years in the service of the man, there had been only one real assassination attempt and that had taken the life of her beloved Trafford.

Of course, she did know how this had happened — the reason most people came undone — bad timing. She had fallen pregnant just as the decision for electing a new general was being decided. Although she hadn't been showing at the time, that rat-bastard, Latimer Willbert, had made sure the judging committee knew. Oh, how they'd painted her transfer to the Imperial Guard as a great honour; saying how it would allow her the time she needed to give birth and then get back into action. She'd accepted it without so much as a murmur of discontent, always the model soldier, and in the years of tedium usually reserved for the elderly housebound, Willbert had weaselled his way to the position of Marshall of Arms, controlling the entire Estrian Imperial Army. Even now, when she had the misfortune of seeing him, he still shot her the same look of arrogant contempt he had reserved specifically for her when they were cadets. The same look he'd worn when, after her transfer, he had whispered in her ear, 'I told you I'd get you eventually, you low-born bitch.'

Whenever she saw him, it was all she could do not to stick her ceremonial lance straight up his self-satisfied arse. But she was a good soldier and soldiers followed orders regardless of personal feelings. Gods knew, if they didn't the whole creaking mess would come tumbling down and there would be no Estria.

The first of the morning watch came noisily through the door.

'... under the bed this time and every flowerpot in the palace!' said a guard. 'Do you know how many fucking flower pots there are in this place? Well, I damn well do now!'

'I just hope the Lord Chancellor shows up soon,' replied another, 'he's the only one who can calm him down these days.'

'Enough!' Cirona bellowed. 'Whether you like it or not, that is the Emperor of the Estrian Empire you're talking about, the foremost of the people you swore a blood oath to protect.'

Both men stood to attention. 'Yes, sir, sorry, sir!' they chorused together.

'Now get some grub and some rest,' Cirona continued, 'those flower pots will still be there when you get back on shift. Dismissed!'

A faint smile crept across their faces and the guards scuttled off. The velvet glove inside the steel gauntlet, discipline without humiliation. That was the key to all great military leadership. She'd been taught that at the academy. Though it was a lesson few in positions of command held to.

Cirona gave a long stretch, she smiled with satisfaction when she felt her muscles ripple. Staying in shape all these years betrayed her slim hope that one day she'd be brought back into active service. *Hogs will fly before then*, she thought. Latimer hated her and the feeling was mutual. If it wasn't for her famed military record he'd probably have her cleaning latrines with her tongue. Picking up her platinum helmet with the cumbersome eagle perched on top, she placed it on her head before striding to the door. She grabbed her lance and began the walk to her position outside the Emperor's chambers. With each step she took, she prayed for the tedium to end. And for the first time in her life she prayed for war.

*

Cirona marched purposefully through the Hall of Remembrance, so called for the vast mural that covered the ceiling overhead. Even after all this time it still took her breath away. It depicted the entire span of human civilisation, from the more recent creation of the Estrian Empire, brought about by conquest, but more often by peaceful negotiation, past the subjugation of the mages and the war that made it necessary, all the way back through the mists of time to when the races of the world had stood together to banish the Old Terrors into the ethereal Void. It was a phantasmagorical smash of history and ancient myth, all told with the emphasis on Estria's importance. And, more specifically, that of the Castria dynastic line which the current emperor was the last direct descendant of.

When she reached the looming double doors which were flanked by two of her colleagues, Cirona noticed the fresh pile of gifts and letters stacked neatly to one side. With no prospect of an heir springing from the loins of Emperor Isembert the Sixth, the branch families of the Estrian nobility sent more and more elaborate gifts to gain his favour. The infighting was bitter and, at times, bloody with all involved more than ready to use any means to undermine each other. *Still, given the current state of the Emperor's mind, she thought, it was more likely he would proclaim one of his treasured luminous fish as the heir apparent.*

Cirona returned the guards' salutes and waited for them to stand down, instead they opened the doors to the throne room.

'The Emperor and Lord Chancellor are awaiting your arrival, Captain Bouchard,' explained one of them.

Somewhat baffled, she advanced into the ceremonial heart of the Estrian Empire.

The brightness of the room dazzled Cirona's eyes as she heard the doors thud shut behind her. Light streamed in through a back wall made entirely of glass, the rays bouncing off the platinum walls and gold colonnades that lined the Imperial throne room. Tinted mercury, kept in place by glass, swirled endlessly around the intricate wave patterns etched into the platinum walls. The floor was a mosaic, representing the Estrian Empire, its landmasses depicted in jade, its rivers in crushed sapphire. The room was crowned with an onyx ceiling studded with stars fashioned from diamonds. At the centre of the room with its back to the glass wall, was the Imperial throne. The massive witch oak chair was crowned with a giant eagle, wings spread wide in an all-encompassing gesture.

The scene was designed to impress upon anyone who witnessed it a sense of awe and the Emperor's supreme command of the earth, the sea, the stars, and the sun. It was an effect completely undone by the shrivelled countenance of the Emperor who sat upon the throne. He was supported by a mass of pillows, covered in blankets and seemingly on the brink of being swallowed whole by the construction that surrounded him.

At the foot of the throne stood the Lord Chancellor, preparing the Emperor's tea. The only person in the Empire who was still able to offer the old man a drink without it having to be sampled by an entire regiment of food tasters. Cirona knelt at the base of the throne and placed her left hand across her chest.

'Your, Majesty,' she said with downcast eyes.

'Pray stand, Major Bouchard,' came the rasping voice of the Emperor. It sounded like grains of sand falling through an hourglass.

At this Cirona stood and bowed appropriately to the Lord Chancellor who returned it with an almost imperceptible incline of his body, a grand gesture coming from him.

'You have been a loyal and dedicated servant to me, these past ten years,' the Emperor continued, 'but it would now seem your diligence is needed elsewhere—' A fit of racking coughs shook him from head to toe. Regaining his breath, he gestured towards the Lord Chancellor to continue for him.

'As His Magnificence was about to say, though I'm sure he would have done it much more loquaciously than I, you are being transferred with immediate effect into my employment.'

Cirona's eyes met the Chancellor's and the flicker of hope she'd long held started to burn brighter.

'My daughter is of an age now where she will be betrothed and start a courtship. As such she will be attending functions and events which will not require my presence. She, of course, will require a personal bodyguard to watch over her at all times. Your impeccable military record, coupled with your composure and quick action during the attempt on the Emperor's life, has led me to believe that you would be best suited to the task at hand.'

The Emperor who had started shuddering at the mention of the assassination attempt was struck with another coughing fit.

'If I may presume to speak again for the Emperor, he would like to extend his most heartfelt thanks to you for your service. The role you are required for should last the duration of my daughter's courtship, at the end of which I shall see you returned to the armed forces, if you so desire, and bestow upon you the rank of general.'

Unable to speak for a few moments, Cirona finally managed to find her tongue. 'Permission to speak, sir?'

'Proceed.'

'I am afraid that the Marshall of Arms would be most disinclined to accept my return to the army. We have … ahem … not always seen eye to eye.'

'I am well aware of this, Major Bouchard, but I am also well acquainted with your file. The Marshall of Arms is a man who bears many grudges. This one, it would seem, has deprived him of an outstanding military mind and graced the Emperor with a preeminent Master Guardsman. However, this lapse in judgement is well within my power to rectify.'

The flame of hope blazed and Cirona felt as if she was floating out of the room, borne upwards on a whirl of elation it should not be possible to achieve without the aid of certain substances.

The Lord Chancellor cleared his throat and continued. 'Please pack your things immediately; a carriage is waiting in the palace stables. You are dismissed, Major.'

Suppressing the urge to kiss the man full on the mouth, Cirona bowed to the Lord Chancellor, then once again knelt to the Emperor. He extended a stick-like hand weighed down by the Estrian signet ring. Cirona kissed the ring, bowed again, turned and seemed to glide out of the room. It was not war, but perhaps the gods listened to prayers after all.

4

'How do I look?' Bellina asked, spinning around dramatically in the dressing room.

'Simply magnificent, my dear; an inspired choice of costume,' gushed Madame Matresca, who was knelt fussing with a loose thread at Bellina's back.

The Lord Chancellor's daughter turned to face the full-length, oval mirror and examined the results. She was dressed in the male costume of Gortrix's high gothic period — a black doublet with puffed shoulders and ruffled sleeves, stitched with interlacing stylised foliage of silver thread, and dark red breeches, the colour of blood under moonlight.

'How about you, Major? What's your opinion?' Bellina enquired.

Major Bouchard, standing some six feet away to the left of the door, simply nodded sharply and returned to staring into the middle distance. It was as if she was trying to terrify and marshal the very atoms of the air. Bellina would not be too surprised if she succeeded in accomplishing this feat after witnessing the effect the major's arrival had had on the Lord Chancellor's palace.

Bouchard had quickly assumed the role of top dog in the small unit that was attached to the Lord Chancellor's residence. Bellina had been astonished at the deference the other guards had paid her. The major had quickly tightened things up. Full inspections were made of the estate three times a day, people directly in contact with Bellina were interviewed and even the cats seemed to have bucked their ideas up and gone on an unprecedented massacre of mice.

Bellina secretly thought her father had allowed the usual tight running of his household to deliberately slip in the weeks prior to the major's arrival — a fact that she first attributed to his seeming exhaustion — to test the new arrival's competence. It would be an unnerving fact if true, but indicative of the forethought that went hand in hand with her father's machinations.

Since then, Bellina had grown accustomed to Bouchard's stares and easy air of command. In the beginning she had relished the freedom the bodyguard seemed to offer. She had been allowed to visit the market district and take in a theatrical performance or two. Even visiting the Tremore tailors on Cloth Cutters Row had been enjoyable, thanks largely to the state of near ecstasy that Bellina's pending betrothal had put Madame Matresca in.

Subsequent days of attempting to engage the major in conversation, though, had been met with monosyllabic utterances and automaton head gestures. This would have been bearable if Major Bouchard hadn't become a giant, ghostly apparition that haunted Bellina's every step.

With the novelty of the first few days of the major's appointment evaporating like warm breath in cold mist, all that was left was the intolerable notion of further constraint on Bellina's already restricted world. The simple wandering of the house and grounds was now accompanied with the ever-present form of Bouchard, a half-glimpsed shadow forever in her wake.

This, coupled with the silent tension during meals with her father since he had told her who she was to be betrothed to, had made the week incredibly trying. At least those meetings were blessedly brief due to the Lord Chancellor's preoccupation with the Burkeshi affair. The awkward near-silence of Major Bouchard's company was an excruciating constant.

'Well, I am glad my choice of costume is met with approval from my female wardens! But alas, it is not yet complete,' Bellina said, grinning mischievously.

'How so, Lady Bellina?' enquired Madame Matresca, looking puzzled.

'Well, as you can see, I am going as the doomed gothic hero, Fasticles. A man so tortured by how he murdered his best friend that his shadow takes the form of his deceased comrade.'

'Yes, I'm familiar with the story, Lady Bellina, which is why the second part of your costume is to be the silk shadow attached to your heels,' replied Matresca.

'Oh, something is going to be fixed to my heels alright. Major Bouchard, you will find your half of the costume in the trunk to the left of the door. Madame Matresca, would you please ensure that, once the major is suitably dressed, the hosiery that will be covering her legs and boots is firmly attached to the shoes I have had specially made.' Bellina fixed her eyes on her bodyguard and watched a small muscle twitch in the side of the woman's jaw.

'My lady Bellina, this will greatly impede my movement and my ability to carry out my primary role—' Bouchard began, through teeth clenched as tight as a barnacle's hold to a ship.

'Major Bouchard! My, my, you can form sentences. Although, not when invited by your employer's daughter,' she interrupted, with exaggerated shock. 'I thought you would appreciate fine Tremoran tailoring accomplishing what you have been trying to achieve this past week.'

'My lady, I will have no choice but to inform your father of this impediment to my duties—'

'Speaking out of turn, once again, tsk, tsk. I thought we disciplined our soldiers better in Estria. Besides, what will you tell him? That you will be a maximum of five feet away from me the entire evening? Perhaps my father will see such an intrusion upon his incredibly strained time as reason to send you back to the Imperial Guard.' Bellina watched a strange spasm pass across Bouchard's face at this last remark, like the death throes of a hyperactive snake.

'As you wish, my lady,' came the major's grudging response.

'Very well, we'd better get to it, there is but an hour till the Lord Exchequer's Annual Costumed Ball and we mustn't be late. Who knows what important piece of gossip we might miss. Oh, how you will so enjoy the nuanced and utterly enthralling conversation of Estrian nobility, Major!' Bellina grinned wolfishly and felt the satisfaction of her minor act of rebellion flood through her.

*

Elvgren leaned back on the plush velvet seating of his private carriage and listened to the clicks and whirls of the automaton horses pulling it. They were a ludicrously expensive showpiece, a whole cavalry regiment could be equipped for the same price, but it was always worth the cost for the looks of astonishment and envy on the faces of his peers. Still, the families further up the line of succession would not be so impressed: his second cousin had remarked how his family gave three to their younger children to ride around the garden on.

The memory caused Elvgren to subconsciously bite his lip so that he tasted the metallic tang of blood on his tongue. *Well*, he thought, *let's see their pompous faces now that my appointment to deputy Lord Chancellor has been made official.* He felt his shame and resentment settle back to the pit of his stomach, replaced with a swell of pride and anticipation that curved his mouth into a smile.

'Are you well, Lord Elvgren?' enquired Benkins, one eyebrow arched so expressively it would have impressed a stretching cat.

'I am in perfectly fine fettle, Benkins. I was merely reflecting on how this will be my first social function as deputy Lord Chancellor.'

'And, the first public event you and your new beloved will be attending together. You do recall her, don't you, my lord? The young lady whose father has seen fit to elevate you above your relations?' In a feat of amazing, facial-muscle control, Benkins' eyebrow had not dropped a fraction of an inch.

'Of course I have not forgotten, Benkins!' Elvgren snapped, though in truth his self-satisfaction had momentarily pushed the Lady Bellina Ressa from his mind.

'I do hope you have thought over all the implications of your current situation, my lord. You and your parents can be very impulsive. Especially when it comes to the eternal battle to up your relatives. Lady Bellina, though not entirely without merits, comes with a lot of ... extra complications.'

'I am aware of that but, in perfect frankness, I would marry a one-legged fishmonger from Bottom Barrow if it gave me an opportunity such as this.' Elvgren sighed and slid, if possible, even further down his chair and looked across at his manservant. 'In truth, Lady Bellina would not even have crossed my mind in terms of potential brides — that hardly needs to be stated. You have been in my family's service some forty years now Benkins, have you not?'

Benkins reflexively ran his hand through his dyed hair. 'That is true, my lord.'

'Then you know, as well as I, with what contempt the minor branch families are held by those closer in line to the Imperial Throne. Lesser nobles, like me, are not even considered worthy to hold a piss bucket for government ministers, let alone trouble their thoughts when considering the succession. The only man who has circumvented this elitism is the Lord Chancellor himself and everyone knows how remarkable he is.'

'Yes, my lord, that is quite true, but to speak freely, I doubt we'll see his kind again.'

'Oh, such subtle condemnation of my abilities, Benkins,' Elvgren pouted. 'That is why the Lord Chancellor is showing me the ropes. The upper families know as well as everyone else that the Emperor is just a show title and real power resides in government, and all of that government's power resides with the Lord Chancellor.' Elvgren straightened himself in his seat, eyes gleaming. 'Imagine the looks on their faces when I, with my betrothed on my arm, make the rounds as they are forced to shake my hand!'

'As long as no one is concealing daggers up their sleeves, my lord.'

'Oh Benkins, you worry too much. The uppers wouldn't dare.'

'I was thinking more of your prospective bride. She is well known for her, shall we say, feistiness.'

They spent the rest of the uphill journey in silence as Elvgren pondered what terrors a riled cognopath may be able to inflict on him.

Finally, the carriage came to a halt at the front steps to the Lord Exchequer's palace. Benkins exited the car first and held the door for his master. Lord Elvgren sprung forth, the gravel crunching beneath his feet.

'Shall I go forth and announce us, my lord?' Benkins asked.

'No, no, Benkins. I am waiting for something.'

'Your lady love?'

'Ahem, no, just a little amusement I have planned. Now, off you go to the kitchens and try not to get too drunk!'

'As you wish, my lord.' And with that Benkins sauntered off, following the pathway to the servant's entrance at the back of the palace.

A few moments later another elegant carriage, driven under more conventional horsepower, stopped behind Elvgren's own. Both doors flew open and out stepped four men in costumes that matched the young lord's.

*

The suspended cable car made its way leisurely up the short distance from the Lord Chancellor's palace to the Lord Exchequer's. The mode of transport had been Lady Bellina's choice. Cirona had never had a head for heights but she couldn't resist a peek out at Victory, the Imperial Capital, spread below them.

To the east she could see the steaming tower stacks of the industrial district. The sinuous coils of magically infused smog belching from them like the smoke from a morpium addict's pipe. In front of the factories and workhouses lay the tightly packed alleys and tenements of the low-born. This realm of the less fortunate was itself separated into sub-sections, with the architecture reflecting the various states of destitution that the people there had achieved.

In the middle sat Builder's Bulge, where the craftsmen and guild labourers lived. The houses were made of bricks and mortar, as well kept as the tenants could afford to keep them. Butted against this and extending to the northern section of the city wall, was the sprawling mess of Skelms Den. Here lay the homes of every miscreant and ne'er-do-well in the city — the brothels, gang hideouts and taverns where you could find a man who'd slit a throat for less than the price of a loaf of bread. The City Watch had long since given up on entering the place, except when a particularly fat bribe was thrown their way. Instead, they focused on trying to keep the worst of it from spilling out into the rest of the city. Closest to the East Gate was Bottom Barrow where she had been born and home to the orphanage where she was raised. Here, the shanties were constructed out of whatever detritus could be found, jostling against each other like fat men fighting over a seat.

She sighed inwardly and brought her eyes across the moonlit silver sickle of the Tollfaith river, past the neat terraced houses of the merchants and artisans, all the way up the steeply ascending Olphant Hill. Here, the palaces and mansions of the great and the good of Estria lay dotted around like elaborate dolls' houses left strewn by a careless child.

At the very top, on a wide plateau, was the Imperial Palace, her home for the last ten years. She'd lived at the very bottom of her home city and the very top, but where did she fit now? She'd been given another nanny's job, though the new surroundings and jaunts in to the city meant the tedium was somewhat interrupted. She looked across to her ward and saw Bellina staring out at the city, her arm resting on the brass handrail. The young girl looked entirely bewitched by the scene before her, eyes wide and mouth slightly agape. There was a loneliness in those eyes though, and a powerful, simmering rage.

As the Lord Chancellor had informed Cirona, his daughter certainly was difficult. During their first trip into the market together, Bellina had tried to give her the slip on five occasions. Each time Cirona had reappeared, the girl had smiled sweetly, but her eyes had flashed like an owl deprived of a mouse. Cirona couldn't say she either liked or disliked Bellina but she'd start to lean towards the latter if the girl kept playing spiteful little jokes, like the costume. Hopefully, a few more weeks of professional, stoic silence would help get the message across that she was the girl's bodyguard, not her friend. Years of watching brothers in arms die had made it painfully clear to Cirona that growing attached to anyone was an invitation to pain. The one time she had let her guard down in the past fifteen years had been with Trafford, the shattered fragments of her soul *still* hadn't knit back together.

As the bittersweet memories came surging forward like a berserkers' charge, Cirona felt the airborne carriage come to a bone shuddering halt.

'Come then, my living shade,' said Bellina. 'A night of stealing conversations about the neurosis of the high-born of Estria awaits.'

Cirona gave a curt nod and tried her best to match movements with the young lady as Bellina deliberately walked in awkward alternating rhythms. Gritting her teeth, Cirona decided, on reflection, she didn't like the little brat after all.

*

Elvgren and his four almost identically dressed counterparts, stepped onto the mezzanine of the ballroom. He looked down into the cavernous room and observed how the attendees had already separated themselves into their various cliques and factions. A string quartet played unobtrusively from the far end of the room, merely providing background music before the real revels began. A few intrepid individuals had already begun to circle and twirl around each other on the black and white marble floor beneath three enormous chandeliers which drooped from the ceiling like glass willows.

'Ok, chaps, let's just check everyone's on the same page for our bit of theatre,' Elvgren whispered. 'Wait until just after the Lord Exchequer begins his speech then start your little disagreement. I'll come over, give you a thorough admonishment and escort you out, just like we discussed at the tavern. Everyone will whoop, cheer, slap me on the back *and* you can look forward to a month's worth of drinks on me. All clear?'

The four men nodded, their faces covered by masks of black satin. Though his companions' disguises covered their features, with only a slit for the eyes, Elvgren had made sure he allowed most of his own face to be visible. What was the point of a ball if you weren't going to be seen? He took the opportunity to quickly make sure the rest of the costume was looking the part. The whole quintet wore black breeches topped with shirts and waistcoats of a similar colour with wide brimmed riding hats sitting jauntily on their heads. They looked the very image of the Wintrim Five, highwaymen celebrated in plays and romances up and down the Empire.

It wasn't the flashiest outfit Elvgren had ever worn to the Lord Exchequer's Ball, but it was the only way he had been able to get his fellows in without any fuss. His gang was composed of four fellow captains, all new-money children of bankers and guild masters. Ordinarily, they would not have been let within a hundred feet of the ball. As such, his four drinking companions had jumped at the chance to play a role in another of the young lord's grandstanding performances *and* gain entrance to one of the highlights of the Estrian social calendar.

'Right then, lads, I'm off to find the ivory mind-melter. You mingle and enjoy the hospitalities. Just make sure you are front and centre when you start your ruckus. That way all eyes will be on me.'

5

Bellina had ensconced herself just to the left of the string quartet's slightly elevated podium. She'd heard all the usual whispers of mind-melter and thought-pilferer, along with the sniggers that accompanied them. Even after all these years it still smarted. Not in the way that it used to when she would hide under the banquet tables and cry, but more in an eye-gouging, face-pulping sort of way.

She was alone except, of course, for her physically attached shadow, a little jape she'd come to regret once Bouchard had started to counteract her arrhythmic walking with the advantage of her considerable bulk. They had reached a silent compromise when going down the stairs in fear for their lives and dignity.

She took a sip from her wine glass and saw the figure of her betrothed warped and bent by the fluting of the crystal. He was making his way across the room towards her with extravagant slaps on the back and near kisses of hands extended to him. He moved, like all nobles did, as if he were gliding. *Well, it's not hard to move weightlessly when you have nothing but air in your skull*, she thought. He finally managed to complete his grand tour of the ballroom and stopped by her side. She felt the eyes of his fellow nobles discreetly turn upon them and caught the blatantly poisonous look from Lady Hortense.

Following Estrian courtship ritual, Elvgren knelt and Bellina extended her hand towards him. He kissed the flesh of her hand in a display of intimacy that was expected between courting couples.

'A small token, my lady,' Elvgren said, looking up at her and producing a silver brooch in the shape of a swan, a symbol of their commitment. 'May I, my love?'

Bellina, with a forced beatific smile on her face, nodded. Elvgren stood up and pinned the trinket to the lapels of her doublet.

'I offer this as a symbol of my devotion,' Elvgren purred, in what Bellina assumed he thought was the most irresistible voice any woman had ever heard. She looked up and met her father's gaze. Fighting back the delightful temptation to spurn the token and crown her already spectacular accomplishments in embarrassing noble fops, Bellina followed protocol. She curtseyed and retrieved her betrothal token from her pocket, a platinum ring also in the shape of a swan. Taking Elvgren's hand in hers, she slipped the ring onto his finger.

'With this I confirm and extend my devotion,' Bellina intoned.

They took each other's hands gently and kissed on the cheek. Bellina was assaulted by his perfume. *By the gods*, she mused, *he smells like two florists who have attacked one other with lavender.*

Having completed their betrothal ritual with faultless etiquette, the couple turned to face the assemblage, with Bellina curtseying and Elvgren bowing. Polite applause rippled round the room and Bellina noted Hortense's gaggle of friends tapping just two fingers against the palms of their hands. *A bold act of reserved disapproval*, she thought; *why do we bother with an army when we could send a squadron of high-born girls to shoot waspish glances at our foes?* The applause soon ended and the guests returned to their frivolous gossiping.

'Well, here we are, my beloved,' Elvgren said, tilting his head to one side. 'Would you care to dance?'

'I'm afraid my costume won't allow such freedom of movement,' another small bonus Bellina had thought of when choosing her outfit. 'You will have to suffer my company and conversation instead,' she said, with a smile of pure sweetness.

'Nothing concerning you, my lady, could ever be considered a sufferance!'

'Please stop that verbal effluence you consider conversation, my lord. If this *arrangement* is going to be tolerable, let's keep the three-penny romance for when someone is in earshot.'

'It would seem your reputation for coarseness is well earned, my lady. What do you intend us to do then? Stand in silence?' Elvgren hissed in exasperation.

'Oh no, beloved! You can twitter on about anything that may pass through your mind. I, meanwhile, will smile, nod, and occupy myself by attempting to count how many diamond shards there are on that chandelier.'

'This is quite insufferable. I have never been spoken to by anyone in this manner! Let alone a woman!'

'Get used to it. Or would you like to stomp out like a petulant child in front of all your peers? Oh, and the upper houses.' Bellina inwardly revelled at the contortions that passed across Lord Elvgren's face. *This is fun*, she thought. Insulting nobles who could storm off after a few utterances was all well and good, but this one had nowhere to go. Why hadn't she got betrothed sooner?

*

Cirona listened with mild bemusement as Lord Elvgren attempted to have a one-sided conversation with Lady Bellina, a conversation the young lady only entered when she took particular exception to something.

After a few minutes she tuned out of their verbal sparring and cast her eyes around the room. She couldn't see any obvious guards hidden amongst the revellers. She felt her guts tighten and hoped that the head of the Lord Exchequer's security had the sense to place a few inconspicuous and capable men in the throng.

Gods, how she hated costume balls! So many variables, so many people who could be anyone. More than anything, she hated not being in control. When she was Master Guardsman, she would have put her men into overdrive for an event like this. The household would have been triple checked, the guest list thoroughly vetted and approved and all attendees made to remove any face-concealing masks to confirm identity. She would have known if a tinder mouse had so much as squeaked out a fart.

Most of all though, she would have known her men, their strengths and weaknesses: who spent a little too much time in a bottle, which of them had gambling debts. Anyone who might be tempted to accept a bag of coin to sneak a lover or a friend in for a noble would have been relieved of duty for the night.

She felt her blood pounding like a tribal drum and her breath getting short. *Calm down*, she told herself. *You are not in charge of the entire place, just one girl five feet from you, focus on her.* Gradually the machinations of her body returned to normal.

*

After twenty interminable minutes of trying to get Lady Bellina to engage in any form of civil conversation, Elvgren was glad to see the Lord Exchequer tap his glass and raise his hand for silence. The man's countenance certainly reflected the position he held. He was a short chap whose spread of gut, after many years of trying, had finally managed to match his height. A double chin was doing its best to smother a third beneath it and small piggy eyes were set into a pink bladder of a face.

'Ladies and gentlemen, a brief moment of your time,' the Lord Exchequer began in a hoarse wheeze. 'Thank you, one and all, for attending my little get together, an event made doubly auspicious thanks to the formal beginning of courtship between the esteemed Lady Bellina and Lord Elvgren.'

He paused here to allow the raising of glasses and applause to subside. Elvgren took the opportunity to see if his men were in position. He located them in the front of the mass of people who had formed a semicircle around the Lord Exchequer. His stomach did a somersault. *This is going to be good.* The thrill of anticipated adulation made his skin tingle.

'Now, if you will all join me in a toast to our exalted Emperor Isembert the Sixth... I say, what's going on there?'

On cue Elvgren's little charade kicked off. Two of the men had started an ungainly tussle, while the remaining two tried to restrain them. *The curtains have opened and the stage is set,* he thought, *time for the lead man to take the stage.* 'Make way!' He bellowed at the top of his lungs, and watched with satisfaction as the crowd parted before him. He stepped into the middle of the fray grabbing the two would-be pugilists. 'How dare you interrupt such an august occasion? You have come here on my vouching and you create this unseemly scene? Outside all of you. Now!'

Elvgren could see all eyes upon him and heard cries of 'Good show!' 'Biff him round the chops' and 'How dare they embarrass, Lord Elvgren'. The last cheer came from the Lord Exchequer, himself. Elvgren grabbed a fistful of both of their shirts and turned to drag them towards the exit, but was met with a weighty refusal to comply. Elvgren turned to face them again. 'I say, chaps,' he whispered, lips barely moving, 'what's the game? Jolly good show, quite convincing and all that. There's no need to extend the amateur dramatics, it's not real, eh?'

At this the two men tried to push past him. Elvgren, still holding their tunics, lost his footing and tumbled backwards. All three men sprawled on the floor, whilst two, very real, daggers spun away from them.

*

A feeling of unease rose in Cirona's stomach which burst into alert adrenaline as she watched the blades whirl across the marble floor in a blur of silver. The party descended into chaos, the nobility of the Estrian Empire letting all pretence at manners slip, clawing and fighting each other to get to the exit.

She quickly closed the distance between her and Bellina and that was when she saw them. The two men dressed like those sprawled on the floor, making their way towards the Lord Exchequer with the consummate ease of expert cutpurses. They weaved through the crowd like fish darting upstream and were soon within a few feet of the rotund man. No one was coming to the Lord Exchequer's aid; clearly the security chief did not possess a lick of sense after all. The Lord Chancellor came running towards them.

'Major Bouchard, quickly to the Lord Exchequer. I will stay with Bellina,' he ordered, brandishing a short sword of his own in his hand.

'Yes, sir!' she hollered over the thunderous noise of the ballroom.

She turned to run forgetting the costume and stumbled to the floor. Cursing, she drew her own blade and slashed herself free. In an instant, she was on her feet, barrelling through the panicked flight of the highborn.

The stumble had cost her precious seconds and the men had already cornered the Lord Exchequer, joined now by their previously prone companions. Time slowed as she realised she wouldn't make it. Their blades rose and descended like pendulums, sinking easily into the lord's fleshy mass. They attacked with fury, torrents of blood pouring from their victim like the sluicing out of an abattoir. The Lord Exchequer fell to his knees, his arms reaching out for an invisible saviour.

Cirona looked from side to side. The guards were finally arriving in the ballroom. Some tried to struggle past the fleeing guests while others stared in paralysed horror at the scene. No one was going to get to her aid quick enough. She lunged the last few paces towards the assassins, striking the one closest to her squarely between the shoulder blades with her sword. She withdrew her weapon with a soft squelch and pushed the man to the floor.

The remaining three rounded on her: one to her left, one to her right, the third in front of her, the bubbling corpse of the Lord Exchequer between them. Surprisingly, this was the one who attacked first. He placed his foot on the body and launched himself at her, screaming. She blocked his plunging blade by smacking her shoulder into the fold of his elbow. At the same time, she continued her twisting motion and slashed her blade through the man's cheek, lodging it in his skull.

The remaining two didn't waste any time, their blades swept towards her. Unable to retrieve her weapon, Cirona crouched, using the body of the slain assassin to shield herself. She could feel her opponent's blades penetrating their former comrade. Seizing the brief window of opportunity available to her, she pulled her short sword free and swung it with all her might into an assailant's lower leg. She heard the impact, like wood splintering, as she shattered his shin, watching as he crumpled to the floor. Cirona rolled out from under her cadaverous shield, pulling her blade free at the same time. She sprang to her feet and thrust the sword through the crippled man's neck.

Withdrawing her blade, she stood face-to-face with the last murderer. He held his sword out towards her, his arm trembling slightly and she sensed his hesitation. He turned to flee but she was on him quickly, tackling him to the floor. She wrestled him round to face her as she sat astride his chest. Pinning his arms down with an iron grip, she gave a forceful downward jerk and snapped them, causing his weapon to trickle from his grasp. Cirona ripped the mask from his face and was met with the unmistakable pale brown skin and blue eyes of a Burkeshi.

'Speak, you fucking bastard! Who sent you?' she yelled, spit flying onto his face.

'I will tell you nothing, you Estrian *durch*. The embrace of Mother Darkness awaits!'

A fevered look filled his eyes, he clamped his jaw down with the force of a descending portcullis, biting into a capsule of poison. Pain contorted his body. He gurgled, retched and spluttered, drowning on his own blood. A thin ribbon of it traced a path from the side of his mouth while frothy pink bubbles covered his lips.

The adrenaline fled Cirona's body and she swallowed back the bile rising in her throat. *Gods*, she thought, *now this is a fucking mess.*

6

The morning after the Lord Exchequer's murder, the sky brooded like a murderous mercenary. Elvgren stood outside the Lord Chancellor's office at the Palace of Administration, chewing his bottom lip. Gods, how much did the man know about his little prank? The only thing the Lord Chancellor had said to him in the aftermath of the ball was that he would send for him in the morning, after which he had led Bellina away with the glory-stealing Major Bouchard trailing in their wake.

She had jumped into the fray before he'd had a chance to properly compose himself. Of *course*, he was more than capable of dealing with barbaric desert folk with sand still in their breeches. If he'd had his sabres with him the Lord Exchequer would still be amongst the ranks of the living. Yes, it was all the costume's fault, no room for sabres there, that's why he hadn't acted. He fussed nervously with his hair and suppressed the maggot of doubt that crawled through his intestines.

The wait was interminable. Elvgren's mind raced, filled with the punishments the Lord Chancellor could have in store. Thankfully, the door finally opened and out stepped the man himself. He was of a height with Elvgren, making his stare all the more threatening.

'My lord,' Elvgren said, bowing so low his nose almost touched the ground.

'Stand up, Lovitz, all the bowing and scraping in the world won't help avoid the shitstorm you have unleashed!' The Lord Chancellor's voice echoed around the hallway.

The clerks and bureaucrats, who had hitherto been walking up the hall, found the nearest doorway and scuttled through it. Elvgren feared this was not a good sign.

'Follow me. Time is leaking like a drunk's piss and the quorum is waiting,' the Lord Chancellor said, immediately setting off at pace.

Elvgren had to jog to keep up. The faces of former ministers and chancellors stared down at him from portraits; not one of them embodied even a hair's width of the command and fury that emanated from the current Lord Chancellor.

'Do you know why I chose you to be Bellina's betrothed and my protégé?' The Lord Chancellor's voice was quieter, but somehow it carried even more power.

'No, my lord.'

'Of course you don't, you witless fucking moron! I chose you because you are an idiot. An idiot that was the right kind of handsome and charming to represent me at events and functions I do not have the time, or the inclination, to attend. I chose you because the combined weight of all the thoughts you have had in your entire life would barely cause a ripple of disturbance.'

Elvgren's insides cringed like a scolded mongrel. 'Lord Chancellor, it was merely a joke! I had arranged for some of my middle-born acquaintances to wear those costumes. I have no idea what happened to them or how this occurred. If anyone's to blame, it's them!'

The Lord Chancellor stopped dead and rounded on him. 'Their fault? Their fault! Don't you dare try to weasel your way out of this. Your equally idiotic friends were found bound and gagged in a ditch. I have spent the morning interviewing them and have managed to piece together something of what occurred. I want you to think, Lovitz, before I have to spell out for you how last night's event transpired. Really think. Let's start with where you planned this *joke*.' He spat the last word from his mouth like a dart.

'Well, we planned it out at one of our favourite taverns, we were incredibly discreet though! We made sure no one was in earshot,' the young lord offered meekly.

'So, you strolled into a tavern, *known* for security and privacy, and laid down the plan to get four men, in complete disguise, into one of the most select and secure events in the Estrian social calendar. Fresh from your appointment as my deputy, this is the first thing you decide to do. It is clear that not even a shred of intelligence occupies the space between your ears, otherwise you would have realised that your new position was going to make you a target.'

'Lord Chancellor, please! I would have known if I was followed or something was amiss. I was a captain in the Imperial Army!'

'Firstly, you were a captain solely through birth and your parent's money. All you had to do was stumble onto the escalating staircase of privilege and try not to fall on your arse! Gods, you jumped-up little prick. You haven't even seen active service!' The tumult of thunderous rage and profanity that spilled from the Lord Chancellor's mouth was completely at odds with the statuesque calm of his demeanour. 'Secondly, *you* would have known you were followed? Gods save me. Our agents extricate sensitive information from the heart of our enemies' seats of power. Do you not suppose the Burkeshis have similar skilled resources at their disposal? How you conducted yourself must have made their souls dance with joy! According to the account I have gleaned from your fellow morons, you thoroughly discussed every aspect of your plan at the tavern. After that the assassins simply had to select a few men of roughly the same size and build, set up a simple ambush and then stroll into a ballroom filled with mouth-watering targets.'

In all his life Elvgren had never been spoken to in this manner. He felt fury and shame all at once. The dishonour to his family, through his destruction of their good fortune, weighed down on him. He collapsed to his knees, hands locked together like mating worms. 'Please, your lordship! I will accept any punishment you inflict on me but please allow me a chance to redeem myself!'

'Oh, you'll be punished alright. You will be at my beck and call, day and night. If I say jump off the Brengorn Mountain, you'll do it and pay for the clean-up. I am going to break you down into the most pliable dribbling idiot in all of Estria. You will come to need my direct consent to take a shit. Are we clear?'

'Yes, my lord,' Elvgren replied, voice quivering.

'And as for the chance to redeem yourself, it may come sooner than you think.'

*

The mahogany double doors of the private assembly room for the quorum of the Estrian Empire, were pulled open by two soldiers. Their bronze helmets, white gloves and blue uniforms were immaculate. They snapped to attention and did not move an inch until Elvgren and the Lord Chancellor strode past, then they closed the door without so much as a backwards glance.

Elvgren observed the room that was the heart of the Estrian Empire's government. Walls panelled with walnut and edged with gold rose to a ceiling twenty feet above. Elaborate platinum light sconces, shaped to resemble drooping foliage and more than capable of illuminating the cavernous space, lined the walls. Occupying much of the room were two large tables. One of them was long and rectangular, spanning from one wall to the other. Along this table were seated the ministers of Estria. Elvgren's skin itched when he noticed the seat left vacant by the Lord Exchequer. The table was set directly below three monumental latticed windows, that on a finer day, would have bathed the room in sunlight.

The second table was set ten feet in front of this. Its semi-circular form was almost equal in span to the first and was orientated so that those who sat around its outer edge, would be face-to-face with those in residence at the first bench. This table was surrounded by the eight delegates representing the countries of the Empire; their clerks and advisors seated at their sides.

The Lord Chancellor took his place at the centre of the rectangular table and motioned for Elvgren to take up the seat next to his.

'Esteemed ministers, lords and delegates,' the Lord Chancellor began, his voice instantly quelling the bubbling stream of hushed conversation. 'I thank you all for making it here on such short notice. As you know, last night the Lord Exchequer was murdered by Burkeshi assassins. This is a matter of importance to the whole Empire. As such, each of you is entitled to a say on how we proceed. Firstly, I will allow the Minister for Foreign Affairs to summarise our current predicament. Kester, if you please...'

Turning his head at an angle his neck did not agree with, Elvgren managed to glimpse Kester. He was a short man of slight build and was almost swallowed by the black minister's habit he wore. He stroked a goatee, the colour of wheat in sunlight, before he rested his elbows on the table, linking his hands.

'Lords, ministers and delegates. I will speak frankly. The Burkeshi affair is fast becoming a considerable problem,' Kester began, his chin inclined towards his chest, eyes penetrating the room like a night hawk. 'As you well know, we have not paid much heed to Burkesh — we have seen no need to. In the last ten years, however, the growth of their military capabilities, as well as their organisational skills, has been astonishing. They have caught us unawares and, I fear to admit, they may know more about our machinations than we do theirs.'

A murmur of bewilderment swept through the assembly.

Kester raised his hand for quiet. 'The small fragments of intelligence we have gleaned are discomforting. A council of twelve kaffars has been assembled by Arch Vizier Marmossa, their purpose unknown.

We also have little knowledge of what powers a kaffar might possess. Up until recently, they would wander the desert waste, from here to there, revered as wise men, never staying in one place too long,' Kester paused for breath. 'The attacks on our trading stations have been well organised. As is their blockade. In regards to last night's assassination, the Burkeshi have claimed it was the work of radicals who follow Marmossa's new cult which worships Varl Dressera, otherwise known as Mother Darkness. I, and the other ministers, believe that all of this is intended to provoke us into attack, to gain sympathy to their cause from the countries of the central continent. Unfortunately, I have no more to add. Lord Chancellor?'

'Thank you, Minister. Who would like to take the floor first?'

Elvgren watched the Tremoran delegate stand up. He was the son of the Duke of Tremore, possessing his father's height and louche demeanour. He was dressed in the height of fashion and Elvgren estimated that the cost of his outfit could have paid fifty labourers' wages for a month.

'Lord Chancellor, esteemed and honourable colleagues. I would like to be the voice of caution before the more bloodthirsty amongst us are given a chance to vent their opinions,' he began, lazily rolling the words around his mouth before delivery. 'We in Tremore greatly appreciate the magnitude of the crime that has been committed *but* we would first explore more tactful options than an all-out assault. As you are aware, my father, the High Duke, has only just finished putting down a minor rebellion in the south of our country. Thus, our troops would not be dispatched easily and, my father fears, the rebels would seize upon the opportunity to destabilise us further.' The duke's son returned to his seat.

'Thank you delegate Vontanza,' said the Chancellor. 'Your concerns are noted.'

The next to stand was the delegate from Narvale. He was a man of medium height but possessed a demonic width to his chest and shoulders. A cloak of black bear fur was draped across him, clasped together by a chain of finely wrought gold. He held up his hand and Elvgren observed that at least two or three rings, adorned with a variety of precious stones, occupied each finger of his rather fearsome looking hands.

'Lord Chancellor, and the rest of you pissants. I am sick of listening to the whining and excuses that flow from the mouth of this young coward. We have been attacked in our own bloody front parlour! This is an act of aggression and should be met with a decisive kick up the arse. Give me leave and I will have ten thousand of my ravagers and berserkers sailing for Burkesh.' The force of the Narvglander's words made his drooping, blonde moustache quiver.

Delegate Vontanza leapt to his feet. 'My lords, as usual the barbaric north proposes we attack. As a delegate of Tremore, and therefore better mannered than he, I would refrain from reminding my lords of the disaster that occurred the last time they were let off the leash in Timboko.'

'Disaster! You snivelling shit! We secured the region and subdued the natives, the blood of my brothers spent in payment for your luxuries and profits!' He was quivering with rage. His bodyguard, a man of equal breadth and more impressive height, stood behind him, stroking the handle of a small axe.

'Oh, and *you* have not enjoyed the fruits of the Empire's labour?' spat back Vontanza. 'You stand there dripping with enough jewellery to offend a whoremonger! We should have left you to your stinking hovels, shoving berries up your noses, instead of offering you parity with your betters!'

'Please gentlemen, calm yourselves,' broke in the Gortrix representative. 'I suggest we send in a battalion of automatons, use modern, enlightened accomplishments to give the sand-lovers a short, sharp shock and be on our way.'

'Heathen!' bellowed the delegate from Escambria. 'It is your godlessness and time spent worshiping machines and science that have brought this judgement from the gods upon us!'

'Oh really, you self-righteous hypocrite! If we had not devoted ourselves to the enhancement of humanity through rationale and logic, we'd still be sacrificing chickens every time someone sprained an ankle. Worse yet, we'd still be slaves to the mages instead of *them* doing our bidding, powering the Empire!'

The voices in the room were growing louder as each party entered the fray.

'Our fleet stands ready,' shouted the Pevontess delegate. 'We should break the blockade with superior naval strength.'

'Please,' snorted a heavily accented voice derisively. 'You witless Pevontess fishmongers could barely sail a toy boat out of a puddle. If you want this blockade broken, the Sylvantain fleet would accomplish the job in half the time!'

'ENOUGH!' roared the Lord Chancellor.

All argument stopped. Elvgren looked around in wonder at the complete control the Lord Chancellor had over the quorum.

'I had hoped that the graveness of the situation would stop this meeting from descending into the usual back-biting, pettiness and insult.' He paused, rubbing his eyes and running a hand over his bald pate. 'Let me try to address some of the madness that just spilled forth. Use of the automatons is out of the question. We are barely producing enough sortilenergy to power our major cities—'

At this, there was another burst of concerned chatter.

'This is the first the quorum has heard of this, Lord Chancellor,' said the Gortrixian delegate with barely concealed terror. 'What is being done to remedy the problem? How, by the gods, did it come to be?'

'That is a matter for another day, but it is part of the reason we have been more active in attempting to capture kaffars.' The Lord Chancellor shot a look at the room, daring anyone to press him on the subject. 'In regard to the statement made by our Escambrian representative, it's such tosh as to not be worth the breath. *But*, for the record, all religious rites are routinely observed. Claristas ensure that at every temple.'

The Escambrian nodded, allowing himself to be placated for the time being.

'Now, I have thought long and hard about our response and propose a plan of caution *and* attack.' He inhaled deeply ribcage rising visibly. 'To send a fleet or an armed response would cause a backlash from the countries of the central continent, lands which will be of great strategic importance should war ultimately break out. Therefore, I table my proposal: I would like to send a party under the guise of a diplomatic mission. A mission which, in truth, will be an undercover operation of great subtlety and danger. My daughter, Bellina's ability to glean information from the minds of our enemies is central to this plot so she will act as envoy.'

'If you will excuse my abruptness, my lord,' ventured the Pevontess delegate. 'Surely, Master Alcastus would be more appropriate. He is the foremost cognopath in the Empire.'

A thin smile spread across the lips of the Lord Chancellor, like a fox who'd spied a preoccupied rabbit. Elvgren flinched at the sight of it.

'As of this morning, that is no longer an honour Alcastus can claim right to. He *was* the most powerful.'

7

Several hours before the meeting of the quorum, Bellina stood outside the door to the study and felt a thrill of excitement. Today would be the day. She had tried her best to compose herself after the insanity of the night before and was as prepared as she could be — well, as prepared as anyone who had just witnessed the slaying of five people, four of them by her personal bodyguard, could be.

She had, of course, seen people killed before, executed at the gallows, but last night was different. Bellina had watched the whole thing as if in a dream — the bleeding, blubbery mass of the Lord Exchequer, streams of blood pouring out of him, Cirona's life or death struggle with the Burkeshis — and had felt eerily calm. At the time, it had seemed like a bad play which relied on too much action and gore. It wasn't until her father had led her back to their home that the shivering had begun. A few stiff Pevontess brandies were required before she regained some composure, at odds with the unflinching Cirona who had resumed her place in the shadows close by, as if nothing had happened.

Her father had flown into a tempest of activity as soon as they had arrived home — the scribograph in constant motion, receiving and sending messages to all corners of the Empire. This was when he had told her his plan, that today her power restraint would be set to its lowest and she would surpass Alcastus.

Her fingers trembled in anticipation. She turned the handle, entering the room. Alcastus stood with his back to the door, the tea service already laid out on the table.

'Master Alcastus?' Bellina enquired deferentially. *By the end of this morning, I will never have to call him that again*, she thought, having to suppress the venom from appearing in her eyes.

'Ah, my lady. Please forgive me, I was somewhat preoccupied. Daydreams are the maker of true nightmares as Konvig the Bard would have said. Please, let us be seated. And Major Bouchard, if you would kindly make sure you are not in the way.'

In Bellina's excitement she had completely forgotten the ever-present Bouchard. The major, without complaint, stood sentry in the corner of the room. How could a woman, who had effortlessly killed four men the night before, accept orders with such compliance? Another mystery about her silent minder that she would probably never solve.

'Your father has informed me of his plan although, I must say, I think it rather dangerous to send a cognopath with no field experience on such a mission. I *can* see the logic behind it — you appear less threatening, I suppose.'

We'll see how unthreatening I appear in a few minutes, she thought.

'As such, he has ordered me to give you the commander's test. A successful completion will earn you the title of "Master". Are you ready for the verbal part?'

'Yes,' Bellina replied.

'Very well. At what distance will a cognopath's power restraints automatically lock out? And what would occur should a cognopath gain unlawful access to their power control?'

'The restraint will lock out at a distance of fifty feet. If a cognopath gained possession of their control conduit, the failsafe device could be initiated and they would be incapacitated or killed, depending on the severity of the offence.'

'Good. How should one approach an attempt to retrieve information from another mind?'

'In the case of someone with no psychic protection: one must tread very carefully. Initial contact should be made in as unobtrusive a way as possible. A psychic landscape should be constructed quickly to protect the mind of the cognopath and the target. Once this is established, the psychic centre, wherein the target's secrets will be held, should be found.'

'Excellent. And what if the mind has been protected? And in what way could protection be achieved?'

'Firstly, a mind can be guarded by a thought protector which will take the form of an item of jewellery. This can be circumvented with sufficient mental strength, depending on the quality of the item. The mind can also be protected by creating psychic landscapes, where defences will be placed which must be overcome.'

'Adequate. There are more ways to bypass both, but time is pressing. How can a cognopath listen to the thoughts of others without being consumed by the noise?'

'By ensuring only one target is under scrutiny at a time and only slightly dampening the cognopathic restraint.'

'Well, I am satisfied with your answers, Lady Bellina. There are, of course, a myriad of other questions, options and variables, but the Lord Chancellor has instructed me to keep this brief.'

Praise be, Bellina thought.

'First of all, I must inform you that, after today, your control conduit will be in the possession of Major Bouchard.'

Outraged, Bellina blurted out, 'Excuse my boldness, Master Alcastus, but those who have attained the rank of master control their own restraints!'

'That is not the case, Lady Bellina. It is a privilege only five people have ever earned, loyalty to the Empire had to be proven beyond any doubt. Even then, we are not expected to fully unleash our powers. It is a token gesture of respect.'

'Even so, Master, I would still expect, when I am successful, to be given—'

'*If* you are successful, my lady, *if.* And I was not finished. Your father feels that if you were seen in possession of your control conduit, the ruse would quickly be up. He expected that you would not be happy about this and said you were to consider it your test of devotion.'

'My devotion to the Empire is absolute, as my father well knows! I can't see myself defecting, can you?'

Alcastus' demeanour changed dramatically. He leaned forward fixing his eyes on hers. 'You presume too much, Lady Bellina. After you have been in real peril, after you have met the glare of your enemy, after you have heard the screams of those around you ringing in your ears and through your brain so that you would do anything to make it all stop. Only then, will you understand why a test of devotion is necessary.' He sighed and pulled away from her, eyes misting with a look of utter abjection.

Bellina had never seen the old man so emotional.

'Forgive me, my lady. There are many things that can go catastrophically wrong on even the most routine of missions. Are you ready for the psychic part of the test? And I really do mean test. This will be different than before, all my power will be bent on stopping you. At the lowest level of restraint there is real danger of serious harm.'

'I am ready,' Bellina replied. This was what she had been waiting for since she was five years old, when he had first invaded the sanctity of her mind. His sudden and unexpected emotion had put her out of step, briefly. *Why has he chosen today to be human?* she thought. As quickly as the doubt rose she pushed it down, remembering the violation of their first psychic encounters.

'Then, shall we begin?' Alcastus leaned back in his usual seat opposite her.

Bellina copied the motion. She breathed deeply and their eyes met.

*

Bellina's eyes opened to the sight of the marshes that marked the beginning of Alcastus' psychic defences. The stench of rotting plant life and stale water filled her nostrils. A thick fog hung in the air making it impossible to see even a few paces ahead. If the old man thought that simply impeding her visibility would thwart her, he was in for a shock.

She threaded her way along the pathway with consummate ease — not too much further to the jungle. She turned right expecting to see the first of the giant trees loom into view. Instead, she continued to feel the soft squelch of saturated mud and grass underfoot.

What the hell had happened? She was sure she had gone the right way. Or was she? The fog was starting to get to her, it seemed denser now; almost alive.

Bellina cast her eyes around to see if there was anything she could latch onto to give her some sense of place. There were footprints in the murky mud. Gods — was something ahead of her, waiting? She knelt to examine them further. Dismay flooded through her. The footprints were hers: she had come back on herself.

Bellina's thoughts ran frantically through her mind. How could she get out of this? What did she need to do? Height, she needed a vantage point. Somewhere above the blinding fog.

She guided her thoughts towards the ground, willing a hill to form. With satisfaction, she felt the earth begin to move. Alarmingly though, it was moving downwards. Bellina watched in horror as the grey, stagnant water rose above her ankles. Frantic, she tried to pull her legs free.

The fog began to lift. Bellina could see that she was at the centre of a vast and rapidly descending crater of marshland. The water was past her shoulders, touching her neck. Then she saw him.

Alcastus appeared, like a ghost in a cheap play with wisps of fog wrapping around him. Terror flooded through her. He'd never set anything as deadly as this before. Gods, how badly had she overestimated her power?

'I am sorry, Bellina, but your father's plan is madness,' he said. 'I do this for your own good.' Struggling to speak, she found her mouth caked with mud. His misty blue eyes bored into her with a pity that stung her soul. Bellina let out a strangled cry, gurgling, her head sank beneath the water.

The world around her was a mesh of greys and greens, thick roots of marsh plants entangled her arms. Gods, this wasn't supposed to happen. She was supposed to win.

Feeling tiny, nothing but a child, engulfed by the same helplessness from her childhood—

NO! The thought echoed through her with the vibration of a battle drum. No, this was not going to happen. These three-penny theatrics were not going to stop her. No. This would be her vengeance. Renewed confidence stirred deep within her. That, and undiluted rage.

The water around her was changing, bubbling. Bubbling gave way to boiling, steaming. In a rush the water evaporated, leaving her standing in the middle of the crater. Unchecked, her power rolled off her in twisting coils of white mist. She caught the look of fear on Alcastus' face in the split second before he vanished.

Rising, she hovered above the ground, and then she shot forward. The world around her seemed to blister and crack. Everything along her path was burning, trails of debris from the landscape followed in her wake. Soon, trees and vines replaced the clay and grass of the swamp. Faster and faster, she flew, roaring past the hydrabasilisk, the creature torn apart with a wave of her hand.

The beach opened out before her and she paused, her feet returning to solid ground. The castle had lost its predatory menace. Bellina was the bird of prey now; *it* was a cowering shrew. All she needed were some talons. The psychic world bent to her whim effortlessly. Sand rose, meshing with the collected detritus, forming a goliath. Together, they marched forward.

Tens of thousands of soldiers streamed from the castle gates and were smashed to pieces.

A few survivors hacked pathetically at the sand giant's monumental base whilst she began her destruction of the castle. The black stone walls crumbled and fell beneath the giant's hands. It clawed at the castle viciously, euphorically, like a starving man devouring a meal.

Bellina rose to the top of her monster's head. She observed the destruction with a drunken glee.

In a stone courtyard, at the heart of the castle, crouched the old man. He held his head between his hands and rocked backwards and forwards.

'Please. Stop, please,' he begged, not towards her but to the air in front of him. Bellina heard it all the same.

'How does it feel, Master?' her voice boomed, vibrating every atom. 'How does it feel to be helpless? How does it feel to be powerless to protect yourself? I was *five* when you violated the privacy of my head. Did you stop? Did you listen to my pleas?'

Alcastus looked around in desperation, finally locating Bellina. 'Please, please, my lady. I only did it to make you strong.'

'I would say you were successful! This, though, is the end, *Master.*'

Together, Bellina and her creation strode into the courtyard. She scanned the scene for Alcastus' memory stronghold as the old man wept on the stone floor.

On a trestle table, she found it. A small wooden music box, partially hidden by desiccated stone blocks. She floated to the ground and took the delicate casket in her hands.

She wound her way through the devastation to stand before Alcastus. His expression was a mix of shock and terror, partially hidden behind the spread of his fingers. Sobs bubbled from his throat. Bellina looked him squarely in the eyes and opened the box. His screams echoed around the desolation of his mind.

*

The assembly room was filled with a stunned silence. Elvgren looked at the faces of each man. Like him, they were trying to digest the news they had just received.

'I take it there are no further objections to the choice of Lady Bellina?' asked the Lord Chancellor.

Not so much as a murmur broke the stillness that had settled over the quorum.

'Good. Major Bouchard will be responsible for the safety of my daughter and head of security. The rest of the diplomatic mission will consist of Lord Kester and a few men-at-arms — not too many as the ruse must, of course, be maintained. On a final note, deputy Lord Chancellor Lovitz has also volunteered his services to the collective, in hope of redemption for some recent errors of judgement.' The Lord Chancellor paused. 'Are there any objections? If not, the plan will be put into play immediately'

The delegates and their assistants looked at each other like men who had just lost the contents of their purses to a street hustler. No objections were raised, except by the silent, inner voice of Elvgren Lovitz.

8

Cirona gazed up in awe at the iron hull ship that would be their home for the next fortnight. It sat in the docks on the River Tollfaith, a black testament to Estria's scientific and engineering advances. With its giant paddle wheels, it barely fit between the banks of the wide river. Magical miasma already belched from its wrought iron funnel. The ship seemed to want to devour the world around it. *Not unlike the minds of the men who built it*, she thought.

Her mind cast back to the first time she had boarded a ship like this. That vessel had been a touch smaller than the one that now engulfed her vision, but it had still provided enough room for a hundred soldiers. The smell of stale sweat in the cabin she had shared with her military family came streaming back to her. Cramped space and lack of privacy had forged a stronger bond between some of them, while others had grown snappy, discipline becoming a problem. Cirona had been in the former camp. The friendships she had formed on that crossing, amidst talk of winning glory and being made generals on their return, filling a vacuum in her soul that she hadn't known was there.

All this changed when they learned the reality of how martial glory was won. The fury, the stink, the madness. Screams, blood everywhere, where was up and who was down. Men dead and dying. Women dead and dying. Gods help them, children dead and dying. The rage, the rush through a town wall, foreign faces filled with hate, spitting and hissing as they came at the Estrian soldiers. Taking the town, the rape, the destruction, the looting. Finding one of her new comrades with their head caved in like a deflated pig's bladder, piss, shit and blood mingling in the light of a crimson sunset.

This? This was glory? She told herself that it couldn't be. Where was the honour? The bringing of civilisation to the uncivilised? Where was it all when soldiers played dice for the stolen possessions of the dead innocents lying at their feet? She told herself she would run, not be a part of it, but she never did. Instead, she won a commendation for bravery and *her* first promotion — however much she reviled war, her maggot-riddled core loved it.

Cirona turned her eyes to the assemblage of people who would form the diplomatic mission. Six clerical staff—not part of the mission itself— fussed and scurried around, checking all was in order before departure, while Lord Kester was busy harrying the dock hands. The selected soldiers, who she had no power to choose on such short notice, stood to one side, chatting and examining their weapons — *probably trying to work out who has the biggest*, she thought. Next to, but somewhat away from the gaggle, were Lord Elvgren and his parents. He stood stiff to attention while they spoke words she couldn't hear, words clearly delivered with cool aristocraticindifference. If there was one person Cirona dearly wished was not part of the entourage, it was him. The scale of the arrogance and stupidity that had resulted in the death of the Lord Exchequer was heart stopping. Although the Lord Chancellor had explained his reasons for adding Lovitz to the party, promising he would be little more than a dogsbody, she still saw him as a massive liability. Liabilities got people killed and, having seen how the skirmish at the ball had paralysed him, what would he do if things really went to shit?

Finally, she looked towards the Lord Chancellor and Bellina, both deep in animated conversation. The love and affection the girl felt for him was palpable and he returned it in his face and eyes.

Since taking up her post at his residence, Cirona had come to deeply respect and fear the man. His cunning was astonishing. As were his organisational skills. He had put together all of this in the space of two days. And *this* was only one of the many plates he had spinning. His eyes, his *eyes*. They were what really chilled her. She had met his gaze and seen a hollow compunction to do whatever he thought was right, like an automaton with the skin of a murderer stretched across the cold metal. Now though, those eyes shone with love. How could they? With what he had commanded her to do?

Cirona watched, seeing the familial warmth flow back and forth between the pair. Warmth she had never known as a child or even as a mother. Her stomach turned as the faces of Trafford and her daughter swam before her. She fought the memories back down, down as far as she could push them. Past her core to the cavern filled with loss and regret.

*

Bellina looked into the eyes of her father. She examined the rippling creases that lined his face as his smile spread before turning to a wistful frown.

'Well, Bellina,' he said. 'I'm sorry.'

In all her life, she had never heard her father apologise.

'What in the world for, Father?' she replied, unable to suppress a hint of shock.

'For... well... for all of this. When you came into mine and your mother's life, I loved you more than I ever thought possible.'

'Lord Chancellor, you are in danger of appearing human!'

'Please, none of your snark. Let me finish. I loved you, we both loved you, and after your mother died you became ever more precious to me. I fear it has been a burden.'

'Oh yes, the tyranny of a father's love. How could I ever bear such a heavy load!' she said, rolling her eyes.

'When your powers first started to manifest themselves, I didn't know what to do. A cognopath born outside of the breeding ground, had not been heard of for decades, and yet, there you were. Just know that I never wanted this for you. To be a tool, a lever.'

'You wanted a princess and, instead, you got a cutlery-bending mind-melter you mean?'

'No, no! You know damn well that's not what I mean. I'm sorry about your training. I just wanted to help you control it, at first, but after Alcastus told me how powerful you were, I knew that someday you would be needed for something like this. So, I prepared you as best I could. I hoped this day would be much further down *both* our roads.'

Bellina felt her emotions well up inside her. 'Come on, you rotten old goat, enough of this sappy crap. I've got a multanate to infiltrate.' She wrapped her arms around his middle and could feel his ribs. Gods, how all of this was taking its toll on him. Bellina felt her father's arms reach around her slender frame and the warmth of his breath as he leaned forward to kiss her forehead.

She would do this for him: take some of that worry away, even if it was only a little bit. This would not be another thing to shorten his years and strip the rest of the hair from his head. Her tears soaked into his greatcoat. 'I will make you proud, Father.'

'You always do.'

*

Elvgren lay on his bunk in the pitiful excuse for a cabin that had been assigned to him. He listened to the sound of the great iron ship, alive around him, and thought of his parents.

His last sight of them had been two tiny specks receding into the distance. It felt like that was the view of them he'd had his entire life. Even at his departure on a mission of great importance and danger, they had barely shown a flicker of emotion. They were, of course, particularly unhappy with him for the Lord Exchequer affair, although the death of a senior and respected statesman paled in comparison to their personal shame and dishonour. His mother had stood resolute, jaw firmly clenched as his father had wittered on about the great honour of the Lovitz name. How one great-grandfather had stormed this, how another had commanded that, how there was no room for more of their son's accomplished failure. His mother had chimed in, commenting that it was their fault, that they had coddled him, pampered him. Well, if scornful derision was her idea of coddling then the enslaved mages were as loved as he was.

That was how it had been his whole life. His parents constructing more and more elaborate ways to keep him from getting underfoot — first a nanny, then Benkins, then the arms training. It was as if a mere second in his company would strike them down with the pox. All of this changed, though, with the sudden and unexpected turn of events which saw him appointed as deputy Lord Chancellor. Oh, *then* they'd developed a sudden and forceful interest in him.

They'd never understood his little eccentricities, the drinking and carousing. They were of the old guard, a noble branch family with a small atom of blood passed down, thousands of years ago, from the great hero Amlith Castria, subjugator of the Old Terrors. Now Amlith was merely the subjugator of artists' brushes, as Estrian nobility fought harder and harder to best each other with epic murals proclaiming their lineage to him.

No, the humourless pair thought of fun as an abstract concept. Time-wasting that got in the way of being honourable. *What's the point of being rich if you don't flaunt it or enjoy it?* he thought. He'd show them though. He was going to show them all. The thought of the thrill he would get when he shoved his parents' faces into the unparalleled success he was going to achieve, rose up in him like a hissing snake. Yes, he'd show them *and* the ever-so-wise Lord Chancellor. The look of glee in the old man's eyes when he told Elvgren he would be subordinate to everyone else on the voyage, calling it a pilgrimage, like the ones pious lunaticswent on. But, instead of choosing self-denial and masochism, his would be enforced. He was stripped of luxury, as attested by the plain wooden chest he'd had been issued to put his personal belongings in.

Enough was enough, he told himself. Lord Elvgren Lovitz, former captain and current deputy Lord Chancellor was not a self-reflective moper, but a man of action! He sat bolt upright, smacking his head on the small shelf above his bed, and then whirled himself round, banging his left knee on the wall of the coffin-like space. Thoroughly annoyed, he strode out of the cabin, looking for a victim to take it out on.

Clambering up through the hatchway, he stood manfully on the deck. The stench of the Tollfaith river was more bearable now that it flowed through the green fields of the Estrian countryside. Briefly, he watched the little hamlets and farmsteads slip by.

All around him the ship bustled with life. Even though the magically fuelled iron hull steamers did not require half as many hands to run as a traditional sail ship, there were still at least twenty sailors bustling about, fulfilling duties he could only guess at.

He saw the captain through the window of the steering cabin and, with an amiable smile, waved. The wizened old prune merely tilted his head a fraction of an inch, a movement so slight that it was only recognisable by the disturbance it produced in the captain's white nest of a beard. The affront that had propelled him out of his cabin, now had more faggots of disrespect thrown onto the blaze. Deciding it was best not to inflict his anger on the man in charge of the mystifying process which kept them afloat, Elvgren chose to take his frustration elsewhere.

Looking around, he soon found his victims. The soldiers that had been sent to accompany the envoy were lazing on the foredeck, trying not to get in the way. Dressing the men down for slackness would assert his authority and, more to the point, it would cheer him up. 'You there, man, what do you think you're doing?' Elvgren shouted, noticing appreciably how some of the people on deck turned to witness his display. The men sat in a semicircle, playing cards. It was the man in middle of the seated trio who Elvgren addressed.

'It would appear we are playing cards, my lord,' he replied, a crooked smile exposing gaps where teeth should have been.

'Do you have any idea who I am, you miserable cur? On your feet, all of you, and look damned sharpish about it!'

'We know who you are alright,' replied the soldier, remaining seated, 'A puffed up little worm's cock who thinks spinning round in a bloody training circle is a real fight. Heard you fell on yer arse and pissed yer britches when you caught a gander at them Burkeshis, at the ball.'

'How dare you!' Elvgren screamed, hearing an unmanly shrill emanate from his throat.

'How dare I? Lord Chancellor had a little word with us before we left. Said to make you as uncomfortable as possible. Now, if ye would kindly piss off, I think Jasper's so deep in the shit he's about desperate enough to wager a night with his wife.' At this, the men on the floor roared with laughter.

Dumbfounded, Elvgren just stood there, the red heat of his cheeks burning like a merry fire in a family home. He spun away on his heel as the beginnings of tears misted his eyes. That miserable old fucker didn't mean to just steal his comfort, he meant to steal his dignity as well. It was then, for the first time, that Elvgren understood the *true* depth of the Lord Chancellor's punishment.

9

Bellina awoke to the sound of the ship's dawn chorus: feet banging on the deck. Three days had passed in boredom on the *Prudence*. The Tollfaith river had reached its mouth, spilling out into the sea like drunks at closing time. The night before, during dinner, the captain had informed Bellina that they were making good time and were half a day's sail from the Varash coast. His broad smile had indicated this was an excellent thing, though it had meant about as much sense as a Mandiran riddle to Bellina.

She had tried her best to find things to amuse herself with. Conversation with Major Bouchard was, of course, out of the question. She couldn't be seen fraternising with anyone on the ship not of officer's rank, which was a shame because they seemed to be having quite a lot of fun. Mainly at the expense of Lord Elvgren.

The betrothed couple had said all of five words to each other since the start of the voyage, which Bellina was more than happy with. Since his humiliating altercation with the soldiers, Elvgren had spent most of his time below deck. Whenever he did emerge, however, his life was made a misery. The three soldiers were intent on carrying out her father's suggestion as if it were an order. They had taken to calling him "Gren the Hen", then just "Hen" and now finally "Mother Hen". In fact, Bellina would be just in time for the morning show if she got a move on.

Making her way past the sleeping Bouchard, who occupied the cot next to hers, Bellina slipped soundlessly out of the door.

It was just past dawn when she made her way from her large cabin, large meaning that not all her movements resulted in fresh bruises. On deck, the soldiers were already up and waiting. This was partially thanks to Bouchard's discipline, though she hadn't ordered them to lay off the young lord. *She enjoys it as much as I do*, Bellina thought. The other reason they were up and still on deck, was that certain calls of nature could simply not be answered below. Despite the size of the ship, one was expected to make one's toilet on deck, the single indoor privy being reserved for Bellina and Cirona, to preserve their modesty.

Bellina looked the soldiers over. The three card players were of Estrian stock, pale brown or blonde hair atop their heads, with the build of farmhands and labourers. More and more of these types were joining the army when they realised the Imperial Capital wasn't all they expected it to be. The soldiers occupied their usual spot on the deck: in front of the hatchway which Elvgren would, sooner or later, have to emerge from. They sat joking with each other and polishing their boots.

Bellina couldn't help herself. Stealing a quick glance around her, making sure no one else would see, she approached the men.

'Ahem!' she said.

At the sight of Bellina the three men sprang to attention snapping sharp salutes. She let out a laugh at the sight of the soldiers in stockinged feet, the boot polish rolling across the deck. 'At ease, gentlemen, neither the major nor my father will spring out of my arse in the next five seconds ... you might want to put down that brush.'

The man on the right had smeared black polish across his face in his rush to salute and now looked like a chimney sweep. He gave a sheepish grin and dropped the brush to the side.

'Milady Ressa. I hopes yer not 'ere to give out to us over the treatment of yer betrothed?' The ringleader said, a smile spreading across his face.

'Whatever could you mean, soldier?' she said, returning an impish smile of her own.

'Well, I was per'aps thinking that my lady was not too happy with some of our brotherly bantering with Lord Elvgren.'

'No, no. I am not *happy*,' she said, suddenly changing to her most commandingtone. Bellina watched puzzlement and anxiety spread across their faces. 'You're too easy on him by half.' They visibly filled with relief, like they'd been pumped by a pair of bellows.

The rattle of the hatch interrupted them.

'Sorry, me lady,' said the soldier in the centre. 'Time to insult our betters. Begging yer pardon, course.'

The hatch doors burst open and out sprung Major Bouchard. Her head swivelled to and fro and, for a second, Bellina thought it may make a complete circle. Bouchard's eyes came to rest on her, anger passed across the major's face as she surveyed the scene. If Bellina had thought that the soldiers were quick when they stood to attention for her, she was astonished at the speed with which they adopted the pose now.'

'Care to explain yourselves, soldiers?' said Bouchard, her voice like molten steel.

'Major Bouchard,' cut in Bellina, 'I was merely making pleasant conversation with these fine gentlemen, while I awaited your *verbose* company.'

Bouchard inhaled, nostrils flaring just a fraction. 'Fine. Gather your things, soldiers, and get below decks. You will be confined to your quarters for the rest of the day.'

'Yes, sir, thank you, sir!' they chorused.

The two women moved to the port rail. 'Well that's my fun ruined for the morning,' Bellina sighed to the major, though she kept the hatchway in sight, just in case. Bouchard gave a disapproving grunt in reply, prompting Bellina to change tack. 'What do you make of the men, Major?' Bouchard looked her dead in the eyes. Bellina met the stare nonchalantly but her insides went through a dizzying plummet. Fortunately, the major's look shifted from irritation to thoughtfulness.

'They're feckless and not used to proper discipline. It certainly wasn't like this in my day,' Bouchard said, letting out a short sigh. 'I would not have chosen these men but, due to the rush to get all of this going, Minister Kester took on the duty.'

The mysterious Minister Kester, Bellina thought. In the previous three days aboard ship, he had confined himself mostly to his quarters with complaints of a stomach illness. The opinion was that he had no sea legs, something the sailors found highly amusing. While she imagined the state of Minister Kester's vomit-covered cabin, Elvgren, finally, made an appearance.

Due to the major's rebuke, the trio of soldiers contented themselves with catcalls and chicken noises as they passed the young lord on their way below decks. Elvgren, surprised by their restraint, scuttled off.

*

It was mid-afternoon on the fifth day at sea. The sky had turned a putrid grey and the sea was rolling like a stomach's first warning sign before a catastrophic puke.

Along the bobbing deck of the *Prudence*, Cirona and Bellina were taking a walk. *Well, a pale imitation of a walk*, Cirona thought. She watched the young girl flitting about in front of her, a nod to a deckhand here, a little smile for an officer there, she really did play her part well. Though, she was beginning to think that it wasn't an act. She'd spent enough time watching Bellina to realise the girl didn't suffer any shit. Just the night before she had torn into an officer at dinner for being a pompous arse and Cirona had been grateful when, red-faced, he had shut his noise. *No*, she thought, *Bellina Ressa would not wave and smile if she didn't want to.* It was something she admired in the girl.

Cirona and Bellina had just passed another sailor, who they both nodded politely to, when a sound like a mob trying to force their insides through their mouths smacked them around the head. As they reached the bow, Cirona could see that this, in fact, was what was happening. Five sailors were in various states of prostration before them. One was kneeling, another supporting themselves with their hands and the final three just lay flat on their faces. The acidic smell of vomit filled Cirona's nostrils and she felt her own stomach lurch. In the corner of her eye she saw Bellina turn an even paler shade of white, but, to her credit, the girl held on to the contents of her gut. The captain and his first mate were quickly on the scene.

'Gads dammit, Captain, it's the black gut is what it is!' said the first mate.

'It most certainly is not black gut! There hasn't been a case of it on an Estrian ship for thirty years, and keep your voice down you imbecil— Oh, Lady Bellina, Major Bouchard, I must apologise,' the captain said, catching sight of them.

'What in the name of the gods is going on, Captain?' Bellina asked.

'Nothing for you to worry about, my good lady. Probably just some tainted meat, that's all. Nothing for you two to concern yourselves with. Anyone who's eaten at my table has had food from different stores,' the captain said. He was trying to affect a cheerful tone, but sounded like a man with a sword in his bowels telling himself it was just a scratch.

'Where the hell is the ship's doctor?' the captain continued.

'Being sick, sir,' came the first mate's reply.

'For the love of... Fine, get all remaining hands on deck cleaning this mess up. Then get these men below decks and tell the others they will be doing double shifts. I'll have to set us on course back to Varash. If we make good time we could arrive by evening two days hence. At least there we can get some medical help or take on fresh hands.'

'You can't be meaning to put into Tavarar, Captain?'

'Unfortunately, we have no choice. At the very least we'll have to take on untainted supplies. Now, be off.'

'Aye aye, Captain.'

'Ladies, if you will excuse me, I need to go and alter our course.'

'Certainly, Captain,' Bellina said.

Cirona saw the gaggle of soldiers at the front of the ship. The men were clearly worried and she wasn't too thrilled either. Anyone who had been on campaign was terrified of black gut, a sickness capable of claiming more lives than battles. She followed Bellina away from the scene, inwardly praying that the sailors really had been struck down by off meat.

*

Glasses clinked as the captain's dinner guests raised another solemn toast, this one to the health of the Emperor. It was the evening of the fifth day and four bottles of very fine Pevontess wine had been disposed of.

Elvgren stared down at his barely touched food. A small green fowl lay with a tiny piece extracted from it. He'd pushed the rest of the food around his plate, trying to give the impression of having eaten. The whole meal had the feeling of a wake, the crew's sickness hanging above the gathering like a grim spectre.

'No appetite, Lord Elvgren?' the captain asked, cheeks flushed by the wine.

'I am afraid I have had little desire for food during our voyage, Captain Yervy.' This was very true, thanks to the constant motion and the harassment by the soldiers. Of course, the possibility of the meal vacating him from both ends at pace had also quashed any hint of hunger.

Giving a shrug, the captain turned his attention to Bellina.

Elvgren swept his eyes around the room. It was the largest on the ship, though that wasn't saying very much. The Lovitz mansion had bigger privies. Despite the restricted space, the captain had tried to make it as handsome as possible. The small dining table and cushioned velvet chairs were dark mahogany. *Comfortable enough for a master tradesman but hardly befitting nobility*, he thought. There was a neatly turned bed to the back of the cabin with a travel weary sailor's chest at its foot. A desk was covered in maps and charts and a family portrait hung above it — the captain, his wife, a teenage son and two younger daughters. Despite its lack of grandeur, there was a cosiness to the room that all the cavernous space of his family pile had never managed to achieve. The cabin had become very familiar to him during the past five daysElvgren had secretly started to enjoy its confines.

This evening, the table was only occupied by himself, Bellina, Bouchard, the captain and the first mate, the mystery illness having now spread to the other officers and two more of the crew. His betrothed was as flushed with wine as the captain and the first mate, though the major had merely sipped at one glass all night.

'Tell us, Captain, what shall we find in Port Tavarar? You did not seem overly keen to anchor there,' Bellina enquired, slurring just a touch.

The captain's face grew agitated. 'Truth be told, my lady, I would not make port in Tavarar under normal circumstances. It is less than reputable.'

'It's a shithole, you mean?'

The captain chuckled. 'Your profanity could give some of my crew a run for their money, Lady Bellina! But yes, that is what I mean.'

'It can't be that bad, Captain! The Imperial City is no bed of roses you know.'

'True, true. But at least there is some semblance of order. Varashis are not known for their respect of the law. Tavarar is where they express their contempt most strongly.' The captain paused, deep in thought for a moment 'When I was a young lad I was in the merchant navy. Fresh off my first voyage, the captain put in at Tavarar where he had a debt with a gambling house. The rest of the crew decided it would be a lark to take myself and the other young'uns out for a night on the town. We went from bar to bar, down streets as narrow as a virgin's fan—err … some narrow streets. We were well liquored up now and decided to try our hands at a game of chance. One thing led to another, can't remember who said what, but there was something about cheating. Twelve hells broke loose … saw the petty officer's throat slit from ear-to-ear.' The captain mimed the death stroke. 'Me and another lad, Wimbur, can't recall his last name for the life o' me, ran like a couple o' spooked hares. We bolted down an alley, assuming it was a shortcut, but two big bastards blocked us off. Thought I was done for! Then one thwaps Wimbur on his skull and stuffs a bag over his head. Then they turn to me — can't picture the faces no more, just the smell of garlic

— they turn and say "too ugly", butchering the common tongue like a hog. Then BANG, he clouts me one, out like a light.' Again, the captain mimicked the action, tapping his fist lightly against his jaw.

'Gods, Captain, what happened to the lad?' Elvgren said, unable to stop himself.

The captain turned his head slowly, a man trying to get his brain to catch up with the rest of the world.

'I got back to the ship the next morning, smelling like walking sin. Told the whole story to the captain. Nothing he can do, he says, City Watch would've been bribed, we'd never be able to buy 'im back. "Back from where?" says I. "From the fleshmarket," he says, "too many eastern lords have deep pockets and a fancy for pretty, young boys. Especially blonde ones." After that we set sail and I said a silent prayer of thanks for being an ugly bugger.' The captain finished his tale, then his glass.

'What a horrible story, Captain!' said Bellina. 'I can't believe that sort of thing still goes on in the world.'

'Who are we to be judging, my lady, when we enslave an *entire* race of people to fuel our empire?... Ah, never mind. I fear I have taken one too many. Don't let my story scare you though, you'll have no need to set foot in that sliver of crap.'

'Oh I wasn't worried for me. I was thinking of blondie over there!' Bellina turned to Elvgren, a self-satisfied smirk on her lips.

He shot her an acidic look but made a mental note to see if there was any hair dye on board.

*

The second day of the ship backtracking to Varash, was eerily quiet. Cirona had watched as the crew fell, one by one. The first to be struck down were now starting to die. The few healthy hands, assisted with unease by Cirona and the soldiers, were charged with commiting the dead to the sea.

Cirona and the first mate were struggling to carry the body of a young man up the ladder to the hatchway. After much grunting and undignified tussling of the poor corpse, they staggered onto the foredeck. They carried him up to the ship's rail.

The captain stood with a further three bodies at his feet; he held a small, leather-bound book of prayer in his trembling hand. He was in conversation with Bellina who put her hand on his arm and gave it a reassuring squeeze. She saw Cirona, spoke a last word to the captain and wandered over.

'How is the captain, my lady?' Cirona asked.

'As well as can be expected, I suppose. He just told me this is the most men he's lost in his whole career.'

'Black gut is a terrible thing, Lady Bellina. I have seen it take out a whole squadron.'

The pair broke off their conversation. Those able were standing in a small group in front of the captain. Three pale sailors, the first mate, Bellina, Cirona and the soldiers made up the feeble mourning party. Elvgren had been deployed to take food to the rapidly deteriorating Lord Kester.

'Those who mourn,' the captain began, 'have come to pay witness to the final passage of these brave souls. We pray to the holy four, to Firuter, Gaindor, Cantrive and Aquanas Above all, we pray to Father Light, that by his benevolence these honourable souls will be led past the Weeping Veil to peace. May his light confirm their path and keep them from Mother Darkness, creator and destroyer. Peace be.'

'Peace be,' Cirona heard herself murmur along with the rest.

10

Later that evening Bellina, Elvgren and Cirona left the captain's table after a meagre dinner. By now, the only people spared the illness were the three of them, the soldiers, the captain and the first mate. The captain had tried his best to sound chipper, informing them that they would be at Tavarar by sun-up if not sooner. Horror at what had befallen his ship lurked at the back of his eyes though. The heaving sea and rolling thunder, seemed to Bellina, like additional poor omens.

The trio made the short walk to their cabins and bid each other a terse goodnight. Bellina settled into a fitful sleep.

She was walking through a marsh. No, *the* marsh, Alcastus' marsh. The breath caught in her throat. It was cold, freezing. She shivered uncontrollably. Figures rose from the water. Some were bloated corpses, saturated flesh dripping from their bones. Others were in better states of preservation. They began to walk towards her, disjointed, like spiders with broken legs. She tried to scream but her mouth was covered with a metal plate.

The first of the terrors loomed before her. She saw the unmistakable likeness of Alcastus, his mouth fixed in a silent scream. He reached towards her. She recoiled, turned and ran straight into figures resembling the soldiers on board. They clawed at her, pulling her side to side. The world lurched left and right, slowly at first, then faster and faster.

Bellina hit the floor of her cabin with a dull thump. She blinked, lifted her head and tasted blood.

'Lady Bellina! Are you alright?' cried the major.

Bellina attempted to say something witty about taking naps on the floor, but only a groggy 'uughngh' came out. She eventually managed to collect her wits. 'What time is it, Major?'

'An hour before dawn, my lady.'

There was a sudden ear-splitting screech of metal grinding against something, then the whole world turned upside down. Whatever had caused the impact sent the pair smashing into the wall.

Bellina shook the stars from her eyes and tried to stand. She tottered unsteadily to her feet with the assistance of the major and found that everything was leaning slightly. 'By the gods! The whole ship is listing.'

'We should check on the others,' Cirona said.

They dressed quickly and fought their way to the passageway against the camber of the leaning ship. The passage was lit by faltering lights. They made their way to Elvgren's cabin.

'Lord Elvgren! Lord Elvgren, are you alright?' the major called, pounding on the door. When there was no response she forced her way in.

Elvgren's cabin was in a state of disarray but there was no sign of him. Panic flooded through Bellina. *Where the hell is he?*

They stumbled to Minister Kester's cabin. It was Bellina's turn to bang on the door, this time. 'Minister Kester! Open the door.'

The door creaked open and snatches of light fell across Kester's face. Bellina stared at it in horror. The skin was tearing away in vicious red slashes.

'Good gods, Minister Kester! What has happened to your face?' Bellina said.

'The sorcery is wearing off too soon,' he answered. 'A pity.' He flung the door back and stepped towards them, pointing the blade of a rapier at Bellina. 'It seems I need a new skin sooner than expected. For that, I will need your heart.'

*

Elvgren lay on his bed, waiting. The hours had crawled by agonisingly but now it was time to strike. He figured it must be an hour and a half before dawn, possibly two, the time when most people would be in the middle of a deep sleep. He got up and slipped the iron bar from underneath his bed. *Let's see how funny those fuckers think they are when they're walking with a limp for the rest of their lives*, he thought.

He stole lightly into the passageway. The ship was lurching quite a bit and he prayed to the gods that it wouldn't disturb anyone's sleep too much. He crept down the passageway making his way towards the soldiers' sleeping quarters.

He opened the door as quietly as he could. Peering round the side of it, his heart sank. The room was empty. *Damn it, where are they?* Well if he couldn't cripple them, he could at least get them in trouble for being out of bed.

He crept back down the passageway until he was outside the captain's cabin. The door was slightly ajar and he could hear suppressed whispers. Elvgren cautiously peeked through the gap. He saw the shadows of two men looming over the captain's bed. Gods, could it be the soldiers? What the twelve hells were they doing?

One of the men stood at the captain's head, he reached forward and clamped his hand over the sleeping man's mouth. The captain's eyes flashed open, wide with terror. The man with the hand on his mouth put his finger to his lips and shushed him like a mother to a baby. Elvgren heard a sword being drawn. Almost quicker than Elvgren could comprehend, the second man thrust it through the captain's throat. For a few brief seconds the captain was a caught fish, flailing wildly. Then he was still.

Gods save me, what the hell am I going to do? Elvgren thought. He needed to move, get to Bouchard. He tried willing his legs to move but it was the damned ball all over again. His body trembled and the iron bar clattered to the floor.

The sound caught the attention of the murderers and they both turned towards the door. Elvgren struggled to believe what he saw. Surely not? It couldn't be? Illumination poured across their faces and his fears were confirmed. Two of the soldiers met his wide-eyed stare. *Fuck, fuck, fuck*, he screamed inwardly. At last his legs found their strength and he ran, not knowing nor caring where he was going. And where was the other one, the ringleader, his chief tormentor?

As if to answer his question, the toothless soldier appeare from the hatchway. The man advanced slowly, wearing that same gappy smile. Elvgren was trapped. He backed up but the other soldiers blocked his escape. The three men pressed in on him. What the twelve hells had happened to their faces? It looked like they had lost a fight with a wild cat. Huge bleeding scars covered their features, strips of skin hanging on by a thread. He tried to scream, tried to make any kind of sound. All that came out was a thin squeak. He felt the leader's blade touch him lightly, cold through the fabric of his shirt.

'Anything to say, yer lordship?' Toothless said, his voice a terrifying chord, like two men speaking in unison, but coming from one throat. 'No? Very well then, I will enjoy eating your heart.'

As he raised his blade, Elvgren closed his eyes.

At that moment, the ship lurched violently and threw all four of them to the floor. Elvgren, adrenaline flowing, got to his feet first and ran for the ladder to the deck. He could hear the men rising and chasing him. He burst through the hatchway and rain whipped his face. The wind howled around him like the cries of the insane, while the world refused to stay still. In the distance, he could see the lights of Port Tavarar. He had to do something: raise the alarm, move the ship, make it go faster, anything.

He sprinted across the deck towards the control cabin and locked the door behind him. The body of the first mate lay in a pool of blood on the floor. Elvgren vomited. Through the cabin windows, he saw the three men advancing at a leisurely pace, laughing and pointing. He panicked, grabbing at everything in his reach. He pulled at a lever and felt the ship begin to move faster. Not fast enough. The men were outside the door. Calling to him, mocking him. He pushed the lever down as far as it would go.

The ship was now hurtling through the crashing waves at breakneck speed. Elvgren saw the tiny specks of light grow bigger and brighter. He could see the outline of the port. Rows of houses rose steeply from the bottom of a stone banked quay, their lights twinkling in the darkness. In horror, he watched the distant concept of the stone wall become a distinct certainty. Elvgren tried to spin the wheel to the right. Too late. There was a sound like a dying whale as the ship's side first scraped then smashed into the wall. The ship listed forcefully to the left and Elvgren felt the glass shatter around him as he was thrown through the window.

*

'Get back, my lady!' Cirona yelled. She stumbled the few feet between them and managed to put herself between Bellina and Kester. The point of his blade separated from hers by a fraction.

'What kind of devilry is this, Kester?' Cirona said.

'Oh, this?' Kester said, stroking a piece of flapping skin. 'Just some magic, courtesy of Arch Vizier Marmossa. You Estrians think you have the world sewn up but you couldn't even begin to imagine half the things I've seen.'

Gods, there was no room to fight, she hoped he was a talker. It would buy some time to come up with the next move. 'Whatever the hells you are I'm getting some answers. How long have you been in the Burkeshi's pay, Kester?'

'Kester?' replied the imposter. 'Kester is dead. Just one of the many faces I have assumed. His heart made a poor meal. I fear I won't have the stomach for yours, Major, but the girl's will be just right.' He reached his free hand to his face and started to peel. The flesh came away with a dry tearing sound, an old book being torn for a fire.

Cirona watched, horrified but unable to look away. Bellina vomited, clinging to Cirona's shirt for support with trembling arms. When all the flesh was peeled away, a brown face stared back at her. The irises of his eyes spun, miniature tornadoes of colour before settling into a pale blue. There was a sound like wood snapping. The man's, the *thing*'s, bones were rippling under his skin like an undulating river. He had grown in stature, taller now, more muscular. Throughout these contortions his blade hadn't dropped an inch.

'It was a shame I started to deteriorate before the others. Having to stay locked in that cabin, I've had no exercise. I shall look to remedy that now.'

The Burkeshi sprang forward. Cirona parried his thrust and jumped back.

'Major, no!' Bellina cried. Too late, Cirona hit the small frame of the girl and they both tumbled to the floor.

'Almost too easy, Major. But one should never double check a gift from Mother Darkness.' The Burkeshi raised his blade preparing to strike, its tip touching the low ceiling. His face a picture of happiness.

Cirona kicked her legs out in a vicious thrust, connecting with the man's bollocks. She jumped to her feet heaving Bellina up bodily and ran for the ladder to the foredeck.

*

Elvgren opened his eyes. The world reeled about him, a carousel of confusion. A wave of nausea washed over him. He retched but nothing came up. Rising unsteadily to his feet, he found everything was leaning slightly to port.

Head still groggy, he surveyed the scene. Some way off, two of the decomposing soldiers lay prone on the deck, the third lay just a few feet from him. The face of a Burkeshi looked up at Elvgren from a puddle of blood and skin. The skull was caved in on one side where it had collided with the guard rail. 'What in the twelve hells is going on here?' he muttered. The smell of death mingled with the stench of burning.

Flames and black tentacles of smoke rose from the ship's stern. He listened to the sound of wood crackling as the fire devoured it.

Suddenly, the two prone bodies began to rise, leaving ribbons of skin tangled on the deck. They shook their heads and their gaze fell on Elvgren. Smiling, revealing sharp pointed teeth, they came at him.

Elvgren felt his legs tremble and buckle, all his strength deserting him. A few more feet now and it would be over. Gods, he hoped it would be quick. A banging, scuffling sound carried from the ship's hatchway. His assailants turned to see what was happening.

Cursing, Major Bouchard and Bellina stumbled on to deck. Their eyes fell on the Burkeshis and then on him.

'Lord Elvgren, you're alive!' said Bellina.

'Not for much longer!' one of the Burkeshis hissed, racing towards Lovitz.

'Shit!' Elvgren heard Bouchard cry. The man filled his vision, closer, closer. He heard a dull thwack. His assailant spun and fell, Bouchard's thrown sword having struck him on his shoulder muscle. The two women sprinted towards Elvgren whilst the other Burkeshi lunged at the major. She grabbed him and they fell to the deck.

'Are you hurt?' Bellina said, the voice coming to him from far away.

'What? No, no,' he heard himself say.

'You've got to stand!'

'Can't,' he replied, watching the fire's haze shimmer below the dark, rain-filled, sky. It was beautiful. Then hands — he felt hands pulling at him. A pale white face, dark hair clinging to a scalp. *Why was she crying? Oh, they were raindrops.* A slap, stinging his cheek. 'What the hell was that for?' Elvgren said, and then, 'Oh... Thanks.' His senses were pulled back into focus just in time to see Bouchard fling the assailant from her. The man went careering into the other Burkeshi, who had just got to his feet.

The major ran over to her travelling companions.

'MOVE!' she screamed and grabbed them both, encouraging Elvgren's feet to run. She led them up the slight incline, to the starboard guard rail. 'Come on!' she yelled, pulling herself and Bellina over the rail and beckoning to him.

He took her hand and caught a glimpse of a third Burkeshi helping the others to their feet. A strong wave hit the ship, making it lean more severely to port.

'On three, let go,' Bouchard said. 'One, two, three....'

*

Bellina felt her body sliding down the ship, the rivets scratching her and tearing her clothes. She saw the wooden planks of a pier come into view and turned her body just in time to take the impact on her shoulder. Still, the force of the fall filled every nerve in her body with pain. Spots of light danced in front of her eyes as the major's face swam into view.

'My lady? Can you hear me?' Cirona said.

Bellina nodded.

'To your feet, quickly then.'

She felt Major Bouchard's arm slide under hers, helping her to her feet. Bellina saw a gaggle of onlookers a hundred paces away at the entrance to the pier. They pointed and talked excitedly but did nothing to help. With Cirona's support they made their way to Elvgren who had managed to struggle to his feet. They huddled together.

'Listen to me,' the major began, having to shout over the storm. 'I don't know how long we've got, but this has gone to shit. I will hold them off—'

'Major, they can't possibly still be moving!' Bellina interjected.

'Lady Bellina, I have just seen a man's skin fall from him. I've seen his bones change their bloody shape in front of my eyes, the list of things I still think impossible is shrinking by the fucking second.' Lightning flashed, a white scar across the sky, illuminating the major's face. Her jaw set tight, brows furrowed. 'Until I see their bodies in front of me, I won't take anything for granted. Go, I will hold them off. Three days' walk along the coast from Tavarar there is a town called Dronkor. A man called Melek lives there, he's an ex-army engineer. Get to him, tell him what's happened and get word to your father. Trust no one else with this, we may not be enemies with Varash but we're not friends either. Now repeat it to me.'

'Dronkor, Melek,' Bellina and Elvgren said.

'Good now get—'

'By the gods, look!' Elvgren shouted.

Bellina turned her head towards the ship. Three black shapes were hissing down the hull. They fell gracefully to the pier.

'Go. Now. Run!' Cirona shouted pushing at Bellina and turning to the Burkeshis.

Bellina tried to say something, anything, but no words would come.

She turned and started to run, following Elvgren. Every atom of the air filled with a sound like a giant striking a drum. Bellina and Elvgren froze. The ship's store of gunpowder had ignited, blowing a massive hole in the side before it rolled completely on to its side. Molten shrapnel rained down, sizzling as it hit the wet, wooden pier.

An immense creaking followed in the aftermath of the explosion and Bellina saw that the mast had snapped. It balanced like an acrobat for a second that seemed like eternity, before plummeting, smashing the pier in half just five feet from her.

Elvgren stared back from the other side. 'Jump!' he screamed.

She ran towards the gap and leapt. The toes of her right foot touched the other side of the pier. It was the only part of her that did. Elvgren snatched at air as gravity pulled her backwards. Time slowed. She saw Elvgren's face, eyes wide with shock. She registered her arm outstretched. It reminded her of the Lord Exchequer and the little good the gesture had done him. The air rushed up around her, billowing out her clothes. The last thing she felt was an impact on the back of her head, her brain registered it for a half second. Then everything went black.

11

Elvgren stared helplessly as he watched the woman he was betrothed to plummet towards the sea. He saw her arm stretch out to him, a look of puzzled shock on her face. He flinched when her head struck one of the pier's support struts before her body cartwheeled into the gloom.

What should he do? What the fuck should he do? Dronkor, Melek. The words echoed round his head, advice from another life. He stood up and ran. He ran to the end of the pier, he ran past the onlookers who shouted and grabbed at him. Barrelling through them, he ran, ran like the Old Terrors were loose and bent on his destruction.

Buildings, bars, people, whirled past him in a blur. Some voices called after him, others laughed. His feet pounded the cobbled path making them ache. He ducked down streets and alleys, not knowing or caring where he was going. Dronkor, Melek. Where was Melek? Who was Dronkor? No time, run, run.

His brain urged his legs onwards telling them to ignore the fire burning in his thighs and calves. The street he was heading down turned into an alley. It was dark, his feet caught on something and he went sprawling to the floor. He raised his face from the ground, pushing up on skinned palms and knees, and spat a mouthful of blood onto the cobbles. Something shuffled in the corner of his eye. A lantern shone at the end of the alleyway. A boy, thirteen or fourteen, sat on a barrel, lazily holding the light source. The boy held the lantern up so the light fell across Elvgren's face. The glare burned his eyes, he raised a hand to block it.

'Estrian, eh?' came the sing-song voice of the young lad.

Elvgren nodded, shafts of light spilling through his spread fingers.

'Looks like you could use a friend,' the boy continued.

'Gods yes, thank you, thank you!' Elvgren blubbered back.

'Well, you won't find one here.' The boy shifted his eyes to something behind Elvgren and nodded.

Elvgren turned. Two huge men were coming towards him. Their faces scarred autobiographies of misdeed. One leaned forward and placed his hand under the young lord's chin, lifting it. The smell of tobacco and dirt was strong.

'Pretty,' the man said, the other nodded approvingly.

Elvgren saw the small, coarse sack in the man's left hand. 'Please, please! Gods no! I'm a lord, my family will pay anything to get me back. Just gods, please no,' he sobbed.

'That's what they all say,' the man said, the rank stench of cheap wine clinging to his breath.

Everything went dark as the sack was thrust over Elvgren's head. He heard himself scream and the men laughing. The rough fabric rubbed against his face.

'Let's get him back to the boss,' the boy said.

Elvgren tasted the saltiness of his tears and felt the warmth of his piss trickling down his leg.

*

The sound of the mast crashing into the pier attacked her ears and sent a shudder through her body. Cirona didn't turn to look, couldn't afford to take her eyes off the men. The false Kester still held his rapier, the other two brandished large scimitars. She had nothing. Her adversaries spread out in a semicircle. *Fuck it*, she thought. Cirona dived at the Burkeshi to her left catching him by surprise. She felt the satisfying connection of her shoulder with the man's gut. He stumbled backwards. She caught his wrist, twisted his arm behind his back and heard it snap. The blade fell from his hand, clanging against the wood. She gave the man a sharp punch to the kidneys and swept his legs away. All of this happened in a heartbeat, but the other two were on her. She ducked and rolled to the left, picking up the curved blade as she did. She came up in a crouch, ready. At least now she had something to work with.

The fake Kester slashed at her. She flicked his sword away with her own and whirled her arm back just in time to parry a blow from the other. The floored Burkeshi righted himself and joined his companions. Attack followed attack. Cirona's world shrunk to three paces around her. She drew on every trick she'd ever learned, from the army *and* from the street. Still, she was barely holding them off. Got to even the odds, she thought. She spun on her heel, her scimitar knocking back all the attacker's swords at once. It bought her a second. She swung her sword arm back round catching the nearest one to her on the forearm. Her blade bit deep into the flesh and ground against the bone. He roared in pain. She spun around to his back. Grabbing the greasy, dark, curls of his hair, pulling his head back, she opened his throat.

Cirona pushed the dying man to the ground and eyed the remaining two whilst grinding her heel into the prone Burkeshi's head. *This, this is fucking it*, she thought. The bloodlust flowed through her, the thrill, the adrenaline. She charged like a berserker. Fake Kester and the other stood side by side. *That's not gonna fucking help you now*, she thought. Fake Kester stepped forward. Still charging, she knocked his arm away and smashed her elbow into his face, flattening his nose.

She pushed on to the one she had cut in the shoulder on the ship. His left arm hung uselessly at his side but he still looked capable, confident. *Time to relieve you of that assumption.* She pressed in, attacking with fury and pace. He was fending her off but retreating. She feigned a blow to his head, pulling back instead. The Burkeshi took the bait. He lunged in. She knew it was going to hurt but she no longer cared. His sword hilt collided with her stomach. Grabbing his shirt, pulling him forward, her blade sank deep, deep into his gut. She savoured the shock on his face as she twisted the blade and pulled it up towards his chest.

Pulling her sword out, she was just in time to turn and block the slash from fake Kester. He bore down on her, the point of his sword scratching her neck, pushing with all his weight but she was equal to it. She pushed back and sent him stumbling a few feet.

'It would seem your fearsome reputation is well earned, Major. This has been a fun little exercise, but I'm afraid it's over,' said the Burkeshi.

'What the fuck are you talking about? I'm still standing and two of your fellow sand-eaters are dead,' Cirona spat.

He smirked at her. 'Ah, Major, Major. Did you expect us to fight fair? Our blades are poisoned. Soon you'll go numb, in a few days you'll die in exquisite agony.'

'Bollocks,' she said, but her body felt like lead. *Dammit no. NO!* She fell to her knees, scimitar dropping from her hand.

He advanced, crouching on his haunches to look into her eyes. 'See, I told you. Oh, one more thing before you go. I know about your mission, your real mission, that is. I'm sure the Arch Vizier will find it most intriguing.'

Lies, how could he know? Gods! Can't let him go, she thought.

He leaned close and whispered in her ear. 'May the embrace of Varl Dressera, Mother of Darkness, bring you peace.'

With the last of her strength she leant her head forward and bit into his neck. He spasmed in pain and tried to pull away but she set her jaw tight. With a snap of her head she pulled back taking a massive chunk of the Burkeshi's throat with her. She watched the blood pump from a torn artery as he fell to his back. He writhed for a few seconds, then was still.

Fuzzy white crept from the corner of her eyes till it filled them. She slumped forward and didn't even feel the wooden planks break her nose.

*

Bellina felt the freezing cold of the sea before she even opened her eyes. She felt something else as well, something hard. She willed her eyes open. Her vision was blurred and her head swam, but she could make out the piece of wood that had saved her life. It was part of the smashed pier, three large planks of jagged wood. Her body lay on it, feet dangling in the water as icy swells of seawater rushed at her sides. At least it was keeping her afloat.

It was still dark. The storm had abated and a pale sliver of moon fought its way through the clouds. Bellina raised her head and tried to look around her. Pain shot through her body. Her head ached, her shoulder was bruised, but the worst pain emanated from her ribs. From the way she was resting on the planks, she realised she must have hit the boards full on. Judging from the snakes of agony that shot in all directions from that region, her mid-section had absorbed most of the fall.

Gritting her teeth against the pain, Bellina managed to raise her head a few inches. The gentle bobbing of her unintentional raft made it hard to focus but, eventually, her eyes adjusted to the movement and the dark.

Far off, she could make out the gigantic, capsized bulk of the *Prudence*. Huge gouts of smoke and fire belched from it, like a contented dragon after a feast. Nestled against its hull was the shattered pier, parts of which were also blazing merrily. Tiny dots moved around the pier, swarming over the ship. *Scavengers more likely then helpers*, she thought. *Gods ... Cirona and Elvgren! Were they still there? What had happened?* She tried to call out but the effort made her head spin, and she collapsed back into unconsciousness.

*

The sun was high in the heavens when Bellina next opened her eyes. Though it was still hidden behind thin clouds, the sight gave her some cheer. *So, I'm still alive.* A thirst raged in her throat, her tongue abrasive and rough. She pushed the sensation to the back of her mind and tried to move again. The pain made her gasp and it was a few minutes before her breathing returned to normal.

Where the hell was she? If Bellina squinted her eyes she could just make out the shore. Gods, surely a ship of some kind must be ploughing these waters? She turned her head to both sides but she saw no sails on the horizon. The cost of the effort was to send her head tumbling back to the planks. *A ship has to come by soon*, she thought.

A day passed. The scorching sun beat upon her ragged body. Her thirst was a constant urge, pressing on her, blocking out everything except a tiny flicker of hope. *A ship must come, it must.* Bellina clung to the thought as tightly as she clung to the planks.

Hours passed, or perhaps they were minutes, she couldn't tell. Time had lost all meaning, lost like she had lost sight of the shore. The tide bore her further and further out to sea.

The vastness of the water was claustrophobic, smothering, overbearing in its size and importance. *A bit like my father*, she thought, *without the underlying tenderness.* She tried to conjure an image of her father but the picture wouldn't form. She could smell him though: tobacco, tea, and musty old books. She sobbed but no tears flowed, all she did was make a horrible braying sound that wracked her broken ribs.

Bellina drifted in and out of consciousness. She knew it was sunset by the rushing onset of cold that the night brought, and knew it was morning by the stinging sensation of her sunburn greeting its creator's rays.

A ship. Dronkor, Melek. These things seemed distantly important, a half-heard message from another time. Faces swam in her mind, Cirona, Elvgren, her father, but their skin was peeling away.

As if from far away, she heard a sound, a horn maybe. She opened her eyes and saw the water scythed apart like Father Light parting the Weeping Veil. She wasn't religious but she prayed then, prayed that he would keep Mother Darkness at bay. There were more sounds — shouts, calls. She felt her little collection of planks sway and bob, more and more forcefully. A dark grey wall filled her vision; the Veil perhaps? But it didn't shimmer like the scriptures said.

Bellina's eyes closed. She felt hands bearing her upwards, the Father carrying her to the Eternal. *The Eternal was certainly noisy*, she thought.

Her back pressed against something hard. Rising like the ascension of a poorly kept portcullis, her eyelids opened. Light filled her vision. The shadow of a head came into view, sunlight surrounding it in a halo of diffused rays.

'Close your eyes, little dove, you are safe now,' said a voice. It was a deep, rich bass.

'Dronkor... Melek.' Bellina's voice rasped like from an animated corpse.

'Welcome, Dronkor Melek! I am Captain Barboza. I welcome you to my kingdom on the sea. Welcome to the good ship — *Scampering Vagabond*!'

12

Sounds of unfamiliar languages made their way through the rough sack to Elvgren's ears. The voices chattered excitedly as he felt himself pushed against a wall, something cold and metallic was clamped around his wrists. Then the bag was removed.

The light temporarily blinded him before his eyes adjusted to the brightness. He was in a large room. Simple oil torches, fuelled by stinking, garwhale blubber, lit the windowless scene and he guessed he must be underground. The room stank of damp and stale alcohol, the former coming from the patches of mould covering the walls and the latter, possibly, from the dubious piles of barrels scattered around the floor. Or maybe the stench came from the men themselves, if the flagon strewn table was anything to go by. His three captors sat around it, laughing and chatting while they poured drinks from a large, leather-bound vessel. A fire burned merrily behind them; the scene resembled a bizarre family reunion.

A door banged open somewhere at the back of the room. The three at the table jumped to attention. *Just like men used to do for me*, Elvgren thought. A huge, bear-like man strode to the head of the table.

'What is so big deal that I had mustjump from sweet embrace of Gontara?' he asked.

'We found pretty one, boss!' one of the other men said.

'Really, Jadir? Or will this one be like last, pretty as your mother's sagging tits?'

'Is true, boss. I think may we even square things with Faultwright for us,' said the boy who Elvgren remembered from the alleyway.

'Well, if *you* say so, Dargo, I believe. Let's look at him then,' the boss said. He strode towards Elvgren like a king, completely in command of all around him. He was imposing, with thick black hair protruding from any exposed area of flesh. He leaned towards Elvgren, dark eyes sat atop a crooked nose and his lower jaw was covered in a thicket of beard. A smile broke through the tangle and unleashed chipped, discoloured teeth. 'Well, well. This was a good night's work you've been having!'

'Sir, please, I am a lord of Estria! Whatever you're thinking to do with me, the reward for my return would be far greater!' Elvgren found the courage to say.

The boss laughed heartily. 'Oh really? Could it help me settle debt to biggest criminal in city full of them? I thinkno. Even if some sliver true, you, my friend, are going to be ticket to bigger things.'

Elvgren began to sob.

'Please, no tears, handsome boy; you must keep face pretty for auction in ten days.'

'F ... fuck y ... ya... you ... you stinking Varashi shitstain!' Elvgren stammered out, surprised at himself.

'Tut, tut. Such tongue will not be doing. Perhaps I cut out?'

Elvgren's eyes grew wide and he shook his head.

'No? Good. But no food or drink for you, my *lord*. See if rumble belly and scratchy throat stop your noise.' The boss turned away and went back to the table.

Elvgren sat slumped against the wall in semi-darkness. The gang had produced a large joint of meat that was spitting beautifully over the fire, grease dripping into the flames with a crackling sizzle. The wine was flowing easily too and, before long, the grown men passed out.

The young boy, Dargo, was still alert and bright-eyed, despite the revels. He sighed theatrically at his captors and lifted his light frame from his seat. He wandered over, carrying his plate and a cup of wine. 'Hungry?' he asked.

Elvgren's stomach answered for him.

'Ah! Sounds like it. Here you go.' Dargo set the plate and cup in front of Elvgren's cuffed hands.

He had to shift himself a little, but there was enough slack from the chains connecting him to the wall to get at the sustenance. Elvgren began to shovel the food into his face as fast as his manacled hands would allow him. He stopped mid-chew and eyeballed the boy suspiciously.

'Don't worry: it's not poisoned!' Dargo laughed and Elvgren renewed his assault. Once the plate was empty, Dargo continued. 'For what it's worth, I'm sorry,' he said

'Well that sets it all straight then!' Elvgren replied.

'Look, if it weren't for Faultwright, we would have just robbed you, given you a bang on the head to remember Tavarar and sent you on your way.' Dargo continued.

'How comforting. Don't usually dabble in the flesh trade then, eh?'

'Not much. Too much trouble and our gang ain't got the connections to tie up all the problems it creates.' Dargo stroked his smooth tanned face thoughtfully.

'Where are you from?' Elvgren asked.

'Tremore originally. Took to sea after my mother died. Fell in as a cabin boy, fell out in the world's arsehole.'

'How did you get involved in all... *this*?' Elvgren carried on, enjoying having someone to talk to.

'Oh, the gang? Well a boy's gotta eat and I've always been pretty nimble. So, I started cutting purses. Good at it too. Then one day I lifted a purse from some big bastard, turned out to be the boss. Was just about to make my get away when old Jadir, over there, grabbed me.' Dargo acted this out with a yank of his collar. 'Thought I was done for, finished. But the boss jus' laughed, said anyone who could rob *him* had to be useful. They took me in and here we are.'

'Heart-warming,' Elvgren said.

'Well, it ain't much but it's what I got. Look, it might not be much consolation, but some of the rich fuckers with a taste for pretty boys treat their bed sharers like little princes. Don't hide 'em away or nothing. That kind of thing's not as frowned upon here in Varash,' Dargo said.

'How lovely! Bend over, dear boy, and this time try not to let your furs tickle my balls.' Elvgren shook his head. 'Thank you for your tea and sympathy, boy, but you can leave me alone now.'

'Fine. Just wanted to offer a little solace to a fellow former servant of the great and wondrous Estrian Empire. Funny how it's not around when you need it.' Dargo stood up and brushed off his knees. He walked, without a sound, to a small hammock hanging from the far wall.

It wasn't long before Elvgren heard the gentle rhythm of the boy's snoring. The young lord curled himself up into a ball hugging his knees and tried to remember if his mother had ever hugged him in his life.

*

Cirona saw the smiling face of Trafford. He was cradling their baby in his arms and cooing at it softly. Cirona felt a smile on her face then she saw blood slowly staining the front of his uniform. It spread out from a small burnt hole just above his heart. She started to wail. Two men in cowls appeared at Trafford's side; they turned him and gently led him away. *No!* She could hear herself call after them but they were deaf to her cries. All that was left was the stench of blood.

The smell still filled her nostrils as her eyes opened. She was staring upwards at a low ceiling. Turning her head, she saw a table covered with flasks and tubes. Cotton wadding, grown fat with blood, drooped over its edge.

A man turned from a chair just in front of the table and fixed his eyes on her, eyes enlarged by the spectacles that perched on his narrow nose. 'Ah, you're finally awake!' he said, his voice as soft as velvet.

'Where...' Cirona tried to say, through a furred throat.

'Where are you? Who am I? I'm sure your mind is positively racing with questions, my dear. I shall answer them in good time, but first, perhaps a drink?'

The small man rose, his delicate hands cupped a wooden bowl which he brought to her mouth. Cirona drank gratefully, feeling the slight sting of the liquid passing over her cracked lips. She drained the contents of the bowl and laid her head back.

'Now for your questions. I am Silas Trevelbert, chief medificer to Gulgarno's School of Gladiatorial Combat. The finest, and most profitable, combatant based spectacle in all of Varash.'

'A gladiator school? I don't suppose you took me in out of the kindness of your hearts then?' Cirona said.

'Ha, ha, no. You're quite right. My master, and yours now, heard tale of a large Estrian woman who killed three Burkeshis single-handedly. He considered the expense of your treatment a risk worth taking and here you are!' Silas paused taking a sip from a small cup he had procured for himself.

'Ah, the well-known charity of the Varashis. They see a person dying on the floor and the first thing they do is work out how much they can get for the meat.'

'Come now, madam. Don't be sour! If it wasn't for our master's hospitality, and my considerable skills, you would be another corpse floating on the sea. Been plenty of those since your ship went down,' another small sip. 'You are alive, and will be given a chance to win glory and perhaps even your freedom. What more could a woman who was staring into the Weeping Veil want?'

'How long have I been out and where the hells am I?' Cirona asked.

'You have been unconscious some ten days now. I was beginning to worry that you may never wake. That would have been a most unfortunate conversation to have with the master,' Silas said. 'As for where you are presently, well, I think *that* can remain a secret. Lots of people get funny ideas when they know how close, or far, they are from something familiar.'

Dammit, this wouldn't do: she had to get to Dronkor. 'Was there anyone else with me when I was found? And where the hells are my belongings?' Cirona said, her fatigued mind finally wondering where Bellina's cognopathic power control had gone.

'Your meagre belongings are gone, my lady. Well, all except this,' Silas said dangling the power control bracelet and an ornate key on a chain in front of her. 'Do not worry I shall return them, though how they escaped the prying fingers of the miscreants who brought you in, I will never know,' he said placing the bracelet back on Cirona's wrist and the key round her neck. 'As for if there was anybody found with you at the time, to the best of my knowledge there was not, madam.' He shook his head to emphasise his words. 'Now, I think that's quite enough questions. The sleeping draught should be taking effect soon and you will need your strength. You'll be expected to begin training as soon as you can. Our master has a great many remarkable qualities but patience is not one of them.'

'You fuck....' Cirona started to say. Her head was heavy and sleep was calling. She felt her eyelids droop and prayed to the gods that Elvgren and Bellina had not fallen prey to the many dangers of Tavarar.

*

Bellina paused mid-scrub to look down at her raw hands. Only a few hours of the monotonous chore and her fingers were already chapped and sore. Until then she had never thought about the effort it took to get clean plates to her table at home. If she ever got back she would never take it for granted again.

'Chop, chop, Belle. Those pots ain't gonna clean 'emselves and I wanna see my face in that one!' said Bandrick, the ship's cook.

'I'm looking at your face now and, quite frankly, you don't!' replied Bellina.

'Oho! A saucy one, eh? Best not to piss off the cook on a ship, love, never know what might turn up in yer grub,' Bandrick chuckled before going off to busy himself elsewhere. He was a jolly sort as most people on board seemed to be, an attitude that came from the captain.

Ah, Captain Barboza! Now there was a most intriguing man. It had taken Bellina the best part of a week to recover from her ordeal. During that time she was allowed to take up the first mate's cabin. The captain himself had taken pains to bring her food and her first sight of him was something she was never likely to forget. Stooping so low he was almost doubled over, he came through the door. To say he was a giant of a man would be a lie, Bellina thought that there must be small mountains somewhere which were envious of him, and his height matched his width. His skin was as black as onyx, a native of Bakori she found out, with shining eyes. His attire was even more remarkable than his physical appearance. He was dressed in bright white breeches and a pink greatcoat. All of this capped off with a spectacular, blonde, pompadour wig.

The sight of his physical appearance, combined with his dress, forced Bellina to suppress her laughter. His voice though, his voice was pure gold. It was the same voice she had heard when she was first rescued but now she was well enough to truly appreciate it. It was like the warmth of brandy running through her body, comforting, strengthening. His voice seemed to make her very bones vibrate pleasantly; she could have listened to that voice for hours.

Which is precisely what she had been made to do. Barboza questioned her at length. Who was she? Where had she come from? How had she ended up adrift? Having regained enough of her wits, Bellina decided to tell the man half-truths; easier that way to avoid being caught in the massive tapestries that lies could become. She told him her name was Belle and that she had been travelling as a maid to a lord. Their ship had stopped at Tavarar for supplies and she had been knocked from the pier in a storm. Barboza seemed to believe the story but that was when things got complicated.

Bellina asked some questions of her own. Were they far from Varash and could she be taken as close as possible to Tavarar or Dronkor? The captain told her that unfortunately his ship would not be returning to Varash for a while as his business took him elsewhere. She asked him what type of business that was and he told her it was fortune.

'The *Scampering Vagabond* is a ship of fortune, a pirate ship. A floating kingdom of free men and women who refuse the constricting laws of dry land,' he said. If Bellina desired and his travels took him there, he would drop her off at Varash but, until then, she would have to be part of his crew and work for her passage.

He painted a beautiful picture of his democracy on the high seas, his silky voice making the whole notion very romantic. Then he set her to scrubbing pots.

Well, that was just one of her duties as cabin girl. Sweeping and scrubbing floors, bringing food and drink to the captain's table, peeling vegetables — it was a servant's life and it made her bristle with indignation. It also brought the reality of what she had left behind into sharp focus. If scrubbing pans was what it took to get her to Varash, then scrub pans she would.

Bellina was in a committed fury to this activity when she heard a voice speak hesitantly behind her. 'If you put a dab of vinegar on the brush it won't take half as long.'

She turned towards the friendly advice. A young man stood before her. Twenty if he was a day. His height was above average, with a solid looking frame. He had a thick neck and jaw, a fine stubble covering the latter. He wasn't a handsome youth, his eyes were a little too far apart and his teeth were ever so slightly crooked, but he would not have trouble finding a wife. Bellina arched her eyebrows at him and delivered her most condescending look. 'Do you presume, boy, to tell me how to scrub a bloody pot?'

'Oh no, no, I just thought that... You see... I—' the boy stuttered.

'Yes, yes, what the hells is it?' Bellina said.

'It's just that ... this used to be my job and I know a few tricks that might speed things up for you.' He offered her a nervous smile.

'If I wanted advice from idiots, I would ask for it. Now be off with you: I have work to do.' Bellina turned her back to him. She heard the door close behind her. Waiting a few minutes, she then reached for the glass vial of vinegar.

*

Later that day, Bellina was sitting with her back against the wooden frame of a raised platform. She took her brief moment of respite to observe the *Scampering Vagabond*. It was a small vessel, iron clad, with two masts sprung from the deck to assist when the sortilenergy ran low. The sails were not unfurled at the moment and the ship chugged merrily along under the power of the two spinning side paddles.

The sun was past the mid-point on a hot, clear day and her thoughts drifted. She wondered what had happened to the others. Were they in Dronkor now? Was Cirona hurt? How badly had Elvgren ballsed something up? What else were the kaffars of Burkesh capable of if they could replicate the appearance of others? All this went through her mind together with the fear that the news of what had become of the mission would surely have reached her father by now. How the hells would he take the news with his nerves already so strained? The idea that she could be causing him more pain and worry made her guts spin. That, and the shameful knowledge that after only a few weeks from his watchful eye she was a cabin girl on a pirate ship.

Her musings were disrupted by a shadow looming in front of her. She looked up ready to shoot another waspish riposte at the boy. It wasn't him though. So far, the crew of the *Vagabond* had been at odds with her idea of pirates, but this man confirmed the ship's true purpose.

His eyes stared at her from deep, sunken pits. A matted tangle of hair covered his narrow ratty face and his head sat atop a wiry but muscular body. 'Shouldn't you be working, girl?' he asked, his voice gruff.

'I'm finished scrubbing this bit of deck and was about to start on the upper. Thought I might catch my breath, if it's all the same to you,' Bellina replied.

'Always work to be done on a ship, lass.' He paused, hawking a wad of phlegm onto the deck. 'See? Looks like you missed a bit.' With that he stalked off, laughing.

Bellina's eyes followed him, burning with anger. She stroked absently at her power restraint. One tiny click from its control conduit and she could blow the brains from his skull. The thought was delicious but, with Cirona and the control conduit gods only knew how far away, it was not going to happen.

'That's pretty.'

Bellina turned her head and met the young man's eyes.

'Oh. It's you,' she said. 'It was a gift from my father, I was wondering why no one had tried to take it.' *Not that anyone would be able to get the bloody thing off*, she thought.

'Nah, won't no one try to take it, miss. Cap'n banned anyone from taking shipmates personal art... ar ... artik ...'

'Articles?' she finished for him.

'Yeah that's the word.' He smiled at her sheepishly.

Bellina dearly wanted to tell him to bugger off but curiosity got the better of her. 'Who was that man just now?'

'Oh him. That's Tinker — miserable git. There's a few like him on ship, I'm afraid. Take it upon 'emselves to *initiate* the new crew. Try to stay outta their way and keep your eyes down, they'll soon get bored.'

'Well, I'm not accustomed to keeping my eyes down. Now if you don't mind I've got decks to clean.'

She pulled the brush from her bucket and began to remove the greeny brown present Tinker had left for her.

'Try doing it in circular motions,' the boy offered.

Bellina shot him a look of pure acid at which he flinched and scuttled off. When he had retreated to a safe distance she began to move the camel hair brush in big circles.

*

The sun had finally set and Bellina was trying to get herself comfortable in a hammock. A task she was quickly deciding was impossible. She had finally contorted herself into a position that may have allowed her to sleep when she was tumbled unceremoniously to the floor.

'That one's taken,' a flat female voice intoned.

Bellina turned to face the woman trying not to rub at her throbbing knee. 'Don't see your name on it,' she replied, attempting to sound as threatening as the other woman looked.

'Ain't gotta have my name on it, scrub rat. Just gotta take it.' Malice danced in the woman's eyes.

Bellina scrabbled to her feet and stood face-to-face with her. Well, face-to-chin anyway.

'Wahoo! A fight! Git 'er, Vell,' came a voice from the back of the sleeping quarters.

'Make sure to tear at each other's clothes a bit!' came another voice, followed by laughter.

Bellina looked up into Vell's eyes. She bit her lip to stop it trembling.

'Hang on, Vell! She's new, don't know the rules.' It was the boy again.

'I don't need anyone to fight my battles!' Bellina said to him. Vell used the distraction to belt Bellina round the face. Bellina tumbled to the floor for the second time that evening. She looked up at Vell, blood boiling. The boy placed his hand on her shoulder when she tried to get up but she brushed it away. 'She can have the fucking hammock if she thinks her fat arse will fit in it!' she said, like a dog not knowing when it's beat.

'Get 'er outta here, Holger, before that lip gets well and truly busted,' Vell said to the boy.

'Come on,' Holger whispered to Bellina.

Still keeping her eyes on Vell, she allowed him to lead her away.

'You really don't keep yer eyes down, do ya?' Holger said. 'Come on, I'll show ye where we get to kip.'

He led her to the back of the sleeping quarters, passing full hammocks, their occupants happily snoring. He stopped at the far wall. A scrawny boy of about ten was already curled up, a threadbare blanket wrapped round him.

'Budge up, Midge. Gotta guest,' Holger said, nudging the boy with his boot. The lad looked up sleepily and shuffled over without complaint. Holger settled himself on the floor and then patted a space nearby.

Bellina lowered herself down. The spot was unexpectedly warm, the wood practically radiating heat. The surprise must have registered on her face as Holger grinned.

'Ha! Yeah pretty cosy, ain't it? Right next to the engine room. One of the few perks us young'uns get. Here, have my blanket. I'll get too warm anyway.'

Bellina took the rag. 'Thanks,' she said.

A smile lit his face. 'You're welcome miss...'

'Belle,' she said.

'You're welcome, Miss Belle. Well, better get yer head down, all starts again tomorrow.' With that he yawned and huddled up.

Bellina settled herself a respectable distance from Holger and sank in to the deep untroubled sleep of the exhausted.

13

'Wakey, wakey, handsome boy!' The boss' voice penetrated into Elvgren's dreams of home and pulled his eyelids open. 'Today is the day!'

After ten days on the floor of the gang's subterranean lair, being fed scraps from Dargo, it seemed he was finally to meet his fate as a perfumed rent boy. It had taken the boss longer than expected to set up a meeting with Faultwright, but the Tavarar criminal overlord had finally found the time to accept the gang's gift.

'Let's get you up and washed; you smell like a fucking dog,' the boss said.

'What do you expect when that is how I've been treated?' Elvgren replied.

'Ha, no. We have kept you worse than a dog. Dogs are useful. They catch rats and can be trained to attack. While you, you are just a pretty mouth to feed.' The boss unchained him from the wall, and removed the cuffs from his wrists..

'Dargo, help our young *lord*, with his bath. Make you feel at home, pretty boy? Servants seeing to your whims.' The boss shoved Elvgren towards Dargo laughing like thunder.

Dargo helped him undress until Elvgren stood naked beside the large metal tub in front of the fire.

'Hope you just cold, lordship. I thinks maybe you master will be small disappoint!' Jadir called at him from his seat at the table. The gang laughed. Elvgren tried to look dismissive of their taunts but it's hard to keep your dignity with nowhere to hide.

'Here you are mate, I'll help you in,' Dargo said, offering him his hand. Elvgren refused it, and tried to surmount the high sides of the tub on his own. Unbalancing, he tumbled in sending water everywhere amidst more laughter.

'Hope they don' wanna take you to any balls!' Kotor, the third in command said.

Dargo helped him to scrub and clean his back in the lukewarm water. Then, after Elvgren was out, Dargo passed him a poor excuse for a towel.

Elvgren thought of the big fluffy towels Benkins used to pass him after his bath and the pang for home grew more intense.

Dargo helped him dry his back, legs and arms. 'I think you can reach your own balls, my lord. I'm afraid I'm not in quite so much of a mind to get acquainted with them as some in Varash.'

Elvgren gave him a cool look and finished his drying. Dargo then helped him get into a clean shirt and brown breeches.

'I am thinking now you will do, eh?' the boss said, clapping Elvgren round the shoulder. 'Come now, your carriage awaits!'

'Hang on, boss. Could I have a few words with him before he goes?' Dargo asked.

'Ah, go on. All that feeding and cleaning him has made him feel like a pet to you, no?' the boss paused to laugh. 'Yes, yes, go on then. But quick you must be, yes? Jadir, Kotor, bring him up front when this is over.' Then he strode to the door and left.

'Look, I know it doesn't mean much, but I *am* sorry,' Dargo said.

'Oh, more of your apologies. How about you set out on your skinny arse and find someone else then? Or maybe offer it in place of mine?' Elvgren said.

'Alright, alright, just...' Dargo lost his balance and stumbled into Elvgren. They both went down. Dargo jumped back to his feet and offered Elvgren his hand. After pausing for a moment, the young lord accepted it. He was glad he did. Elvgren felt a small, metal key pressed into his palm. Dargo squeezed his hand. He looked him square in the eye.

'Maybe you will disappear before Faultwright gets you to the fleshmarket. Not before the transaction mind, gotta make sure he can't trace it back to us.' Dargo whispered to him.

'Than—' Elvgren began to say, but Dargo shook his head.

'Go now, you don't keep Faultwright waiting.'

Elvgren gave the boy one last look and tears welled in his eyes.

'No crap like that, eh? Got to look good! Not all red in eye,' Jadir said. Then they led him from the gangs' den.

*

After a long carriage ride Elvgren and his captors stood in front of a large run-down warehouse. The boss went ahead and rapped out a signal on the wood. The large doors slid back and they were ushered inside.

The room stank of barley, which Elvgren thought was probably in the sacks lining the shelves on the walls. The ceiling rose to a great height, from where pigeons looked down on the scene, defecating in appreciation. A man sat at a table which occupied the large, clear space at the centre of the warehouse. Behind him, stood five scary looking individuals who displayed a rather impressive array of weapons. The boss' group walked to the table and the man rose.

'Afternoon, Danker, this the bit of fluff then?' The man was Estrian, tall and mean looking.

'Certainly, it must be, Holt. But where is Master Faultwright?' Danker replied.

'Ain't got time to be dealing with you little piddlers, eh. If his lieutenant ain't good enough for ya, we'll go,' Holt said.

'No, no. Please good sir, no offence was I meaning,' Danker said.

'Good. Right then, bring him up 'ere so I can get a look at him.'

At this Elvgren was marched forward. Holt gave him a thorough appraisal including his teeth, before delivering his verdict.

'Not bad, Danker. Not bad at all. He a real blonde or another one of your dye jobs? That cost you sore with Faultwright when the last one's hair grew out.'

'No, no. No more tricksies from me. I've learnt my lesson,' Danker said, deferentially. Elvgren took some bitter amusement from the boss' servile attitude towards Faultwright's man. 'Well, you are happy, yes? You take him, then me and your boss, we is all on the square,' Danker continued.

'Yeah, well about that, Danker. Thing is, boss don't know I'm 'ere. Think I might just take this little beauty to 'im meself and get a nice bit 'o coin for me troubles.' A satisfied smile spread across Holt's face.

'You stinking son of a whore! Swindling, chalky, swine-fucker! How dare you!' Danker roared.

'Now, now, don't get angry, Danker. You're outnumbered 'ere, use that tiny puddle of ant's piss you call a brain and walk out of here alive. How about... what the fuck is he doing?'

Elvgren had used the distraction of the heated exchange to get the key into his teeth. He had just inserted it into the lock securing his cuffs when the assembly turned on him.

'Stop 'im!' Holt cried.

'Oh no you don't! If I get nothing, you get nothing!' Danker threw the table over into Holt. Jadir and Kotor sprang forward to help their boss take on the men.

'Fuck them, you imbeciles. Two of you get the boy!' Holt shouted as he tried to extricate himself from under the table.

Two men split off from the fray and started towards Elvgren. His blood pounded and his body shook. The key fell from his mouth. He backed away but he soon felt the wall bang into his back.

The men were coming on, laughing. *Why are these people always fucking laughing? Laughing at me, a Lovitz.* He was sick of trembling and pissing his breeches. *Fuck it*, he thought, *if I'm going down, I'm taking someone with me.* He assumed a fighting stance.

A look of surprise passed across the thugs' faces.

'Gonna do something, pretty boy?' one of them said, leering at him.

Elvgren smashed his forehead into the man's nose. It left the lord dazed and sent his attacker tumbling.

'You little fucker!' the other shouted, drawing his sword and charging.

Slow, too slow, Elvgren thought. He let the man set his wild swing in motion before darting to the left, ducking under the strike. He drove his knee into his opponent's gut and the man doubled over. Elvgren brought his cuffed hands down sharply on the man's neck. Unconscious, the sword fell from his grasp. Elvgren stooped to pick it up as a ballistol shot whizzed past his cheek. Just managing to grab the sword, he luxuriated in the feeling of power that flowed into him as he stood up. The first man was back on his feet, smoke trailing from his ballistol. He saw Elvgren brandishing the sword and gave up on trying to refill his weapon. He dropped the shot and powder on the floor and pulled a small mace from his belt.

'Your move, shitface,' Elvgren sang at him. The sword made him feel complete, unstoppable, the fastest blade in Estria had rediscovered his form.

This one was more wary though and circled him slowly. Elvgren danced forward and back, trying to draw the man into a premature strike. It wasn't forthcoming. *Fine then, I'll go.* He shot forward, surprising the man with his speed. During his sparring matches, he would have played this advantage up and showboated, now he was pure business.

Without any hesitation he thrust the sword through the man's gut. His opponent gasped in shock, his blood trickling over Elvgren's hands. Pulling the sword loose, he let the man fall to the floor. Picking up the key, he unchained his hands. The scuffle continued up ahead. He turned to escape through the open door, then stopped. Perhaps Danker's gang might be of some use to him. He had no money or food. He ran back into the fight.

Holt and Danker were at loggerheads, as were Jadir and Kotor with their opponents. Charging in, he slid his blade into the small of Kotor's assailant's back. Without waiting, he stormed towards Jadir's fight. His new foe saw him coming and forced some distance between himself and Jadir. Elvgren kept running, the man swung at empty air as the young lord rolled under the strike slashing into his opponent's shin. The man stumbled forward and Elvgren plunged the sword through his neck. Jadir stared in wonder at Elvgren, who nodded at him.

The young lord continued to Danker's side. Holt, seeing the numbers were against him, dropped his weapon.

'Alright Danker, you win. You wouldn't hurt old Holt, would ya? Come on, what would Mr. Faultwright think if one of his … er … most trusted men didn't return to his nurturing bosom?'

Danker looked thoughtful and started to lower his weapon. 'Perhaps you are being right? You can—'

Elvgren cut him off. 'Hang on *boss*. Didn't this ratshit say that no one knew where he was? Lots of places a man like you could end up eh, Holt? Brothels, gambling dens … face down in the sea?'

A smile spread across Danker's face. 'Right you are being boy, right you are being. This is end for you Holt, I think. I will be makeingsure to bury you under some shit.'

Holt turned and scrabbled to get away but Danker stamped heavily on the man's ankle. There was a snap and a scream. Holt fell on his belly. Danker sat on his back, pulled his head up and slit his throat.

'Well boy, it would seem you are not being so useless after all. Would you like a place in our little family?'

Elvgren nodded.

'Very good. Then you shall have your fair share of the loot we take from the corpses. Oh, and welcome, brother!' Danker extended his hand to Elvgren, who shook it.

14

Cirona stood on a covered veranda looking down at her fellow gladiators training. The heat beat down relentlessly, a deluge of sweat poured down her back and *she* was in the shade. Gods only knew how the poor bastards on the hard, sandy ground below her felt. *I'll find out soon enough*, she thought. The sleeping draught Silas had given her had been potent but it had not stopped her dreams, merely trapped her in them. Last night her baby and Trafford had been accompanied by Bellina before being taken away by the cowled figures. As such, her sleep had been far from restful. She was beginning to think that she may be able to sleep standing when a door opened behind her. Cirona turned and saw two men. One was Silas, she guessed the other was her new master.

Gulgarno was listening to the medificer. One eyebrow, atop a fleshy slab of face, raised in question at whatever Silas was saying. If size was an indicator of such things, then Gulgarno was an extremely successful proprietor of death sport. His features were small and dainty, hemmed in by the jowly fat that surrounded them. As he spoke to Silas, the fat jiggled and rippled around his mouth. Cirona's eyes scanned down the man's frame. She could see now why the doors of the gladiator school were so wide. His gut pressed urgently against his silk robes, quite a feat considering there was probably enough material to cover a small village. From his torso, large formless legs extended to his bloated feet. Gulgarno raised his hands in a gesture that told Silas their conversation was over. As he stretched out his arms, flesh drooped like theatre curtains. His fat fingers were covered in rings that Cirona felt sure would never come off. Silas saw himself out. Gulgarno waddled towards her. He stopped a few feet away and Cirona's vision was engulfed by the sphere of blubber.

'Aha! My newest acquisition. Good morning,' Gulgarno said.

Cirona nodded in reply.

'Silas tells me your recovery is complete, well, enough for *me* anyway. Pray tell me what you think of my charges toiling in the training yard.'

'They seem ... well drilled,' Cirona said.

'Of course, they are! You don't become the most successful gladiator school in Varash without looking after your cattle well. Hopefully you will make a good addition to the herd.'

It made her skin itch to be referred to in such a way. She bit the inside of her cheek to stop herself from punching him. She could tear his throat out on the spot but she wouldn't get far. No one got as fat as him without investing heavily in their own self-preservation.

'Ah, now there is the look! Want to punch me and claw at me. Well save that feeling, hang on to it, use it to win yourself glory and fortune, perhaps even your freedom — once I've made a return on my investment, of course.'

'At least I wasn't cheap,' she said.

'Quite the contrary. I just hope my scouts were right about your fighting ability!'

'So, you're telling me that your men saw me fighting three Burkeshis on a collapsed pier while a boat exploded around me, and their first thought was to sell me to you? Don't you think someone will come looking for me?'

'A lot of things get lost in Tavarar. Plus, whoever you work for won't be looking for you *here*.' He let out a satisfied little chuckle.

'What makes you so sure?' she asked.

'This and that, that and this. But enough questions from you. Let's see how you do in the yard!'

Cirona was deep in thought as she left the veranda and followed him down the stairs. Gulgarno must have some idea where she was from, the *Prudence* was obviously an Estrian naval vessel. Surely, someone would at *least* come asking questions about her? He seemed so confident though, and a man like him would make sure to cover his tracks. *For fuck's sake*, she thought, *I've just got to concentrate on getting out of here for now.*

As Cirona reached the training area she really took in how well fortified Gulgarno had made his gladiator school. The rectangular training area was surrounded by massive sandstone walls. On top of these stood a hundred, maybe more, armed guards, watching the gladiators intently from towers and walkways. Each corner was topped by a huge watchtower. *How the hells could she escape this?*

Gulgarno and Cirona swept into the yard. The fat man observed the training, nodding appreciatively. The trainers nodded back while the gladiators continued their drills as if he wasn't there. After a while they came to a halt by two men who were sparring with dulled weapons which couldn't cut but could damn well hurt. One of the men was of mixed heritage, like so many in Varash. The other was unmistakably Burkeshi. *Oh, you have got to be kidding me?*

'Reveeker, come here,' Gulgarno said. The Burkeshi put down his weapon and walked towards them. The other man went off with a trainer.

Standing a good head taller than her, the Burkeshi's muscles were well toned and oiled. Cirona noticed that the sides of his hair had turned to grey. A large scar ran from his chest to his abdomen. *The man must be tough to survive the kind of life that gives you scars like that one.*

'Reveeker, would you please spar with ... oh dear, I'm afraid I don't know your name, my woman?' Gulgarno said, eyes glittering with amusement at something.

'Cirona,' she said, deciding that if he did some digging on her name, it might give him pause for thought.

'Yes, that's it. Major Cirona Bouchard. Can't believe I forgot the name for one of Estria's most famed soldiers.' Gulgarno snickered.

'How the fuck do you know my—' She was cut off by the sharp sting of a whip against her back. She turned to see a middle-aged man of medium build with rodent-like features. He held the lash in his hand, his eyes burning with spite.

'Hold your tongue woman,' the man spat.

'Yes, yes, Barag. That's enough. I'm sure the major here will get well acquainted with your whip in due course.' Gulgarno turned back to Cirona and the Burkeshi, Barag leered menacingly over the fat man's shoulder. 'Now, if you two assets would indulge me ...' he continued, pointing Cirona and Reveeker towards the training square.

'I fear a woman fresh from the sickbed won't be much sport, Master ... but as you wish,' Reveeker said.

The pain from the whip had subsided, leaving behind anger and confusion. What the fuck was going on? How in the twelve hells did Gulgarno know her name? How much else did he know? *Dammit all*, she thought, anger rising to fury. 'You want sport?' Cirona spat at Reveeker. 'I'll fucking give you sport, sand-shagger. Got pretty handy at killing you brown bastards in my time.'

'There now! That's the spirit, Major. Off you go then,' Gulgarno said.

Reveeker extended his arm towards the practice square, like a butler inviting her to dine.

She strode to one side of the square and picked up the blunt longsword left by the Burkeshi's previous opponent. Reveeker stood across from her and raised his weapon in salute. Her fury went past its tipping point and she charged. Their swords met with a dull clang. He sprang back, gaining himself some room and tossed his weapon from hand to hand, an old Burkeshi trick for deceiving an opponent's eyes. Cirona swung her sword at him and used her momentum to throw a punch at his face. He blocked her sword, ducked the blow and gave her a sharp smack to the stomach with his fist. She swung the butt of her sword downwards grazing his cheek as he pulled back.

The pair circled each other, looking for openings. By the look of frustration on Reveeker's face, he was as stumped as she was.

Reveeker tried to break the stalemate with a horizontal stroke. Cirona parried his blade downwards and threw a strong kick into his thigh. He switched his blade into his other hand with the speed of an alley cat and delivered a sharp blow to her knee. Cirona spun, pain flaring in her leg. She managed to pirouette on her standing heel and come full circle just in time to block Reveeker's blade.

They stood, locked together, both pressing on their swords with all their strength, spit escaping with their grunts of effort. Cirona allowed herself to fall backwards. Surprised by the sudden lack of resistance, Reveeker stumbled forward. As they both fell Cirona planted a foot in his sternum and pushed, sending him spinning away.

He landed a few feet from her, sword clattering from his hand. She rushed in and planted a boot on his wrist. Swearing in Burkeshi, he used his free arm to drill a vicious punch into the same knee he'd hit earlier. Cirona crumpled and Reveeker followed up with a punch to her sword wrist. Now unarmed, they each swung a vicious punch at the other's head. They both connected, sprawling simultaneously onto the sand.

Claps and cheers erupted from the gladiators, all of whom had stopped to watch. Cirona hefted herself to her knees, trying to shake the spots from her vision. A shadow fell over her. Reveeker stood with his hand extended, smiling. It was like the smile of a wine connoisseur who had just enjoyed a particularly fine vintage. She smiled back and he helped her to her feet. Cirona looked him in the eyes and they both nodded.

'Not bad for a half-dead Estrian wench!' Reveeker said, smiling.

'Same to you, you canker-ridden, old sand-shit.'

'Yes, yes, save the mutual appreciation society for later,' Gulgarno cut in, throwing his puffy hands into the air. 'Reveeker show her the ropes, I have business to attend to.'

With that he waddled away. Cirona watched him and visualised sticking a spear straight up his arse.

*

Elvgren woke in a puddle of his own vomit. His head pounded, his eyes ached and it felt like a skut rat had crawled down his throat. What the hells had happened? It took him a few seconds, and then the events of the previous night's revels swam into his mind. Flushed with the success of escaping death and the haul of loot they had pilfered from Faultwright's men, Danker had proposed a feast. Dargo was sent to get meat and ale, while Kotor and Jadir talked to Elvgren, in awe of his heroics. When Dargo returned he wasn't alone.

Fifteen other men accompanied him. This, apparently, was the rest of the gang. The whoremongers, cutpurses and smugglers who carried out the jobs beneath the boss and his lieutenants. They too had been informed of Elvgren's exploits and they welcomed him into the fold with open arms. Drinking companionably with the men who had just tried to sell him for the pleasure of whatever lord cared to pay most for his arse, felt strange but Elvgren thought he deserved a drink. And how he had drunk. He allowed the usual remorse of the hangover to flow through him, swearing an oath to never drink again. Then he pulled himself to his feet and waited for the bottle-strewn floor to come back into focus.

'Finally up, eh?' came the call from Danker. 'You Estrians cannot be handling your drink. Last one to rise. Lucky you were saving of my life or else I try to sell you all over again!'

Danker's laughter rolled round the room making Elvgren's head throb. His eyes swept the room. It was empty of everyone but him and the boss.

'Come. Sit,' Danker said, pushing a chair towards him with his foot.

Elvgren collapsed into it gratefully.

'Yesterday you were accepting of my offer of brotherhood,' Danker said.

Elvgren nodded, half regretting his adrenaline fuelled decision.

'Good this is being. Now bound you are to me.'

'Hang on a minute, what do you mean?'

'You have been seeing of sensitive informations. You know our faces and you know where we are living. There are also other issues now arising. We cannot allow you to leave.'

'Well, I'm afraid I've got somewhere to be,' Elvgren said. The thrill of his hard-won freedom lending him courage.

'Ah, you are thinking of finding your friends? The others who were on your ship, yes?'

'How the hells do you know that?' Elvgren said.

'Here, be seeing for yourself.' Danker threw a newsprint to him across the table.

Elvgren picked it up. It was the *Imperial Chronicler*, he scanned the headline: "Naval Vessel Sunk Off Coast of Timboko". Surely this was a joke? Elvgren devoured the rest of the article. It said that the Estrian naval vessel, *Prudence*, had been lost somewhere off the coast of Timboko. That a search party from Estria was out in force, looking for any survivors. It mentioned the Lord Chancellor's concern for the safety of the diplomatic mission and his daughter. It mentioned them all, providing descriptions.

Gods dammit, Elvgren thought, *they're looking in the wrong fucking place. How the hell had the facts got so skewed?*

'I am not good at the reading, but Dargo has told me the tale. How the description you are matching. In fact, one of our men was witness to the whole thing.'

'Gods, what did he see?' Elvgren said.

'My man, he told me that a woman fought and killed ten Burkeshi single-handed. She is then collapsing. After that, away she was carried by some people also in the business of flesh.'

'That's Major Bouchard. Who took her, does he know?'

'The men who are taking her, they are known. They work for an owner of gladiators, of course they are operating under Faultwright's care. No one does this kind of business without him being consenting.'

'There was another with us … a girl. She fell from the pier.'

'No news there is of her.'

'Then if this is the case, I really do have to go. I must get news back to Estria!'

'This we thought might be being in your mind. But allow you to go we will not. You are family now. Think. Powerful men have been twisting at this tale. My man has met them.'

'Who were they?'

'Some were men of Faultwright, others were Burkeshi. Good coin they paid to shut mouths. Add that Estria is not loved in Varash and that is how these lies are in the paper news.' Danker sat back in his chair and stroked his chin. 'You save my life otherwise out you would be going onto the street. This is an almighty up fuck.' Danker paused and looked deep into Elvgren's eyes. 'A debt of blood, now, I owe you. I will help you best I can, but give up you must on this.' The boss stabbed a finger at the paper.

Elvgren sat back, the world reeling. What in the name of the gods should he do? Danker was more than right, whoever could pull off this shit was powerful. Terrifyingly powerful. His sense of honour stung him and he thought of the reproachful looks from his family if they were here. *Fuck it, there is nothing I can do for now.* 'Boss Danker, I accept your offer gratefully,'

'Good, my mind you put it at ease,' Danker said grinning.

Gotta play for time, thought Elvgren, *find out more information*. He knew where he would have to start: Faultwright.

15

Bellina sat side by side with Holger in the galley. A steadily rising pile of scrubbed potatoes lay at their feet. They sat in friendly silence, absorbed in the pleasant monotony of their task. Four more days had passed on the *Scampering Vagabond*, and Bellina had quickly adjusted to life on board — the unwritten rules, the superstitions, and the hard graft of the work. Each night she practically collapsed on the cabin floor next to Holger and Midge but she was finding that she was remarkably content. She felt free, despite the confines of the ship. There was work to be done, people to talk to and, in some cases, people to avoid. Best of all, there were no nobles to look down on her, no furtive glances thrown at the restraint on her arm, just casual acceptance. Even if, to some of the crew, that meant she was accepted as bottom of the pile.

In her free moments she would contemplate the crew of the ship. It was worlds apart from the strict regime of the *Prudence*. The men and women joked, laughed, gambled, occasionally fought, but all abided to the good-natured rule of Captain Barboza. Bellina had watched him most of all. The captain would stride around the ship with his first mate, Crenshaw, chatting here, inspecting there. His favourite activity was standing theatrically at the prow of the ship pointing into the distance. Or to shake things up he would sometimes do this from the stern. He was never at the wheel like poor Captain Yervy, leaving this task to Crenshaw ... or anyone else for that matter. *Gives him more time to look dramatic I suppose*, thought Bellina.

'Done!' Holger said, tossing his last potato onto the pile.

'Oh, congratulations! I shall send a scribogram to the Emperor and see you receive suitable commendation for your heroic deeds!' Bellina quipped.

'Ha, alright, Belle. While you're at it would you see if he could grant me a small dukedom? Nothing fancy mind! I know my place,' Holger said, smiling.

Bellina smiled back. *Nice to finally meet someone with a sense of humour*, she thought.

Holger pulled out a box of matches and sat with the back of his head to the wall. He pulled one out of the box and began to twirl it around his fingers absently.

'I didn't know you smoked,' Bellina said.

'What? Oh... I don't.'

'Why do you keep matches on you then?'

Holger sat for a moment, deep in thought. 'Just a good luck charm is all. Makes me feel safe if I've got 'em on me,' he said, a furtive smile creasing his face. 'Well then, Belle, I'd better get back on deck, sure someone needs a hand somewhere.'

'Thanks, Holger, see you at grub time.' She watched him walk out the door. She was left alone with her peeling and curiosity. What had caused him to adopt such a strange talisman? A few minutes passed and she heard the door open again. 'Ah, Holger, no one else got any use for you either?' Bellina said.

'Nah, lover boy's occupied darling.'

Bellina turned to see Tinker and Vell in the narrow aisle of the galley.

'What the fuck do you two want?' Bellina said, panic rising like a snake.

'Well, Vell 'ere still ain't too 'appy 'bout your disrespect the other night. Ain't that right, Vell?' Tinker said.

'Couldn't o' put it better meself, Tinker,' Vell replied.

'Thought we'd come down and rectify that. Would 'ave done it sooner but that Narvale fuckwit's been following you round like a little lost lamb.'

'Got 'im nice an' occupied now though. Gives us a bit o' time to proper educate ye like,' Vell said.

'Go fuck yourself with a rusty nail!' Bellina spat jumping to her feet.

'Now it's just that kinda language gonna make this worse, las—'

Bellina cut him off by throwing a large bottle at his head, missing by a fraction of an inch.

'You damned bitch! Get 'er!' Tinker cried.

Bellina backed down the galley, brandishing the small knife she had been peeling with.

'Ha! You gotta be kidding girl. Think you might need a bigger knife.' Vell laughed.

They both advanced on her. Tinker went to grab at her hand and she slashed his palm with the blade. While she did this, Vell grabbed her other hand. Bellina tried to swing the blade at her but Tinker caught her arm. He squeezed her wrist viciously making her let go of the knife.

With his free hand, Tinker slapped Bellina round the face. Dots danced before her eyes and her cheek stung. Vell threw a sweeping punch to her stomach. Bellina doubled over in pain. Tinker punched her on the side of her neck and she went sprawling.

'That's it you little bitch: on yer knees. Now if you have dreams of being able to chew yer food again you better lick my boots,' Vell said, dangling her foot in Bellina's face.

Bellina crawled towards her and sank her teeth into the back of Vell's calf. The woman howled in pain. Tinker punched Bellina in the ribs, forcing her to let go. He pulled her to her feet and stood behind her, pinning her arms. Vell hobbled towards her.

'Real bit o' work, eh? Let's see if my old mate 'ere can't take some o' that spirit outta ye,' Vell said, slipping knuckledusters onto her hand.

Fuck, Bellina thought. Surely someone would have heard the racket they had created? 'Barboza, will toss you overboard for this! Know what? Worse than that I will fucking get you, I *will* get you,' Bellina cried.

'You? I'm some kinda scared o' you, ain't I. What a joke.' Vell laughed harshly. 'As for that posing idiot, Barboza, we know quite a bit about 'im. Certain things he most definitely doesn't want to get out. Yeah, all things considered, I think I'm take the risk.' Vell drew her fist back. Bellina closed her eyes and tensed her body for the blow.

'What the fuck do you think you are doing?' Holger screamed from the doorway.

Vell turned, stunned, and Tinker loosened his grip. Bellina took the opportunity to stamp down on the man's foot with all her might. He hollered in pain and let go.

'Fuck off, boy. No concern o' yours, weren't planning to mess up the bits you're interested in,' said Vell.

'FUCKING BITCH!' Holger roared. He rushed down the galley and, with a brutality Bellina never expected from him, landed a punch square on Vell's nose.

Vell fell backwards into Bellina, sending them both tumbling into the hopping Tinker.

Holger pulled Bellina back to her feet. 'Belle are you—' Holger began.

'Hold that thought,' Bellina said. She turned back to the pair kicking and stamping in a fury. Senseless curses tumbled from her mouth until Holger pulled her off.

'Easy, Belle, easy. You give 'em theirs, but there are rules,' Holger said.

'Fuck your rules!' Bellina screamed, anger still pounding like a drum in her blood.

'Look, Cap'n don't mind a bit o' fighting but kicking each other to death ain't on the cards. Now take a couple o'deep breaths,' Holger said.

Bellina listened and felt her pulse begin to return to normal.

'Now we best get some help. Cap'n will want to hold a vote on this.'

*

Bellina stood on deck with the rest of the assembled crew. Captain Barboza and the others had listened to both Bellina's and her attackers' accounts. Tinker and Vell had come up with a story, claiming that Bellina had set upon them with a knife when they went to the galley to get an apple. Holger had informed everyone how he had seen the pair skulking off and followed them. He then described the scene he had found.

'Well, we have heard from all involved,' Barboza said, 'What say ye men: who do you find guilty? Raise your right hand to condemn the young lady, Belle, and your left for Tinker and Vell.'

The raising of hands was evenly split.

'Hmm. Then t'would seem I have the final say,' Barboza said, prowling up and down, clearly relishing the performance. 'By the looks of it both parties got a fair share of each other. Therefore, I propose half rations for all involved. What say you my fine crew of democrats?'

'Aye, aye, Captain!' the crew called in unison.

'Then it's decided. The four of you shake hands, the matter is closed. Any further attacks on each other will be met with the lash. Are we clear?'

The four combatants nodded their heads.

'Good. Now shake.'

They all shook hands, each of the quartet trying to outdo the other in damning glares.

'Now, all hands back to their duties,' the captain commanded.

The crew dispersed till there was just Holger and Bellina. He turned to look at her. Bellina's lip was swollen and her face was bruised from the slap. Her ribs ached and she couldn't turn her neck without pain. Still though, she couldn't help but smile when Holger spoke.

'Well, now I know not to piss *you* off!'

*

The common room of the gladiator school hummed with life. Men, and a few women, drank and ate. The sound of their happy chatter filled the room, a sound distinctly at odds with Cirona's mood. She sat on her own in a corner of the room, a large mug of very fine ale, barely touched, in front of her. Cirona rolled her shoulder muscles and a pleasant rush of warmth flowed through them. The expert massage she had received had rubbed and pounded out every knot and tangle. The scent of rosemary and canther leaf wafted from her skin.

If the gladiators were slaves, they were well kept slaves. Cirona had always imagined that the gladiator schools she had heard about would be filled with discontented men burning for freedom. It came as a great surprise to her to find that some of the combatants had enrolled *themselves* in the school. Most though, like Cirona, had been bought.

'A rencat for your thoughts, Major,' Reveeker said, appearing at her table.

'Please, Rev, don't call me that,' Cirona said. And she meant it.

The title she had once taken so much pride in was now nothing but a bitter reminder of her long list of failures.

'Sorry, Rona, no pain meant. Come, tell me what is on your mind.'

Cirona looked at him thoughtfully. During the past couple of days she had formed a friendship with the Burkeshi, thanks largely to them both sharing a military background. In fact, they had spent the first night after their spar exchanging stories and comparing battle scars.

'It's just all of this,' she said, waving her arm at the room, 'Can't marry up all the merriment with men who might have to fight each other to the death.'

'Hmm, well if you think this is a revel you should see this place the night before a contest,' Reveeker said. He paused, then added, 'We don't always fight to the death. That's just for a special attraction. Wouldn't do to have your investments continually slitting each other's throats.'

'Really?' Cirona said.

'Ha! You Estrians. You really don't pay any mind to what goes on around you, do you? As long as your ships and merchants can trade as they please, us unwashed foreign types can indulge in whatever uncivilised activities we desire,' Reveeker said, his laugh betraying a hint of bitterness. 'You wait and see, Rona. We are just one part of a huge pageant. There will be executions, novelty bouts, animal fights, all rounded off with our display.'

'I can't wait!' she said with exaggerated excitement. 'Ah gods dammit! Sorry, Rev, don't mean to be so...'

'Miserable?' he finished for her.

'Yeah, s'pose so.' Cirona took a long swig from her mug.

'You are as entitled to your misery as anyone else. And damn well never apologise for it. But I will listen if you want to talk,' Reveeker said, taking a seat across from her.

Cirona thought about it for a moment. She wasn't one for talking about her feelings, not really out of stoicism, more because she had learned that few people actually listened, but the regret and worry that had been building inside her needed an outlet. 'I was on a... mission,' she began, 'ran into a bit of trouble ... ah, twelve hells, a lot of trouble. Saw some things I wouldn't even have dreamed possible!' Cirona ran a hand over her face as the image of the shape-shifters attacked her mind. She wondered if Reveeker would know what they were. She decided not to pursue it now. Pushing the thought away, she continued. 'S'posed to be guarding this girl. Shit went south and I lost her. No idea if she's dead or alive, safe or in trouble. And here I am, getting rub-downs, top grub and the finest Pevontess ale.'

'You can't think like that, Rona. Tell me: what do you reckon this girl's chances are of keeping herself alive?'

'She'd probably stay alive out of damned stubbornness. Got a hot streak running through her alright! Gave me a damn run for my money, let me tell you. She's strong, don't take no shit from no one. I'd give her better odds of surviving than someone else who was with us,' Cirona said.

'What is this girl to you? If I am not mistaken, that glint in your eye, the tone to your voice ... seems like pride.'

Dammit, she thought, *he's right! The little madam has wormed her way in.*

'Was she kin?' Rev continued.

Cirona felt her heart drop. 'No, no. Just a... charge. Employed to look after her, nothing more. She just reminds me of someone I lost.'

'Lives like ours are full of loss, Rona. Don't make it any easier though, I myself... ah damn it, never mind. Wouldn't do to have two old soldiers balling their eyes out,' he said with a wistful smile.

'I suppose not. But you've heard my woes, be unfair to not listen to yours.'

'It's, well... why not.' Rev took a long slug from his ale cup. 'It was back when I was still with the army, about six years ago. Been with them all my life, didn't know any different. Watched everything grow under the Grand Multan and Marmossa. Saw my tiny little village in the arse end of nowhere turn into a great big town. Things were good, they were better than good. Money poured in from establishing the Grand Multanate, loads of work.

'Then one day we get sent into this city, against one of the last multans still fighting. *Vaksa!* Did they fight! Every soul in the place had a weapon, women and children too. Now, I have killed a lot of people, not saying it with pride just a fact, but those kids they ... they tore at my soul. I told my general that my men weren't in the business of killing kids. He asked if I was refusing to carry out an order. I said if he could find a man willing to do it, then he could have my command.' Rev paused and drained his cup. 'Well find him he did, led the charge himself on a hospital where the kids had holed up. That night I walked through the town. Those tiny bodies piled high and deep. I walked over and, I'll never forget it, one of them had this tiny little toy rabbit in her hand. And it just hit me. That was it: I knew I was through. I always believed, always, that I was doing what was best for my country. But how the hell could I justify this?'

'Fuck, Rev, that's some heavy shit.'

'Oh, I'm not done. To punish me for what I had done, my family were rounded up. Wife and daughter. Taken, put on show with me. Gave me a choice, shoot my wife or they would kill us all. What could I do? She told me to do it, I did. They took my girl away to be raised in the temple, to atone for my sins, a servant of Mother Darkness. Me they sold as a slave. Got passed from pillar to post and, well, here I am.' Reveeker finished his story, eyes shimmering.

'Gods, I'm sorry, Rev. That's, well, there aren't even words.'

'She was a good woman, the best. Didn't cry. Held it together the whole time for me and our daughter. My girl, my angel, she liked rabbits too.' He stopped and punched his leg. 'Anyway, enough of this.

Get some rest or get drunk. I know what I'm going to do. Goodnight.'

Reveeker strode to the nearest ale cask and filled a large tankard. *So much pain and loss*, she thought. *Gods what a life*. Maybe that was the fate of people like her and Rev. She hoped to the gods it wasn't, but she was starting to feel like you could never escape the horrors you experience in life; she couldn't even manage it in her sleep. Sleep that was calling to her now.

Cirona rubbed her eyes, forcing them open. Exhaustion sang through her body but she didn't want to answer. Didn't want the dreams to come.

*

Elvgren stood at the top of the steep hill that Tavarar was built on. A wide brimmed hat covered his head, offering him shade from the heat and obscuring his face. He had spent the best part of the day roaming the narrow streets and alleys of the town. From the slums and bazaars of the lower reaches to the large manors that clung to the hillside like fleas to a dog. He was accompanying Jadir, Dargo and a few others, collecting loan payments. Danker may have sworn to protect him, but Elvgren was still expected to pay his way.

'One more,' Jadir said, as the gang rounded a corner in a better part of the merchant district.

They came to a stop outside a large store front. The window was blacked out but eye-catching letters, written large in gold, proclaimed: Master Chemistician, Aldous Groteak.

'You go. Tired now. Take boy and gets money,' Jadir said, pointing to Elvgren and Dargo.

Elvgren looked at Dargo who glanced back nonchalantly. 'Don't you think it would be more *intimidating* if there were more of us?' he said, feeling uneasy.

'No. You gotta work. Boss said. You watched us, it's simple. Ask for money, they no give money you threaten and bang stuff. Easy,' Jadir said, his tone indicating that there would be no further discussion on the matter.

'Fine, fine! Come on, Dargo.' Elvgren turned towards the shop. After seeing some of the lowlifes and thugs the gang had got money out of today, a timid little potion brewer in a nice part of town shouldn't pose any problems. Elvgren pushed the door open and stalked into the room. Dargo followed, shutting the door. A myriad of chemical concoctions filled his nostrils, bitter and suffocating. He cast a menacing look at the old man who sat at the counter before walking around the shop.

The room was filled with cabinets. Row upon row of shelves stuffed with flasks and vials, cork stoppers preventing the foul-looking liquids from escaping. Glass jars lined the top shelves, each containing a pickled animal, forlorn specimens floating in preservatives. The eye of a giant boar toad stared down at him, distorted and condescending. It reminded him of his mother.

Dargo sauntered over to Elvgren. 'You gonna do something, my *lord*, or are you thinking of making a purchase?'

'I'm just waiting for the right moment. Building suspense, you know.'

'Oh yeah, the old codger is a bundle of nerves,' Dargo said, jerking his head at the chemistician.

The old man sniffed derisively and flicked through the pages of a newsprint. If he was scared he was wasted in his profession: the stage would have been a better calling.

'Well, if you're so bloody terrifying why don't you do something?' Elvgren hissed.

'Fine.' The young boy walked up to the counter and coughed.

The old man looked up. 'Can I help you, boy?'

'I've come for the money.'

'What money? Get out of here, you cheeky little fuck. I've run this shop for forty years, not going to get shaken down by a child!' he spat.

'Fine then. Got a lot of glass things in here. Glass gets broke real easy, don't it Gren? Why not give this man a demonstration?'

Elvgren dangled a long thin vial from his hand. He let go, catching it clumsily in mid-air as the chemistician screamed.

'That's gorrel brew, you idiot! You'll gas us all!'

Elvgren returned the vial to the shelf and tried to look like the last thirty seconds hadn't happened.

'Even more reason to give Danker his money. If not, we'll smash all your little brews,' Dargo said.

'Danker! That miserable shit! Alright, alright. Let me get the coin.' The old man shuffled off to the back of the shop.

Elvgren strode over and stood behind the boy. 'Good show!'

'Yeah, no thanks to you! Try and read the labels on bottles you're gonna throw around in a potion master's house, eh?'

Elvgren flushed with anger and shot him a cool stare.

A few minutes later the man returned and dumped a large bag of coins on the table with a thud. 'There you go. Oh wait, there are a few more coins under the counter.' The chemistician reached down.

Elvgren couldn't say what made him do it but he reflexively pushed Dargo aside as the old man shot up. Time seemed to slow and Elvgren watched a silvery liquid arc from the container in the old man's hand. The substance splashed across his face. A thin trickle, like the run-off from a painter's brush, slid from his left eyebrow to the crease of his mouth. Then it started to burn.

The world became a screaming black mess of noise and agony. He heard Dargo curse and scuffle with the old man. He felt a blow smash into his nose but from where it came he couldn't tell. The door of the shop slammed open. More fighting, swearing, bangs. Elvgren heard it all from his position crumpled on the ground. The world coming to him through a wall of pain. He passed out.

The next thing Elvgren saw when he opened his eye was Danker. He looked down at him chuckling.

'I think no one will be recognising you now, eh?'

16

Bellina stared out to sea from the port rail of the ship. The sound of the side paddles turning came to her from below. She looked down towards the noise and saw the trail of foam the *Scampering Vagabond* left in its wake. Her eyes scanned the horizon.

Nothing. Three weeks at sea and nothing. Holger had told her that there was no chance of making port until they'd won some plunder. Aquinas, goddess of water, or the Cruel Mistress as the sailors called her, had not sent them a gift. She was beginning to think she would be forever trapped on the ship, always looking over her shoulder for her enemies. Although Tinker and Vell had held true to their promise and not touched her, a cruel prank from one of their friends was never far away. Bellina's musings were shattered by a call from the crow's nest.

'Merchant ship, dead ahead!' Midge called down.

'How far off, lad?' Barboza asked.

''Bout twenty minutes, Captain. She's going slow. Laying heavy in the water!'

'Ha ha! A fat sow ready to drop her piglets! All hands on deck!' Barboza cried. The message passed through the ship till the whole crew was assembled. 'Right, my beauties, the Mistress has seen fit to throw us a juicy morsel. Are we ones to shun her divine meal?'

'No, Captain!' The crew chorused.

'Well let's show our teeth. Loose the sail. Everyone to your stations!'

'Aye, aye Captain!'

The ship was a blur of activity. Bellina caught Holger's eye. 'Where are we to hide ourselves then?'

'Ha. Nowhere I'm afraid. I'll be up front on the first boarding. Another perk of being bottom of the heap. The veteran hands sing a bold tale but you don't become an old pirate by charging into the fray,' Holger said.

'Oh! I didn't realise. Good luck then ... I suppose?' Bellina said. She felt a cord of worry knot itself in her stomach. Holger's steadfast friendship was one of the few things keeping her going.

'Don't worry, be back before you know it.' He turned to walk off.

'Holger!' she called.

'Yeah?'

'Holger... be safe, alright?'

'What do you think I'm gonna do? Stick my gut out and run into the first blade I see?'

'Fair enough, smart arse! Go and get yourself skewered.' They both laughed, then he was off.

Having no function to serve, Bellina watched the cargo ship grow bigger in her vision and noticed its Estrian colours. *Fantastic*, she thought drily, *aiding in the capture of one of my own.*

Her introspection was soon over. The frightened ship was too loaded down to escape the *Scampering Vagabond*.

They pulled up alongside the merchant ship. Barboza strode to the side rail. 'Who is your Captain?' he bellowed.

'I am!' came the call of a man with a steely look in his eye.

'Surrender your valuables to us now and no blood need be spilt,' Barboza said.

'How about I give you this in surrender!' the merchant captain replied, making an obscene gesture.

Bellina stood just to the side of Captain Barboza and Crenshaw. She willed the captain to look at her, recognise her, but he didn't look in her direction. *Can't bloody well dance for him*, she thought.

'Very well Captain, you leave me no choice. Take the ship! Attack!' Barboza commanded.

The *Vagabond*'s crew threw boarding lines. Men shot balliskets from the upper deck and fire was returned. Crenshaw tried to get Bellina below decks but she refused.

The pirates swarmed over the merchant ship like wasps on a rotting piece of fruit. Bellina could just make out the straw-coloured stubble of Holger's hair. The fighting was fiercest around the captain, the merchant sailors' poor skill at arms quickly becoming apparent. The *Scampering Vagabond* crew hemmed them in to groups, forcing them to put down their weapons.

Barboza made his way to the captured ship. The merchant crew sat huddled in the centre of the deck. 'We are not murderers,' the captain began, 'We only want your goods. No man here shall be harmed as long as there is no more resistance.' As he spoke, the rest of his crew returned to the deck. They looked angry. Tinker took the lead.

'Ain't fuck all to plunder, Cap'n. Hold's full of fertiliser. Nowhere we could offload it in enough bulk to make a decent coin,' Tinker said.

'Damnation! Valuables then, personal belongings, gold teeth ... anything. You see it, you take it. As for *you* Captain, you are lucky none of my crew were injured or I would personally slit your throat,' Barboza said, looming over his merchant counterpart.

Bellina couldn't stop herself laughing at the sight of the giant Bakori, blonde pompadour gleaming, scowling into the face of the defeated captain.

The captain of the merchant vessel turned towards her and hollered across the gap between the ships. 'Something funny girl... By the gods, it can't be!' he said, jaw hanging loose in astonishment. He stared straight at her. 'Lady Ressa!'

'What are you blathering about man? That's Belle, our cabin girl,' Barboza said.

'Cabin girl? Cabin Girl! That's the Lord Chancellor of Estria's daughter. The Empire mourns for her as we speak! Her ship was sunk off the coast of Timboko and here she appears in your clutches, you damned villain!'

'How can you be so sure?' Barboza said, a hint of interest appearing in his voice.

'Saw her once when she accompanied her father on a tour of the shipyards. If you don't believe me, tell me this: does she wear a bracelet in the form of an eagle, studded with an emerald, a ruby and a sapphire?'

'She does!'

'That's her cognopathic restraint, you fucking moron. Didn't you wonder about it?'

Cries of alarm came from the *Scampering Vagabond*'s crew. A mind-melter. Thought thief. She felt their eyes turn towards her. She couldn't meet Holger's gaze.

'She told me she was a serving girl for a rich lord. I merely thought she might have provided, *ahem*, certain services that gained her such a bauble,' Barboza said.

Bellina stared indignantly at the man, then she went back to holding her breath.

The merchant captain laughed maniacally and screamed. 'You sea rats will swing for this! Just you wait till news of this reaches Estria!'

You fucking idiot, Bellina thought, *you couldn't just keep your mouth shut and sail off, getting news back to Estria. Oh no! You think you're a hero in a play, you even talk like one.*

'Hmmm, I think not. Crenshaw dispose of these men and scupper this ship of shit,' Barboza said.

'You promised us no harm. How dare you call yourself a captain? A man's word is as good as his bond!' the merchant captain cried.

'Tell that to your Father Light. I'm going back to my ship to speak with the priceless treasure that has floated auspiciously into our lives.'

Barboza locked eyes with Bellina and she felt her legs start to give. Bellina tasted the bitter tang from the cloying fog of Captain Barboza's perfume. She watched the huge man prowl about the cabin. The opulence of the compartment was staggering. Every inch of the small space shone with gold. A small, round table covered in trinkets and bottles of scent sat in front of her. The walls were hung with rich Paltont carpets, lions rampaging across them in a fury of platinum thread. To her left, a mahogany wardrobe swallowed the space instead of just occupying it. A door was ajar, vivid silks and cloth peeked out cautiously.

'Hmmm... is something wrong with your port, my lady?' Barboza said.

'No! It is very fine, thank you,' Bellina replied, taking a dainty sip of the ludicrously rich drink.

'This is most unexpected. A glorious piece of fortuitousness so carelessly thrown into my lap! Why, good lady, did you not tell me of your superior birth sooner?'

'I wasn't sure who was a friend, or how much of my tale it was safe to tell. After the events of my recent past, well ... I take nothing for granted.'

'Yes, yes, most prudent. 'Twould seem you inherited your father's famed shrewdness.'

There was a pause in the conversation, both of them searching for words.

Finally, Bellina said, 'Well, there it is, Captain. You know who I am. As much as I appreciate a good port, I would very much like to find out where in the Father's name we go from here?'

Barboza paused and looked at her. 'Go? Why, my precious little dove, we take you home. Home to your father and the rich reward that must surely await your saviour! And, if a reward is not immediately forthcoming, I'm not adverse to ransoming you as a hostage.'

The captain took a seat across from her, beaming. *At least I'll be going home*, she thought. Yes, going home, tail tucked firmly between her legs, a failure. She hadn't even set foot on Burkeshi soil, let alone stolen the secrets from the minds of the country's top officials. But she had to face the reality of the situation. She was alone, probably completely now her cognopathic ability had been revealed. She had no money and no clue as to where she was. Bellina thought of her father. She wanted to see his face again, even if it was disappointed. She wanted to soothe any added stress her failure had caused him.

'Good then, Captain, I suppose we have a plan.' Bellina paused. 'Though your crew seemed far from thrilled about having a cognopath on board, even one as lucrative as I.' Bellina had lived with scorn and derision all her life but the coupling of a confined ship and two pissed-off crewmates with the ammunition to bring others to their side, did not strike her as a mix for a happy sail home.

'Bah! Let me worry about that, Lady Belle, sorry, Lady Bellina. You may have my cabin, as befits your status. I shall take Crenshaw's. You need never set foot on deck again, if that is your wish.'

'I'm no coward, Captain. And it's certainly not the first time people have baulked at what I am.'

'Very well. I give you free rein of the ship. Well, within reason. Don't go mucking about in the engine room or anything like that. Of course, you are relieved of any duties. Can't have you returning to you father with the calloused hands of a deck scrub!'

There was a knock at the door.

'Enter!' the captain boomed.

Crenshaw's head appeared around the door. 'Ready to scupper the merchant vessel, sir,' he said.

'Very well. My lady, would you like to witness the fireworks?' Barboza asked.

'I can't hide in here forever,' she replied. Bellina strode out on to the ship's deck with her head held high. Looks of contempt and fear burned into her. She caught Midge's gaze, his eyes wide with terror. Holger stood to the side of him, looking determinedly at the floor. If Bellina had an Estrian penny for every response like that she had received, she would be richer than the Emperor. Still, seeing such a reaction in people she considered friends cut deeper than she ever thought it would.

Bellina, the captain and Crenshaw walked to the starboard rail. Barboza gave the order and a thunderous broadside fired into the merchant vessel.

She watched the ship slowly sink, taking with it the brief window of freedom her anonymity had given her.

17

The smell of sweat floated on the air. Grunts and bangs resounded around the training yard as Cirona and Reveeker sat side by side, slumped under an awning. The idea was to provide the gladiators with shade from the blistering sun though, in truth, it just provided a place to boil alive.

Two more weeks had passed at the school, her days filled with training, her nights with terrors. Each day she seemed to wake more exhausted than the previous. Her fatigue had not helped her to come up with an escape plan. Guilt and worry gnawed at her insides.

What would Trafford have done? What would he think of her closest friend in this place being a Burkeshi? He probably would have tried to fight his way out and died in the attempt, so wrapped up had he been in his sense of duty. He had never learned that there were things worth living for beyond protecting pampered Estrian nobles. Even his love for her had been dutiful. Maybe that was why he could stand by and watch, without a word of protest, as their daughter was taken away by *them*. What use was duty now though? Man and child gone. Duty and honour taking them both. Ever since, she had tried to live her life to that creed of honour but it rang more hollow with each passing day. Maybe she should accept the life of a gladiator and live in the comfort of her gilded cage. Maybe, if not for Bellina. The image of the young lady was burned into her mind. She clung to it, turning it into a symbol for never losing anyone again. She believed in her heart that the girl was alive and she wouldn't give up until she found her.

Her thoughts returned to the present as excited chatter sprang to life. Cirona looked up to see the immense bulk of Gulgarno struggling across the yard. Since her initial day in the training yard this was the first time she had seen him descend into the gladiator's pit.

'Something's up.' Reveeker said. 'Better go and find out why the Lord of Drippings has paid us a visit.'

Cirona nodded her head in agreement. They made their way towards the growing crowd.

'Settle down my little money-spinners, settle down,' Gulgarno began. 'The day you have all been awaiting is here. We have a tournament.' A babble of voices rose. 'It commences in a week's time but there is an unusual stipulation.' The fat man paused for dramatic effect. His delight at their attention shone in his piggy eyes. 'The games are being held in dual honour of the Prince of Varashi's eighteenth birthday *and* to celebrate Amlith Day. As such, the prince has been allowed to decide the theme and structure.' A murmur of concern ran through the crowd causing Gulgarno's delight to shine even brighter. 'The young prince wishes to see something unprecedented. Therefore, the games will include a gladiatorial tournament of eight fighters, with each round being fought to the death.' Cries of outrage rang out and it took a few sharp lashes from Barag's whip to settle the crowd down. 'That is not the only thing to consider,' Gulgarno continued once the tumult had eased. 'The weapons used in each round will be subject to lottery. There will, undoubtedly, be joke weapons. The prince is well known for his … sense of humour.' He flashed his own smile to emphasise this, his teeth tiny daggers of white. 'Now I wouldn't normally consider such a request, you know I like to make a return on my herd before sending them to slaughter. The prince has offered me *substantial* incentive though, enough to replace a hundred of you. So... who would like to volunteer to be one of the eight?'

The gladiators were silent. Furtive looks shot between them. Finally, one woman called out.

'What's the prize?'

'Oh, the prize, yes. Well there is a fight purse of ten thousand rencats. And what was the other thing?... Ah yes! Freedom for the winner.' Gulgarno grinned at the storm of agitation he had created. 'Well then, who would like to volunteer now?'

Cirona was the first from the throng to step forward, closely followed by Reveeker.

*

The young man stood in front of a grime covered, full-length mirror. He did not like what he saw. Elvgren stared at his reflection and saw a stranger stare back. The track of the chemistician's acid had left a thin scar from above the ridge of his left brow down to the corner of his mouth. The imperfection shone a sickly pink. He lifted a finger and ran it down the mark, pausing where his left eye should be. Now just a ragged hollow permanently stitched shut in a ghoulish wink. Elvgren then shifted his fingers over to the crooked hump of his nose. It was bent to the right as if trying to escape the burnt out eye. Elvgren shuddered, remembering the goo of his dissolving eyeball mingling with his tears.

In the weeks since though, there had been no more tears. The first thing he had done upon seeing himself was shave his head down to stubble. He hadn't cried, he hadn't wailed, just told Dargo to get the razor and help. He felt different. Fuck, he was different. With the loss of his looks he felt his insides harden. There was no more fear, just a cold determination.

Since the visit to the chemistician's shop Elvgren had been brooding. Every day, he got up and used his free time to perform the same ritual: searching for information. Knowing that he wasn't as recognisable, Danker allowed him to roam freely around town when he didn't have any jobs on. Most of the gang's activities required the cover of darkness so he tended to have the days to himself. He turned away from the mirror, got dressed and threw on his hooded travel cloak — a ludicrously oversized gift from Kotor — and exited the den.

He had spent the last few days frequenting the taverns and dives of Tavarar but he could find no information about what had happened the night the *Prudence* sank. His questions about the event were met with looks of fear and dread. His feet led him down the winding streets of the town. Passing the merchant district, he saw the gleaming letters of the chemistician's shop. He gritted his teeth and carried on. Since the gang's visit to the shop, the proprietors of the area had pooled their money and gone to Faultwright for protection. As such, Danker had told his men not to set foot in the place. It cut Elvgren's insides to be denied revenge for his disfigurement but he had to stay focused on finding out what the hells had happened to his companions.

Of course, he would know for himself if he hadn't been such a bloody coward. The dishonour of his flight stung his soul. He should have done something, anything. The old Elvgren would have consoled himself with the fact that Cirona had ordered him to leave, convinced himself that he was not to blame, but that man was dead. The lesson had come with a steep price though, and he wasn't going to let it be in vain. The events played out again and again in his mind. Sometimes he dived in after Bellina, other times he fought off the Burkeshis with Cirona. No matter how much he fantasised, the truth was still the same. He had run.

That had been another change since his injury: when he lost his eye, he lost touch with the superficial things he had thought so important. Preening and strutting around had got him into a world of shit, minutes away from being the plaything of some Midderland noble. His lack of courage had cost him his eye, Cirona and Bellina. For all he knew he was the only one who had any chance of getting news back to Estria.

Subconsciously his feet had taken him to the waterfront. He looked out to the pier, at the workmen sawing and hammering, replacing the smashed timbers. They were almost finished. Then it would be like nothing had ever come to pass here. Elvgren was genuinely shocked by how the truth had been suppressed so thoroughly. Whoever had the power to orchestrate all of this was a force to be reckoned with.

He walked up to the waterfront. The harbour walls plunged downwards; dark, wet and covered in green scum. He leant on the guardrail and stared across the ocean to home. Somewhere across the water his mother and father were going about their lives. Were they in mourning? Did they miss him? Had they gnashed their teeth and pulled out their hair? Elvgren doubted it very much. He was sure they would have adorned the house in black and made sure the windows were covered, just the right level of mourning that tradition required. They would have made offerings to the gods but had they made them in the hopes of his survival or to help ease his passage through the Weeping Veil?

Elvgren was broken from his reflection by the voices of two dockers. Due to the Burkeshi blockade on Estrian merchant ships, there were many of their kind to be found on Tavarar's harbour front. They were a surly bunch of unemployed men who spent most of their time drinking and cursing Estria and Burkesh in equal measure so he was quite surprised at the cheerful tone from these two.

'Ah but it's gonna be a grand affair, mate. You seen this bill they just put up?' one said, a squeak in his voice.

'Nah, woz it say?' came the deep voice of the other.

Elvgren turned and tried look like he wasn't listening in. The pair were standing by a wall some five feet away, their attention focused on an advertising bill. Elvgren squinted his eyes to read it.

"Yondapolis' Grand Amlith Day Celebrations!
Executions, performances and a tournament to the death

from the famed Gulgarno's School of Gladiatorial Combat."

'It's gonna be a good one this year, eh? Prince Hivat's eighteenth as well as all the regular shit. S'posed to be his idea this tournament to the death thingy,' said squeaky.

'Yeah?'

'Yeah. Rumour has it as well,' squeaky continued, leaning towards his friend conspiratorially, 'that bird who killed all them Burkeshis on the pier is gonna be fighting.'

'Shut up ye bloody idiot! If one of Faultwright's lot cop you talking like that, there'll be murder,' his friend hissed.

'Oh fuck! Good point. Actually though, on the topic of Tavarar's favourite citizen, how in the twelve hells is he gonna rig the betting this year?'

'Ye got me there. Can't really rig a death fight can ye. Anyway, what time is it?'

'Looks like it's just past noon. Fancy a drink?' The two wandered off.

Elvgren's mind spun with the new information, a plan began to form in his mind.

18

There was only a week till Amlith Day and Elvgren did not have much time to get his plan into motion. There wasn't much to go on, just an overheard rumour that Cirona would be a combatant in the Varash capital's celebrations, but it was all he had.

The first stage of his plan was to get an audience with Faultwright. This was proving difficult. The crime boss never set foot in Tavarar, all his machinations were carried out by his subordinates. There were a lot of them but it was hard to get one alone; always in pairs, always watchful. It had been a frustrating few days of half chances slipping through his fingers.

Now it was about four in the morning. Danker's gang had finished their own brand of skulduggery for the night, the boss and his lieutenants were fast asleep in a drunken stupor. He couldn't let any of them know what he was up to. Elvgren was sure they wouldn't appreciate him trying to pull on Faultwright's tail but he had to find a way to meet the crime boss. Elvgren slipped from his cot, still wearing his day clothes. He tiptoed through the sea of empty bottles strewn across the floor, past the snoring gang. Reaching the door undetected, he almost tripped over Dargo who was sat cross legged in front of the exit.

'Goin' somewhere, Gren?' the young boy asked.

'Just catching some air, Dar. That pie is *not* sitting right,' he replied.

Dargo looked at him suspiciously. 'Is that so? Not your first walk in the wee hours this week though, eh? I know where you've been going each night. Been following. Taking a lot of interest in Mr. Faultwright's operations, aren't you?'

Shit, Elvgren though. He hadn't stopped to think whether Dargo was asleep before he set out each night, he'd been so damn preoccupied with the rest of the gang. 'Fine. Then you know that my little excursions have been fruitless,' he said, deciding on honesty. It was true as well. All the boy could really report back was that Elvgren had spent the small hours of the past few days crouching in alleys getting a sore arse. 'Well, Dargo, is there going to be a problem here? Would you sell out the valiant man who saved your face from looking like a melted candle? That's bloody gratitude that is—'

'Who said anything 'bout telling the boss? Just curious is all. No one's ever had the balls round here to even dream of taking on Faultwright. I think it's piss poor. Don't see why the rest of us should have to live off his scraps,' Dargo said, his eyes burning with a childish passion. 'I want in on whatever it is you're up to.'

Elvgren was stunned. Should he allow the boy to come with him? If anything, two idiots would be better than one. 'I won't lie, Dargo, this is going to be dangerous. And I'm not doing it for the boss' benefit. This work is purely for me.'

'Fine,' he replied, his round face flushed with anger. 'I'm sick of his holier than thou attitude, anyway. Throwing his weight around but never coming up with anything juicy. I bring in more money cutting purses than the loan sharks do but it's Dargo who has to sleep in the fucking corner, Dargo the errand boy running out for more booze for him to piss my earnings away on. Nah, all things considered, I fancy doing something for myself as well.'

'Well. That was quite the speech. Didn't know you could string that many words together without needing a nap.'

'Go fuck yourself, Gren.' A little smile flashed on the boy's face.

'Come on then, my young squire. The forgotten hours are wasting,' Elvgren said.

They both left the den as quietly as a moth farts.

*

Elvgren caught sight of the signal from Dargo: two of Faultwright's men approaching.

It had taken at least an hour to make their way to one of Faultwright's storehouses. A further thirty minutes had been spent observing the guards' routine. Dargo had been invaluable for this task; he melted into the shadows as he sneaked around spaces Elvgren would never fit.

Finally, with the promise of dawn, Faultwright's guards had whittled down to a mere two. *If* he'd interpreted Dargo's signal correctly. Elvgren hoped he'd remembered the signals properly and that the one just now hadn't been "run for your life". He peeked round the corner of the stone wall. The alley they had chosen for their ambush was a good way down a wide road that led to the warehouse. He breathed a sigh of relief when he saw Dargo approaching just two burly men then his guts tightened with the realisation that there was still a lot to do before the plan could be considered a success.

He watched as the boy walked up to the men and engaged them in conversation. The two men pushed him away and he ran off about six feet then ran back to them, cheekily lifting one of their jingling purses. One of the men stood laughing while the other gave chase. Dargo ran towards Elvgren and darted down the alley. A few seconds later the man sprinted round the corner.

'Got yer now, you little shit, that's a fucking dead en—' Elvgren grabbed the man's shirt and slammed him into a wall. He pressed the point of his sabre to the man's throat.

'Don't make a damn sound,' Elvgren hissed. Keeping the blade to the man's throat, he led him further down the alley. The man was sweating like a hog, his eyes wide with terror.

'Look, I ain't got nothing else, eh? The boy's already got me purse,' he squeaked.

'I told you to keep quiet. I'm not looking to take anything else from you. I want you to take something from me: a message to your boss. Tell him the one-eyed lord wishes to meet him. Inform your master I'll await his arrival two nights hence at the Cantering Horse. Tell him to dress smartly and to be there prompt at eleven.'

'You gotta be fucking mad, boy. The boss will have your guts for this.'

'Tell him that I have a business proposition. No tricks. I just want to borrow his ear for an hour. Understand?'

The man nodded.

'Good.' Elvgren gave the man a blow between his eyes with the butt of his sword. The guard collapsed to the ground, unconscious.

'Better get going, Gren, the other one's bound to come looking soon,' Dargo said.

They both scaled a high wall at the end of the alley and ran like wild horses. They ran for a full fifteen minutes before they came skittering to a halt. Elvgren gasped for breath, while Dargo stood laughing.

'Well that's gonna put the fox amongst the hens, eh?' said the boy.

'We're... not... done... yet,' Elvgren managed to gasp.

*

The sun was just clearing the horizon as Elvgren and Dargo stood outside Aldous Groteak's shop. Elvgren relished that his plan included a splinter of revenge. He looked up and saw the curtains were still drawn in the living quarters.

'Shall we?' Elvgren asked.

'Sure thing, boss,' Dargo replied, then set about picking the lock on the door.

In just a few minutes, a testament to Dargo's skill, the pair were looking down on the sleeping form of the old chemistician. Dargo held a small knife to the man's throat and Elvgren slapped Aldous' face.

'Gwaaarhgh...' The old man started before falling silent at the sensation of the knife against his throat. His eyes went wide in recognition of Elvgren.

'Hello, Master Groteak. Are you well?' Elvgren asked.

'Wh... what the he... hells do you want?' the chemistician stammered.

'Remember me, eh? Don't worry, I just require a small token. Not a grand thing in exchange for an eye.' Elvgren paused, lifting his eyepatch to give Aldous a good look at the damage 'I need a potion. One that will simulate the effects of death. Would you happen to have any in stock?'

'I... might have something. Worm's foil. It would render the taker in a death-like state for about three hours. Please take it. I am... I'm sorry about your eye. Please don't hurt me.'

'Sorry? You're fucking sorry. Well isn't it fantastic how apologies make body parts re-grow, eh? I'm not going to hurt you.' A look of relief appeared on Aldous' face. 'But he is,' Elvgren said. He clamped his hand over the man's mouth as Dargo flicked his blade down the man's left eye.

Elvgren and Dargo walked back companionably to the gang's den. The sun was finally up and it looked like it would be a fine day. They crept inside, happy to see that Danker and the rest were still asleep. Elvgren paused in front of the mirror. It was funny the things you were capable of when you no longer recognised you own reflection.

*

Elvgren's cup of ale was half drunk. He twitched it back and forth with his fingers. It was already half past eleven and still no one had approached him. He had decided to go alone to the Cantering Horse, in case there was any foul play. So far, it appeared that there would be no play of any kind. Still though, he twitched every time the door opened and he continually eyed the other tavern patrons, each one a potential threat. Elvgren started to think maybe this little scheme hadn't been such a good idea after all.

Another hour rolled slowly past before he decided to give up. He drained the dregs from his cup and walked out the door. Making his way along the cobbled road that led back to the den, he heard the clopping of hooves behind him. The carriage overtook and came to a halt. A door flew open and a face it would have been kind to describe as unsavoury looked out at him.

'You the one-eyed lord?' the man asked. Elvgren nodded. 'Get in.'

Elvgren stood in fearful contemplation for a moment before getting into the carriage. He sat across from a slight man who looked like an accountant. The man who had hailed him slammed the door shut and banged on the roof for the driver to carry on.

'So, the one-eyed lord, eh? I wouldn't normally have my interest piqued by a piece of theatre as crude as you pulled the other night but I was wondering if you might be the same lord who has been described in all the newsprints?' The slight man said, polishing a pair of small, round spectacles before perching them on the bridge of his nose.

'That would be correct Mr...'

'Faultwright, boy. You know damn well who I am, don't play cute. It's a funny thing, isn't it? The whole of Estria looking for you and you throw yourself into my lap. Especially knowing I've had a hand in the deception that has the Empire looking in the wrong place. I was curious to see if you were brave or just insane in seeking me out.'

Elvgren thought it was probably a little of both. 'I merely wish to discuss a business opportunity with you. My mental capacity was not lost with my eye.'

'Yes, you are not quite as handsome as you once were. It would seem my adopted home town has shown you its own particular brand of hospitality. But what makes you think I would not take you straight to the Burkeshis? They were most keen on discovering your whereabouts when they paid me to help with their deception and already furious to find that Major Bouchard had been plucked from their grasp.'

'Why in the twelve hells are you helping them? You're clearly of Estrian descent.'

A curious, thin smile spread across Faultwright's face. 'Hah. You really are a pampered noble aren't you, boy? Never had to work for anything in your life. Enjoying the fruits of the Empire while others sweat and bleed to maintain it. It's like a ravenous beast, devouring and chewing up the people who keep it all spinning. I'm just one of the many people it threw up. I have no love for my home country. It gave me nothing and took the little I did have.' He paused letting his tirade subside and delicately wiped the froth away from the corner of his mouth. 'Besides, I am a businessman and the Burkeshis paid very well for a service I could provide. I have no great empathy towards them either. Which is why I assisted in the transporting of the major. I am a man of my word and Gulgarno also pays for my services.'

'So, that's it to you? Just business. Our ships are blockaded, trade strangled, war threatened and all you can think of is who can pay you the most. Where's your honour man?'

'Don't talk to me about honour. Honour doesn't put food in your stomach or keep you warm. It's a sham. One that keeps people in their place. But I did not come here to digress into philosophic discourse. I came out of curiosity which has been satisfied. You are alive, I now possess this information and shall see what rewards I can gain from it.'

'Wait, please, Mr. Faultwright. Hear me out. I have heard you rig the betting at the annual Amlith games. I have a scheme that could make you a lot of money. Think of it as just another business deal if you wish.' It was a risk. Elvgren was relying on the idle chatter of out-of-work dockhands but he had to act now.

'Money I have, boy. But I would be interested to hear how you plan to rig a fight to the death?' Faultwright looked at Elvgren like an owl hovering over its next meal.

This is it, he thought, *all or nothing*. 'If I pull this off, I ask for my freedom and that of a boy called Dargo, also the major, if I can secure it. In addition, I want ten thousand rencats.'

'I may be curious, boy, and I admire your balls, but that is a steep ask,' Faultwright said with a little laugh.

'I am aware of that. But I also have some information you might find interesting. I know what became of your right-hand man. Holt, was it? And I know who did the becoming,' Elvgren said.

Faultwright fixed him with a look of cold curiosity. 'You have my attention, boy. Go on.'

19

Gulgarno's cart, full of gladiators, trundled along the stone road to Yondapolis, the capital of Varash. Cirona and the rest of the combatants sat in silence. None of them knew what to say to the people they would be trying to kill in a few hours. They had been travelling since the night beforeand it had been a long ride. The sun was fresh over the horizon as they rounded a hill and the capital came into view through the hard-topped wagon's windows.

The ground fell away into a deep valley, a few mansions clinging to the sides. Cirona's eyes were led down to the vast sprawl of Yondapolis. It spread like an abscess, its streets snaking out and infecting the surrounding brown fields. The wide River Var cut through the mess, spilling out to the sea, shimmering in the distance. And then she saw it.

The grand coliseum stood out even from this distance. The vast walls rose to a staggering height, lined with columns of white marble. The flag of Varash, flew from its sides. It was said that the structure could hold a hundred thousand souls and Cirona didn't have a hard time believing it. Sitting at the very heart of the city, the tiny people carousing around it gave the impression that it moved, a pulsing heart of stone.

'It's quite a sight, is it not?' Reveeker said to Cirona.

'A lovely place to watch humans kill each other for sport. Seems a waste to use something so grand for something so shitty,' she replied. They fell back into silence, the same silence that had accompanied them since they had both volunteered for the fight. 'Look, Rev, I... I don't know what to say. This is madness, but I will do anything to get back to the girl I told you about,' Cirona said, summoning the courage to break the silence.

'I know. I shouldn't have been so distant either, but you know why I want my freedom too. Sounds stupid to say it. A reason for wanting to be free. You've seen the life a gladiator can lead. Money, glory, adulation: it turns many heads.' Rev sighed. 'But I have waited a long time for this opportunity — six years, six! If you think you need to get out after the short time you've been with Gulgarno, then how do you think I feel?'

'All I can say is good luck then. If we meet, I will try my best to kill you,' Cirona said, meeting him dead in the eye.

'See if you can, you stinking Estrian *kifet*,' he replied with a grin.

'Same to you, you sun-baked shit.' They chuckled together, both happy to have made their peace. Now Cirona would have no regrets if she had to kill him.

She cast her eyes around at the rest of her potential victims: a stocky Narvglander stroked his plaited moustache, two Carthanians spoke together in a whisper, a young boy, one of the gladiators who had enrolled freely to the school, chewed nervously at his thumb nail, a leathery Bakori woman was asleep and a giant by the name of Gengarth, a native of Paltont, was eating dates. The bleakness of the scene hit her. By the end of the day only one of them would be left alive, rich and free. Cirona began to think of all the stories that would end today, all the hopes and dreams. No time for that, though. She had her own hopes and she was damned well going to fight for them. Still, it left a bitter taste in her mouth. She had killed countless men and women in her career but that had always been in the heat of battle. You never fucking shared a wagon with your enemy before you got to the scrap. *Fuck, I hope I don't have to fight that kid.*

*

There was a soft knock on the cabin door. Bellina stirred beneath the silk sheets. 'Ngnnh... come in,' she mumbled, rubbing at her eyes. She rubbed them again when she saw Holger standing in the doorway.

'Morning,' he said sheepishly, moving into the room and setting down a pot of steaming tea on the table.

Since the revelation of her powers, she had not spoken to the boy. 'Ah. Watch yourself. You've descended into the mind-melter's pit! I never thought you possessed such bravery,' she sneered at him.

'I'm sorry Bel... I mean, my lady. It's just shock, is all. You share a delightful piece of floorboard with someone and you think you know them,' he said with a hopeful smile.

Bellina didn't respond in kind. 'Well, if there is nothing else, get out.'

'I ... well ... I just...' Holger stammered.

'What? Want to say you're sorry? That it doesn't bother you, we can still be friends just so long as no one else sees you? I don't need you and I don't need your piddling sympathy or whatever the hells it is you're trying to do here. Just go.'

'Belle, please! I know I haven't been a good friend and I'm sorry. Know it's not worth nothing, won't be healing any wounds, but I just wanted to say it even if you don't want to hear it. I know how you feel. Kind of anyway, I've got...' He paused, his eyes looked into hers. She watched him as he fished around for whatever it was he wanted to say. 'Enjoy your tea. Oh, and peace be. It's Amlith Day.' With that, he turned and walked from the room, taking whatever else he was about to say with him.

Bellina hugged her knees. Why? Why was it so hard? All her life, she had never had anyone to call a friend. She had been tutored at home, closeted away like a barmy old aunt. She knew her father had meant well but the seclusion had only enhanced how weird she was to her peers.

Uncalled for, the first time she had gone to a function with her father, where there would be other children, smashed to the front of her mind. She had been about seven and so excited, wittering on endlessly to Madame Matresca about how many new friends she would make. Her lady-in-waiting had smiled and nodded while she plaited her hair and helped her with her new frock. Then she had stood back, beaming, and told her how pretty she looked, to mind her manners and enjoy herself.

Bellina had skipped up the path to the manor — *gods, whose was it?* — holding her father's hand, an excited babble of chatter still tumbling from her mouth. Her father looked down with an indulgent smile and told her not to speak too fast to the other boys and girls. Then they had gone into the reception room. She saw the other children playing games in the corner and begged her father to let her go. He did. She ran over like a puppy, all ungraceful motion, before she remembered her instructions and tried to glide across the room like Madame did. She curtseyed to the other children and they laughed. Had she done something wrong?

'It thinks it's human.' and 'Bet it pees itself. Quick let's run away before she melts our brains.' They ran off. She chased them, pleading. 'Please, please can I play too? I don't melt brains. I'm a good girl.' 'You're a dirty mind melting poohead,' a girl shouted at her. 'Poohead. Ha ha ha.' The tears stung Bellina's face. She ran for cover. That was the first time she hid under the table during a party and it became her favourite hiding place for many years.

Bellina watched the drops of her tears fall onto the sheets, turning into dark circles on the silk. She cried and cried like she hadn't done in years. Why had she allowed herself to hope? Gods dammit what a balls-up. Her breath heaved in her chest and her body shuddered. She completely gave in to the sobs until there were no more tears.

Only then did Bellina get herself dressed and go up on deck, just like she had forced herself to do every day since the crew had learned her secret. Some cursed, others spat audibly onto the deck but all eyes followed her. She saw Barboza standing at the prow, pointing into the distance. This time he actually had something to point at.

A black rift darkened the sky ahead. The clouds rolled and she could see sparks of lightning shoot through them like the veins on an old woman's wrist.

'Bad weather coming, my lady,' Barboza said.

'Can we outrun it?' Bellina asked.

'Alas no! It's coming on at pace. We'll just have time to lash everything down before it really fucks us. Perhaps it would be best to stay in your cabin.'

For once Bellina agreed.

*

The gang's den was silent except for the snores. Elvgren sat in a chair by the fire and contemplated the hell that was coming, a hell that he had summoned.

Faultwright had accepted the terms of the deal once he had been told the truth about what happened to Holt. Well, not the whole truth. Elvgren had fudged the events a smidge and painted himself out of the slaughter. And now, just past dawn, he waited for the men to come.

Right on cue the door flew open. Ten of Faultwright's men came charging in, pulling the sleeping gang to their feet. A few scuffles broke out but were quickly subdued.

'What is being the meaning of this?' Danker cried.

'Shut up you fucking rotter! Did ye think there would be no reckoning for what you did to Holt?' one of the men holding Danker said.

'You are talking nonsense, eh? I know nothing! Who is this Holt?'

'Don't play dumb. Your boy there showed us the bodies himself, after he told us what happened,' added another man, who had Jadir pinned to the floor.

'Is this true?' Danker said, looking at Elvgren.

Elvgren felt a pang of guilt flood through him but he didn't have time for such things. He had to get to Cirona, had to do something to make amends for the night the *Prudence* sank. He reminded himself that this man had tried to sell him, that if it hadn't been for Elvgren, Danker would be dead anyway. Still, he knew it was a cold thing he did and the fate that now awaited Danker did not bear thinking about. 'It's true, Danker,' he said, trying to not let a quiver enter his voice. 'I could say I'm sorry, but I know that doesn't mean shit when someone else holds your fate in their hands. When Faultwright heard it was you who had done away with Holt, well, let's just say that how he felt about your previous debt to him pales in comparison.'

'You little fuck-shit! It was him, it was all him!' Danker screamed.

'Alright, Danker, you must think we was born yesterday. No way that streak of Estrian piss killed some of our best men,' said the man holding Danker as he led him from the room. Jadir and Kotor were led out raging behind him.

'Wait!' Elvgren shouted as a man began to carry Dargo out of the room. The boy was kicking, biting and scratching but the man may as well have been made from granite for all the good it did. 'The boy is to be spared,' Elvgren said. The man put Dargo down, shrugged his shoulders and followed the rest out of the door.

Dargo kicked Elvgren hard in the shin and set upon him, arms pumping and legs kicking.

'Dargo! Dargo! Get off, just listen to me, please?' Elvgren said wrestling himself free of the boy and pinning his arms.

'You fucking traitor, how could you? I thought you were just gonna tell Faultwright about your betting scheme. How could you?'

'I know Dargo, this is not my finest hour. Just listen!' Elvgren shouted as the boy writhed in his grasp. 'Look, I don't have much time. I have to be in Yondapolis by midday at the latest. Are you in? You can have half the take for the job, five thousand rencats. But I need your help. After that, you can go wherever you please. You'll certainly have the funds.'

''S not about funds. This is my home. Where would I go? With you?'

'I don't know if that's possible, I won't lie. There are a lot of things to consider. All I can say is that I asked them to leave you alone but once I'm gone I don't know what Faultwright will do. Hells I don't know what he might do to me even if this works. But I have got to do this and I have got to go now. Are you coming?' Elvgren looked in to the boy's eyes. It was true that he didn't trust Faultwright. The whole thing was one big gamble but he had to see it through.

'I guess I don't have much of a choice, do I?' Dargo said.

Did anybody? Elvgren thought to himself.

20

Barboza had not been lying about the weather. Bellina clung frantically to the side of the bed as the ship convulsed to and fro. The storm had been raging for thirty minutes though it felt like hours. A particularly violent swell unprised her grip and sent her sprawling onto the floor. 'Gods damn it,' she cried as a large, jewelled bracelet slid from a shelf onto her head, the pain adding to her frayed nerves. She had always enjoyed a good storm from the safety of her home but being trapped in the middle of one was deeply troubling. Bellina felt like a mouse caught by a spiteful cat, prey batted around before being finished off.

She heard shouting from the passageway. Angry voices, loud and harsh, but she couldn't make out the words. There was a sharp banging on the cabin door and before she had mustered her wits to respond it was thrown open by two of the ship's crew, a couple of Tinker and Vell's cronies.

'What the hells is it?' Bellina asked. *Were they sinking?*

'Shut your noise, witch, and do as we say or things will get painful for yer,' one of the men said. He pulled out a knife while his companion hoisted her to her feet. Despite the rolling of the ship they managed to keep her in check with the point of a knife in the small of her back. Before long they had climbed onto the deck.

If Bellina had been scared in the relative shelter of her cabin, her legs gave way at what she saw outside. The sky was a swirling mass of green and yellow, spitting out silver tongues of lightning. Thunder boomed around her, shaking every bone in her body, and giant swells pounded the deck. She was led over to where the crew were gathered and was shoved through the middle of them. Their eyes were filled with hate as they spat and cursed at her. She was pushed in front of them and fell to her knees. It was Captain Barboza who helped her up again so that she stood next to him and his first mate.

Tinker came to the front of the assembled crew and bellowed over the storm. 'Shipmates, we have all bought in to this black devil's democracy. The best thing about it is we get to choose our leader.

Barboza has let us down. The moment we found out about that fucking mind-melter we should have thrown her into the sea!'

'You treacherous dog! This is mutiny!' Barboza howled.

'Nah, I think you'll find this is called an election. Who here agrees we toss the lot of 'em overboard and appease the Cruel Mistress?'

'Aye!' the crew sang back.

Bellina saw a scuffle break out, then Holger was thrown forward, his nose bloody.

'Ah, if it ain't the lovesick puppy,' Tinker said. 'If you wanna live boy, I'd get over her and quick!'

'This is fucking madness, Tinker! This shit isn't her doing!' Holger shouted.

'Madness, is it? Ever since she came aboard we've been cursed. Not a decent piece of plunder and now this fucking storm. Nah, it's not madness, this is the wrath of the goddess. She won't bear the mind-fucker's weight!'

The crew cheered in agreement. Holger tried to charge at him but the ship rocked and he was thrown back. Vell pointed the tip of her blade at his throat and led him over to Bellina and the others.

'Looks like we've got one more to add to our offering then,' Tinker said, laughing. 'Come on men, the quicker we're shot of them, the quicker this storm will end!'

The crew advanced. They harried Bellina and the others towards the starboard rail.

'You piece of shit, Tinker!' Barboza cried. 'I'll get you for this, you wait and fucking see!'

Bellina could just make out Holger and Crenshaw amongst the mad tangle of the mob. It was taking twelve men to force Barboza from the ship, fighting as fiercely as he was. There was a sound like the snap of a giant's whip. Bellina looked up to see a support line holding one of the small boarding boats to the ship had come loose. Inside the craft, Midge sawed furiously at the other line.

'What the fuck is that boy doing?' Tinker cried.

Midge, seeing that he'd been spotted, started to hack at the taut rope as if the Old Terrors were after him.

'Get up there and stop him!' Vell shrieked. But it was too late, the boat swung like a pendulum for a few brief seconds before another vicious wave provided enough force to send it crashing into the water.

'Little shit's trying to save 'em,' one of the crew called. 'Better slit their throats before sending 'em to the goddess!'

Vell advanced towards Bellina. 'Oh, it would be my honour,' she sneered.

A great roar came from the massive frame of Barboza. Men scattered from him as he flew into a berserker's rage. More men rushed to subdue him. Bellina used the distraction to kick Vell sharply in the groin. She fought the last couple of paces to the rail and threw herself over.

Bellina hit the water with breath-stealing force. She had barely a fraction of a second to register the freezing chill before her momentum dragged her beneath the waves. She fought her way back up, her head breaking the surface, struggling for air, her body convulsing from the cold. As she tried to keep herself afloat, she caught sight of the boat Midge had dropped into the water. It looked close but it may as well have been on the other side of the world. *Where are the others?* she thought, before she was dragged beneath the raging waves again.

The world turned the colour of aged stone, dark grey and unforgiving. Her struggle made her think of her psychic battle with Alcastus. Had he recovered his wits yet? Or had she damaged his mind beyond repair. The thought of her arrogant treatment of him, how he had cowered before her, stung at her soul. At least then she had been able to use her powers to free herself, bend the psychic world to her whim. Now she was at the mercy of the elements, she prayed that they showed more clemency than she had to her former teacher. Air escaped her lungs in an explosion of bubbles. Her body reflexively tried to breathe and she tasted the salty tang of the sea fill her mouth, she quickly clasped her jaw shut. Panic flooded through her, she made another effort to get to the surface. Her muscles screamed at her in agony but she refused to heed them. She reached up, stretching every sinew to reach the shimmering ceiling of water. Her lungs cried for air again and her body gave in. The sea rushed into her throat before she could stop it.

When she was a child, Bellina had choked on a small sweet. The terror and the panic she had felt then were the same, but this time there was no one to turn her upside down and get the foreign thing out of her. She flailed weightlessly beneath the waves, the surface taunting her with its proximity. Her vision began to blur and a blackness came, stealing in from the corners of her eyes.

Something grabbed her hand, firm and warm. She was hauled up through the roiling sea before being pulled into the small boat where she retched and heaved the water out of her. Holger and Midge had her by her arms while Barboza and Crenshaw did battle with the oars. She crouched on her knees in the belly of the vessel and threw up everything inside her. Holger patted her firmly on the back while Midge tried to steady himself against the fierceness of the sea.

'Are you alright?' Holger asked.

Bellina wanted to answer back with something sarcastic but she could only nod. Holger moved over to Crenshaw to help with the rowing. Their wet clothes clung to their skin, shoulder muscles bulging with the strain. Considering the difficulty they were having, it was amazing that they had managed to get the boat over to her. The small vessel was being smashed from all sides by the waves, tossed to and fro as if the giant crests of water were playing catch with it.

Bellina felt a tightness around her middle and looked down to see Midge clutching her, a lost toddler who had found his mother. She held him close while they both hunkered down in the boat. She felt the warmth of his tears against the chill of her skin. Bellina stroked his hair and sang a faltering song in his ear — a song of home.

*

Cirona and the other gladiators were led through the crowds that had built up around the arena. It seemed like the whole city had turned out for the event. There were merchants selling food at an outrageous price, ale and wine men filling clay cups for revellers, bettakers screaming odds at the top of their lungs. Cirona watched it all through the slatted eye holes of her face mask. Gulgarno had insisted she wear it in case anyone recognised her but she thought there was no fear of that. If Tavarar was a mash of different races from across the world, Yondapolis was the complete opposite. All the faces she saw, cheering or jeering, belonged to Varashis. The common tongue was spoken here but only when necessary for trade and, even *then*, the words were spat out with disgust. Due to countless clashes over the years, the Varashis bore a legacy of hate for all things Estrian. Only the superiority of Estrian technology held them back from all-out war. *No,* Cirona thought, *I will find no friends here.*

The combatants finally reached the backstage area of the arena, a stunning space to live out your last moments. It was a large, square room, the walls lined with veined marble; the floor, a beautiful mosaic of gladiators standing triumphant, the red squares of blood having a particular vibrancy. Velvet couches were scattered invitingly around the room and a banqueting table, filled with delicacies and wine, took up the centre space.

Cirona was now sure that they would spend the time before their duels in each other's company. More time to observe and humanise the people she would have to kill if she was going to survive. She began to feel anxious, her breath coming in ragged bursts through the metal mask. She reached behind her head to rip it free but Barag grabbed her hand.

'No. That stays on till you are dead or till you win,' he said, before wandering off to the table of food.

Gods, why had she agreed to this? Why hadn't she thought of some other way to get free? The madness of it all swept over her. This wasn't right, it wasn't who she was. She couldn't stand in front of thousands of people and kill for sport. She felt faint, her legs began to give way. A hand touched her back, supporting her. It was Reveeker. He guided her over to one of the couches and sat her down.

'Come now, Rona,' he said to her kindly. 'Steady yourself. The first time I was to fight at a tournament, panic tried to claim me too and I didn't have to wear a ridiculous mask.'

'I can't do this, Rev. I can't. Get me out of here, please,' she said, the panic creeping round her throat like a noose. There was no escape, no way out she could see. The fighting had been so remote when she was at the school. Even on the wagon ride it still seemed like a dream. Now though, in this waiting room that was decked out like a pleasure parlour, the reality stared her in the face.

'Look woman, you are here. This is it. In a minute, they will call two names and those people will fight till one is dead. I don't say this to be comforting, but to wake you up. Find the woman who fought me like a leoguar. Find her and bring her out, or you *will* die!' Reveeker stared deep into her eyes as he said the words, jaw clenched tight.

She looked deep inside her. Looked as hard as she could: but the fight wasn't there. Her mind was filled with Trafford, Bellina and her child. Her beautiful, perfect girl. How could she find the woman she needed to survive when that woman was the reason none of those people were here now?

'Rona, come; they are calling the first names,' Reveeker said as if from another world.

*

Elvgren and Dargo had ridden like the Old Terrors were at their back. They had been forced to abandon their horses at the edge of the city due to the crowds flooding the streets and were fighting their way across the bridge over the River Var. The suffocating smell of the waterway which doubled as Yondapolis' main sewer outlet bombarded their nostrils. The Varashis who surrounded them were clearly not bothered by the stench; many walked along eating honey-baked dormice on thin skewers.

Ahead, the great arena of Drastos, the Varashi god of war, dominated the view. Elvgren had always marvelled at how occasions like Amlith Day, celebrated to honour the defeat of the Old Terrors, were held worldwide amidst so many differences in religion and culture. It was as if the events that took place a thousand years before had been absorbed into the blood of humanity so that, even when the events had passed into legend, some small, inherited memory had survived. *A bit like the common tongue*, he thought. People across the world still spoke it, even though they now had their own languages.

'Are we almost — hey watch your fucking self — there?' Dargo said, as he was bashed mid-sentence by a corpulent Varashi. The man hissed something back in his native tongue and sauntered off.

'Yeah, almost,' Elvgren called back. Truthfully, he had thought they were almost there thirty minutes ago, the immense size of the arena had skewed his sense of distance.

They were squashed in like tinned meat, the crowd carrying them along untilfinally they could see the multitude of entrances to the arena. The space in front of the building was a vast circle and, blessedly, there was plenty of room to move. The pair were shot out of the seething crush of human flesh like a ball from a ballisket. They both stopped and took a minute to breathe in air that wasn't coming to them second-hand.

At the centre of the circular space was a large fountain. Huge, bronze fish sprayed each other in a dazzling criss-cross of water. Elvgren gestured Dargo over to it. They had made it but now came the risky part. 'Right, Dar, I'm going to change into my costume; think there are enough people to not get noticed if I'm discree—what the hells is all that noise about?' Elvgren was interrupted by a sudden eruption of sound. Men stood on boxes calling out to the crowd in Varashi, then the common tongue. 'What the hells are they saying, Dargo?'

'I think they just said the games are about to start,' Dargo replied, eyebrow raised.

'Shit, shit, shit!' Elvgren looked at a sundial timepiece that studded the wall of the arena. There were still thirty more minutes till twelve. *Oh, how delightful, they have decided to start early this year*, he thought. 'Damn it all to the fucking Void! We still have to meet with Faultwright's men by the back entrance. Hopefully, they have all got the message to the bet-takers but, if the major is drawn to fight first, we're done.'

'Well then genius, you had better get a move on!' Dargo replied.

21

The breath stuck in Cirona's lungs as she waited for the names to be called. A man dressed in gold ceremonial robes plunged his hand into a bronze cauldron.

'The first contestant will be... Griffith of Tavarar!'

Cirona looked around. The young boy who had been nervously chewing his thumbnail pointed his finger to his chest. He looked at the man drawing the names and then at Barag with terrified, questioning eyes. Barag nodded. Griffith stood up on uncertain legs and made his way towards the man in gold.

'The next contestant will be... the Estrian woman!'

Cirona felt the life go out of her. This had to be a joke, the fates couldn't be so cruel.

Barag fixed his eyes on her. 'Move, woman,' he commanded.

Cirona's mouth was dry, she tried to lick her lips but was foiled by the tightness of the face mask. She rose to her feet and joined Griffith.

'Well then,' the man in gold began, 'we will make our way to the arena floor without further ado, the prince is most anxious to see—'

'Hold on one minute. No one's going anywhere just yet!' a voice called across the room.

All eyes turned towards it. A medificer, dressed in the traditional white cowl and mask shaped like a bird, was striding across the room. A small apprentice wearing a grey cloak accompanied him.

'What is this all about?' Barag bellowed.

'The proper examinations have not been carried out yet. The fight must be postponed while I make sure these two are in good condition,' the medificer explained.

'The prince will not stand for this. The games must not be delayed!' the man in gold said.

'Who the hells do you think sent me down here to do the check-up? The prince wants to make sure they are in perfect condition so that they put on a performance befitting such an auspicious occasion. If you want to bother him by questioning his own commands, then by all means go and ask.'

The man's face contorted as he battled with the choice. 'I will give you fifteen minutes,' he said before stalking off, muttering.

'You, man,' the medificer said, pointing to Barag. 'Take us to a private room where I may carry out my examination. I will see the woman first.'

A petulant look passed over Barag's face, before he grudgingly led them into a side room.

'This will be adequate. You may leave,' the medificer said with a dismissive wave. Barag exited the room, muttering about bloody medificers and their attitudes.

Cirona was left in the room with the healer and his apprentice. The room itself was sparse, ridiculously so compared to the waiting room, with just a simple wooden chair and table in it. Relief flooded through Cirona and she started to talk in a mad babble. 'Thank the gods. I can't go out there, Medic! I just can't, you've got to find a way. I can't breathe, I can't—'

'I'm afraid you must, Major. There are a lot of very important people backing you to die.' The medificer pulled his mask away.

Cirona stared in amazement and horror at the face of Elvgren Lovitz. But it wasn't the face she remembered. A hideous pink scar, partially obscured by an eyepatch, slashed down his face. His nose was crooked, his cheeks sunken and hard. He looked like a starving wolf. 'Lord Elvgren... what... how...?' she spluttered.

'Major, I know you must have a lot of questions but there isn't time. Here, quickly. You must drink this potion,' Elvgren said, brandishing a vial of sludgy brown liquid in front of her face.

'What in the twelve hells is that?'

'It's a potion called worm's foil. It will put you in a near-death state for about three hours. Hopefully that will be enough time for us to escape. Now quickly, please,' Elvgren said.

Cirona took the bottle gingerly. At that moment, she would have eaten shit if it would have got her out of the tournament. She downed the contents in one.

'You will know the potion is working when you start to feel... euphoric,' he said.

'Wonderful, my lord! You will get me off my ever-loving tits before your death poison works its magic. How thoughtful. How am I supposed to go out there and fight if I'm not in my right mind?'

'Don't worry, just go out and... I don't know, play fight or something.

I'll have a word with your opponent. The lad didn't look too keen to be out there himself,' he said.

'So, I just flail about a bit then collapse in a heap. Oh, fantastic. How long does this muck take to work anyway?' Cirona said, her relief turning to anger.

'I ... um... don't actually know...'

'You don't... you don't fucking know. I should have known this was too good to be true. Another of Lord Lovitz's balls-ups, although I suppose nothing could top the Lord Exchequer's Ball now, could it!'

'If you have a better idea I'd like to hear it. I have gone to *considerable* trouble to get here, sacrificed a lot for this, and you want to throw a strop? Fine, stick your fingers down your throat, puke it up and take your chances!' Elvgren said, a look of deep hurt on his face.

Cirona regretted her words. Gods, the idiot must have been through the twelve hells to be here, if his face was anything to go by.

'I'm sorry, Elvgren. I really don't want to do this; what if there is a mistake, a slip of the blade? I don't want to kill that boy and I certainly don't want him to kill me.'

'It won't come to that. This is what you do isn't it? You better go now, I don't think I can put off my other examinations any longer. But please trust me, I know it's hard. I will get us out of this,' he said, a hint of pleading in his voice.

'Do you know what became of the Lady Bellina?' Cirona asked, remembering how she had sent the pair off together.

'I think that's a conversation best left for later. You need to concentrate on the job at hand,' Elvgren replied.

She did not like the sound of that, or the look on the young lord's face as he said it. He was right though, she had to stay focused. One thing at a time. 'Ok, *Medic*. See you later, I suppose,' she said in resignation. There really were no other options. She tried to put the image of the bleeding Lord Exchequer out of her mind.

'Be careful, Major,' Elvgren said to her with a nod of his head.

Cirona turned for the door then a thought struck her. 'Wait a minute! Rev! I've got a friend, a Burkeshi. Let him know what's happening. See if you can help him too.'

'A Burkeshi? A bloody Burkeshi! Are you mad, woman?'

'I know how it sounds but he is a good man. Speak to him, see what you can do.' With that Cirona exited the room leaving the young lord with an incredulous look on his face. She swallowed hard then closed the door behind her.

*

Elvgren watched the major leave the room, his nerves as taut as a cable. It had been a close thing getting into the waiting room on time, if it hadn't been for the assistance of Faultwright's inside men they would never have made it. Elvgren had been stunned by how many of the arena's security guards were on the take from the Tavarar crime lord. They had followed his instructions to the letter, clearing a way through the crowds for him and Dargo before alerting the bet-takers. By now, the majority of the revellers would have thrown their money at the ludicrously long odds on Major Bouchard, while those in the know would be putting their money on her opponent. It was a win-win for Faultwright. The peasants and merchant classes would empty their pockets on a bet with no chance. Meanwhile, the Varashi nobility would be greatly appreciative of the tip-off. It seemed like a flawless plan.

Then again, he had thought that before the blunder that had cost the Lord Exchequer's life and sent him into the hell of the past weeks. Elvgren certainly couldn't blame the major for doubting him but it stung all the same. He blocked those thoughts out. He was here now, that was what mattered. And he still had a lot of work to do. 'Ok, Dargo, go and get the major's opponent. Let's fill him in on the plan,' Elvgren said.

'What if he just runs off and tells someone? Maybe that ugly fella with the whip who saw us in?'

'All we can do is hope that he is as reluctant to fight as he looks.'

'It's been a hell of a lot of trouble to come down to a hope, Gren,' Dargo said, before going to get the boy.

Fuck it all, he thought. He really hadn't figured out all the angles, so much had been taken on assumption. He forced the doubt deep down. No way back now, all he could do was ride out the storm and hope he came up on dry land.

Thankfully, the major's opponent was more than happy to be handed a free pass into the next round. He even asked Elvgren if there was any more worm's foil. The look on his face when Elvgren said there was no more was heart-rending. *Poor bastard*, he thought, his mind flitting back to his own brush with capture and slavery. He couldn't save everyone though.

Elvgren and Dargo saw the rest of the gladiators quickly, as they would have to be out on the arena floor before the fight finished to find out where the major's body would be taken. They did their best to sound like medificers: rambling on about humours and the moon. Neither knew what the hells they were saying but they quickly realised that the uniform and a condescending manner made their patients more than cooperative. Finally, the only one left was the Burkeshi.

'So, you must be Rev,' Elvgren said, once Dargo had seen the huge man in and shut the door.

'My name is Reveeker, yes. But how did you come to know this, Medic?'

Elvgren once again took off his face mask. He watched as the man drew back ever so slightly. 'Major Bouchard seemed to think you could be trusted. Though I have serious doubts that any Burkeshi is deserving of that sentiment,' Elvgren said, half expecting the man's face to begin peeling away.

'Well, I have no love for my homeland anymore. My own people sold me into the life I lead know. But who in the hells are you anyway?'

'I was one of the major's companions before... well, before all of this. I have come to rescue her. She has taken a potion that will simulate her death. Then we have a wagon waiting to take us away. She asked me to tell you this and to help you. Though I don't really see how.'

'That's quite a lot of information to take in. Of course, I desire my freedom but unless you have another potion hidden up your arse then I don't see what you can do to help me either.'

Elvgren felt a burning anger in his stomach. How dare this stinking sand-shit speak to *him* like that? But, the major *had* asked him. 'Look, I don't have all the answers. In fact, I don't have half of them. I offered you help, you give me insults. Frankly, that is not helpful,' he said.

The Burkeshi cast his eyes down. 'I am sorry. I am pleased that Cirona would think of me at a time like this. If there is anything I can do, I will help. Perhaps we can all find a way out of this.'

'Let's hope so. Anyway, we'd better go and see how the major is doing. Her fight must be under way by now. Is there anywhere we can watch from?' Elvgren asked.

'There is an observation stand for participants and trainers just by the entrance to the arena floor. I will show you,' Reveeker said as Elvgren put his mask back on.

After a short walk down a dark tunnel, they came to the small stand. *It would have been a great seat if you weren't watching someone you knew battle for their life*, Elvgren thought. Although the stand was small and already close to full with the assembled combatants and trainers, it was positioned right on the arena floor. The roar of the crowd was ear shattering. The steeply rising stands made the seating in the Estrian training ground look pitiful. Elvgren looked up at the sea of humanity crammed into the seats. In the middle of the left stand, some twenty rows above the arena floor, was the royal box. The prince and his retainers stared intently at the unfolding spectacle.

Elvgren shifted his eyes down to the floor. It was a large circle of compacted red earth. That was it. There would be no other distractions for the gladiators today. No traps or other obstacles to avoid. Elvgren was glad of this as he had no idea how the potion would affect the major. His attention was drawn to the centre of the circle. Bouchard and her opponent stood with the man in the gold robes. The crowd fell silent and the man spoke, his voice carried by the incredible acoustics. He spoke first in Varashi then in the common tongue.

'Ladies and gentlemen. The tournament of death, a double celebration in honour of Amlith Day and His Highness, Prince Hivat of Varash's eighteenth birthday, is about to commence!'

22

The sea was calm, finally. The beautiful sight of the sun's rays glistening on the crest of the waves was a stark contrast to the terror the small boat had faced. The battle to keep the boat from capsizing had been immense. The three men toiling with all their might to fight against the swells. Then, afterwhat felt like a lifetime, the storm had passed as suddenly as it had arrived.

Bellina and the rest sat exhausted on the wooden planks of the small vessel. The gentle motion of the boat had sent Midge to sleep while still clutching at Bellina's dress. She stroked his back absently. The whole time she had been on board the *Scampering Vagabond*, the young boy had been a mystery, saying few words and staying out of people's way. She looked down at their unlikely saviour; his head rested in her lap, his rhythmic breathing tickling her legs.

With the passing of the storm and the immediate threat to their lives behind them, Bellina's mind turned to what the hells they were going to do now. They had no water, no food and gods only knew where they were. She hoped that Barboza was as good at navigating as he was at pointing. 'Captain Barboza?' Bellina asked, giving voice to her thoughts. 'Where in the twelve hells are we?'

'Hmmm, a fine question my lady,' Barboza said, standing up. His massive frame made the craft rock more energetically. He walked to the front of the boat and stood impressively. He placed his foot on the prow and pointed out to sea. 'If I am not very much mistaken, the land of Paltont is but a day's sailing in that direction,' he said, his voice carrying an unquestionable air of certainty, as if he dared the country not to be where he was pointing.

'For the love of the gods, Bar, give it up!' Crenshaw said, propping himself up on his elbows.

'What do you mean, Mr Crenshaw?' Bellina asked.

'The man can as much sail a boat as I can shit diamonds. He's been bluffing the whole time,' Crenshaw replied.

'Captain, is this true?' Bellina asked, spinning back round to face Barboza. The giant man looked down, his face a picture of abject shame.

'I am afraid so, sweet lady. I couldn't tell a capstan from a privy. I meant no one any harm, privateering is just the latest on my list of many occupations, I thought the booty would set me up for life. On that front, I was sorely mistaken,' he said, sorrow resonating through his rich tones.

'How in the world did you ever become the captain?' Bellina said, her brain struggling to comprehend what she was hearing.

'It was simple, really. I have very strong views on democracy as you may have gathered. When the last captain was disposed of—'

'Hang on,' Bellina said, 'you mean the *Scampering Vagabond*'s crew have mutinied before. And this wasn't troubling to you?'

'Well, I never intended to stay for very long, a few months at most. Then I would be away on my twinkling toes with a chest full of loot. Anyway, as I was saying, I offered the crew equal shares and say on everything. After the veritable despotism of the previous captain — a miserly swine who demanded a forty percent cut for himself — I seemed like a good choice, I suppose. I have always had a way with words.'

'A way with words? You should have seen his Asvertine. The crowds in Carthania couldn't get enough of it,' Crenshaw said.

'Wait a minute. Asvertine? As in *Drenteel and Asvertine*, the play?' Bellina asked, her voice betraying her total amazement.

'Yes. I was an actor in a past life, as well as many other things. As such, I found it incredibly easy to portray a captain — it's amazing how much you can get away with if you act as if you are entitled to command. And when it came to the sailing bit, well, I had Crenshaw here pick up the necessary lingo and knowledge and there you have it!' Barboza finished, throwing up his hands.

Bellina reeled back against the side of the boat, stunned. She had been sailing on a ship for the past weeks with an out-of-work actor who fancied a turn as a pirate. *Fuck the storm*, she thought, *it's a small miracle we stayed afloat for a day*. Bellina looked across at Holger, the revelation seemed to have had the same effect on him. They all sat in silence for some time. There was another thorny issue: Holger. In her heart, she was grateful to him for coming to her defence but she had always had a hard time climbing back down from her high horse. When he looked up at her and offered her a small smile, she narrowed her eyes at him. Then she turned back to the others. 'I would just like to take the opportunity to say thank you, *Mr* Barboza and Mr Crenshaw. Whatever your occupations, you saved my life and I am grateful. That thanks also extends to Midge — though I think we all owe him that and a damn sight more — and... you Holger. Thank you,' Bellina said, hiding her fellingsbehind formality.

'Don't mention it,' Holger said. 'What was I gonna do, let you drown? Although, I thought witches were supposed to float.' He shot her a cheeky smile.

'I could extend the same expectation of survival to you, Master Holger. That inflated bladder you call a head is too buoyant to allow you to drown,' she replied. They both laughed as Barboza and Crenshaw looked on in bewilderment.

Bellina felt better for making the peace but that still did not change the fact that they were adrift in a boat with three cabin crew and two fake sailors.

'So, does anyone actually know where we are?' Holger asked, looking at the ex-first mate of the *Vagabond*.

'Last time I checked the ship's chart we were somewhere off the coast of Etvora. About a half day's sail,' Crenshaw replied, scratching at the straw-coloured stubble on his chin.

'That's not too far from Varash, is it?' Bellina asked, trying to dredge up a mental world map.

'Nah, it's not,' Holger said. 'Damned close depending on where you put into port, problem is we have to get to land first.'

'I think I might be able to navigate us there,' volunteered Crenshaw, 'but it's gonna take a hell of a lot of luck. One more storm like that and we're done for. Plus, I'm gonna need the stars to go by, so we'll have to wait for nightfall and hope the sky stays clear.'

'Then I suppose we have no choice but to wait,' Bellina said, not relishing the prospect of spending a sun-baked day floating on the sea.

'Does anyone fancy hearing a one-man version of *Drenteel and Asvertine*?' asked Barboza, hopeful. 'I know all the parts!'

*

Cirona stood in the centre of the arena. She was beginning to feel... strange. She was standing next to the man in the golden robes — he was saying something but she couldn't understand it. The strength of the sun beating down from a cloudless sky was overwhelming. The roar of the crowd smashed into her like cannon fire and her mouth was drier than the compacted sand at her feet. She tried to focus her eyes on her opponent. What was his name? *Griffin, that's silly*, she thought, as a laugh escaped her lips. The gold man looked at her: his face twirled and wouldn't settle. He said something else and then she had a parasol in her hand. *What the hells is this for*, she thought? The man in gold was leaving. The griffin boy stood pointing a spear at her. *That's going to get someone hurt.*

The next thing she knew, Cirona was floating, flying high above the arena. A rush of adrenaline flew through her. Gods, what a feeling!

It didn't last.

She was falling, plummeting. The sensation made her stomach turn. The ground rose to meet her. Where was she? The ground was a sea of flames, scorching her legs and feet. Had she died? She vaguely remembered something about a potion and dying. Had it actually killed her? Fuck! Oh fuck no, was this one of the hells? Had she missed the Veil and gone into the Void? Mountains with human faces trapped in them wailed at her in agony. This was a hell! Maybe the fifth one. Wasn't there some description of a land of fire and mountains in the scriptures?

If this is the fifth hell, she thought, *that must be Henderoth: the fifth of the Old Terrors, banished into the Void*. She swallowed in horror at the thing. It had a human form but its skin was covered in scales. Cirona looked into its face. The visage was melting, sliding but never falling off. There were no eyes and a yawning cavern where its mouth should be, tiny little teeth glinting.

Panic spread through her as the Terror came forward. No, no! Stay away! She could hear herself scream. Still, it came on, sucking air through its mouth. She started to back away but fell on her arse. It jabbed a jet black spear covered in unblinking eyes at her. What could she do? She stared into the crowd and she saw Trafford's face trapped in the stone of the mountain. He was howling like all the rest. Then she saw Bellina. Why? Why? She wasn't dead, was she? Finally, she saw the face of her daughter.

Her hands twisted into balls of fury. The child was pure, innocent, she never would have ended up here, whatever became of her. Cirona's attention returned to the fucking thing that was taunting her, playing with her. No more! No fucking more. She leapt forward, snarling and hissing. If this *was* the fifth Terror then, today, she was going to show him there were human terrors too. Her hands were empty but that didn't matter. The thing backed away. Oh no, that's not gonna do you any good. He jabbed the spear at her. She grabbed it feeling some of the eyes explode beneath her grip. They wrestled for possession of it. Back and forth. Back and forth. Cirona made a mad wrench backwards. The demon let go of the weapon and went spinning away. It landed on its feet hissing. She lunged, missing its head by inches. It scuttled away again. It was wary now, not advancing. Fine. She launched the spear at it, grazing its thigh. Black ooze seeped out, thick like treacle.

It was frozen now, afraid of the sight of its own blood. She landed a punch to its face. It flew across the arena floor. Before it could recover, she straddled its middle, punching and punching at its face. More of its treacle blood flowed from its rippling countenance. Cirona put her hands around its throat and squeezed. She bent forward, her face close to the Terror's. It raised its head to meet her. Sounds came out of its mouth, like it was trying to talk. Still she squeezed.

Suddenly her hands were far away. No strength in them. Her head spun and her stomach heaved. She threw up blood. It covered her hands, mingling with that of the monster's. Her blood came alive where it met the Terror's blood. It writhed and seethed, spreading up her hands, her arms. It wrapped itself around her throat, covered her face and eyes. Then everything went black.

*

A wave of disbelief washed over Elvgren. What in the world was the major doing? Elvgren had watched the fight unfold with his breath held. If Bouchard's battle had started with comedy it looked like it was going to finish with tragedy.

She had begun the bout looking up to the heavens, arms outstretched like a bird in flight. Laughter had come from the crowds at this. Next, her opponent had advanced tentatively, she had recoiled and fell. The young man had poked at her with the spear, after that she had flown into a fury.

Elvgren's stomach knotted tight as the major mounted her opponent's chest and began to pummel his face. Gods, what had that potion done to her? If she didn't stop soon she would kill the boy. If that happened the whole damn thing would be done for. Without the help from Faultwright's men he could see no way that any of them would make it out of the arena alive.

'What the fuck is she doing, Gren?' Dargo whispered to him.

'I don't know,' he replied.

'We've got to do something. Now,' Dargo said.

Elvgren's mind spun. What the hells could they do? The arena had its own official medificer on the floor of combat to inspect the combatants, Elvgren and Dargo had no authority to run out and put a stop to a fight. He searched for a solution but none came. 'There's nothing we can do except hope the potion kicks in soon,' Elvgren said, gripping the railing tightly.

'There's that word again, eh? Fucking lot of things riding on your hope,' the boy replied.

Their eyes returned to the fight. Bouchard was now throttling Griffith. The boy was trying to plead with her but, wherever her mind was now, she was deaf to his words. Suddenly, the major's body began to convulse, a stream of blood poured from her mouth. That didn't look good. *Damn it all*, Elvgren hadn't even thought that the chemistician might have lied to him. He kept watching, everything riding on what happened in the next few moments.

The major, still astride Griffith, looked at her hands. Her head lolled backwards and her body twitched violently, before she finally slumped to the ground.

The man in the golden robes approached the pair. Griffith stared at him in wide-eyed terror, then the boy looked back at the body of Major Bouchard and he scrabbled away on his arse. The floor-side medificer ran over to Bouchard's body. He examined it for a few moments and shook his head. The golden announcer crossed his arms over his head, signifying that the fight was over. He pulled Griffith to his feet, raising the boy's hand in the air. There was polite applause from the bewildered crowd. The prince in the royal box did not look amused. He turned to a fat man and delivered an unmistakable verbal tirade.

While Elvgren had been watching the prince, he hadn't noticed that a group of men with a stretcher had already appeared on the arena floor to take away the body. *Shit*, he thought, *I need to get out there*. Dargo had already sprinted ahead and was mingled inconspicuously with the small group taking the body away. Elvgren started to hurry towards them when a hand clamped down on his shoulder, the grip biting into his muscles.

'Where do you think you're going, *Medic*?'

Elvgren turned to see the man with the whip. 'I am going to inspect the body. Humours in balance and all that,' he replied, trying to sound convincing.

'You know as much about fucking humours as I do, you bloody fraud.'

Elvgren felt the point of a knife digging into the base of his spine. 'Now, move. Gulgarno wants a word with you.'

Elvgren looked to Rev and the other spectators in the small stand. He looked imploringly at them.

'Wait a minute, Barag,' the Burkeshi said. 'I know his whole plan. I am sure Master Gulgarno would like to speak with me too.'

Fucking, stinking sand-puke! You could never trust a Burkeshi, why the hells had he listened to the major? For all he knew, she had already been off her head when she asked him to help the man.

Barag led Elvgren and Reveeker back down the tunnel to where the fat man waited with five guards, their backs to the main entrance.

'Well, well. If it isn't the medificer who delayed our little celebration,' said Gulgarno. 'Barag, get that mask off him so we can get a look at the fraud's face.'

Barag ripped the mask from Elvgren, the metal clasps at the back tearing at his hair.

'An ugly little bastard for a medic, aren't you boy? How Barag fell for your mummer's farce I will never know. He shall feel the sting of his own lash tonight, for that.'

Gulgarno's right-hand man shot a menacing look at Elvgren.

'I suppose I can show some leniency towards you though, Barag. In the end, you alerted me to this carry on,' Gulgarno turned his piggy eyes back to Elvgren. 'I am assuming you had something to do with the pitiful display we just witnessed. Though quite what you did eludes me.'

'I may be of assistance there, Master,' Reveeker said.

Elvgren swallowed hard. *Gods, don't let him tell*, he thought.

'This lad posed as a medificer. He gave Major Bouchard a potion to simulate death, with the idea of spiriting her away. He tried to get me in on his scheme as well. I believe he is trying to influence the outcome of the matches for the bet-takers.'

'You fucking Burkeshi bastard. That woman trusted you, wanted to help you, and this, *this* is how you repay her?' Elvgren spat at Rev. The man simply shrugged in response. Elvgren's mind reeled as the whole world seemed to fall apart around him. This was it. The jig was up. At least he had restored a small part of his honour. Though that was little comfort at this precise moment.

'Thank you, Reveeker. Your honesty shall be rewarded. I will see that you do not get a joke weapon in your bout. As for you, boy, you are in for a—waaarghh!' Gulgarno's tirade was cut short by the sudden appearance of a knife at his throat.

Dargo dangled from the fleshy mass of the man, one arm just about managing to get around the flabby neck and multiple chins, the other pointing the blade. His scrawny legs swung about, his body completely obscured by Gulgarno's girth. Under different circumstances the scene would have been comical. 'Anyone moves and the fat fucker gets it,' Dargo said.

Barag made a move forward and Reveeker smashed his fist into his face. He picked up the man's weapon and placed a foot on his chest.

'Now, all of you put down your weapons and back the fuck away,' Dargo said as the guards looked for instruction.

'Do as the boy says!' Gulgarno squealed.

Elvgren regained his composure and sauntered forward. 'It would seem we have you at a disadvantage, Master Gulgarno. Dargo, where is the major's body?'

'Already loaded on the wagon, Gren. Had to grease a few palms. Said we needed it for dissection. Came back to see where you were and saw the welcoming party,' Dargo replied.

Elvgren felt incredibly grateful that the boy had chosen to come with him. He looked directly into the fat man's eyes.

'It has been a distinct pleasure, good man, but I really must go. Enjoy the rest of your tournament,' Elvgren said, giving the gladiator proprietor a friendly pat on the cheek. For an instant, he felt like his old self again.

'You'll swing for this, you little shits,' Gulgarno hissed. 'That woman is my property, this is robbery!'

'We'll take our chances thanks. The Burkeshi's coming too,' Dargo said.

'No he's not. The sand-fucker just sold us out,' Elvgren replied.

'I saw the boy coming down the hall you dolt! I was stalling for time!' Reveeker said. Elvgren was not convinced.

'Look, Gren, I just saw that friend of yours beat the living shit out of her opponent. I don't wanna be the one to tell her we didn't help

155

this bloke when we had the opportunity,' Dargo said.

'Fine, the Burkeshi comes too,' Elvgren said, against his better judgement. 'Now we really have to leave.'

Dargo slid off Gulgarno's back. He tiptoed backwards still pointing the knife. Reveeker and Elvgren walked past Gulgarno and into the doorway. The trio crouched, looking out at the bustling scene.

'Run,' Elvgren whispered.

23

The rhythmic sound of the oars was strangely soothing. This was a stark contrast to the back-breaking effort it took to use them. Bellina sat at Holger's side helping with the right oar, while Barboza pulled the left one alone. Midge was at the prow of the small vessel watching for any hint of land, while Crenshaw commanded the rudder. His navigational skills had been a revelation. He plotted their course by the stars with an instrument he had retrieved from under a seat in the boat. Bellina had never seen anything like it before, but Crenshaw seemed to know what he was doing; he was evenwhistling a little ditty.

'That's a nice tune, Mr Crenshaw. What is it?' Bellina asked through her gasping breaths.

'Just a lullaby me mam would sing me, gods rest her soul, always reminds me of home.'

Home, now there was something. Bellina's head filled with images of hers. The Lord Chancellor's study, Madam Matresca, the beautiful library and the roaring fires. At that moment, in the clutching chill of the evening, she missed those most of all.

'How much further now?' Holger called to Crenshaw.

'Should be there soon. You two let me know when it gets too much and we can swap places for a bit.'

'I'm fine for now, thanks,' came Holger's reply.

'How about you, my lady?'

'A small respite would be most welcome,' Bellina answered.

'Come over here then.'

Bellina extracted herself from the rowing bench and made her way over to Crenshaw.

He placed her hand on the rudder. 'Now, just make sure she stays straight and you'll be fine,' he told her before seating himself in the place she just vacated.

Bellina held the rudder so tight her knuckles whitened but she soon realised the sea was as placid as it looked. Her mind began to wander. Had either of her travelling companions made it? What was going on back in Estria? Why had that merchant captain said the *Prudence* was lost on the Timbokan coast? The questions swam round her mind till she felt dizzy.

'Not too much dreaming there, my lady, eh?' Crenshaw called out.

'Sorry,' she replied. 'Help me keep my mind from drifting, Mr Crenshaw. How did you and our former captain meet each other? If you don't mind me saying, it seems an unlikely alliance.'

'Ha! I suppose it does to an outsider but me and Bar have been together twenty years or so. Getting into scrapes since we was lads. Ain't that right, fella?' Crenshaw said.

Barboza merely grunted in reply, consumed with his task.

'Didn't you think his latest scheme was a tad foolish?' she continued.

'Nah, not really. To be honest with ye, this has been one of our more sedate adventures.'

Bellina marvelled at how you could live a life that considered being thrown into the sea in the middle of a storm "sedate".

The group drifted back into silence for some time before the peace was shattered by Midge's thin call.

'Land Ho!'

*

Elvgren, Dargo and Reveeker sprinted away from the arena. Their hard-topped wagon was waiting, along with one of Faultwright's men.

'The woman and the gold are on—Hey! What the fuck?' The man looked perplexed as the trio barrelled past him.

'Many thanks! If you see a group of angry men coming this way trip them up, would you?' Elvgren called over his shoulder.

They clambered onto the elevated seat at the front of the vehicle. Elvgren, sitting in the middle, took the reins and snapped the grazing horses to life. A tumultuous sound came to them from behind.

'Get this thing going, boy. They're on us,' Reveeker said, looking back over his shoulder.

Elvgren didn't need further prompting. He clipped the horses into a gallop and they were off.

The streets were now practically deserted and the wagon hurtled, unimpeded, through Yondapolis. They were speeding into the centre of the citywhen the first riders appeared.

'Fuck. They're gaining on us, Gren!' Dargo shouted.

'I know, but unless you've got a bow and arrow concealed on your person I don't know what we can do about that,' Elvgren cried.

'Turn left, now, boy!' Reveeker said.

In his confusion and panic Elvgren turned right. They careened into the Grand Bazaar. A few terrified shoppers dived out of their way as the wagon rushed through the massive covered market. The smell of a thousand different spices assaulted Elvgren's nose, tickling it into a sneeze. Merchants looked on in astonishment as the wagon sped past, the pursuing riders gaining every second.

'How many are there?' he shouted.

''Bout five I think—Gren, look out!' Dargo screamed.

Two merchants were carrying a heavy crate of apples across their path. They hollered and jumped to the side, Elvgren *just* managed to pass the dropped container. The back of the wagon clipped the crate, unleashing a deluge of apples. A cry of dismay and a heavy thump came from behind him.

'Four riders now,' Reveeker said.

They continued on their devastating path through the market, collapsing stools and stands with their wild careening.

'Exit's just ahead, boy,' warned Reveeker. 'This time, take the fucking *left*.'

They skittered out of the bazaar sending more startled passers-by leaping for safety. One of the riders caught up to the side of the wagon. Dargo slashed out at him with his small knife as the man tried to get closer. The rider withdrew and prepared himself for another charge. He came in for his attack and Dargo leant out to fend him off. The man grabbed the boy's sleeve and pulled.

'Help!' the boy cried as he teetered with only his toes touching the boards of the carriage seat.

Elvgren reached over with one of his hands, not daring to let go of the reins completely. There followed a vicious tug of war between him and the rider.

'Ah gods, look out! A wall!' Dargo shouted.

The rider's attention turned to the road ahead, a look of puzzlement crossing his face when he saw no wall. The boy took the split second he had gained to sink his teeth into the man's hand. With a holler of pain, the man let go, sending Dargo sprawling back into the wagon.

'Thanks for the help, Burkeshi,' Elvgren spat.

'I have problems of my own, boy!' Reveeker replied from above. While Elvgren and Dargo had been struggling with the horseman, he had climbed up to the roof of the wagon to deal with another rider.

'Oh, for the love of... Dar, be a good chap and take the reins,' Elvgren said. He wasn't sure what he was going to do but two against one made for better odds. Scrambling on to the top of the wagon, he marvelled at how the two men were able to stand, let alone fight. But fighting they were, or had been, the pair were now locked in a snarling embrace. They wrestled on the bouncing roof, spinning each other like dance partners. Elvgren crawled over, too afraid to stand. He sank his teeth into the rider's ankle, eliciting a cry of pain before Reveeker landed a hard punch to the jaw, sending the man flying.

Still, two riders came on, with more pouring from every street they passed.

'I can see the city gate!' Dargo called.

So did the riders. They screamed in Varashi to the guards stationed atop the massive structure. Panic erupted and the guards began to turn a large pulley. The gate to the city of Yondapolis started an angry, screeching descent.

Dargo screamed incoherently and whipped the reins in a mad panic. Curses came from the watchmen as the gate jammed a quarter of the way down. Reveeker dropped to his stomach, next to Elvgren and the coach shot through the gate, the spiked base tearing at their clothes. At that moment, the gate came back to life. It dropped to the ground with a sound like a thousand cats squalling, trapping the pursuers inside the city walls.

Arrows thudded harmlessly into the ground behind the wagon, accompanied by more shouting. Dargo whooped with joy and Reveeker looked at Elvgren, grinning.

But Elvgren was staring towards the city. The massive arena loomed in the distance, its arched walls staring back at him like a disapproving aunt. *It can disapprove all it wants*, Elvgren thought. He certainly wouldn't be coming back. He had no desire to ever lay eyes on the city again.

*

The small horse Bellina rode, ambled calmly along the dirt path. The animal's owner, a clarista of Father Light, walked beside her. Two days into their trek they had encountered the clarista on the Varashi road. He was on a mission to convert the heathen inhabitants of the land to the call of the Lumanist faith. Bellina feared this would be a quest beyond his reach. The man was pleasant enough though, and he had a horse. The soles of her shoes bore the fallout from the miles they had trudged since landing on the Etvoran shore — she was very glad it was her turn to ride. The rest of the group followed behind. Midge sat astride Barboza's shoulders, the giant man telling the boy another fanciful tale of his deeds. Holger and Crenshaw walked alongside, chatting amiably.

Their journey for the past three days had been uneventful, blessedly so, so too had been their arrival in Etvora. The small boat had come ashore in a sleepy little fishing village close to the Varashi border. The villagers had been more than charitable. The women fussed and clucked around Bellina, helping her to bathe, scolding her affectionately in the common tongue like a mother would have. The whole group had been given clothes except for Barboza for whom they couldn't find anything to fit. Instead, they had given his clothes a thorough washing. They had been well fed and well looked after and it was with a great deal of reluctance that the group set off on their journey to Dronkor. But Bellina *had* to get there, she was desperate for news of Elvgren and Cirona. Hells, for all she knew they could have been sitting comfortably in a nice tavern for the past few weeks. Even if they weren't there, she still needed to get word back to her father.

They journeyed along the dirt road, headingtowards Dronkor. Bellina had marvelled at a world untouched by the power of sortilenergy. There were no galvanic lights, no magic-fuelled heating, no miasma stacks piercing the sky and belching out magic-infused smog. For the first time, she recognised what a privileged part of the world she came from. Of course, many people in Estria could not afford to pay for sortilenergy but, nevertheless, even remote villages could purchase vorotorium cells — the large transportable containers of sortilenergy providing them with access to its benefits. *This*, she thought, *was why Estria was the envy of the world.*

'Dear lady,' Barboza asked, 'is it perhaps time for another of us to take a turn in the saddle?'

She looked at the man and had to fight not to laugh. His blonde wig had survived their ordeal but was rather worse for wear, stray strands sticking out at odd angles all over the place. The villagers had offered to repair it but he had refused to take it off.

'I think you're right, Mr Barboza. Midge, would you like to ride next?'

'Yes please, Belle!' the boy replied, scrambling down Barboza in excitement, adding further trauma to the wig.

'Good lady, the boy has been using *me* as his beast of burden for some time. I think this is most unfair.' the former captain said, with the beginnings of a sulk forming on his face.

'You'll live Bar, you'll live,' said Crenshaw 'Let the lad ride. We owe him our bloody lives... oh s'cuse the language, Brother.'

'No need, Mr Crenshaw,' replied the clarista. 'I have heard a lot worse on my travels, most of it directed at me.'

On they continued, the red earth path snaking its way through the Varashi countryside. They passed little white homesteads with flat roofs, farmers ploughing their fields and women fetching water. It was a sweet respite from the horror of Bellina's recent past.

Holger moved up to walk beside her. He opened his mouth to speak and then closed it. He looked at her, his face scrunched in confusion, mouth moving strangely as he searched for words.

'Oh for goodness sake, Holger, what is it?' she said, unable to stand the torment his face was going through.

'I... I don't really know how to put it,' he said.

A flicker of worry and excitement swept over her, though she couldn't place where the emotions had come from.

'When did you first start noticing your powers?'

Whatever she had been expecting him to say, it certainly wasn't that. 'Er... when I was about five.'

'What happened?'

'One morning I was sat playing in the dirt. The gardener was digging up a new flower bed and I was getting in the way, making mud castles. Next thing, I could hear him talking but his mouth wasn't moving. It was like he was speaking directly into my skull. He was pondering over what would be the best arrangement for the new flowers. I didn't know what to make of it but I just shrugged it off, like you do when you're little.

'From then on, though, it got worse. After a few weeks I could hear everyone around me speaking even when they weren't. I told my father about it. I was crying and asking him to make everyone be quiet. He understood straight away what was going on, he'd had lots of dealings with cognopaths in his line of work. That's when my training started.' Bellina felt her blood run cold at the memory. 'Why do you ask?'

Again, Holger's face went through a bout of frenzied motion. 'I was just curious. It must have been hard to have all that thrown at you so young,' he said, looking at her thoughtfully. 'I can under—'

Holger was cut off before he could finish.

'How much further now, good Brother?' Barboza called, eyeing the horse longingly.

'Not long now. The town of Dronkor should come into view very soon.'

The moment passed with the interruption and whatever Holger was about to say passed with it. Bellina looked at him. He had sunk into a reflective silence and pulled out his box of matches, staring intently at them. They were new ones he had picked up in Etvora, his old box ruined after their dip in the sea. Bellina had thought that the original box was what held the good luck but it seemed any box would do. 'Do you know, Holger, no one has ever asked me about my powers before. Were you worried I was going to read your mind?' she said with a smile.

'I am now!' he said giving her a playful push. 'But, no, I know you wouldn't do that. You're a good person, Belle, I trust you.'

Bellina felt a rush of emotions and didn't know what to do with them. Should she hug him, shake his hand, tousle his hair? She couldn't think of an appropriate response so she gave him a jab on the arm. Holger feigned agony and went tumbling to the side of the road. He looked up at her from the roadside ditch. 'Thanks for taking an interest,' she added.

'If that's how you thank people, I'll not do you any favours!'

They both looked at each other and laughed. Bellina held her hand out and helped him back to his feet.

The group carried on along the path, heading up a steep hill. When they reached the crest of it Bellina could see a small town. From this height it resembled a model and she extended her hand, pretending to pick up one of the buildings.

'Aha! And lo weary travellers, your journey is at an end,' the clarista said.

'That's the tenth passage in the Book of Radiance... if I'm not mistaken,' Bellina said.

'Quite so, my lady, you know your scriptures well. You must be from a good family.'

'Oh. The best,' she replied.

24

Elvgren sat by the major's bedside. Her breathing was sharp and shallow, much the same as it had been since the signs of life had returned to her a week ago. However, there was still no sign of consciousness.

After their arrival in Dronkor, they had immediately gone in search of a good tavern where they could rest. The money they had earned from Faultwright bought them the time of a real medificer. He had poked and prodded, hummed and ahhed, applied some leeches, handed them a potion, then left whilst prattling on about a depletion of black bile. Elvgren and the others were wary of giving Cirona another potion so it was still untouched.

The door to the room opened and Reveeker entered. 'Any change?'

The sight of the Burkeshi made his skin itch but he still replied. 'Sadly not.' He looked at the pale, clammy body of the major and felt his gut whirl. 'I'm going out for some air.' Elvgren rose from his chair and put on his light coat.

Outside, he traced the path that he had walked every day since their arrival. He strolled down the narrow, cobbled streets of the town, past white, single-storey stucco houses. He wondered where Dargo had got himself off to? Probably out cheating the town's children at cards again. The young boy had not taken long to find his way into mischief. He had insisted on buying a set of the finest clothes with his share of the money, complete with a tall hat and a walking cane topped with gold. He resembled a miniature whoremonger. A small group of local children followed him about, enthralled.

Elvgren continued walking, the streets widening as he came to the merchant district. Soon he would be at Melek's and, in his mind's eye, he could already see the former army engineer shrugging his shoulders and saying there had been no news. This had become part of his daily ritual.

On his first visit, Elvgren had learned a lot. The Estrian search party had now been called off and the members of the diplomatic mission were proclaimed lost at sea. There seemed no way of getting a message about the true events to the Lord Chancellor. Melek had said that all the usual channels of communication with Estria were cut off. Estrian merchant ships were under constant attack — the Burkeshis blaming pirates — and the Empire's navy had been recalled. War looked imminent. As such, there was a lack of ships going to and from Estria. Melek could think of no one he trusted enough to carry a message of such importance and they couldn't try for it themselves with the major in her current state. *Damn it all*, he thought, *Major, please wake up!* He prayed to all the gods that she would but, so far, it was having as much effect as the medic's leeches.

He finally arrived at Melek's store front and pushed the door open, preparing himself for more disappointment.

*

Dronkor has a rustic charm I suppose but it certainly doesn't have the amenities an Estrian would expect even if he was an engineer, Bellina thought, *but that's probably the point.*

The bright sun beat down lazily on the town square — a large rectangular space with the typical red earth of Varash packed hard for its floor. A lone citron tree occupied its heart, surrounded by a circle of stone slabs. Cats slept idly in its shade, in fact it seemed like the whole town was asleep.

'So, we come to the parting of ways,' said the clarista. 'Stay safe and peace be.'

'Thank you Brother, and peace be to you,' Bellina replied.

They left the man of faith assembling his preaching stool and set off in search of Melek. A few questions later, they had the directions they needed.

Bellina stood before the door of an unassuming building that was nestled between the premises of a chandler and a baker. No identification adorned its front. She turned the handle of the door, her heart jumping. This was it: she was about to find out if there was anybody left to find.

The door opened into a sparse room. The floor was uncarpeted, exposing wooden planks. At the far side of the room was a desk with a bell on it, behind that was a sturdy wrought iron door. She rang the bell with the rest of her companions standing awkwardly behind her.

An eye slit in the door shot open with a sound like a ballistol firing.

Two hard eyes stared out of the gap. 'State your business,' a voice said from behind the door.

'I... I am a friend of Major Cirona Bouchard. I have come to find news of her, if there is any to find,' Bellina replied.

The clanking of many locks and bolts being undone reverberated around them. The door swung back on well-oiled hinges. A man of medium build came out, his dark hair, deep tan and easy swagger marked him as a Tremoran. 'Pray forgive me, my lady, you can never be too safe in my line of work. I am Melek, and I most humbly place myself at your service,' he said, bowing low.

'My forgiveness is not needed, good sir, as no offence was taken,' Bellina replied, returning the bow with a curtsy as etiquette dictated.

'Am I right in presuming that you are the Lady Bellina Ressa, daughter of our most wise Lord Chancellor?' Melek said.

Bellina had been expecting many things from the engineer but faultless manners was not one of them. Then a more pressing thought struck her. 'Yes, that is me but, if you will excuse me good sir, how came you by my name and title? Have you received word from Major Bouchard?' Bellina replied.

'Not from the major herself, unfortunately. According to Lord Elvgren Lovitz who tends to her, she has taken most unwell. Nothing seems to be alleviating her malady,' he said with a look of deepest sorrow on his face.

'Lord Elvgren is here too? If you would excuse my rudeness I would like to meet them straight away, , will you direct me to where they are staying?'

'Of course, my lady, I would not presume to steal upon your time, though to keep it would most certainly be a joy. Lord Elvgren and his party are staying at the Gal Danstoupolous Inn, not fifteen minutes' walk from here if you follow the main road. You won't miss it as it's one of the few buodings in town with more than a single storey.'

'My eternal thanks, good sir. I look forward to our next meeting,' Bellina said with another curtsy.

'As do I, my lady. Until then,' Melek said, bowing once again. He glided across the floor to see them out.

Bellina was in a state of confusion and not just thanks to the bizarre formality of her meeting with Melek. Cirona was ill; how bad was it and what had caused it? What did he mean by *Lord Elvgren's party*? That would imply that he and Cirona were not alone.

She caught Holger's eye. He was looking at her with a look of surprise on his face. 'What's the matter?' Bellina asked him.

'I think that was the first time I met the *Lady* Bellina. I must say it's a marked improvement from your usual manner,' he said grinning like a buffoon.

'I shall have to fix that, make up for all that protocol, eh?' Bellina replied making a gesture so obscene it would have made a docker blush.

25

Elvgren was by the major's bedside again, a book open but unread on his lap.

Knocking softly, the proprietor of the inn, Danstoupolous, entered. 'There are, eh, some guests, eh, here to see you.' The old man wheezed from climbing the stairs.

He stood aside and Elvgren's heart almost stopped. Bellina stepped forward, a gang of rather strange companions bustling in behind her: one large, black man barely fitting through the door, a young boy of perhaps ten or eleven, a wiry fellow with sandy hair and a young man whose eyes were fixed intently on Bellina. Elvgren took an instant dislike to him *and* that intense look. He had not been enamoured with his betrothal to Bellina but the worm of his soul wouldn't allow for anyone else to have designs on her. That aside, he was sure she would have mentioned their courtship to this boy.

'Lord Elvgren! What in the hells happened to your face?' she cried.

Elvgren had wondered what her reaction to his new countenance would be and the look of horror in her eyes gave him his answer. 'Much has happened since our parting. For you too, if that motley bunch are anything to go by,' he replied gesturing at her companions.

'Motley? You young cur!' the large, black man said, his voice resonating with indignation. 'I am Gambiko Barboza, actor, soldier of fortune and most recently captain of the floating democracy: the good ship *Scampering Vagabond*!'

'Please, Mr. Barboza. Now is not the time,' Bellina said, turning her eyes towards the prone form of Bouchard. She fell to her knees beside the bed, tears forming in her eyes.

Guilt squimed in Elvgren's gut and he felt like he had just been scraped off the privy floor. Now would come the hard part. 'I think it's time we shared our tales of woe, my lady.'

*

Hours passed as the pair recounted their tales to each other and the sun was high in the sky when they finished.

'And so, there you have it,' Bellina said, a flush in her cheeks from the exertion of her long recount. 'As soon as we heard of your whereabouts from Melek we came as quick as we could,'

The door to the room opened and Dargo and Reveeker came in, chatting away. The boy had formed an easy bond with the Burkeshi that Elvgren wasn't able, or didn't want, to emulate. 'Hello Rev! Looks like we got company,' Dargo said, doffing his hat and bowing to the assembly.

'Lady Bellina, everyone else, this is Dargo and Reveeker who, as you've heard, played a large part in our being here at all,' Elvgren said.

'So, this is the lady who Cirona was willing to sacrifice so much for. It is an honour,' Reveeker said, offering a bow of his own,.

'The honour is entirely mine, good sir,' Bellina replied.

'Bloody hell, Gren! You didn't tell me the bird was a looker!' Dargo exclaimed winking at Bellina.

Elvgren noticed a look of anger quickly pass across Holger's face. *Interesting.*

The pair introduced themselves to the rest. Barboza stood to shake Reveeker's hand, the Bakori standing half a head taller than the impressively sized Burkeshi.

'Then I suppose it's time to consider our next step. Cirona's advice would be most helpful now,' Bellina said.

Elvgren watched her take the major's hand, squeezing it tightly.

'Major Bouchard? Cirona, please come back to us,' she said. The major's face twitched and her eyelids spasmed. Bellina snapped her head round to Elvgren in astonishment.

'Keep going, my lady!' he told her, stepping forward in surprise. 'That's the most response we've got out of her the whole time we've been here.'

'Cirona? Can you hear me, Major?'

*

Inky blackness surrounded Cirona. An aching nothingness. She was there and not there. Sometimes she thought she could hear voices far away, like music carried on a breeze. Images began to form, bulging from the black, rippling and distorting the nothingness.

The dining room of the orphanage, where she spent her youth, wobbled before popping into focus. The room was deserted, grey stone floor and walls, the long narrow tables, the arse-numbing benches. Miserable children would eat miserably at them. The food devoured, as only people who know the brittle punch of hunger can. This wouldn't be achieved in a mad rush but with methodical scraping and licking, wasting nothing.

The vision changed and Cirona saw herself and was herself, in that peculiar contradiction that only dreams can bring. She was eight years of age and sat in her place at the table, her bowl and the square of stale bread that every orphan was given in front of her.

The governors of the orphanage insisted that that the orphans gave thanks before the meal. She felt her stomach cry in protest and looked at the governors. They were not cruel men and women, merely disinterested. This was their job, nothing more. The Estrian government paid for institutions such as this, but the payment did not require the custodians to show affection.

The short prayer was finally over. She lifted her spoon, determined to savour every slurp of the thin carrot soup. A larger boy walked past and took her bread, he looked back, smirking. That had been the first time she had felt the power of her rage and seen what it could do. For a few seconds, she had no memory of anything. The next thing she could remember was being pulled away by two of the governors, the boy's face a bloody ruin.

She had been punished, of course, but it hadn't stopped the anger. The fights became more and more frequent. The smallest infraction could set her off. By the time she was fourteen she had become the same as the bully whose face she smashed. The sight of her was terrifying to the other children and a part of her loved it.

Cirona took to straying further and further afield to satisfy her need to fight. Drinking in the hot rush of her fury.

After a particularly brutal attack on a young lad, she had another meeting with the governors. They told her they could not stand her presence at the orphanage any longer and that there was a man who would like to see her. She watched him walk into the room, the buttons on his uniform gleaming. He asked if she would like to join the military academy. She said yes.

The world of the vision twirled faster. Glimpses came to her. Her joy at the army appreciating her. The beautiful security of the academy's routine Her feuds with Latimer Willbert. The first battle she took part in. The freezing land of Narvale, men like bears attacking and attacking. The first time she met Trafford. The first time they had kissed, the first time they had made love. The look on his face when she told him she was pregnant, not joy or anger, just a bland acceptance. Giving birth, the pain of it. The brilliant heart-soaring happiness when she saw her daughter's face. The emptiness when she was taken. The fight with Trafford before he died, the last words she would speak to him. The Emperor, Castros Del Var's insurgents, the would-be assassins, the shot from the ballistol. The pathetic hole in Trafford's chest that had taken him across the Weeping Veil.

The visions became the merest snatches of things. Faces, sounds, smells. The Lord Chancellor. A deal made. A key. Blood. Skin peeling. An oath. Something rotten. Bellina, calling and calling. The vague sense of herself reached towards the girl's voice. Stretching and stretching.

Cirona's eyelids cracked open. Light rushed in, relentless. The sound of voices, like people talking underwater came to her. Her eyes focused. Bellina's face stared down at her. There were tears in the girl's eyes.

*

The ragtag collection of people took up residence at the inn while they waited for Cirona to recover her strength. The medificer had forbidden her any undue stress at such a nascent stage of her recovery. But Cirona was in a thoroughly foul mood. She couldn't remember ever having to lie in bed due to illness and there were things to do. The others took turns to sit with her, any attempt she made to gain more than the most basic of information was met with soft cooing sounds and instruction to not strain herself, like a mother to a child.

One day, Reveeker sat dozing in the chair by her bed. They had chatted briefly but her snappiness had made him quickly abandon the endeavour. Closing her eyes, she had pretended to sleep, while Rev succumbed to the real thing.

There came a soft knock on the door. She snapped her eyes shut and feigned slumber again. Reveeker woke with a start, stumbled across the room and answered the knock.

'How is the enchantress this evening?' that was Elvgren's voice.

'Her strength is growing, but her mood is still... trying,' Rev said.

'Delightful. What young man wouldn't wish to spend a fine evening in the company of a tetchy invalid?' Elvgren replied.

Cirona smarted at the remark but she knew she owed the idiot a considerable amount of slack.

'Good night then, lad,' Reveeker said. His footsteps started away but were suddenly halted.

'You really should address me as *Lord*, you know.' There was a second of loaded silence.

'Oh, should I now. And *why* pray tell should I do that. This is not Estria and you are no lord over me.'

'We are not intimate and we never will be. I am tolerating your presence for the sake of the major. And while you are living here on my rencat, I feel you should drop the lad and boy bollocks when you address me.'

Another pause. Cirona almost laughed aloud at the thought of how Rev's face must look.

'Very well. Goodnight, *vaksa silem*,' Reveeker said, his footsteps stomping away.

'What the hells does that mean? Come back here and use the common tongue you fucking shit!'

'Shut up you two! Some of us are trying to get to bloody sleep!' Dargo called out from his room.

Cirona heard Elvgren mutter to himself and close the door. She waited till he had seated himself in the chair beside her before she addressed him. 'Quite a display of diplomacy, deputy Lord Chancellor,' she said.

He gave a small start.

Obviously her feigned sleep had been convincing.

'Ah, Major. I'm sorry, did we wake you?' he asked after a few deep breaths.

'Being referred to as a tetchy invalid tends to draw you from your dreams.'

'Bugger... sorry Major, I meant no offence. It's been a damned shitty day.'

'Forget it, I have. I know I'm not the life and soul of the ball at the minute. What's the news?' she asked, more in hope than expectation.

'Sorry Major, medic's orders,' he replied throwing up his hands. They fell into an awkward silence.

'Alright then. If the weakling can't take the strain of what's going on right *now*, will you tell me what happened the night the *Prudence* sank?' A strange look passed over Elvgren's face. She could see he was chewing on the inside of his cheek.

'I... well...' he began.

'Oh, get on with it. I'll die of old age at this rate,' she said.

Elvgren exhaled audibly. 'Alright, alright. You told us to run, get away. We tried, the mast of the *Prudence* smashed into the pier. I was to one side of it, the lady Bellina on the other. She tried to jump across, but she fell. Then...'

'Yes? Then?'

'I saw that she had knocked herself out as she fell. I ran to some steps that led down to the water. I could see her. I swam out a little way but the tide was too strong. I ran back for help. That was when I was captured..'

She looked at him. One eye, shattered nose. He had proved his worth, shocked her with his resourcefulness. The idiot had come good. 'Thank you, Gren. For that, and for getting me here. You've done yourself and your family proud.'

He looked down in embarrassment. 'Don't mention it,' he mumbled.

Her mood lifted slightly and they chatted for a while. Elvgren even read to her for a bit. She listened to the sound of his voice. A pleasant breeze drifted in from the window, a smell not unlike lavender carried on the air. It wasn't long before Cirona drifted in to a genuine, and dreamless, sleep.

26

The breakfast table at the inn was loaded with a steaming pot of tea and a selection of sweet delicacies. Bellina had a cup in front of her, enjoying its warmth in her hands. Around the table were Elvgren, Dargo and Reveeker. Midge, Barboza, Holger and Crenshaw were out, taking a stroll in the morning air.

The conversation had been heated; as it had been for all of Cirona's convalescence. Each person chewing over the facts of their current predicament till the words were soup in their brains. How could they get word back home? Should they hire a boat and sail back? Did the Burkeshis know they were here? On and on the discussion circled, never changing and always returning to the blunt conclusion that they were fucked.

'Surely, we would be safe to sail home in a boat of our own,' said Elvgren. 'We more than have the funds for it.'

'As I have stated, I have no intention of going to Estria,' replied Rev. 'And, with the news from Melek about the pirates and the Burkeshi blockade, your *lordship*, I would not like our chances by sea.'

'Reveeker is right, Elvgren,' intervened Bellina. 'If the ships of the Grand Imperial Trading Company are not sailing, that is a bad sign. I would have expected Estria to decommission its entire naval fleet before ordering the trading ships to stop.'

'No one bloody well wants to hear my suggestions,' chimed in Dargo. 'Half that money is mine. You lot aren't gonna use it to go sailing off into the wide blue yonder.'

'Dar, how many times have I told you: there are no mermaid islands in the Larulian Ocean,' Elvgren said in exasperation.

Dargo pouted and took a bite of an almond pastry, chewing the treat rebelliously.

'So, this is how you morons have been spending your days, eh? Bickering pointlessly over a pot of tea like a group of nattering fishwives?'

The group turned to see Cirona struggling down the stairs.

'Please, Major, don't overexert yourself!' Elvgren called to her.

She waved her hand to stop his fussing. 'Sick of lying around in that bed. Wanted to make it to the privy on my own for once. Seeing as I have managed that feat of heroism, I'm sure I can sort this mess out,' she said, making it to the foot of the stairs. She stood for a moment, regaining her breath, then walked tentatively to the table. 'Right, I'm here now and I won't be turned away. What is our current situation?'

There was a pause as everyone looked at each other.

If Cirona was well enough to make it downstairs it was probably alright to tell her, Bellina thought. She nodded to Elvgren.

'The Estrian fleet has returned home, the merchant vessels have also stopped sailing. Meanwhile the Burkeshis control all trade coming from the eastern continent. We have no way to get a message to the Lord Chancellor and, even if we did, we have no way to assure him that it originates from us. Oh, and we have all been pronounced dead, just to put a little cherry on the top of it.'

The major looked deep in thought for a moment. 'Hmm. It's a damn shame we can't get hold of a Scribograph."

Bellina watched as the major's brow furrowed.

'Hang on a second,' the major exclaimed 'The answer is staring us in the bloody face. In fact, she's sipping tea right in front of us!' She pointed at Bellina.

'Me? What can I do?'

'Create a psychic link and talk to him face-to-face? Or mind to mind rather.'

'Oh! It's that simple, is it? I shut my eyes, think happy thoughts of my childhood and I'm instantly in conversation with someone across a bloody ocean,' Bellina replied. *Gods*, she thought, *the amount people understood about cognopaths would barely fill a saucer.*

'Is there really no way you could make contact?' Reveeker asked.

'There is a technique for communicating mind to mind over long distances but I have never attempted anything from this far away. The most I managed during my training was from my home to the School of Cognometry which is just outside the city walls.'

'Anything is worth a try at this point eh, Bellina?' said Elvgren. 'We can't go on like this, doing nothing till we're all caught up in the middle of a war we could have helped avoid.'

'Fine, I will give it a shot; but I'm not promising anything. Cirona, you will have to allow me full access to my cognopathic abilities.'

'Of course, I wi—hang on, has anyone seen the control conduit?'

'You have got to be fucking kidding!' Elvgren screamed in exasperation.

Bellina stared at the major's right wrist, a faint tan line showed where the control conduit had been.

'I had it on me the whole time I was with Gulgarno's, right up until the games. I can't think—' Cirona was interrupted by the sight of the conduit dangling from Dargo's hands.

'Um, is this what you're all going on about?' he said.

'You little shit! When did you get that?' Elvgren shouted.

'Took it when we shifted her body off the arena floor, got this key too. Dunno why you're getting all tetchy with me. If I hadn't, some other bugger would have lifted it,' Dargo said, his face a picture of petulance.

'The boy's right, Elvgren,' intervened Reveeker. 'He has done well.' 'Good job, pass them over quick would you?' Cirona said quickly tucking thekey out of sight before slipping on the control conduit.

Dargo beamed from ear-to-ear and handed the conduit over to Cirona who attached it onto her wrist.'Ok Bellina, are you ready?'

All eyes fell upon her, watching with a mixture of fear and fascination. 'Yes,' she lied. She watched as Cirona clicked the gem suppressing her cognopathic powers, three times. The precious stone glowed and Bellina's bracelet responded in kind. She closed her eyes and concentrated.

*

The psychic landscape formed in her mind. Bellina stood on a circular expanse of marshy ground. The outer extremity of the circle was masked by a thick, roiling mist from which sinuous tendrils of ribbon trailed away. It was the centre of her social hub, each ribbon representing someone she had strong feelings towards. The ribbons fluttered before her, like flags caught in the breeze. The contrast of colours was brilliant: burgundy, cerulean, copper. She tried to remember the rules. How could she pluck her father's ribbon from this mess? It had been a very long time since she had visited this place and she had only done it then as part of her training.

The knowledge came back to her with a force that almost bowled her over: the length of the ribbon represented the amount of time she had known the person. She reached out and they snapped taut in response. She noticed the beginnings of new tendrils, short and stubby, but the one that belonged to her father was impossible to miss — its unmatched length trailed from the distant mist to where she stood.

That ribbon was a deep red. Bellina took it in her hand and wrapped it in coils around her forearm, pulling until it pulled back and she shot forward, the mist whizzing past her in a sickening blur. She closed her eyes, engulfed in darkness for a time.

When she opened them again she was standing in a vast room full of complicated machinery. Brass instruments shone, levers poked up invitingly, dials whirled and there was a faint clicking sound. It resembled a computation factory, where the copper instruction cards for automatons were created.

She had not generated this psychic landscape which meant her father must have created it with the help of a cognopath. It was his defence against mental attack. The idea that he might have felt the need of it in order to keep her out pinched at her. She quickly pushed the thought away — her father had many enemies and they would use any means of attack him. The more she thought about it, the more she realised that, with her father's level of shrewdness, she should have expected to encounter such a place.

'Father? Father!' The sound of a handle being turned came from behind her. She spun round and there he was.

Her father looked at her in disbelief, jaw agape. 'My darling... how in the...'

'I've finally managed to make you speechless. Now there's a thing,' Bellina said, rushing forward, flinging her arms around him. Even in the psychic realm he retained his familiar smell.

'I had gone beyond all hope that you were alive, my girl,' he said, embracing her back.

'It was betwixt and between on many occasions but I have survived. Lord Elvgren and Cirona have managed to remain this side of the Weeping Veil as well.'

'Where are you now? What happened? Gods, I'm completely befuddled. You're alive!'

His smile was bigger than any she had ever seen upon his face. 'We are in the town of Dronkor, in Varash. There was sabotage from the outset. Some of the soldiers and Lord Kester turned out to be Burkeshi imposters. I know this sounds impossible but they had somehow taken on the forms of our people.'

'It doesn't sound too impossible, I am afraid. We discovered the bodies of Kester and the soldiers a week after your departure. The hearts missing. We tried to get a message to the ship but it was impossible — some other kaffar devilry, no doubt.'

'I expect so. I think them capable of anything now. So much has happened but I don't know how long I will be able to keep up the psychic link. We are at a crossroads, we have funds but no idea of what to do next.' Her father began to pace up and down. His brow creased in thought. The familiar action made her heart leap for joy.

'I will have to ask you to go on,' he replied.

It was Bellina's turn to stand agape now. 'Go on? But we no longer have the smokescreen of the diplomatic mission to hide behind!'

'I know, my love, but it seems there is a great deal we do not know about the inner workings of the Burkeshis. Frankly, I'm astonished at the breadth of their reach. I assume they have had some hand in spreading false information about what became of you so I shall spread some of my own. Possibly find some decoy bodies and put them on show, convince them that you're really dead..'

'Father what you ask is incredibly dangerous. I don't know if I can convince the others. I am having a hard enough time convincing myself.'

He looked at her with a sadness that tore at her heart. 'Bellina, I know this is something I should not force upon you. Something is afoot, something big, and for once I don't know what it is. We need to know. As cold as it sounds, this is what you have been training for.' He paused and placed a hand on her shoulder before continuing. 'It goes without saying, this mission is now covert. Head to the country of Chenta. The city of Krangoon is, for all intents and purposes, Estrian. There is a military outpost on the mountain border between Chenta and Burkesh. I will notify them of your arrival and get them to offer any assistance they can. They should be able to get you to the Burkeshi capital. I will contact our intelligence operative there and inform him about all this. From now on, you be discreet and cover your movements.'

Bellina felt dumbstruck. Secretly, she had dreamed of returning home. Pride flared within her though. Her father had asked and she was still determined to help him, to lift some of the great weight from his shoulders. 'Very well, father. I will do as you ask. I will tell the others.'

'Thank you. If you need to contact me, use this method if you cannot find access to a scribograph, if you send a scribogram use the word ebullient so I know it's you. Oh, one more thing. Tell the major her plant is well cared for. I expect to take a cutting on her return.'

'As you wish,' Bellina said. She puzzled at the words but assumed it was a coded message that the major would understand.

'Go now, my brave girl. And know this: I am truly sorry. Sorry for this and sorry for... well, I'm sorry.' His face carried a look of deep despair.

'Don't worry. I won't let you down.'

She gave him once last squeeze then pulled at the ribbon still wrapped around her arm, disconnecting her from the psychic world.

*

Bellina's eyes snapped open and she saw the others looking down at her. She was lying on the floor and could feel blood trickling from her nose.

'Bellina? Bellina? Are you alright? Damn it. Elvgren, get some water!' Cirona said.

'I'm alright, I'm alright. Stop fussing,' Bellina replied, struggling into a sitting position.

'Did you speak with your father?' the major asked

'Yes ... I was able to speak with him.'

'And what does he say?' Elvgren asked, hovering at her side with a glass.

'He said, we go on.'

There was an intake of breath. Elvgren looked at Cirona who returned his look of confusion.

'We are to make our way to Chenta, make for an outpo—' she began, but was cut off by a ringing sound that grew louder and louder in her ears.

'Don't talk. Rest. We will take you upstairs to bed,' Cirona said, scooping her up.

'Major... he said your plant is... looked after and... want a cutting...' she managed to say. Just before she drifted into unconsciousness she observed the look that passed over Cirona's face. It was a peculiar mix of elation and anxiety.

*

That night the whole group gathered in Elvgren's room. Cirona watched the rabble they had collected with affection. They all looked at the pale form of Bellina, waiting for her to deliver her news. The message she had already delivered to Cirona, before falling unconscious, had given her delight and heartache in equal measure. If what the girl had said was true, the Lord Chancellor had found her daughter. That would mean that he intended for her to carry out his orders to the letter. Her stomach twisted at the thought. *Not now*, she told herself, *one thing at a time.*

'My father's orders are clear,' began Bellina. 'He has asked me, Lord Elvgren and Major Bouchard to carry on to Burkesh. We have all agreed to it, some more readily than others.' She stared pointedly at Elvgren who seemed to find something very interesting to look at on the floor. 'We have no right to entangle anyone else in what comes next. We all owe you our lives and for that we are grateful. We must go on but we need to ask what *you* would like to do.' The girl finished and spread her arms out to the assembly.

Barboza and Crenshaw exchanged looks of concern, Midge looked at the faces of Holger and Reveeker, Dargo was thoughtful and Elvgren continued to stare at the floor. The earlier conversation between the three remaining members of the diplomatic mission had ended with the young lord stomping off.

'I'll come, if you'll have me. Always wanted to see the world, plus someone's gotta keep an eye on muggins 'ere,' Dargo said, jabbing a thumb at Elvgren.

'I have no desire to go to Burkesh' said Barboza. 'I'm not well loved there. But I will offer my, and Crenshaw's, assistance for some of the journey. At a price, naturally.'

Crenshaw nodded in agreement.

'I want to stay with the captain,' Midge said.

'So you shall boy. I would not turn you away for all the tea in Chenta,' Barboza replied, giving Midge a massive smile.

'I think I'll come with you,' said Holger. 'Don't know what help I can be but I know a little about a lot.'

'They say that's a dangerous thing, don't they?' Elvgren remarked, a dark look in his eyes.

Holger returned the look with his jaw set tight and shrugged.

'I think it goes without saying that I will come with you,' Reveeker said. 'There are things that need to be put right in Burkesh for me.'

Cirona was certainly glad to hear that as, so far, their covert team included an urchin and a love-struck young man, though Bellina seemed oblivious to Holger's feelings. 'Thanks, everybody. Now we get to the bones of it. We need a plan to get to Chenta. Ideas?'

'Sailing would be risky but achievable,' volunteered Crenshaw. 'I think I'd be able to get us there in one piece. Only problem would be how tight the Burkeshis are monitoring the ports.'

''Ow 'bout we take one o'them hot air things? That looks like a right laugh,' Dargo said, eyes bright with enthusiasm.

'For the love of the gods, Dargo!' Elvgren replied hotly. 'How the hells would we manage to get one across an ocean? I suppose you also have a method of controlling the wind, should we get in the air?'

The little lord's in a right flap this evening, Cirona thought.

'Well screw you an' all, Gren. Only mentioned it 'cos that Melek fella is always prattling on 'bout his.'

'What do you mean, Dar?' Bellina asked.

'Just that we got to talking one day. I was saying it was a shame we couldn't just fly up like the birds and do as we please, shitting on people and what not, and he says that he's been up there. Got some contraption he's been working on so you can sail around in the sky.'

'Fuck me! Don't tell me that crazy git done it!' Cirona exclaimed.

'What are you saying, Rona?' Rev asked her.

'Melek. He was an engineer, brilliant at it as well. Was a noble and some kind of inventor before he was forced to join the Imperial Army.'

'What do you mean *forced*?' Elvgren asked.

'He was a bit on the dodgy side. Worked for some unsavoury sorts. Even for that fucking shit Castros Del Var.'

'You mean the terrorist? The one who tried to shoot the Emperor?' Bellina said.

'Some would call him a freedom fighter. Particularly those from less prestigious births than some of the people present here,' Barboza said.

Cirona most certainly did not see it that way. She fought her anger down.

'Look this isn't a philosophical debate. What's this got to do with flying?' Crenshaw said, clearly sensing her anger and trying to dissuade a confrontation.

'You're right, let's get back to the point,' said Cirona, shaking it off. 'He was sentenced to death for conspiracy. But if there is one thing us Estrians are, its opportunists. They dragged him in to work for the military instead of executing him. Anyway, he had this idea about using hot air balloons to fly over enemy encampments and drop bombs and decided to try it. Up he goes in this bloody thing, like he'd stuck a Sylvantain gondola to the bottom of a pig's bladder. Ends up getting blown down in enemy territory. Me and my men were sent in to retrieve him. We saved his life but the whole thing shook him up good. He asked us to say he had died, killed in the crash. I wasn't too keen, told him he would swing if he weren't careful. So, he gets this strange look in his eye. Says he'll serve but as a soldier in my company. He'd grown some kind of bizarre attachment to me on the trek back, I think he thought I could keep him safe. Said he'd carry on with his work in the field. The higher ups let him as he was refusing to do anything without me.

'Two years he was with us. He improved our weapons, forded rivers with all kinds of contraptions I won't pretend to understand. After that tour of service, he decided he'd had enough of military work. Convinced the top brass to let him retire somewhere out of the way if he still sent them things he'd been working on. We kept up a correspondence. He told me he had set up here in Dronkor. He'd started to get paranoid and thought this was a nice, out-of-the-way place to hide himself. And there you have it.'

'So, what you're saying is that this might not be as fanciful as it first appears,' Crenshaw said.

'What I'm saying is that tomorrow we go and see a man about a flying ship.'

27

After a fitful night dreaming about flying boats falling out of the sky, Elvgren had woken up in an even worse mood. Whilst they walked towards Melek's, he thought about the man who had instigated this ridiculous state of affairs. The Lord Chancellor's order to continue was selfish and unreasonable. It might well be easy to command others into danger from your bony arse in Estria but it was quite another thing to be the one who actually had to go and do it. The only reason he had finally agreed to carry on was the thought of being Lord Chancellor one day. It was a thought he hadn't had for a while, one that was too much to give up on. He'd been so caught up in merely surviving the ignominious events that had befallen him that he had spent little time dwelling on the prize awaiting him at the end of the adventure. Visions of glory, honour and, at long last, the respect of his parents filled his inner eye. There would be parades, balls, banquets. It would be him looking down in disdain on his mother and father, their roles reversed. All the put-downs and jibes he'd endured from them. *'Oh, you'll never be as grand or fantastic as your brother, peace be,'* he heard his mother's voice resound in his mind. No, what *could* measure up to the serene perfection of Jeremias Lovitz, fucking peace be? What peace had he ever had, haunted by the ghost of his brother's memory all his life. Haunted by a man he had never even met. No, he wasn't going to think about this. He pummelled the spectre of his brother deep down inside him. No one needed to know about *him*.

He tried to distract himself by imagining his glorious return but he couldn't. This was why he never thought about Jeremias, his brother's saintly ideal always ruined his equilibrium. Why had he started to think about him now, after so much time? *Let it go; deep, deep down*, he thought.

He tried to make his mind blank. A small part of his brain gnawed at him like a maggot. Run, take the money and your chances. He could leave everyone to it and escape the madness descending around him. The idea was more than tempting. He took a deep breath to steady his nerves. He had to go on, for his honour, for himself, to finally have something of his own, not just second-hand dreams that belonged to a dead man. He mulled over how guilty he had felt about running after the *Prudence* sank; he then imagined that magnified by a hundred.

'What's eating you, Gren?' Dargo asked.

'Wha... oh nothing, Dar. Just thinking. Actually, I forgot to thank you properly for suggesting flying as our method of travel,' Elvgren said, giving the boy a light punch on the arm.

'Oi! Watch it you. Bloody nerve! Save your arse how many times and I get a punch on me arm? Anyway, ye gotta admit: flying? Flying! Come on,' he said, his body going into excited spasms.

Elvgren looked at Dargo. The boy was dressed in an outfit that wouldn't be out of place in the smoking room of a gentlemen's club while strolling around an arid Varashi town. A smile spread across his face. The little git had got to him, he couldn't imagine the lad not being around anymore. 'I suppose you're right, Dargo. Flying will be... well I won't stretch to fun, but how about interesting, eh?'

'That's the spirit, boss!' Dargo replied. He began to puff himself up like a giant balloon and stomp about.

It was easy for Elvgren to forget how young the boy was, especially when the lad was holding knives to people's throats. Elvgren pretended to prime and load a ballisket, then shot at the Dargo balloon. The boy mimed an explosion, complete with sound effects ending in a loud farting noise. 'Dargo, are you sure about all this?' Elvgren asked. The boy looked thoughtful for a moment.

'Got nothing else,' he said, shrugging.

'Absolutely nothing? No one at all back in Estria?'

'Nah, all gone. Me mum got taken by the pox, never knew me dad. Had an older brother, looked after me. Then sickness got him and he died as well. *You* did for Danker and the rest.'

'Ah, sorry about that, Dargo. I... well there's not much more I can say, I suppose.'

'Don't worry. It's a sorry state of affairs when you consider whoremongers and loan sharks as your family. Never would have lasted anyway. Something would have got 'em eventually, just thankful I fell in with a decent lot.'

'You... you have me, you know. I promise.'

'Hah! What a curse!' he said laughing his little head off.

Probably not too far from the truth though, Elvgren thought.

They finally made it to Melek's. The inventor performed his usual scrutiny from behind the door before whirling through the locks, making a tremendous sound, banging, swearing, until the door finally flew open. Melek stood sucking at his thumb, which he had evidently caught on one of the bolts.

'Major Bouchard! What a singular joy! How, pray tell, are you feeling?' he asked, engaging Cirona in an awkward hug.

'Not too bad, Melek. Thanks for all your help.'

'Not at all, not at all! I would do anything in my power to assist you.'

'That's certainly good to hear. We need you to get us to Chenta.'

'Chenta? If you will pardon my rudeness, what for?'

'Can't tell you, Melek. Sorry. Now, will you help us, even if you don't know why we're going there?'

'Of course, but I do not see any way that I can. I am not in the possession of a ship.'

'What about an airship?' Bouchard said.

Elvgren watched Melek's face. If he thought Dargo had been excited about flying, then it paled in comparison to the glee that shone from the inventor's eyes.

*

The parched red soil of an unused field stretched out before Bellina's eyes. The only thing to be seen for miles was a large ramshackle storehouse. The long walk to Melek's airship had taken hours and the sun was sitting high in the sky.

'Come, come, my would-be aeronauts. We have almost arrived!' Melek shouted at the group, who were lagging behind.

Though they were all interested in the man's contraption, their curiosity did not hold the power to spur them on. Reveeker led the straggling group. Barboza stomped behind Bellina and Holger, muttering under his breath, whilst Crenshaw suppressed laughter at his friend's expense. Dargo dragged his feet in the way only a young adolescent can. Elvgren, Cirona and Midge brought up the rear.

'So an airship, eh?' said Holger.

'Let's hope so and the deranged git doesn't have a sheep's bladder with a box tied to it in there,' she said, making Holger laugh. He had been one of the keenest to accompany them on the next stage of their journey and she was glad. The young man had become a close friend and it was nice to have someone of a similar age to talk to. Especially, seeing as Elvgren never had been, nor never would be, her first port of call for a chat. He had changed during his trials and had certainly proved himself but they didn't have anything in common. Sometimes, when she caught him looking at her, she noted it was with the eye of a man coveting a trophy, all selfish greed. It was an unsettling expression. Come to think of it, Holger was prone to a strange look in his eyes as well. She banished the thought, deciding not to examine it now.

Her attention turned to Cirona, who was chatting away with Midge. The major had been displaying a motherly side she would not have credited the military woman with when they first met. Bellina wondered what sort of a mother Cirona would have made. Probably a good one, at least, better than none at all. Bellina's small amount of knowledge about her own mother came from a few brief conversations with her father. He did not like to speak of Lady Tabitha Ressa and had extended the silence on the subject over the entire house. There was only one painting of her in their home. Bellina pictured it hanging over the fire in the drawing room, a distant look in the eyes of the woman who had brought her into the world.

*

They stopped outside the large doors to the warehouse. One was hanging off its hinges, making a bashing sound as it swung in the breeze.

'Ladies and gentlemen, boys and girls,' Melek said with pride as he pulled open the doors. 'Behold! The first of its kind, the aeronautical ship: *The Sighing Wind!*'

Bellina shared a look with Holger and turned to see how everyone else had reacted.

They looked underwhelmed too. The floor of the warehouse was covered in dark brown canvas. A small wooden gondola with a covered roof lay towards the rear of the storeroom. That was it.

'Is this all?' Dargo said, not hiding his disappointment bordering on anger.

'What in the name of the gods do you mean by that?' Melek asked.

''S not quite what I was expecting.'

'This is the future, my boy. Don't you see? We shall loose our worldly shackles and enter the realms of the gods.'

''Tis just a load of material and a troublingly small carriage,' Barboza said.

'For the love of... Major, why have you inflicted people of such puny imaginations upon me?' Melek said, his hands on his hips, a look of consternation on his face.

'I think I will require some selling on this one too, Melek,' Cirona replied.

'Very well. The material, as you so unimaginatively put it, is the balloon that shall bear us aloft. It will be filled with the gas that is emitted by the mineral, aquidifex, when it is burned. Once the balloon is full, I shall attach the gondola and we will be on our way, my brave voyagers, into the unknown,' Melek said, his eyes misting over.

'Well, as far as I'm aware old chap that's the same as a regular hot air balloon. Saw one last year at the Imperial Exhibition, some fella called Groven rode up in it then came down. Took passengers too, as far as I recall,' Elvgren said.

'Bah! Don't speak to me of that talentless hack. A feeble mind with no aptitude for natural philosophy. All that type of balloon can do is go up and then float wherever the wind takes it. But not mine! Oh no, no, no. This has a great tharg engine, powered with sortilenergy. It is truly a testament to the greatness of Estria,' Melek said, clapping his hands.

'How the hells do you propose to get a bloody great tharg engine in there? Half the bottom deck of the *Vagabond* was taken up with hers,' Holger said, surprising Bellina. He was usually a very quiet member at the many meetings they had; it had seemed to her that he didn't like talking in front of groups of people very much.

'At last, praise be to the Father for sending me someone with an ounce of intelligence!' Melek cried, throwing his hands in the air and looking to the heavens.

Bellina wasn't sure she liked the new enthused engineer; he was distinctly ruder than he was in his home.

'Come with me, I will show you. Quickly now, come on!' he continued, already striding down the warehouse.

They followed him. He stopped briefly to pull a lever on the wall and artificial light flooded the warehouse. For the first time they could see the ceiling and upper half of the storage space.

A wooden catwalk lined the walls of the building. High up, on the left side, Bellina saw what she assumed must be his workstation. What was truly staggering though was the massive ship-like structure that dangled from the ceiling on taut cables. A large tharg engine was attached to its hull, the brass and copper pistons, crankshafts, and pressure cylinders shining like an ocean at sunrise. Vast objects that looked like giant oars fashioned from canvas protruded from the sides of the vessel. There were three on each side and a small screw propeller on the back. Melek pulled another lever and the whole thing started to descend.

'As you can see, the engine does not need to fit inside the vessel, instead it attaches to the base of the vessel,' Melek explained.

'Hang on, if that's the airship then what the hells is that thing over there?' Holger said, pointing to the tiny vessel they had first noticed at the back of the barn.

'That? Oh, that is just an old gondola from a previous model. I have converted it into a privy.'

'I think I can speak for all of us when I say I am grateful for that,' cried Barboza. 'I would not attempt to leave the sweet embrace of the ground in something that is barely fit for a shithouse. But that engine, by the gods! Can such a thing really work in that position?'

'It most certainly can. In fact, it is a necessity. The, ah, aquidifex must be burnt at a controlled temperature and, the, er, intense heat from a tharg engine can prove…explosive.. As I have found out.'

There was silence as Bellina and the group considered the implications of an unhappy mix of heat and gas whilst sailing the sky. Eventually the silence was broken.

'How do you propose to land the thing, old boy?' Elvgren said.

'Well, once it's aloft so shall it stay. Entry and exit to the vessel will be via a rope.' The answer seemed to satisfy Elvgren.

'How are you going to power it though, Mr. Delagrond? There is no access to sortilenergy in Varash,' Bellina said.

'That is not strictly true. I have — at not inconsiderable cost — had vorotorium cells shipped to myself. Each is charged with the power of the mages but, thanks to a few of my own modifications, the amount of sortilenergy they can hold has been increased tenfold and they now have the output of a large vorotorium generator. I have also been able to reduce the size of the cells considerably.' Melek led them over to a small box on a wooden workbench, which he lifted.

Beneath it, sat a modified cell. A small glass orb, about the size of a cannonball, sat on a silver, circular base, it was topped off in a similar fashion. A variety of tubes, connecting points and cables extended from the cell like the tendrils of a plant. Bellina's eyes were drawn back to the glass. She watched as the forcibly extracted mage power filled the space, the swirling, purple cloud, throbbing within the orb. Small flashes of galvanic energy arced out from its core sporadically. *Gods, a few improvements ... the man is a genius,* she thought. Since she had been a young girl Bellina had been fascinated by machiney that fuelled the Estrain empire. She knew the vorotorium generators that most middle-class and upper-class houses used had to have a room in the basement specially constructed. Generators and portable cells came in a variety of sizes, the amount of power they could emit diminished with the size. But to have increased the output *and* decreased the size by this much ... In the midst of her musing, Bellina felt a tug on her arm. She turned to see Midge peering out from behind her, his eyes wide, chin trembling.

'What's the matter Midge? Did you never see the generator on board the *Vagabond?*' Holger asked. The boy shook his head.

'There is no need for fear young man! The sortilenergy is quite tame, much the same as the damned race that produces it,' Melek said, but the boy still shied away.

'I think it would be best if you covered it back up, Melek?' Cirona said. Once he had done so, she continued. 'This is all very impressive but does it work? And when can it set off?'

'It will most definitely work, Major, have no fear. As for setting off I would need four hours to inflate the balloon.'

'Start your preparations immediately, if you would be so kind. We shall return to town to gather our things and get supplies.'

'As you wish, Major, but I will require some help. Would anyone care to volunteer?'

Barboza, Crenshaw, Holger and Dargo stepped forward.

'I ain't traipsing all the bloody way back to Dronkor,' Dargo said. 'Get me stuff from the inn, Gren.'

'You lazy little... if anything gets left behind, don't blame me,' Elvgren replied.

'That settles it then. Melek, we will see you back here tonight,' Cirona said.

'There's no need for that Major. *I* will pick *you* up.'

28

The sun was setting on the town of Dronkor but the market stalls were still open and very busy. Revekeer and Elvgren headed for the inn to gather the group's personal effects while Bellina, Midge and Cirona made their way through the crowd, picking out the choicest vegetables and haggling for better deals.

Cirona spent a long time selecting a sword she felt comfortable with. When she finally found one she liked, she tested it for weight and balance with a few practice cuts that made Bellina wince. After that, they visited more food stalls looking for preserves and other items that would survive a long journey — the Varashis had not begun dealing in the canned goods that were starting to become available in Estria.

Bellina was watching Cirona haggle aggressively in the common tongue with a stallholder over the price of some cured ham.

'Four rencats for this sliver of pig? You've got to be joking. I wouldn't charge that to a mage! I'll give you half a rencat.'

'No. Four. That is price. You pay or go. Damn Estrian, this is free market, you not tell me how to run stool!'

'Not everything is a bloody political battle you miserable old scrotum, the price of that ham is fucking robbery. Think you can get one over on me? Think again. I'll offer two and that's 'cos I'm in a hurry.'

'Two? Two rencats! This is best ham in all of Dronkor. People beg for this and I say it is gone, they offer ten rencats just for slice.'

'Then Varashis are more stupid than I imagined...'

Bellina sighed and looked at Midge, tuning out the heated bartering. 'Shall we go and see if there are any sweets, Midge?' she offered, desperate to get away from the scene that was now attracting amused onlookers. The young boy's eyes lit up and he nodded.

They snaked their way through the crowd, Midge darting around the legs of customers in too much of a rush to pay him any heed. She held him by the hand and helped to lead him through. They burst free of the crowd in front of the confectionary stall. Rows upon rows of sugary delights covered the stand: Paltont honeyed pears, flavoured jellies in the shape of birds, raw sugar cane from Timboko and even some chocolates from the Estria. Midge's eyes were as wide as dinner plates as he leaned over the counter trying to make his choice. Bellina smiled at him, watching him nibble samples offered by the cheerful vendor.

Midge was one of the biggest mysteries in the group, no one had any idea about his past. Even Barboza didn't know anything about him. All he could say was that Midge was already on board the *Scampering Vagabond* when he and Crenshaw joined the crew. Holger said that he had heard Midge mumbling protests in his sleep and once the boy had woken up shouting out in an unknown tongue. But Midge could not be enticed to speak about any of it.

The assortment of sweets the youngster had selected was just being poured into a small bag when there was a commotion behind them. Bellina turned around and saw people were crowding around where Cirona had been shopping. Suddenly, there was a bang like a ballistol going off. The crowd tried to get away in a mad crush. People fell. There were screams and shouts.

'Take my hand, Midge, we'd better find Cirona,' Bellina said, turning back to where the boy had been standing a few seconds before.

The space was empty.

A cold feeling settled in her stomach, like an icy hand was squeezing her gut. 'Midge! Midge!' she shouted at the top of her lungs. She turned in every direction, the colours and the sounds of the chaotic market overwhelming her. Bellina felt faint. She turned to the stallholder.

'Where did the boy go? Did you see?' she asked, frantically.

'No see. Looking at that over there. I sorry,' he replied, looking genuinely distraught.

She needed to get to Cirona.

*

Moments before the stampede started, Cirona was still haggling.

'Two and half. Then go, you stinking thief!' the meat vendor said to her.

She felt a flush of some pride for getting him down so low — the Varashis had *special* rates for Estrian visitors. The large crowd that had gathered around her, murmured in appreciation of her bargaining prowess. Suddenly, she felt a cold, hard cylinder nuzzle against the base of her spine — the unmistakable barrel of a ballistol.

'Turn round nice and slow, bitch, or this bastard will be selling your entrails off the front of his stall.'

She recognised Barag's voice, whispering in her ear. *Twelve fucking hells*, she thought, *where did this shit-bag come from?* Cirona had forgotten about Gulgarno and his men. She now prayed to the Father that it wouldn't be a costly oversight. When she turned round, as slowly as she could manage, the crowd caught a glimpse of the weapon and gasped. None of them moved to help, they didn't even look away — the shooting of an Estrian would just be another part of the market's entertainment. *Think, think*, she told herself.

'How did you find us?' she eventually asked, trying to stall for time.

'Not too hard, really. Wasn't word of you for weeks though, otherwise we would've been here sooner. The man who runs the inn you're staying at likes to dabble in a bit of smuggling. Passed on word that a rather strange group of people were frequenting his establishment. Word got around and here we are.'

Fuck it, she had been worried that their bizarre mix-raced assembly would draw attention. Barag had her cornered and two more of Gulgarno's men stood behind him. Escaping through the tightly packed crowd would be quite a feat. 'What do you want?' Stupid question but she needed more time.

'Do you think I'm thick or something? Quit stalling, ain't no one coming to help. Got a couple o' people over at the inn now, dealing with the rest of your lot. Now hand over your weapon and these fine gentlemen will help you get less comfortable,' he said. One of the men behind Barag flexed a piece of rope while the other grinned manacingly.

Cirona's mind raced. Did they have Bellina and Midge? In fact, where the fuck had they got to? What about Elvgren and Rev at the inn? Time to try something unsophisticated.

'REV! REVEEKER! Over here!' she bellowed, looking over her captor's shoulders. Barag flicked his eyes away for a split second but it was enough. She grabbed the outstretched hand that held the ballistol and wrenched it upwards. With a deafening bang, the single shot from its barrel went off.

The twelve hells broke loose around her. The crowd surged in every direction at once. Cirona and Barag went sprawling to the ground. The feet of fleeing people trampled over her prone body, her face smashed into the hard, red earth. Millions of bright lights ignited across her vision and the world reeled. She was going to be crushed to death. *Of all the fucking ways to go*, she thought. She reached out and grabbed at the first thing she could — it was the coat of a running man. She pulled, gaining some purchase and managed to get to her knees. The man was frantically trying to get the coat off and escape. A woman ran past to her left and Cirona grabbed at the coarse fabric of her dress, she could feel it tearing in her grasp. The women let out an otherworldly scream but Cirona managed to pull herself to her feet.

Unfortunately, so did Barag. She glimpsed his hateful eyes through the fleeing Varashis. The crowd around him and his guards was thinning. Gulgarno's men started to advance on her. She tried to pull her sword but the damn thing wouldn't come loose. There was a dull thump and an apple went spinning off Barag's head. Cirona could see the tiny form of Midge behind him, fury written across his face.

'No! Run, Midge, bloody run!' she cried.

'Grab him!' Barag shouted. The two other men snatched the boy roughly, he kicked and bit but to no avail.

'You want him, bitch, come and get him!' Barag laughed over the heads of the crowd.

The three men went barrelling off, sending people flying. She tried to go after them, fighting furiously against the current of the crowd but they were soon lost in the chaos. 'Gods damn it!' She had to find Bellina.

*

'All set?' Elvgren said to Reveeker as he pulled the string tight on a large burlap sack. The big Burkeshi nodded and they both struggled down the stairs with their loads. Elvgren went to the front desk of the inn and rang the little bell.

Danstoupolous appeared, wringing his hands. 'Yes gentlemen, how am I to be helping you?' He looked flushed and a sheen of sweat covered his face.

'Just came to settle the bill, good man. We are to be off. Say, are you feeling alright?' Elvgren asked.

The old man licked his lips. 'Fine, yes, I am fine. Sorry to see such generous guests go. Er ... perhaps you would be wanting a small drink before you leave?'

'No, no old boy. I'm afraid time is pressing. Just the bill.'

'A sip of tea? Some cake? Er … surely no need for you to be going right now.'

'His majesty said to give us the bill. Do it,' Reveeker said.

The old man threw up his hands and leant down to pick up his register. He came up holding a twin-barrelled ballisket. 'Sorry. Many debts,' he said, the barrels trembling.

'What's the bloody meaning of this, Danstoupolous? Put that down before someone gets hurt,' Elvgren said, trying to sound commanding.

'Do it, Varashi. You don't look like you know how to handle that,' Rev added.

'Oh, but we do,' a voice called out from behind Elvgren.

He turned his head and saw a young woman sitting on the first-floor banister. She had a horrible smile. The rest of her face was scarred horribly and her nose was smashed flat. Two men flanked her, aiming balliskets of their own. Elvgren swallowed hard.

'If it isn't the fake medificer and the Burkeshi,' said the woman. 'The old shit down there wasn't lying then. Get yourself out of here man, remember you saw nothing.'

Elvgren heard the front door open and close, then a lock turning. For the first time that evening, he realised that the inn was deserted.

The light from the oil lamps hanging from a dark wooden chandelier formed grotesque shadows behind the ballisket-wielding trio.

'The fat man will be glad to get the Burkeshi back and that military bitch too. Got no real use for you though, scrawny,' she said, flashing a wolfish smile and pointing at Elvgren.

'Who are you, woman? I have many enemies but you are unknown to me,' Reveeker said.

'Dilla is my name and we are bounty hunters. Gulgarno wants you back, we get you back. Some of his lads are out rounding up the rest of your little group.' She gave a little push on the banister and dropped the considerable distance to the floor, landing like an alley cat. Standing up, she stuck her hands in her pockets and walked over to them, whistling.

Elvgren could feel his heart hammering in his chest. He shot a quick look at Reveeker, who stared unblinking, jaw clenched tight. How the hells could he be so calm?

'Right then, big man,' said Dilla, 'hands above your head and up the stairs. I'll deal with this one.'

Elvgren watched in dismay as Reveeker moved towards the staircase, he may not have liked the man but he was more than handy in a fight.

The woman smiled her horrible smile again, up close it was even worse. She had tiny little teeth like a child, terrifying in her scarred countenance. Greasy, lank hair stuck to her forehead, a few strands displaced by her dramatic descent to the floor. She pulled out a knife and Elvgren began to back away. There was not that much room to back into and he soon bumped into the counter.

'I'll enjoy this. Consider myself a bit of an artist. Know exactly where to cut to make it painful but not kill,' she said lunging forward.

Elvgren spun out of her way. *It's just the training ground*, he told himself, *focus, focus!*

'Oho! A lively one. Just makes it more interesting,' she sang, darting at him again.

He twisted his body to let the blade go past him and threw his fist at her jaw. She moved her head instinctively and the blow failed to register.

'You need help boss? Welt's watching the big one.'

'The day I need help to take out a streak o' piss like this, I'd better call it quits!' she replied, crouching forward and twirling her knife in small circles.

Elvgren licked his lips and waited for an opening. He backed up some more and tripped on the edge of the rug in the centre of the inn's reception hall. He fell hard on his back and Dilla pounced on him. She tried to stab the knife into his good eye. He grabbed at her hand and pushed her arm back but the woman was stronger than she looked. In horror, he watched the point of the blade come closer and closer to his eyeball.

Shouts and bangs could be heard coming from the first floor. A ballisket went off, followed by a twanging sound. He looked up as the large, wooden chandelier came hurtling down towards them.

Dilla screamed when the whole weight of the wooden chandeliersmashed into her body. Heavy wood pinned her to Elvgren. The oil lamps shattered with a sound resembling a horde of laughing fairies, all twinkling loveliness. They unleashed a fiery hell. Tiny flecks of flaming oil spat outward, catching anything they touched alight. The collection of small fires began to form a circle around where he was pinned to the floor. He tried to push the woman and the chandelier off him but they were too heavy. Elvgren could feel the woman's warm blood seeping into his clothes and the smell of smoke filled his nostrils. 'Reveeker! Reveeker! Fucking help me!' he screamed over the roaring flames. Elvgren could just about make out the sounds of a scuffle from the hall above him. There was an ear-splitting shriek and both of the remaining bounty hunters fell to the floor. One of them had half of their face blown away, a ruined mess of bloody pulp. The other had broken his neck in the fall, his head twisted round at an unnatural angle.

'Where are you boy? There's too much damned smoke,' Reveeker called out, coughing.

'Don't call me boy!'

'Is this really the time? For *vaksar*'s sake! Just tell me where you are or burn, I don't really care.'

'Alright, alright, I'm trapped beneath the chandelier.'

'Hang on, I'm coming.'

'Well I'm not bloody going anywhere, am I?' Elvgren saw Reveeker coming down the stairs, shimmering in the haze of the fire. The Burkeshi held a rag before his face as he stepped between the pools of flame. He charged through the ring of fire around Elvgren and tried to lift the chandelier. Elvgren heard the red-hot wood singe Reveeker's skin with a sizzle. He watched the man, veins popping out of his neck, straining to get some leverage.

With a heroic effort, the Burkeshi managed to lift the wood just enough to give Elvgren the room to wriggle free. Reveeker helped pull him to his feet and Elvgren could finally appreciate the gravity of their predicament. Tongues of fire licked their way up the wooden interior of the building. The couches and tables in the waiting area were melting away in the intense heat. 'What the fuck do we do now?'

'How about say thanks for saving my life? I would not even be in this situation if I had not come back for you!'

There was a thunderous creaking and the wooden balcony above them collapsed. A supporting strut fell towards them, a pillar of fire. Elvgren dived to the left and accidentally took Reveeker with him. They rolled through the flames across the floor to the foot of the stairs. Elvgren stumbled back to his feet, head spinning.

The Burkeshi looked at him. 'Well, I suppose that can serve as a thank you.'

Elvgren decided it was probably best to keep the truth to himself.

The remains of the balcony started to creak as the heat warped and ravaged the wood. A sea of flames separated Elvgren and Reveeker from the front door.

'Quickly! Upstairs,' Reveeker said.

They sprinted up the stairs and into the room straight in front of them. The Burkeshi opened the window and climbed out onto the sill, beckoning Elvgren to follow, before disappearing.

Elvgren stuck his head out. The inn was one of the tallest buildings in town and the view to the ground made his head spin.

'Climb, you blundering great fool!' Reveeker called down to him. He was already scaling the wall of the building with the ease of a spider.

Elvgren hauled himself out and reached up for a handhold, his palms slick with sweat. The tips of his fingers dug in desperately to the gaps between the stones. He pulled himself up inch by terrifying inch till finally he reached the flat roof of the inn. Standing up, he walked over to Reveeker, coughing and spluttering. Smoke rose high into the sky, billowing from the windows of the building. He could feel the heat through the soles of his boots. A curious whirling sound was coming from somewhere, adding to his state of confusion.

'Where do we go from here?' he asked the Burkeshi, who was staring into the sky.

'Up.'

29

Cirona shoved her way through the rapidly thinning crowd. The citizens of Dronkor were fleeing from the market, the vendors hurriedly packing up their wares. *The town's meagre watch will surely arrive soon*, Cirona thought, *it'll be best to not be around when they do*. Frantically, she looked around her and finally caught sight of Bellina by a fountain, looking dazed.

'Bellina? Bellina? Look at me.'

'Huh, oh, Major, thank the gods you're here! I... I don't know what to do, Midge... he's...'

'Gone? I know. Barag and some of Gulgarno's men took him.'

'No! Who? What the hells do we do?'

'Men from the gladiator school. We get him back. Listen, I'm going to lower your power restraints. You reach out and find him.'

'There are a lot of people ... but I'll try.'

Cirona pressed a gem on the control conduit twice and watched the girl. She saw her turn even paler, reeling back like she'd been slapped.

Bellina scrunched her brows and beads of sweat trickled down her face.

'Can you hear him?' Cirona asked.

'Barely ... there is so much noise.'

'Does he know where he is? What's happening to him?'

'He's frightened. Sobbing... he's moving very fast, uphill ... in a carriage, I think. He glimpsed a bridge in the distance.'

'Shit! They must be taking him out of town by the West Gate. How the fuck are we supposed to catch up to them?'

Suddenly, the air was filled with a terrific whirring sound and a huge shadow passed over them.

Cirona could hardly believe her eyes. The immense elongated balloon of the airship hovered above them. Steam billowed from it like a volcano preparing to erupt. The corkscrew propeller at the back whirled so fast it looked like a perfect circle. A thick rope tumbled down towards them.

'I think this is our ride.' She grabbed Bellina tightly round the middle and took hold of the rope. It shot upwards with breathtaking speed, the town shrinking beneath them, becoming an abstract mess of colours and shapes.

They burst through a trapdoor in the bottom of the airship, which shut behind them with a welcome click. The rope they had just made their dizzying ascent on was attached to a winch on the wooden craft's ceiling which was controlled mechanically with pistons and gears.

'Where is young Midge?' Barboza asked.

'Taken. Gulgarno's men,' Cirona explained, looking around the room. It was more like a study than a ship's cabin — a decent enough space with bookshelves on one side, a bed at the back, a table and chairs. A wall with a single door and round window cut off the space at the far end leading to the control room a door on the left led to the observation deck. 'And where's Melek?'

'Through there,' Holger replied, pointing at the door.

She strode towards it and entered the control room. The engineer sat at a desk covered in brass dials, switches and levers. The arced front of the airship was one curving window.

'Ah, Major! Still attracting trouble, I see,' he said, without turning.

'No time Melek, turn us towards the West Gate and look for a carriage. One of our number has been taken.'

'Certainly madam,' Melek said, performing a series of intricate pulls and flicks.

The airship started to turn gently to port. He pulled a lever and the craft shot forward with a speed that made her body jolt. Cirona stared out of the window, looking down at the world below. They soon passed over the west gate and kept following the road that led from town. It didn't take long forthe fields of Varash to spread out below them like a carpet of dark blood, dismal clutches of trees sped past, the west road traced across the landscape, a sandy snake. 'There they are! Turn more to port!'

The *Sighing Wind* shifted gently. Dust from the speeding wagon clouded the air around it, partially obscuring it form view. Their quarry was a good distance away but the airship was quickly closing the distance.

'There, below us. Good. Melek, can you hold us to the speed of the carriage?'

'Of course, but what are you going to do? The *Sighing Wind* has no weapons.'

'I'm going to go down there and take back what's ours,' Cirona said and stormed back into the other room. The rest of the party watched her, eyes wide, registering an array of emotions.

'Dargo, give me your knife. Reveeker, get over there and operate that winch. Bellina, tell Midge I'm coming.'

'Major, you're not thinking of going down there while we're still in flight?' Elvgren asked as Dargo and the others carried out her orders.

'Damn right I am. Once that carriagegets to another town or city, we're done for. Got to stop them now.' With that she strode over to the rope and nodded at Rev who pulled a lever on the wall. The trapdoor opened and the bracing breeze whipped at her clothes. Her head spun when she looked down — she was not a fan of heights. Cirona thought about how scared Midge must be feeling and put her own fears aside. She wrapped the rope around herself and gave another nod to Rev who pulled a second lever. The rope started to descend. Cirona caught one last glimpse of the gang before dropping towards the fleeing carriage.

In no time, she was swinging in the air, just above the roof of the coach. The driver looked around at her in complete amazement and tried to spur the horses on faster.

Cirona shifted her weight towards the top of the carriage and let go of the rope. She slammed on to the wooden top with a bone-jarring jolt eliciting angry cries from inside. Crawling to the side, she lowered herself over the edge and dropped to the foot board. She grabbed hold of the door handle. Through the window, she could see the fat face of Gulgarno and the rat features of Barag. Midge sat bound and gagged in the middle of the two men. Fury surged within her and she smashed the glass.

Gulgarno screamed like a schoolgirl whilst Barag lunged for the door. He turned the handle, pushing the door and Cirona outwards.

She clung, with bleeding fingers, to the base of the smashed window and tensed for the impact. Her body cracked into the side of the carriage. She could see Barag's face, twisted in anger, leering at her as he smashed the door back and forth. Cirona felt the air knocked out of her but still clung on. He pulled her towards him once more and she stuck her hand through the window, clawing at his face. Falling backwards, he tumbled over the squealing form of Gulgarno. She pulled herself round the door and leapt into the compartment.

'Give. Me. The boy,' she said, Dargo's knife in her hand, ready to strike.

'No! I personally came here to ensure your retrieval and I'm not leaving without you. You are mine, mine damn it! I paid for you. This is outrageous!' Gulgarno rambled with Barag sitting at his feet like the family dog.

Gulgarno tried to move towards her but she stuck the point of the blade into the blubbery flesh around his neck. 'Don't you fucking dare! Hand the boy over now and you get to live. Negotiations are ended. Now you've got about three seconds before I lose my patience and kill you.'

'You can't...'

'One...'

'There are laws...'

'Two...'

'You will be hounded for the rest of...'

'Thre—'

'Fine, fine, take the bloody thing! Too scrawny to entertain me anyway,' Gulgarno said, pushing the boy towards her.

Midge stumbled into her arms tears glistening on his cheeks. The warmth of his tears soaked through to her skin and a lever switched in her mind. She drove the point of the blade into Gulgarno's neck, twisting it to add to the pain. He gurgled and gulped, immense limbs flailing, hands grabbing at his throat. She flicked her wrist and slashed from one side to the other, an arc of blood splattering against the wall.

Barag watched, mouth agog. He cried out in fury and lunged at her. Cirona pushed Midge behind her and slammed her fist into Barag's face. Pinning him to the wall of the carriage, she rained down blow upon blow till he crouched on the floor spitting blood. She sent a vicious kick into his temple and he collapsed. Cirona turned to Midge and pulled the gag from his mouth. His wails washed over her. 'It's alright, it's alright,' she said, hugging the boy tight before undoing his bonds. Crouching down, she looked into his eyes. 'Midge, listen to me. I need you to be brave. Can you do that for me?'

Midge nodded.

'We have to climb onto the roof of this carriage. I'll push you up.' The pair went over to the door and Cirona pushed the scrabbling boy onto the roof before hoisting herself up. The driver looked round at her again. 'Pull over if you want to keep breathing!' she said.

The driver gulped hard and nodded.

'Don't you fucking dare!' Barag roared from inside. 'What's she gonna do? If she kills you, the whole thing will crash!'

Fucking little weasel is tougher than he looks, she thought. They would have to do this the hard way. Cirona stood up on the carriage roof and tried to keep her balance. She clutched Midge close to her side and eyed the swaying rope. It flicked towards her and she grabbed it. The rope started to ascend but jammed about five feet above the carriage. *What the fuck is happening now?* As she swung helplessly on the rope, the bloody form of Barag crawled onto the roof.

'Midge, quickly, climb up the rope!'

The boy extracted himself from her grip and began to shimmy upwards.

Cirona waited until he was a good distance up before beginning her own ascent. There was a sharp pull on her leg and she looked down to see Barag's face snarling up at her. She tried to kick out at him but his grip was iron. The rope jolted and started to ascend. Barag pulled himself up her legs and drove his head into her stomach. She felt the air escape from her lungs and her grip loosen. Thankfully, she was quick to regain her composure, as they were now higher than athree storey house. Barag headbutted her stomach again. She had to do something. An idea came to her. She let go of the rope with one of her hands — their combined weight was now held by just one arm, her muscles trembled under the strain. Using her free hand, she grabbed Barag's dark, greasy hair and whipped his head furiously back and forth. He lost his grip and fell away from her.

Time slowed as Cirona watched Barag plummet to his death. His legs flailed and his arms whirled madly but his hate-filled eyes stayed locked on hers.

30

The ground passed by at an amiable pace. Bellina took it all in, filled with wonder. She had always loved being up high, the cable cars and elevated railway of the Imperial Capital were a sought after treat for her. On the *Sighing Wind*, she could see the whole world pass by, not just a city. She stood on the observation deck of the vessel. The oars were outspread, helping propel and turn the airship, rising and falling with the aid of unseen mechanical hands. *Melek has created a truly marvellous thing*, she thought. Bellina had asked what the engineer intended to do now he knew his airship worked as expected. Riches and fame could be his, the world changed forever. His mind was filled with the military potential though. He described, in great detail, the devastating effect a fleet of airships could have. She pushed the thought away and tried to re-focus on the beauty laid out before her.

'It's quite the rum old thing, this flying lark, eh?'

Bellina turned and was surprised to see Elvgren standing beside her at the airship's rail.

'It certainly is, Lord Elvgren. What brings you out here? I thought heights gave you dizzy spells?'

'Oh, they do but I thought it best we had a talk, a long overdue one, and seeing as only you, Dargo and…that Narvglander have the stomach for coming out here, it seemed the best chance to find you alone.'

'I see. Speak on then.'

'Do you still have your betrothal token?'

'Ha! I am afraid that is long gone. Lost it with the *Prudence*.'

'A convenient excuse,' he said.

Bellina didn't like his tone. 'What do you mean by that?'

'Well, you turn up, ragtag crew in tow *and* an admirer. One who I am beginning to think is unaware of our standing.'

'Admirer? Our standing? What are you on about?'

'You know damn well what I'm on about. That man, Holger, he has eyes for you. I will not stand for it. You are mine… well, what I mean to say, is that we are promised to each other. You must make our situation clear to him. You are a noble, him even daring to think of you in such a way is an affront to your birth. It's enough to have him flogged.'

Bellina reeled from the outburst. Holger was her friend but in the pit of her stomach she knew that Elvgren was only airing a suspicion that her own mind had been keeping at bay. Still, a defensive fury welled up inside her. 'How dare you!' she said, her body shaking with rage. 'I am yours? *Yours*? I am not a fucking possession for you to put up on a bloody shelf. If I was to sleep with a one-legged fisherman it would be no business of yours.'

'That's where you're wrong. You *are* mine and I am yours,' he hissed softly, leaning in.

'Ah, what a privilege, to be next in line to catch the clap from a one-eyed man who's already stuck his cock in half the whores in Estria!' She felt that she had gone too far but, at the same time, she felt the thrill of her anger burning through her.

'You are insufferable! But, and know this, I will have my reward for this venture. The whole bloody lot. You understand me!' Elvgren said, before flouncing back inside.

Bellina stared into the distance and tried her best to get her emotions in check. A reward? A prize? That's what he thought.

'What was all that about?' Holger's voice came to her from behind.

'Oh... nothing. Just his usual rubbish,' Bellina replied, as the young man came to stand next to her.

'What a view! Can't quite believe it, me — flying,' he said, letting out a low whistle.

Bellina turned her head slightly and looked at Holger. A huge grin was spread across his face and his eyes were shining. She found his expression endearing in a childlike way.

'D'ya... d'ya think that mages used to be able to fly?' he asked.

'Probably just another myth. If they could, why didn't they just fly off before they were captured?'

'S'pose so,' he said with a strange little smile. 'Don't let that mouthy idiot get to yer, Belle. Shit spills out every time he opens his mouth.'

'You're telling me. He certainly has a way with people. I've yet to meet a person who has spent thirty minutes in his company and not wanted to punch him.'

Their eyes met and they laughed.

*

'Two claristas and a prince!' Cirona said, slapping down her cards happily. She looked at Reveeker who groaned and threw his cards down.

'I think I will be taking my—' she began, but was cut off by Dargo.

'Not so fast! Not. So. Fast. I am afraid, Major, that I happen to be in possession of the noble duke and two princes. The spoils belong to me,' the boy said, reaching across the table and pulling the small stack of coins towards him.

Well, Cirona thought, *it all belongs to him anyway.* That was a dismal thought. Everything, except the money Dargo had on him, had been lost at the inn. Neither Elvgren nor Reveeker had spoken about what had happened and their already tense relationship seemed to have grown even more strained.

Just then the door to the observation platform burst open and Elvgren stomped angrily across the cabin, before throwing himself down dramatically on the bed.

'What's got into the moody git now? Better go and have a word with him. Oh, and by the way, I know exactly how much coin there is on this table,' Dargo said, casting a suspicious eye over them.

With his departure Rev and Cirona were left alone at the table. Barboza, Crenshaw,Midge and Holger were in the control room — Barboza and Crenshaw, in particular, had developed a deep interest in the *Sighing Wind.*

'I am sure that boy is cheating,' Reveeker said, pushing his pile of cards into the middle of the table.

'Well, he was raised in a den of iniquity. Pretty sure that cheating at cards is just one of his many talents,' she replied. 'So, how are you feeling?'

'About what, Rona?'

'All this. Going home, being swept up in our personal shitstorm, flying? Take your pick.'

'Huh, it *is* a lot to take in, I'll admit. Home. Now there's a word. Burkesh has not been my home for many a year. Probably from before I was sold. It was becoming a dark place even then. I suppose my greatest fear is that there will be nothing left of what I remember, all the places that I have held dear in my heart swept away. Gone, like they never existed.'

'It's a hard thing to go home,' Cirona said, though it was not a feeling she could relate to. The thought suddenly struck her that she had never had a home to call her own — raised in the orphanage, then moving to the bunkhouses of the academy, military camps, the palace... All, somebody else's home. *It's a funny thing,* she thought, *to feel the loss of something I've never had. Maybe now though, after this ... with my daughter ... perhaps?*

'Are you alright, Rona?' Rev asked.

'Yeah, sorry. Just daydreaming, I'm listening.'

'Do not worry. I myself have been caught in many a daytime reverie and you have much to ponder.'

'Tell me about it.'

Their conversation was interrupted by Holger bursting out of the control room. A look of excitement mingled with terror on his face.

'Come and look at this. You can see the bloody scorched earth from up here! Come on!'

Cirona and Reveeker got up and went into the control room.

Midge, Barboza and Crenshaw stood staring out to port through the curved observation window. Their mouths were open and their eyes were wide.

'By the gods!' Cirona heard herself exclaim.

There it was, far off in the distance. The shore of the scorched earth, the vast damned continent where, tens of thousands of years ago, the races of the world had battled the Old Terrors. Above its black cliffs, a permanent cloud swirled. Purples of every hue imaginable rippled and forks of green lightning rained from the skies. That they could witness it from such a distance with the naked eye, was a testament to the magnitude of the storm.

'Is there really treasure there, Captain?' Midge asked Barboza.

'No one knows. The place is cursed and no man with any sense would set foot on its shores. Any who have tried have never returned to tell their tale,' Barboza said, adopting an eerie voice.

Midge trembled and held tightly to the big man's leg.

'Don't worry Midge,' Cirona said. 'We aren't going anywhere near it.' The sight was certainly chilling in a way she couldn't quite fathom, the horror was reflexive. *No time for this superstitious shit, she thought, we'll have enough physical terrors to deal with soon enough.*

*

Bellina looked down at the wide, flat plain that spread beneath them.

The *Sighing Wind* had come to a stop, hovering a safe distance away from the city of Krangoon to allay Melek's worries that his invention might upset the local populace. She took one last look from her aerial viewpoint before walking back inside the airship. In the cabin, those who were going on and those who weren't had split into two groups. Elvgren, Dargo, Cirona, Reveeker and Holger were standing close to the exit hatch. Barboza, Crenshaw, Midge and Melek stood with their backs to the control room.

'So, my lady, this is where we part ways,' Barboza said, with a sad smile.

'I fear so. Sorry we can't pay you for your time,' she said with a wink.

'Do not worry yourself on that front, my lady, I shall send your father a bill,' he replied with a laugh and a bow.

Bellina wasn't sure he was joking. 'Stop bowing, you fool!' She hugged him, her hands unable to complete a full circle around his massive frame. 'And you,' she said, turning her hug on Crenshaw, 'try not to get in too much trouble.'

'That's always the plan, my lady. Not our fault it never works out like that,' Crenshaw said, grinning.

Her heart sinking, she moved on to Midge. The boy looked up at her, tears already filling his eyes.

'Don't go, Lady Belle,' he said, grabbing her around the waist.

Bellina knelt down and he rested his head in the nook of her shoulder. 'I'm sorry, Midge. There is something I have to do,' she said, welling up.

'Enough of this sadness! We will meet again, perhaps in Estria!' Barboza said, pointing dramatically.

'Estria's this way, mate,' Crenshaw said, gently revolving his friend's body so he pointed the right way.

Even Midge had to laugh. Barboza pouted but eventually allowed a smile to light up his face.

Bellina gave Midge one last squeeze and moved along to Melek. The inventor performed an elaborate bow, she curtseyed in response. 'Thank you Melek, for your help. Are you sure about taking him on though?' she said, jerking her thumb at Barboza.

'Absolutely! I won't be able to run everything on board by myself and Messrs Barboza and Crenshaw have been very enthusiastic about learning the workings of the *Sighing Wind*. One day, there will be a fleet of airships just like this one and they will need to be manned by someone.'

Bellina pondered for a moment the kind of mayhem Barboza could reap in a flying machine. Then she moved towards the hatch. The group exited the vessel one by one on the rope, Bellina was the last to leave. She shot one last look at the friends she was leaving behind. Giving them a smile and a nod, she felt her stomach turn as the rope shot downwards.

31

The *Sighing Wind* was a rapidly shrinking dot on the horizon. Elvgren gave one last look at the miraculous airship before turning back to the Krangoon road. The two-day flight across the ocean had not been fun. He hated heights with a passion and, the way the craft had swayed one particular night, he thought that he could not be the only person on board unimpressed with aeronautics.

He looked ahead and saw that he had fallen behind. Melek had set them down a fair distance outside the city of Krangoon. Thankfully, the Chentanese had a better road-building policy than Varash. A broad pathway of expertly cut stones stretched ahead, cutting through the irrigated rice fields. The workers in the fields paid them no mind, accustomed as they were to the comings and goings of Estrians. In fact, Krangoon had one of the largest populations of Estrians on the eastern continent — owing to Chenta, along with Mandira, being the linchpins of the Grand Imperial Trading Company.

He looked at the remaining members of their party. Reveeker and Cirona walked, side by side, absorbed in conversation, Dargo was strutting about behind them and Bellina and Holger took the lead. He chewed his lip as he thought about how his conversation with Bellina had gone. He hadn't intended to be so bullish; he felt shabby about the whole thing. She had to be made to realise that the boy wanted more than friendship though. Elvgren would be damned if he would have her snatched away. This mission and his betrothal to her were his ticket to honour, a chance to finally outshine his brother in the eyes of his family.

After a good two hours' walk, they reached the walls of the city. Two guards stood to attention by the massive entrance. It was known as the Hanging Gate, a place famous throughout the empire, and it was obvious why at close inspection. Spread out across the top of the gate, along the stone wall, were carvings of dragons' heads. From each mouth hung the body of a condemned criminal, the lifeless form swaying in the breeze. It was a testament to the fact that, although the Estrians had a large presence in the city, Chentanese traditions were preserved. They passed beneath the grisly scene and through the gate, without any acknowledgment from the guards.

As they walked along the main thoroughfare of Krangoon, Elvgren remembered from a book his father had given him about the empire's eastern interests that the city was laid out in a grid formation, following some celestial plan. It was an odd thing to see every street ending in a sharp corner, but each to their own. Along the side of the road, tall wooden buildings with pointed roofs rose upwards. The beams supporting the roofs flared outwards, a variety of unnerving mythical creatures were carved into them. They stared down, barely tolerating the presence of the humans beneath them, happy to devour any one of them in the blink of an eye.

The people of Krangoon hustled and bustled around them. Street vendors hawked their wares, and all the other sounds of a thriving city bombarded Elvgren's ears. A food merchant offered him a roasted terrapin served in its own shell, which he politely declined. A gaggle of children swarmed around them asking for money or trying to sell them charms. In fact, it was becoming incredibly difficult to make any progress. Then, without warning, the children ran away to the side of the road and flung themselves, prostrated, on the ground. Elvgren looked left and right, seeing that the rest of the people on the street had followed suit. Some had their heads pressed firmly against the ground while others had theirs raised a bit higher. He realised that the Chentanese could be sorted into groups by their social standing, each one identified by a different variation of the same pose. Elvgren and the rest of his companions stared around them to see what was causing the strange scene.

'Get into the side of the road and bow your head, you imbeciles!' A voice hissed at them.

They turned and saw an Estrian frantically beckoning them over to him. He had the fine clothes and large gut of a well-to-do merchant. They made their way to where he stood.

'Right, stand like I am and bow your head just so,' he said crossing his hands over his stomach and inclining his chin.

They did as instructed, though Reveeker looked about as happy with the situation as Elvgren felt. Before too long, the reason for the deferential poses came into view. A man in a long, silk gown came swaggering down the street. In front of him, two men furiously swept the ground he was about to walk on. Despite the angle of his head,

Elvgren could make out the man's smug look, his almond-shaped eyes taking in the view with an air of complete satisfaction. He stroked at a long thin beard before returning his hands to the billowing expanse of his sleeves. The man and his retinue made their leisurely way onwards.

The merchant who had pulled them aside whistled in relief. 'Bloody close thing that! What in the twelve hells were you thinking?'

'I am sorry, kind sir, we meant no offence,' explained Bellina. 'We have just arrived in Krangoon today. Who was that man?'

'That? That was the Hetong, the governor of the province. All must bow in his presence, though foreigners are allowed some leeway. It was lucky I caught your eye, the locals like nothing more than to see Estrians get a flogging instead of them. Oh, please excuse my manners, I am Melvin Asterbrook, merchant with the Grand Imperial Trading Company. At your service,' he said, bowing.

The rest of the group responded in kind, with Dargo and Holger overdoing it. Reveeker just nodded his head.

Melvin looked at the group with a raised brow. 'Quite a strange gathering you have here,' he said eyeballing the Burkeshi.

'Oh yes, we are on a tour of the Empire's eastern interests. The Burkeshi here is our guide to the region,' Bellina said.

'I am not one to cast doubts on your choice of companions, my lady. Please excuse my rudeness. Well, I am afraid I must be off. If you find that you need help getting to know the city, please look me up.'

'That is most kind Mr. Asterbrook, our utmost thanks to you. Though we do not intend to stay long in Krangoon.'

'A shame. Goodbye, my lady. Gentlemen,' he said, nodding his head at them before setting off down the street.

'That was a damned good bit of fortune and no mistake,' Elvgren said.

'Half an hour in the city and we almost copped a beating. That would have been embarrassing,' Dargo said, scratching his chin.

'What in the name of the gods was that all about?' Holger asked.

'The Chentanese have a very rigid society,' said Reveeker. 'Government bureaucrats work for the Fei Doh, king for want of a better word. He is considered divine, thus, those who carry out his orders are doing the will of the gods and have to be respected.'

'Divine? Why, what a load of old tosh!' Elvgren said.

'Is it so different from what the countries that make up Estrian Empire believe?' Reveeker said.

'We don't consider our kings to be *gods*. Just appointed by them, how the hells is a country supposed to advance if they have to fall to their knees every time some clerk walks down the street? It's a miracle anything gets done around here,' Elvgren said.

'It certainly is, considering half the country's population is also out of their minds on shafi leaf,' Reveeker's said.

Elvgren felt a wave of indignation rush over him. 'How bloody dare you! I suppose storming around slaughtering everyone around you is the best way to subdue a population!'

'Enough, the pair of you,' cut in Cirona. 'We haven't got time to discuss the evils of empires. We need to find supplies and get moving. The longer we stay in one place the more chance we have of being spotted.'

*

The group spent the rest of the day procuring the essentials for the journey ahead. Tailors took their measurements and produced their garments in a matter of hours. They acquired a down-at-heel pair of ballistols and the shot to fire them with before gathering food supplies. The items had all been bought with Dargo's stash of money, which he had loaned out to them at an extortionate rate. He said they could repay him on their return to Estria.

'Think that should do it,' Cirona said, putting some smoked armodile into a kitbag. 'Here Rev, take this bag. Elvgren you take the other.'

'Why is *he* not taking anything?' Elvgren said pointing at Holger.

'For the love of the gods! We are going to take turns. Stop bloody whingeing'

Elvgren pursed his mouth and stared into the distance.

They worked their way through the city towards the East Gate. Reveeker had said the best way to the military outpost was through the jungle, two days' walk from Krangoon. After that it would be a hike up the forested mountains.

When they reached the gate, they found two guards barring the way, their long spears crossed in front of the exit.

'What is the meaning of this?' Reveeker asked.

'Way ahead barred. No one passes this way without the seal of the Hetong,' one of the guards replied.

'Well this is just fantastic. What are we going to do now?' Dargo asked.

'Get the seal, of course,' Reveeker said, matter of factly.

*

The group walked through the portion of the city occupied by the Grand Imperial Trading Company. Stone-fronted buildings in the Estrian style lined the docks and the merchants' families went about their daily business. For Bellina, it was a bittersweet reminder of home.

After asking passers-by a few questions, they had been given directions to Melvin the merchant's office. They had all decided that he was the best person to help them get the Hetong's seal.

They found the building and were shown into Asterbrook's office by a thin, waspish man. He looked askance at them as they passed him and visibly baulked at the sight of Reveeker.

Upon their entry, Melvin looked up from a formidable stack of papers. 'Ah, my travelling friends. You've decided to stay longer in the fair city of Krangoon after all, eh?' he said, his expression amiable.

'Our plans have run into a small snag, I'm afraid old chap,' Elvgren said. 'Damned guards won't let us leave the city through the East Gate. Something about a seal.'

'Hmm. I did not know you intended to travel in that direction. This may be a problem,' Melvin said, stroking his cheek.

'What, pray tell, is the cause for such strict regulations?' Bellina asked.

'It is a decree direct from the Fei Doh. Until the silly business with Burkesh is sorted out, His Divine Magnificence has declared that all gates and roads to Burkesh be placed under the closest scrutiny. As such, only the seal of a Hetong can allow passage and it is most rare for one to be granted. Surely you are not intending to go to Burkesh? The latest news from there is that diplomats and traders are being held to ransom. There has still been no news of Lord Farvenstare and his wife, since their capture,' he said, shooting a loaded glance at Reveeker.

'Ah, you misunderstand us, wehave business at the military outpost on the border, not Burkesh itself and we're in a hurry. We need to get through that gate. Is there any way to meet with the Hetong?' Cirona asked, cutting straight to the point.

'A note from a respected merchant of the Grand Imperial Trading

Company may get you into the Bureaucratic Palace. But it would be, ahem, a bit risky for the merchant in question,' Melvin said with a meaningful look.

'People are the fucking same anywhere. I get yer meaning, here's ten rencats. Now give us a bloody letter,' Dargo said, slamming down his money on the table.

'How uncouth. What gutter was this little rat brought up in? I say! Attempting to bribe a senior trader, it's a scandal,' Melvin said.

Dargo sighed and put down a further ten rencats.

This time the merchant slid the money across the table and pocketed it. 'Give me fifteen minutes and you shall have your letter.'

*

Half an hour later they were striding through the city towards the Bureaucratic Palace.

'This is a good start but what are we going to tell them when we get there? And Dargo, what are you scribbling?' Elvgren said.

'Oh this? This is your bill, just working out how much you lot will owe me when this is all finished. Never realised that espionage would turn out so profitable!' he said with a grin.

'You are a damned reprobate, you know that!' Reveeker said laughing. 'But his *majesty* is right. What *do* we say?'

'Why don't we just tell them what we're about?' Holger said.

Bellina looked at him amused. *There's not a dishonest bone in his body, is there?* 'Fantastic idea!' said Elvgren sarcastically. 'I can just imagine the conversation now: Oh hello, Mr. Official. We're on a mission to steal sensitive information from your neighbours, that could cause you a bit of trouble too, but just be a good chap and let us through.'

'Alight, mate, don't shit your britches. Just a thought. And that tone ain't helpful, is it?' Holger replied, a look of suppressed anger on his face.

'I'll talk to you any damn way I please, you stinking peasant.'

'No, you bloody won't!' spat back Holger, jabbing a finger at Elvgren. 'I don't gotta take any shit from you!'

This is not looking good, Bellina thought.

Thankfully Cirona stepped in. 'All right, that's enough! For all that is holy, why have I been stuck babysitting this nursery of madness? Pack it in, the pair of you. You know, the only reason I let *you* Holger and *you* Dargo come along is because you have proved yourself useful. I am beginning to regret that decision.' Cirona paused, rubbing her forehead. 'Now Elvgren, stop being a prick. And Holger, as much as it pains me to say it he is above you in rank and station. You're a Narvglander, right? So, you know Estrian protocol. It still exists — even here. Oh, and Dargo stop writing that fucking bill! The rate our luck is going, we won't make it to Burkesh, let alone home!' Her tirade over, the major took a deep breath.

The three young men looked as though they had been slapped and Bellina had to suppress her laughter.

'I could nick this seal, so I could,' Dargo said, after a while.

'Thanks for the offer, Dargo,' replied Bellina, 'but we should try not to cause too many international incidents.'

'You are all overthinking this. We go in, ask for the seal, say we are traders. The more you complicate things, the worse it gets,' Reveeker said.

'Rev's right,' added Cirona. 'We keep it simple. Let me and him handle the talking in there. Agreed?'

*

The Bureaucratic Palace was hard to miss. The massive building sat at the heart of a square lake. Wooden bridges with dragon-shaped railings connected the palace to the rest of Krangoon. They passed over one of these and waited by the steps that led into the building. Their papers from the merchant were taken away to be looked over. After a short while, a guard beckoned them in and led them to a pair of elaborately decorated doors, which opened onto a breathtaking inner space.

The walls were carved ivory reliefs made from an unfathomable amount of phantalus tusks. The floor was mahogany, polished to a brilliant sheen. Delicate porcelain vases on plinths formed the borders of a pathway to the centre of the room. There, at a table, sat the Hetong. He was scribbling on some papers, an assistant by his side. The guard led them towards him before withdrawing.

'You wish to speak to me? I do not normally take audience with people stupid enough to fall for Asterbrook's letter scheme. How many do we receive a day, Foo Ta?' the Hetong asked the man to his side.

'At least ten, my lord,' the man replied.

'Yes, that's it. The fat little trademonger makes quite a profit selling his letters of introduction. However, the description of your little collective interested me. A group of Estrians abroad with a Burkeshi? This was something I needed to see.'

'No matter how we gained this audience with your lordship, we are most grateful,' Cirona said. 'I am afraid we have a pressing matter at hand. We are merchants and we require your leave to take the East Gate and make for the Burkeshi mountain crossing.' Cirona said.

At this, the man broke into a fit of laughter. 'Merchants? You are funny, I will give you that. But you are not merchants and I was not born this noon. Tell me, who are you really?'

Bellina's stomach churned. *Damn, we should have thought this through properly*, she mused, their haste had driven them to rash action.

'You have us good sir. You've got us good,' Elvgren said, to everyone's surprise.

Oh no, what the hells is this idiot going to do now? thought Bellina.

Cirona and Rev were looking daggers at him.

Elvgren cleared his throat. 'You happen to have in your chambers, the cream of Estrian nobility.'

'That is enough out of you my *lord*,' Reveeker hissed.

'No, no. I'm afraid it's not. We are nobles from Estria. I am sure we seem a rum old bunch to your eyes but necessity makes strange friends of us all. Myself and the young lady are the children of Lord and Lady Farvenstare. The others you see before you, are our guardians and staff. The boy is my page and the other one is a fool we keep in our employ to amuse us,' Elvgren said pointing at Holger, who clenched his jaw so hard Bellina worried he might break it.

She had to hand it to Elvgren. It was a bold move but it seemed to be having some effect on the Hetong.

'Lord and Lady Farvenstare ... The ones who were taken hostage by Burkeshi bandits?'

'The very same. We are on our way to personally negotiate the ransom and release of our parents. So you see, we are in considerable haste. Isn't that right, sister?' Elvgren said, looking at her.

'Quite so, brother, quite so,' Bellina said, trying her best to sound worried — an emotion not that hard to feign given their current circumstance.

'This is most unusual. I would have to contravene a direct order from the Fei Do himself; like contravening the gods.' He paused a few seconds. 'Foo Ta, leave us for a moment.'

'Your will, Hetong,' Foo Ta said, bowing low before exiting the room.

'It would seem your needs and mine intersect. I have a certain, ahem, understanding with the Estrian captain stationed at the outpost on the mountain border. He usually drops by for his payment most regularly but I have not seen him this past week. I would like you to take a package to him and remind him gently that we are entwined in this deal together, in case he has other ideas,' the Hetong said.

Bellina wasn't sure that she liked the sound of this. She glanced at Cirona who gave the briefest of shrugs.

'Would it not be better to send one of your own men?' Elvgren asked, who looked none too thrilled by how the situation had turned.

'That would unfortunately raise too many questions. These are my terms, accept them or accept you parents' fate,' the Hetong said with a tone of finality.

'It would seem we are your emissaries then, my lord. We will deliver your package in exchange for your authority to travel,' Cirona said.

'Excellent, I will have your passes drawn up immediately. It goes without saying that word of this must be breathed to no one.'

32

Steam rose visibly from the jungle's foliage. Cirona hacked through a dense tangle of vines, the moisture from the plant covering her arm as she worked. With every breath, the humid air strangled the life from her lungs, making each step a major undertaking.

She paused for a moment to let the others catch up. Bellina and Holger joined her first, sweat streaming from their faces. She was in half a mind to say something to the boy herself. His lovesick shadowing of Bellina needed addressed — the girl was showing no sign of dealing with the matter. Though he was going about it in his usual ham-fisted way, Elvgren had a point. Bellina was betrothed to him and that *did* mean something, wherever they were in the world. For the sake of the group Holger needed to be told to save his affections for someone else. Just another job she had no heart for, much like her mission in Burkesh. Cirona fended the thoughts away, knowing that she would play her role if it meant the chance to see her daughter again.

Elvgren arrived behind Bellina and Holger. He was brooding angrily, engaged in a desperate attempt to keep the sweat out of his good eye. Cirona could see him muttering under his breath. The boy's quick thinking back at the Bureaucratic Palace had been inspired but she was not pleased about being the patsy and message bearer of a bloody jumped-up official. She had, therefore, made sure that the extra weight of the Hetong's delivery was added to Elvgren's load.

Bringing up the rear were Reveeker and Dargo. The young boy was chatting excitedly to the Burkeshi. Rev was laughing at something the lad had said and giving him a clap on the back. Dargo beamed from ear-to-ear at the show of affection and started on another wild tale. *He must have been a damned good father*, she thought. Cirona marvelled at the way that Rev could interact with Dargo, especially when she considered what he had lost and *how* he had lost it.

'What's the bloody hold up, Major?' Elvgren puffed. 'And when is someone else going to take their turn with the load?' He had taken the opportunity to slide the burden from his back. He lifted his eye patch to wipe the sweat away from where his left eye should be.

A pang of sympathy passed through her. *Poor fucker*, she thought, regretting her little show of spite in giving him more to carry. 'Holger take the load. Your turn,' she commanded.

The boy went over to Elvgren, a look of anger on his face. Elvgren gave a condescending smile as he let go of the bag, then stretched his shoulders.

Cirona turned away and resumed hacking at the jungle.

*

The group had finally stopped for the night and Bellina's aching body was glad of the rest. They were all huddled around a fire that Cirona and Rev had performed a minor miracle in getting alight. The meagre rations had been handed out. She took a bite from a dry crust of bread and followed it up with a wrestling match between her teeth and a strip of smoked armodile.

The jungle plant life pressed in around her, a green claw that gripped them tight. The trees obscured any possible sighting of the Ganteng Mountains, but Reveeker assured them that they were on the right course. His knowledge of the local landscape and cultures had been invaluable on their journey, it made her think about how little attention Estrians paid to the rest of the world.

Cirona moved round to sit next to her. Bellina was acutely aware of the damp from the decomposing log she sat on seeping through her clothes. *She must have a good reason to leave her small dry patch to come and talk to me.*

'Lady Bellina, I feel we must have a word,' the major said.

'It must be serious! These days you only address me as *Lady* when there's something up,' she said, only half jokingly.

Cirona lowered her voice and continued. 'It's about Holger. He... well, there's no way to say it delicately ... the lad has taken a fancy to you.'

Bellina felt her cheeks redden and was glad of the darkness that hid it.

'We are friends. That's all. There's nothing more to it than that.'

'I don't think that's how he sees it. I also think you like the attention,' Cirona said.

Bellina opened her mouth to object but the major held up a hand to halt her.

'Don't get me wrong. It's only natural, he's not the ugliest bloke in the shuffle by any means. Given how your life has been governed, it's probably the first time you've experienced anything like it. Ha, at your age, in Bottom Barrow, you'd have two nippers swinging from your tits by now. But I digress. My point is: have a chat with him. Tell him about your betrothal. We've got a long way to go and we all have to be reading from the same scripture if we're going to make it. He's coming back from a piss now, I'll leave you to it.'

The major left and went back to her dry spot. Bellina felt a torrent of emotions inside her. She was outraged at the blunt statement of facts that Cirona had just laid out before her. It was accompanied by the sadness of realising that what she had been told was true. Her heart sank when she thought about what she would have to say. Above all else, she didn't want to lose Holger's friendship. The ease with which they chatted and joked had been a thrilling new experience for her — the first time someone not in the employ of her father had been kind and listened. Alas, whatever she thought of the whole thing she *was* betrothed to Elvgren. Bellina had done it for her father and she meant to see it through for his sake. The cloying hands of Estrian protocol reached out for her from half a world away, choking her with rules.

Holger caught her eye and smiled. He wandered over and sat next to her on the log. 'Wouldn't go too far out to answer the call of nature, Belle. Just saw a spider as big as his lordship's head, if you can believe such a thing!' He pointed at Elvgren, laughing.

Bellina let out a laugh of her own, it only made it harder to find the words that she needed to say. 'Holger... there's something we need to discuss.'

'What's up?'

'I... well, I'm just going to say it! Elvgren and I are betrothed. And... you see... any ideas you may have that we might possibly be more than friends, are out of the question,' Bellina said, her voice growing quieter towards the end. She watched Holger's face and, for a split second, she saw a strange flicker pass across it.

Then he broke into his broad smile. 'Oh... I suppose that makes what I've been wanting to say a bit tricky,' he said, running his hand through the short crop of strawberry blonde hair atop his head. 'I don't see you like that, Belle. As a matter of fact, you remind me of my sister, Anhar. You've got the same complexion — different hair though.'

Bellina felt a wave of relief at how he had taken the news, though she discovered that a part of her was rather disappointed. 'Oh! I didn't know you had a sister.'

'Yeah, couple of years younger than me. Tough as nails, just like you. She... she died, few years back. Fell through the ice one winter. I was out mucking around at the time. When I got home me mam told me what happened. Felt the shame of it all these years, should've been there, you know. Kinda why I said I'd come along with ye,' Holger said, his voice cracking slightly.

'I'm sorry, Holger. That's terrible. You can't blame yourself. Was no one else around who could have helped her?'

'Nah. Da died in a stupid skirmish with another village back when we was small. Me mam was never quite right after that. Once we lost Anhar she just came apart. It's why I left home. Joined a ship, legit at first, to send the money back to her. Then I got captured by the first captain of the *Vagabond*. Ain't been in touch since.'

'Do you miss her?' Bellina asked, a part of her pining for the mother she had never known.

'Miss how she was, not how I left her. I know I should've got word to her, sent money, but the opportunity for that is slim on a ship of fortune. Maybe when this is all over, I'll go home. Tell 'er 'bout me adventures. That I helped an honest to goodness lady protect our homeland. Make her proud,' he said trailing off.

He turned his face away and Bellina saw him wipe quickly at his eyes.

'Ah well. Think I'm gonna turn in, Belle. Try to find the least damp spot on the ground. Night.'

He stood up and wandered off, leaving Bellina with the residue of their conversation.

*

Elvgren awoke, covered in sweat. He had been dreaming that the large portrait of his brother, the one above the drawing room fire, had fallen on his head, while his parents stood around laughing. An urgent, pressing sensation come from his bladder. He looked out into the thick darkness of the jungle and felt less than happy to answer its call.

'Dargo? Dargo? Are you awake?' He hissed at the prone boy.

'Wahng... well I bloody am now. Wassa matter?'

'I ... um... need to relieve myself.'

'Sorry, Gren. Not into that kinda thing. Try your intended.'

Elvgren could picture the smirk on the little rat's face. 'You damn well know what I mean, you cheeky git. I am not going out into that wilderness alone!'

'For the love of the gods, man! Just go and piss. I need me beauty sleep.'

'Well, you'll be sleeping a long time to make up for the looks nature cursed *you* with!'

'Whatever, One Eye. Don't let the leoguars eat you,' Dargo said, pulling his coat around him.

Elvgren shot a furtive look into the plants and trees. A primeval fear flooded through him — it was a very real reminder that there were still untamed corners of the world. He mustered up his courage and stepped into the foliage. He went as far as his nerves would carry him — it probably wasn't far enough for politeness but at this point he didn't care. He selected a suitable tree in the gloom and enjoyed the satisfying feeling of his bladder emptying. He closed his eye and sighed in appreciation.

A twig cracked in the undergrowth and he snapped his good eye back open. He turned his head left and right until something caught his attention in the near distance. Two glowing round orbs with tiny, black slits for pupils glared at him through the leaves of a fern. Elvgren felt his breath catch and he stumbled backwards, falling hard on his rear. He glanced back in the direction of the eyes but nothing remained. Dragging himself to his feet, he hurried back to the others. He stood, contemplating waking up the major, then decided against it. *Just my mind playing tricks*, he told himself, *I certainly don't need to add the major's scorn to my embarrassment*. He settled down on the spot he had been sleeping in and drifted into a fitful dream. He was staring up at the portrait of his brother again, only this time the eyes were glowing.

33

It was noon the following day and black clouds threatened between the gaps of the jungle canopy. Cirona didn't like the look of them. A downpour now would be the last thing the group's spirits needed. Elvgren had woken up in a shocking mood and was being taunted by Dargo, the boy dancing away from the blows Elvgren tried to land on him. Looking at Bellina's expression, it appeared she had taken her advice and spoken with Holger. Cirona felt bad about the whole thing but, deep down, she knew it was for the best. Holger seemed troubled himself and she thought of the pain unrequited love could cause. A wave of sympathy washed over her, she wanted to put her arm around him and tell him it would be alright but, from her own experience, Cirona knew the mess young love could leave your insides in. The bad mood had even spread to Reveeker. He stormed ahead of the group hacking at the foliage with unrestrained ferocity. Cirona spurred her legs on and came up by his side.

'Something wrong, Rev?'

'What? Oh sorry, Rona. Had a bad night's sleep is all. I had the strangest dream... ah 'tis nonsense. Pay me no heed,' he said, shaking his head as if trying to rattle the thought from his mind.

'I, for one, slept like a log. If you want to tell me, feel free. I promise not to laugh too hard.'

'Alright, nothing better to do I suppose,' he replied, landing another forceful strike on a vine, decapitating an orchid in the process.

'I was walking home, to my town, though it wasn't my town ... bah, you see dreams are just horse *gavish*,' he said throwing up his hands.

'Go on, Rev, maybe once you've spoken about it your mood will improve. I've got enough on my plate trying to deal with the melodrama of those three,' Cirona said, jerking her thumb over her shoulder towards Holger, Elvgren and Bellina.

'Well, I was walking to my town. Then the sky clouded over, the ground shook and cracked. Black ooze started to rain from the sky and seep up from the earth. Then I saw my daughter. The black stuff was covering her, crawling over her body, choking her. It was... unsettling.

Then there was a howl and I saw a faresk. I... How do I explain it?... They are fell beasts that can be summoned by kaffars. Like huge black hounds, the size of a donkey, with glowing eyes. It looked at me and then dragged my girl away. I tried to run but I was trapped, sinking into the black ooze. Then I woke up with a day of walking through this damned place ahead of me,' Reveeker said.

Cirona looked at the sweat that had formed on his brow while he was speaking and was sure that some of it wasn't just from the humidity. 'That explains it. Don't think I would be a picture of happiness after a night like that. Sorry Rev,' she said, inwardly groaning at the fact she couldn't think of anything better to say.

'Don't worry, Rona. Like I said, just nonsense, and thanks — it helped, even if it was to just hear how mad it sounded out loud!' Reveeker replied with a weak smile. He strode ahead and resumed his assault on the jungle.

*

Night set in again. Elvgren looked up at the towering expanse of stone that loomed overhead. Reveeker had led them to the foot of the mountain and even Elvgren had to begrudgingly give him his admiration at the feat. Quite how the Burkeshi had led them through the maze of jungle, escaped him. They had all agreed to camp at the bottom of the mountain before heading up to the outpost. He settled himself on the ground next to the fire and tried to ignore the protests from his aching body. The stench of rotting jungle fruit assaulted his nose. Reveeker had pointed out one tree that gave off a particularly revolting stench. He assured them that the stinking fruit was delicious but they had all refused to share his meal. The fire blazed happily, unaware that it burned in a wild jungle and not some snug homestead. Night closed around their glowing halo of light, the sounds of the animals the only thing to alert them that there was anything else in the world beyond the campsite. Then, amongst the calling of the birds, there was a blood-chilling cry. It sounded to Elvgren like a cross between a howl and a roar. The hairs on his body stood on end while the group exchanged confused looks.

'What the fuck was that?' Dargo exclaimed, eyes wide.

'Just a leoguar. Sounded far off,' Cirona said, a note of uncertainty in her voice.

'That was no leoguar,' Reveeker said, his eyeballs bulging like they were trying to escape his skull, 'We have to move. Now!'

Before any of them had time to comply with his command another cry rang out and then another. The sound of movement rustled through the foliage. Then Elvgren saw them, the pair of eyes he had seen the night before, only this time they were not alone. At least five pairs peered in at them, forming a semicircle in the jungle.

'What is this? What the hells is going on?' Bellina cried.

'Faresks. Beasts summoned from the beyond to do the bidding of a kaffar,' said Reveeker. 'Shit it all! We have to get away from here!'

'Kaffar? Here?' asked Cirona, alarmed. 'I never dreamed we would run into one now. Hoped we wouldn't at all. Right everyone, draw your weapons and get behind me and Rev. Quickly!'

Elvgren pulled out his sabre and hurried over. A crashing sound came from behind him and he felt powerful jaws clamp round his arm. He screamed in pain and tried to swing his blade, but he couldn't reach. He could smell the creature's rancid breath and looked at the huge teeth that had sunk into his flesh, saliva running from them and mingling with his blood. The fangs were housed in the skull of a giant hound. Its bulbous eyes blazed, features contorted in a sickening snarl. Long, lank, greasy fur hung around its form, twigs, bones and shit meshed into it. Elvgren looked in terror at his companions. Holger stuck a branch into the fire to light it and came tearing towards him, the flame leaving an after-image in its wake. The faresk switched its bite, its fangs closing around the fabric of his shirt, before pulling him through the undergrowth at a startling speed.

'Cirona!' Reveeker shouted. 'Take Dargo and Bellina up the mountain. The stone steps should be close. I will get Elvgren. Holger wait!'

Roots and vines smacked into Elvgren mercilessly as he was dragged away. In the distance, he could make out Holger's flaming branch growing smaller and smaller.

*

Cirona watched Elvgren disappear into the jungle, followed by Holger and Rev. Her heart pounded in her chest but she saw only two pairs of eyes now. The faresks slunk into the light of the fire, the two beasts pawing warily around it.

'Ah shit and fuck it!' Dargo yelled.

A faresk drew closer, muscles visibly bulging beneath its revolting tangle of fur. What the hells should she do? There was no way she could take them both on. 'You heard Rev. We run. Go now! Towards the mountain!' Cirona bellowed. The sound of the pair escaping came to her from behind. Only then did she pull the primed ballistol from her pocket and fire at the closest monster. It jumped away from the shot and the ball merely clipped its side. The same treacly blackness that she had seen come out of the Burkeshi shape-shifters, back on the *Prudence*, cascaded out. Still the creatures advanced. She threw the fired weapon at them, turned and ran. She could hear the footfalls of Dargo and Bellina ahead of her and it wasn't long before she could make out their shapes in the darkness. Cirona crashed through the jungle, vines and plants whipping at her face and arms. Behind her she heard the howls of the faresks, their heavy paws snapping and crunching through the undergrowth.

'I can see the steps!' Bellina shouted.

'Keep going!' She could see the steps too now. They rose straight up from the jungle floor, cut deep into the stone of the mountain. She spurred her burning legs on and went sprawling forward, tripping on a root. Hitting the ground hard, she rolled head-over-heels twice before coming to a halt. She spun round and pulled out her sword.

One of the faresks had outstripped the other and was on her. Jumping towards her as she tried to regain her footing, it knocked her savagely back into the dirt before trying to bite her head with animalistic fury. She jerked away and slammed a fist into the side of its skull. The faresk's head recoiled and she grabbed the fur at the back of its neck, pulling it to one side. She swung her sword in a broad arc and slashed the creature's throat. Black blood spattered across her face, hot and stinking of decay.

Cirona had just enough time to pull herself out from under the immense weight of the beast and then the second one was on her. She crouched low as it accelerated, the creature pouncing through the air in an ease that seemed impossible for its massive bulk. It clamped its fangs into her sword arm and twisted, flinging her to the side. Cirona felt herself spiralling through the air before her breath was knocked from her when she hit a tree.

Her body slid downwards, her back against the trunk. The faresk pounced again, its giant paws pinning her shoulders to the tree. She jolted her head to the left as it went to bite her face. Its skull cracked into the solid wood behind her, some of the strength went out of its hold. She drove her own head into its snout and pushed forward. Grabbing at the fur around its stomach with both her hands, Cirona heaved with all her might and flung the hound through the air. It landed on its back a few feet away. In the blink of an eye, it was charging again. She bent down, grabbing her sword. The faresk leapt once more. She held the sword out in front of her, using the creature's own momentum to skewer her blade through it. It let out a howl that surely came from the Void itself. Despite two feet of steel sticking through its middle, the faresk still made a mad attempt to bite her. Cirona pushed up, twisting as she did. The creature's eyes bulged then whatever had given it life fled. She pulled her sword out of its gut as her legs gave way.

*

The jungle flew past Elvgren in a dark blur. In the distance, he could hear the cries of Reveeker and Holger. The faresk showed no sign of stopping. Elvgren wriggled frantically within his shirt, trying to get the damn thing off and escape the beast's jaws. The cloth was cutting into his neck as he squirmed and he could feel a trickle of blood around his chin. *Twelve hells, what can I do?* Not really registering what he was trying to achieve, Elvgren tried to stick his hands into the undergrowth. Only one of his arms responded, thanks to the vicious bite from the faresk. He dug his fingers into the dirt and leaves, and his grip found what he was after. His hand wrapped around an exposed tree root and he gripped it with all his strength. The faresk continued at the same speed. There was a tearing sound and the fabric of his shirt ripped. Elvgren jumped to his feet, watching the faresk run on for a few feet, momentarily unaware that it had lost its prey. When it realised its mistake, it came skidding to a halt, eyes searching back towards him. Elvgren stood, breathing in ragged bursts, waiting for the giant hound to come at him. His bitten arm hung uselessly by his side.

Before the faresk had time to react, a ball of fire streaked past from behind Elvgren. Flames flickered and trailed in its wake. With a start, he realised it was one of the other creatures.

Holger ran behind it, madly waving a sword. He caught sight of Elvgren. 'They don't like fire,' Holger said, stopping by his side.

The flaming faresk bolted past the one that had been dragging

Elvgren through the jungle. The two young men stood side by side watching the remaining creature.

'What should we do?' Holger asked.

'I really don't know,' Elvgren replied. The creature charged at them and pounced. Elvgren cringed waiting for the impact, sword hanging forgotten in his hand. There was the loud crack of a ballistol being fired. The faresk's head exploded in a shower of gore. Elvgren looked round and saw Reveeker surrounded by the smoke from the fired weapon.

'Don't just stand there, you pair of idiots. We have to go, at least one more of these things is still out there. Head towards the mountain wall. We can climb up — lots of ledges this low down. Gain a bit of distance. Now go!' Reveeker instructed them, sprinting off ahead.

Elvgren and Holger followed him, running as fast as they could manage. Soon they came upon the craggy mountain face. Reveeker was already scaling the cliff with consummate ease. Holger followed suit.

'Hang on! Wait a gods damned minute!' Elvgren shouted, panic flooding through him. 'My arm is fucked. I can't climb.'

Holger and Reveeker looked down at him from their vantage points.

'*Vaksa gavish!* Hold on. I'll come and get you!' Reveeker shouted down. He began to descend and then stopped, a look of terror on his face. He was staring into the darkness behind Elvgren.

Dread rose up like vomit and the young lord turned slowly. The glowing green eyes of countless faresks stared at him. 'For the love of the gods... help!' he squeaked.

A heavy weight thwacked against Elvgren's head. He turned back towards the mountain and saw what had hit him. A thick rope coiled down from a ledge high above.

'Grab it!' a hoarse voice commanded from the darkness.

Elvgren didn't need to be told twice. He grabbed hold. Slowly, he was pulled into the air. The faresks, furious at being deprived of their prey, ran back and forth beneath his dangling feet. They let out their terrible cry, their voices merging into a hideous chord. Elvgren had to draw up his legs to avoid their attempts to jump up and bite him. Inch by inch, the rope crawled towards the ledge. Elvgren's good arm burned, sinews and muscles stretched to their limit. Just when he thought he could hold on no longer, he was pulled over the edge of the precipice where he collapsed face first on to the rock. He gulped in air and writhed in agony, feeling whatever energy had sustained him thus far drain from his body. The pain in both his arms was excruciating.

'Here lad, gimme your hand. The good one, not the one covered in blood.'

Elvgren looked up at the outstretched hand that was offered to him. It was connected to one of the most insane looking people Elvgren had ever seen. Large, unblinking eyes stared out from cavernous sockets. The man's hair was a mess of tangles with a collection of detritus caught in it. A massive bushy beard, that would have been rather fine looking if it wasn't for the state of the rest of him, spanned the distance from his chin to his chest. His clothes were in tatters but Elvgren could see they were once a uniform of the Estrian Imperial Army. At that moment though, Elvgren couldn't care less. He accepted the hand and noticed a small band of silver studded with three precious stones. 'Thank you,' he managed to wheeze.

'Nae problems fella. Ye got any grub?' the man said.

'I'm afraid not. Who in the world are you, my man?'

'Torkwill Burns, cognopath, stationed with the Twenty-third Eastern Division. Sure ye ain't got any food?' Torkwill asked, scratching furiously at his beard.

'No, I am quite sure. What the hells happened to you? Why are you up here?' Elvgren asked, growing more puzzled by the second.

Torkwill darted in close to him and whispered in a mad ramble. 'Is him, man. Dinnae ye see it? Him, the brown devil and his fucking hellhounds. If only they were the worst o' it. But nah, ye won't believe the things the bloody devil has set upon us. Oh no! You'll see, though, you'll see, they're here an' they're coming. Though you won't believe it and then it'll be too late.'

'Who? Who's coming?' Elvgren asked, beginning to wonder if he wasn't better off with the faresks.

'The dead, man! The fucking dead!'

34

Cirona dragged her aching body up the mountain steps until she heard the cries from Dargo and Bellina up ahead — *they must have spotted me*, she thought. The sound of their feet scuffling, came down to her.

'Gods! Cirona are you alright?' Bellina exclaimed.

'Yeah, I'll survive,' she replied, though her arm was trying to tell her otherwise.

Dargo joined Bellina and they both helped the major to her feet. Together they struggled upwards, climbing the last portion of the steps. As they ascended, Cirona could see vast carvings etched into the mountainside. One showed a giant man with huge dangling earlobes, he was fighting a serpent and it looked like he was winning. They battled their way up the last few steps. Finally, the gates of the military outpost stood before them. A high wall of roughly hewn stone bridged the gap in the mountain that the stairway cut through. Tall watchtowers flanked them, staring down questioningly. *Where the hells are the guards?* Cirona thought. She staggered up to the gates and banged on them. 'Hello? Hello? Is anybody there?' she called out, but no reply came back.

'Nobody's home?' Dargo said.

'Bloody looks like it. That's not a good sign at a military outpost. We need to get in there and see what's what.'

'How are we going to accomplish that? The wall has to be at least twenty feet high?' Bellina said.

'We could just go through the door. It's not locked,' Dargo said, pulling the large, bronze handle so that the door swing open.

'Something is very wrong here,' Cirona said. 'Be on your guard and stay behind me.'

'No offence, Major, but your arm don't look too clever,' Dargo said.

'There will be a medical station inside the compound. We'll make our way there first and I'll sort my arm out. Hopefully, there will be someone who can tell us what the fuck is going on here.'

They went through the gate and Cirona took in the scene. Around her, wooden huts stood untouched on a plateau but no lights shone from the widows. The Estrian flag hung limply on a large pole in what was the parade ground. Hundreds of criss-crossing footprints were trampled into the dirt. Cirona looked around and caught sight of the red "x" that marked out the sickbay. She wandered over to it with bated breath, Bellina and Dargo following just behind. The medical building was low and flat-roofed, three steps led up from the ground onto its porch. They climbed them, Cirona cursing every squeaking step. She gripped the door handle and turned it as quietly as she could manage. Cirona peered her head round the door. The room was in chaos, beds were strewn across the floor, blankets and sheets engaged in a frozen fight, vials and other equipment lay smashed and scattered. She tiptoed into the room, hardly daring to move more than an inch at a time. Dark stains were splattered over the walls. The air was filled with a metallic tang and, to her horror, she realised they were blood. The stains were dry so, whatever had happened here, it had been some time ago. Cirona held up her hand, signalling Bellina and Dargo to wait. After a quick search of the building, she found no sign of life. Making her way over to the medic's table, she rummaged through the cabinet above it and found some dressings and alcohol. She applied the alcohol to her wounds, wincing, then fixed the bandage. Her arm still felt numb but some of the pain eased when the bleeding was staunched.

'What the hells happened here?' asked Bellina. 'How can there be so much blood and no bodies?'

Cirona thought it was an excellent question. 'This is some dark shit. Should have been a couple of hundred men stationed here, easy. We'll make our way to the command station and see if there are any clues in the logbook. Then you had better use your powers to contact the others.' Her guts whirled with worry at the thought of what might have befallen Elvgren, Rev and Holger — she had to trust that they were alright for the moment.

Dargo and Bellina pocketed any medical supplies that might prove useful before leaving the sickbay. Together, they stole across the parade ground, adding more footprints to the mad trails already in place.

Cirona made for the largest building — the command station. She hoped to find a scribograph so they could get a message back home. After the turn that the girl took in Varash, she was loathe to put added strain on Bellina's abilities. She went first again, opening the door with the same amount of caution as previously. The command station was in a similar state of disarray as the sickbay. Papers, blood and smashed furniture combined in a tableau of destruction. At the centre of the room, she could see the campaign map, its miniature soldiers bent and broken. Faint light shone through a window at the back of the room illuminating a writing bureau. She crossed the room towards it, followed by the others, and started to rifle through the drawers. Cirona moved aside various memos crusted with blood before the logbook was found.

'What does it say, Major?' Bellina asked, the moonlight from the window making her pale skin glow.

'This is really, really wrong!' Cirona said. She couldn't believe what she was reading.

'Bloody hells, tell us!' Dargo hissed, casting furtive glances around the room, his small knife poised in his hand.

'Nothing... the logbook shows that there's nothing wrong. The last entry was fucking today!' Cirona said, barely managing to keep her voice down. The whirring hum of a vorotorium cell coming to life reached them from the opposite end of the room. She motioned for the pair to stay where they were and made her way towards the sound. It was coming from behind a door, the blue flickering light of the power cell in action spilling out under a gap at the base. She opened the door, a rusty hinge protesting — a sound so easily ignored in normal life, magnified horribly.

The small room was bathed in the glow from the cell, casting everything in a surreal aquamarine. Cirona could see a table and chair at the back of the room. A body was slumped forward in the seat. Strangely, the sight of at least one dead body settled her nerves — the coupling of shit loads of blood and no bodies to account for it was unnerving. She closed the distance to the table. The stench from the woman's rotting flesh filled her nostrils and made her gag. The corpse's head lay unnaturally on the desk, contorted at a bizarre angle. Blood had oozed from her mouth and pooled around her cheek. Her eyes stared, lifeless and cold. The poor woman's hand was still inserted in the scribograph which was perched on the side of the table. *Probably trying to get a message back to Estria when she died*, thought Cirona.

Suddenly, the scribograph sprang into motion, drawing out its message. Startled, Cirona read the fluid calligraphy of the Lord Chancellor. *Have the party arrived yet?* was written across the parchment. She watched in paralysed revulsion as the hand of the dead scribograph operator began to twitch. It moved as if pulled by invisible strings and began to pen its response. *No need to worry, my lord. They have just arrived.*

*

'What the hells do you mean? The dead are coming?' Elvgren asked, mouth slack with amazement.

Holger and Reveeker had now shimmied over the ledge, panting from the climb.

'The dead, man. The dead. I cannae say it any plainer than that, can I?,' whined Torkwill. 'I sensed him though, the mud-skinned fucker, him and his devilry. What the fuck is this? You brought one of the bastards upon us!' he cried, producing a large knife from the waist of his frayed trousers and pointing it at Reveeker.

'Calm down, man. He's with us and means no harm. Has news of our coming not been transmitted to you?' Elvgren said.

'You? Wha? Lemme think on that a moment. We did have word of a party that was s'posed to be coming through. Had orders to accommodate you as best we could, orders direct from the Lord Chancellor. You telling me tha's you?' Torkwill said, his eyes roving between them, filled with suspicion.

'Yes, that would be us, old boy. Now how about we put the knife down, eh?' Elvgren made a motion towards the blade.

'Dinnae you be touching ol' Betsy here. Means more to me than the combined worth o' you lot.' He took a step backwards and ground his teeth furiously. Then, a crazed smile spread across his face as he seemed to come to a decision. 'I remember now, yeah. One o' ye was supposed to only have one good peeper left. S'pose that's you, eh? Well that certainly is a weight off my mind. Woulda been a shame to have to skin the first proper people I seen in weeks.'

'What happened here?' Reveeker said, eyebrows raised quizzically.

'Thought you'd know, eh? Dinnae recognise a kaffar's handy work when ye see it?'

'A kaffar? Are you sure?'

'Sure as I shit every morning. Ain't seen the bastard but I can sense him. Oh aye, I can sense his stinking darkness. An' you have made acquaintance with his hounds,' Torkwill said, spinning round on the spot with outstretched arms.

'This is all most unorthodox,' Reveeker explained. 'The faresks are usually used as omens of death. Kaffars summon them to sniff out the sick in a plague-ridden town and to find the dead bodies so they can stop the spread of disease. Before tonight, I had only seen them attack people who refuse to go with them.'

'Well, they be attacking now, eh? Them *and* the dead.'

'You can't... never in all my days have I seen, or even heard, of a kaffar performing narkifir. Not since...' Reveeker said, running a hand over his head.

'Narkifir? What's that?' Holger asked.

'Necromancy lad,' replied Torkwill. 'The dead walking. Controlled by some fucking mage hidden away somewhere while he makes my brothers in arms dance around an' kill each other. Fucking coward! You hear me? You fucking coward!' he screamed at the mountain, his mouth frothing.

'This is not how kaffars behave!' Reveeker was shocked. 'They are wise men. Healers! At least they were...'

'Where you been? Dinnae work like that now. Arch Vizier Marmossa, he's been training 'em. Turning 'em into weapons.'

'You've gotta be kidding,' cried Holger. 'We can't deal with something like the Mage War again. Oh, fuck no!' He sank to his knees. Even though the Mage War had happened five hundred years before, its scars ran deep in the Empire and every man, woman and child knew of it. In fact, it was the reason there *was* an Estrian empire. Victory, the Imperial Capital, the Un-fallen City, the last stronghold of humanity, had withstood the onslaught. After their final triumph, the country of Estria had expanded, enslaving the mages, using their power to fuel the growing empire's technological advances.

'You be right to cry out, lad,' said Torkwill 'We are on the front fucking lines of it. The colonel reckoned they've been testing out their new weapons on the trading posts. Gotta bit bolder now though, attacking us like this.'

'How many kaffars are there?' Holger said, looking up at him.

'Clean out yer fucking ears, man! I just told ye, eh? One o' them. Just the one,' Torkwill raised a solitary finger to illustrate his point. 'Dinnae need more, do they? Started wi' one bloke who got sick. Two days later — poof, gone! Black shit pouring outta his body. Bang, he's back alive, going crazy. He kills another, then they both start killing. Before we know it whole place is like it. We shoot 'em, we slice 'em. But on they come. No pain, no doubt, no remorse. The perfect fucking battalion.

But old Torkwill, he's clever see. He knows about the devil, knows what he's trying. Felt it when I reached out with me mind. I know the tunnels and the mountains. Ran, hid. They'll never be catching me. Not while I got Betsy and me wits.'

Elvgren doubted that the man's wits could be relied on too heavily. He stood in stunned silence, along with his companions. His brain tried to wrestle the information he had just heard into some kind of sense. It gave up.

Elvgren? Elvgren can you hear me? Are you alright? The voice of Bellina echoed in his skull and he winced, caught off guard. 'Yes ... yes we're fine. Just about, anyway.'

As he spoke, Holger and Reveeker looked at him as if he were as mad as Torkwill.

You don't have to speak out loud, you fool. Argh ... there's no time. Something is wrong. The outpost is empty. The major is fighting a corpse... I... I ... oh gods! Get here quickly, I think there are more coming!

We're coming. Hold on. Bellina? Bellina? he called in his head, but she had gone. He turned to the others. 'We have to go. Bellina, Dargo and the major are being attacked by ... corpses.'

'Nekrolytes. When people are... used that way, they are called nekrolytes,' Reveeker said as if he was talking in his sleep.

'Nekrolytes, corpses, what the fuck does it matter?' Holger shouted. 'We've gotta get up there, now!'

'Torkwill, how do we get up there?' Elvgren asked.

'Ye wannae go up there? You're mad, boy but I'll show ye the way,' Torkwill replied and set off at a startling speed.

Elvgren and the others hurried to keep up.

35

Bellina's lungs were starving of air and she realised she was holding her breath. She forced herself to exhale and watched Cirona cautiously enter the room where the light and sound were coming from.

'This is fucking crazy, Belle. I don't like this at all,' Dargo hissed at her, moonlight catching his eyes.

'I agree, but the major is here. We'll... we'll be fine,' she said, trying to convince herself more than the boy. From the back of the room Bellina could now here the distinct sound of a scribograph in use, a sound that she had grown so accustomed to in her father's study. Seconds passed, drawn out in nerve-shredding fashion. Then came the sound of swearing and scuffling.

Cirona tumbled out through the door slamming it shut behind her. She leant all her weight against it, shoulder pushing at the wood. 'Bellina, I am loosing your restraints. Try to contact the others, tell them... tell them a fucking corpse is attacking us!' That said, she clicked a gem on the control conduit.

'Major, what... what in the world do you mean?' Bellina asked, her blood turning to ice.

'I mean exactly what I said. I haven't got a clue what is going on, but I just saw a dead woman move!'

The banging from behind the door stopped abruptly, it was replaced by the sound of wood splintering. A hand broke through the door and grabbed at Cirona, pulling at the collar of her shirt. Dargo flew across the room and stuck his knife into the hand. Still, it held its grip. The major reached up and struggled to pull herself loose.

The hand shot back and the door burst open. Dargo and Cirona went sprawling across the floor. Standing in the doorway, bathed in blue light, was the corpse of a woman, her head lolling over her left shoulder.

Bellina felt her stomach writhe. *It* moved forward in bursts of twitches and jerks, setting upon Cirona as she was trying to get up. Dargo pounced on its back, stabbing with his knife to no effect. Bellina knew she had to ac, but her body was not responding. Instead, she reached out her mind to Elvgren — strangely he was the first person she thought of. She held the image of him in her mind, the way she had been taught to for short distance cognopathic communication. *Elvgren! Elvgren can you hear me? Are you alright?*

Yes ... yes we're fine. Just about anyway.

Elvgren's reply came back, creating the horrible high-pitched squeal that indicated a person was thinking and speaking at the same time. Strange moans and cries were coming from outside the command station now. The shock of it almost made her lose the connection. She regained her composure. *You don't have to speak out loud, you fool. Argh ... there's no time. Something is wrong. The outpost is empty. The major is fighting a corpse... I... I oh gods! Get here quickly, I think there are more coming!* The door to the outside exploded inwards, the animated corpses of five soldiers toppled in after it. She fought back her fear and disgust and tried to level out her breathing. *I need to be calm for this,* she thought. 'Major! Quickly give me full access to my cognopathic and cognokinetic abilities!'

'I'm a bit busy!' the major replied.

Bellina could see that Cirona had hacked off the corpse's arms, which were now moving independently from its body. One of the limbs had grabbed hold of the major's leg, the other was closing in on Dargo as he backed away.

'Major, do it now! I have an idea!' Bellina screamed as the five newcomers turned their attention towards her. The gems on her restraint seemed to catch fireand she could feel the full breadth of her power flooding through her, making her lightheaded. Bellina focused her mind on the closest corpse, tuning into its mind — or where its mind should be anyway. Its thoughts seemed to be connected by a dark thread with the other corpses. She wasn't trying to read their thoughts though, she was going to blow the brains from their skulls.

It was an incredibly dangerous technique, one that she had barely touched upon in her training. She had a hunch that the black thread controlling the corpses was relying on the brains being intact. The thought had come to her when she noticed that none of the soldiers had suffered any head trauma. Bellina prayed to the gods that she was right and, if this worked, the black thread controlling the corpses would be severed.

She imagined a giant hand above the first soldier's head. Her mind focused on squeezing the imaginary thumb and forefinger around the corpse's skull. Bellina could sense the force of it inside her head, pressure building. In a blast of gore, the dead soldier's head imploded. Bone, brains and black blood showered the room. Sweat streaming down her face, she applied the same force to the other corpses coming towards her. Their heads caved in with a similarly disgusting result. Bellina turned her attention back towards the corpse that was attacking Cirona and Dargo. Again, she bent the force of her mind around the woman's skull. Her vision was blurring under the strain but she held on, focusing every ounce of her will on the corpse. There was a soft, squelching pop as the woman's head finally gave way. Bellina collapsed to the floor, barely clinging to consciousness. The arms that had been attacking the major and Dargo flopped to the floor like caught fish.

'Bellina, are you alright?' Cirona asked, making her way to the girl's side.

'I... yes... I think so.'

'That was amazing!' Dargo cried, 'Pop, pop, pop they went. D'ya see that, Major?' He continued miming an explosion coming from his own head.

'It was damned hard to miss from point blank range, Dar. Come and help me get Bellina up.'

Bellina felt them raise her from the ground. Her body was leaden, heavy, like it didn't belong to her. She tried to step forward and her leg buckled.

'Come on Belle, let's getcha outside,' said Dargo. 'Hope no more of those... things turn up.'

'There's bound to be more. Didn't you say there should be around two hundred soldiers here, Major?'

'Afraid so. That won't be the last of them. Don't think you're going to be able to pull that trick again,' Cirona said, hefting her towards the door.

Bellina felt nauseous, cold sweat enveloping her. The motion brouht on a wave of sickness. 'I probably shouldn't try again for a while. Their... weakness... gotta... destroy the brain,' Bellina heard herself say before the world went black.

*

Torkwill led Elvgren and the rest along a precarious ledge. Elvgren had his back pressed tightly to the side of the mountain, while he shuffled his feet along the narrow outcrop of rock. 'How much further now?' he called out to Torkwill, who seemed to have the balance of an alley cat.

'Not much now, One Eye! Then you'll see. Ho, ho, oh yes,' the man replied, laughing wildly.

Thankfully for Elvgren, the man was right. They came out onto a wide plateau dotted with buildings. He stepped out onto the blessedly wide ground and was soon followed by Reveeker and Holger. Elvgren could see the major and Dargo — Cirona carried Bellina on her back. Dargo came sprinting over to him.

'Fucking dead are moving, Gren!' Dargo said, in a state of high excitement. 'Should've seen your missus. Took out six of 'em with her powers. Bang! Just like that, blew up their heads.'

Elvgren stood dumbfounded for a moment by the boy's carefree attitude to the horrors he had encountered.

'Ye got any grub wee man?' Torkwill asked.

'Whassat? Food? All in the kit bag with the major, not really the time for a snack though, eh? Actually, who the hells are you?'

'Torkwill Burns, cognopath. She your mind-melter, then? That there fainted girl?' he said, pointing in the direction of the Bellina.

'Yes, she's the one you will have been informed about,' Elvgren replied.

'Must be mad strong to burst their heads like that. Wait, ain't she the girl who did for old Alcastus? Ho, ho, gotta shake her hand when she wakes up. Won't be missed in the cognopath compound, that prancing old queen!' Torkwill said with a demonic smile.

The major had now made her way over to Elvgren and the rest of them, Bellina over her shoulder and the kit bag in her hand. 'Who's this?' she asked, panting.

'Another mind-melter apparently, Rona,' replied Dargo. 'Reckons he can't pop their 'eads like Belle did, though. Oh, and he's hungry.'

'You can eat once we're out of here. Fill me in on what's happened on the way.'

'Escape? Ye wanna escape? Only one way left to get down from up here, woman. The lift at the back of there,' Torkwill said, pointing towards the mountain rising above the other side of the outpost. 'Whole mountain is riddled with caves, some kinda Chentanese temple once. But we ain't gonna get through there. That's where they are, see. Where the brown devil has made his home. Controls 'em from somewhere in there he does. Managed to track his stinking darkness that far before he pushed me out of his mind. The rest of the men are in there though, waiting with him, otherwise I woulda been long gone. Oh yes, lass, I woulda been away like the wind!' He danced from foot to foot on the spot to illustrate his point.

'Major? Put me down. I can walk,' Bellina said weakly.

Cirona set her back on her feet. Torkwill rushed across to her shaking her hand violently. The major pushed him back.

'Wha's wrong wi' you, eh? Just wanted to congratulate the young lass for fucking up old Master Bender's brain. Good show what ye did to Alcastus girlie, bloody good,' Torkwill said snapping to attention and saluting.

'I can't say I feel the same way about how I treated him.' Bellina said with a look of sorrow that made Elvgren feel deeply sorry for her.

'Look, this is all well and good but we *have* to find our way through a mountain filled with nekrolytes,' said Reveeker, a rare look of terror on his face. 'We need to go, now. Anywhere other than here!'

'What's a nekrolyte when it's at home?' Dargo asked.

'Them there corpses, Dargo. They're controlled by some kaffar magic,' Holger said shuddering.

'They have a weakness. If you destroy their brains the connection to the kaffar is lost,' Bellina said.

'Ah, that's the trick, eh?' Torkwill said, scratching his chin as if he was contemplating a wall that needed fixing. 'Wondered why they jus' kept coming with a sword in their gullet.'

A low moan carried to the group from across the parade ground. A large group of nekrolytes came stumbling towards them, blocking off the way to the front gate.

'I believe they have just settled which way we go,' Elvgren said.

'Fuck it, let's go into the mountain. Fearsome lot like you won't have any trouble. An' I got ol' Betsy,' Torkwill said, running his fingers over his blade lovingly.

'I ... I do not want any part of these abominations!' Reveeker cried.

'Rev, we've got no choice,' replied Cirona. 'How long does it take to get to this lift, Torkwill?'

''Bout thirty minutes at a good clip.'

'Right, let's go, lead on man. Quickly!'

'Alright, alright woman, dinnae getcha britches all twisted!' Torkwill sprinted away towards the dark mountain peak.

36

The wound on her arm from the faresk's bite throbbed dully. Cirona pushed the pain, as best she could, from her mind. Torkwill was a few feet ahead of her, the rest were following behind. A wide entrance to the mountain opened before them, the stone around it intricately carved. Three fat men adorned the top of the entrance, hands raised in blessing. The feet of the two carved men on the outer edges of the trio extended downwards, pinning hideous serpents and demons to the ground. Sculpted flames smothered the monsters as they struggled against their banishment into the Void.

Cirona hoped this was not a bad omen. It couldn't really get much worse, though. The walking corpses, nekrolytes, whatever you wanted to call them, were almost beyond her comprehension. She realised that their knowledge of a kaffar's powers was woefully inadequate. In all her campaigns, she had never encountered any of their kind but now they were attacking, using Estria's own dead as a weapon. The situation was beyond any of their worst fears. She wondered how the population of Estria would react when they knew their enemies had people of magical capabilities in their ranks. Despite the five-hundred-year gap and the complete subjugation of the mages, even a hint of a magical person loose on Estrian soil was enough to start an empire-wide frenzy. She remembered with horror how that had been one of the instigators for the war against Narvale.

The real reasons had been economical and political, Narvale being full of minerals and metals. To drum up support for the war, the Empire had declared that the old soothsayers, held in high esteem in Narvale, were dangerous. The idea was ludicrous, Cirona doubted they had any magical ability at all. Even if they did, they had shown no inclination to conquer or rule, as the mages had. They were healers who sometimes told a fortune, telling some dim chief that it was a good idea to attack if he saw five skitterlings or some other such nonsense. The ferocity with which the Estrian army had been ordered to attack them had been excessive. Cirona saw in her mind's eye the image of one of the old soothsayers, a woman who must have been well into her sixties, frail, thin. She had wept and pleaded for her life but the soldiers had hacked her apart like a hog. Cirona fought the images away, she needed to stay focused. Her hopes lay with the success of the Lord Chancellor's plan, though she was beginning to worry about the cost of it. Bellina was certainly powerful but the strain on her body was plain to see. *I can't worry about that now, not if I want to see my girl again.*

'Gonna need some light,' Torkwill sang as he kicked a vorotorium cell into life. 'They'll love that though. Oh aye, they'll come streaming now.'

Cirona watched as the galvanic lights flickered on, one by one, illuminating the path through the mountain. The stench of death and decay wafted from the tunnel, the taste of the sour tang causing bile to rise in her throat. The whole group now stood before the entrance. Cirona looked from face to face noting the various degrees of trepidation on each. The most startling was Reveeker's. She had never seen him show even a hint of fear. Now though, he looked like a small child about to receive a dreadful punishment. 'We all set?' she asked.

The group answered with various nods and grunts, while Rev stared unblinking down the lighted tunnel.

Cirona walked over to him. 'Hey, come on man. Need you to stay sharp. Old crazy balls reckons it's a straight run through to the other side. We get in and get out. You gonna be alright?'

He nodded but didn't seem to have been listening.

'Eh? You ready ye mad fuckers?' Torkwill called out.

'Yeah, we're coming,' Cirona replied. 'Elvgren, Holger, keep an eye on Rev. Think he's lost it on this one. Dar, you help Bellina if she needs it, don't let her fob you off neither. If she looks bad give me a shout.' Dargo nodded his head vigorously and Bellina looked affronted. *Well, I'd rather hurt her pride than see her harmed.*

'Sure thing Major, not good for the nerves seeing that big bastard frightened though,' Holger said, pointing to Rev.

Cirona was in complete agreement. She hurried back to the front, just behind Torkwill. The cognopath led them through a short passage that opened out into a large circular space. A massive wall carving occupied the far wall. It was one of the fat men again, this time though, he had changed. He was now part serpent, no legs, just a vast coiled tail. Thousands of carved snakes and lizards poured from his arms. Cirona looked up to see that the ceiling was covered in them. The light from the lamps threw strange shadows, making the whole canopy of stone seem to undulate with movement. Around the outer walls of the cavern were the entrances to seven tunnels. With disgust, she noticed the trails of dried blood and gore that disappeared into them.

'We gotta take this one down the middle here, woman. Then I get me grub, yeah?' Torkwill said.

'Yeah, yeah. Alright, lead on,' Cirona replied. There was a commotion from behind.

'Argh, you fucking rotter!' Elvgren shouted.

'Hold his arms!' Holger called.

Cirona saw the pair desperately trying to keep Reveeker from running.

'*Vaksa!* Get your hands off me you stupid boys! Touch me once more and I will break your arms. I will, I swear to the gods I will!' he screeched, backing away from them, sword in hand.

'Rev? Rev? Look at me. Breathe,' Cirona said, walking towards him with her hand outstretched.

'Rona! No, stay back. I'm sorry, I'm so sorry, but I cannot deal with the nekrolytes. None of you understand. Hundreds of men reanimated and controlled by a kaffar. This is magic of the darkest kind. It should not be possible, it will throw everything out of balance. If they get you, and you become one, it is a fate worse than death. Your soul will never know peace. It is damnation. I... I... aaargh!'

With that Reveeker tore off down one of the tunnels.

'Where the fuck is he going? That's not the right way. Well, he's good as dead now. Can I have his share of the grub?' Torkwill said, scratching absently at his nose.

'What? No, we have to go after him,' said Cirona. 'Bellina, can you stop him or calm him down somehow?'

'Not without causing him pain, Major. Even if I did subdue him, we would then have to carry his rather considerable bulk,' Bellina replied.

'Chose a great time to go off his rocker,' Dargo said, looking down the tunnel. 'But I ain't gonna leave him.'

'Same here,' Holger said.

'He is one of us now,' Bellina added.

They all turned to Elvgren.

'Look, he's the one gone off bloody raving. Don't see why we should have to put ourselves in... why are you all looking at me like that? Oh, for the love of... alright let's go and get him,' he said throwing his hands in the air.

'Ha! I like yer style people. No man left behind, eh? Well let's hope we don't all end up going down,' Torkwill said, running in the direction Reveeker had gone in.

The group sped down the tunnel, their low cries for the Burkeshi echoing back at them. From ahead, they heard a loud roar and headed towards it at fast as they could.

Crouched in a ball at the back of a rectangular room with an altar in it, was Reveeker. Three of the nekrolytes were advancing on him. Cirona tore forward and sliced the top off one of their heads. Holger, Elvgren and Dargo followed, delivering slashes and stabs to the corpses' skulls.

'Rev, get a fucking grip on yourself! Do you think none of us feel like you do?' Cirona shouted at him, her terror and frustration bursting loose. 'Bolting off on your own down dark tunnels is not going to help. We've got to stay together!'

Reveeker simply stared past her, his mouth frozen in a silent scream.

She turned round to see what looked like the rest of the battalion coming along the narrow tunnel. The dead soldiers fought and clawed at each other to get to their targets, some fell and were trampled underfoot. There was no way back now. Cirona looked around frantically for an escape route but none was available.

'Oh, fucking hells! What do we do?' Dargo cried.

'I'm sure there's a secret passage in here,' Torkwill said scanning the room.

'Fantastic: a secret passage so well hidden you can't find it. in the meantime what the hells are we going to do? We can't fight them all,' said Elvgren. 'Do you see what you've done, you fucking Burkeshi scum? You've doomed us all! I told you we should've left him. But, oh no!'

'Oh, be quiet you self-pitying idiot!' Bellina cried. 'There is only one thing we can do. Well, I can do. I will find the kaffar and destroy him,' she continued, a steely look in her eyes.

'Lady Bellina, can you do it?' Cirona said, realising that Bellina could truly be their only chance of survival.

'Yes,' she replied flatly.

'If anyone can do it, I'd put me money on you, lass,' Torkwill called from the back of the room where he was cheking the walls. 'if what you done to these monsters and Alcastus is anything to go by. I can't help though, dinnae have access to me powers and even if I did psychic battles are not my strong suit. You'd be on your own in the filth of that devil's mind.'

Cirona's mind spun. She was supposed to be protecting the girl from harm, not throwing her under its wheels. Oh gods, it was their only choice. 'We will hold them off. Good luck Bellina.'

'Thank you,' Bellina said, seating herself at the back of the room.

Cirona watched the girl close her eyes, drifting away, deep into another world where she could not protect her.

*

The stone floor of the room was icy cold — distracting — through the fabric of her clothes. It was the least of the things Bellina would have to block out if she was to accomplish her goal though. She drew in deep breaths, getting her heart to beat at its normal pace. A bright candle flickered in her mind's eye and she focused on it, closing off all her external senses. The sounds of fighting faded into nothing.

Bellina plunged her consciousness into the flame and became one with it, then she willed herself out of her body. She looked down on the room they were in, everything now represented in the colours and lights of psychic materialisation. The vague white blurs of her companions flashed before her like the after-image from a lantern. She noticed that one of the figures, possibly Holger's, had a slight turquoise hue to it. The nekrolytes appeared to her as a dark mass, more like deep nothingness than simple black. Bellina felt a tremor of fear run through her, understanding Reveeker's fear of the kaffar's human puppets. Every essence of their humanity was gone, there was nothing left. Only hate emanated from their direction but even this didn't belong to them.

Above the black shape of the nekrolytes, hundreds of thin purple strands streamed out. Bellina willed herself to follow the trail they had created. Unhindered by physical concerns, she sped faster than she could comprehend. The strands descended sharply downwards through the stone of the mountain. Her consciousness whizzed through it, concentrated solely on following the trail. The strands came to an end. Bellina could see that they were connected to a thin streak of the most sickening yellow she had ever seen. It throbbed and bubbled like a festering wound. Sickened and scared to her core, she drove her will towards it.

*

The horde of dead soldiers advanced slowly on the group's position. Elvgren stared at the bodies, taking in the different wounds each had suffered. He thought of who they might have been, where they had come from. Now they were dead, worse than dead, if Reveeker was right. He tried not to think about it as he stepped forward and slashed into the head of the nekrolyte in front of him. His injured arm hung uselessly at his side. He noticed, with some annoyance, that the major had found time to clean and bandage a wound of her own. The tunnel that the corpses had followed them down was very narrow, the throng of bodies getting caught in a natural choke point. The nekrolytes spilled out in twos and threes and Dargo, Holger, Cirona and himself picked them off as quickly and efficiently as they could. Torkwill was fiddling about with the altar..

'A bit of help would be nice!' the Major bellowed at the cognopath.

'Keep yer hair on woman I think… he was cut of by the sound of rocks grinding against each other. 'I knew it!' he continued. 'I knew there was a secret entrance around here!'

'Oi, hang on , where's *he* going?' Dargo called.

'I'm going to level the odds lad! You keep them wee nasties busy here!'

Despite longing to take off down the tunnel Torkwill had found Elvgren knew they could go nowhere without Bellina. There was no way he would leave his ticket to greatness for some reanimated corpses to devour, so he kept on slashing.

There was a lull in the fighting and Elvgren looked around the room to see if anyone needed help. So far, the group was managing to stay on top of the nekrolytes, wasting no time and attacking the skull straight away. He glanced at the rear of the room, where Bellina's body sat reclining against the rock. Reveeker was next to her, hugging his knees and shivering from head to toe. *Useless fucking idiot. Bellina is battling for our lives and that sand-fucker is shitting his britches.* He thought of Bellina, wherever her mind had taken her, alone, fighting. A wave of admiration welled up in him. She may have been stubborn, opinionated and strong-willed, but she never gave in. Bellina was nothing like a noble lady of Estria should be and he was starting to think that was *not* such a bad thing.

'Ha ha ha! All set, my beautiful people!' Torkwill said, sprinting back into the room from the secret tunnel.

'What's set?' Cirona asked, pulling her sword from the eye socket of a nekrolyte.

'The charges! What else would I be talking about, eh? Gonna blow these here devils back to the Void!' he shouted, waving his fist at the corpses.

'Charges? Charges? What the hells have you—' Elvgren began, but was cut off by the first distant boom of an explosion.

37

The wave of darkness that hit her consciousness was so dense that it almost severed the connection to the kaffar before it was properly formed. Bellina pushed against the pressure, forcing it back. She began the process of constructing a psychic landscape in which to battle the kaffar. Hoping that the sorcerer had never encountered a cognopath, that she would have complete control of the creation of the psychic space, she was disappointed to find herself wrestling for control of its creation with the kaffar's mind, even though he had no defences in place.

Bellina managed to create part of her favoured psychic landscape. It was an extravagant formal garden complete with a topiary maze, a place she knew every nook and cranny of. The grass, flowers and trees of the lawn all extended in front of her as they should. Fifty paces from where she stood, though, the garden withered and died. Grass giving way to an immense desert of black sand and mountains — the kaffar had created a landscape of his own.

A figure appeared where the garden turned into the sand. Bellina swallowed hard and walked towards it. A tall man with an elongated neck stood before her. His face was thin and gaunt, he had the sunken cheeks of a cadaver. Circles of black paint had been drawn around his eyes, the whites staring out starkly. There was a series of small circular dents on his forehead. She felt her breath catch as she realised they were the tell-tale signs of trepanning.

'So, this is a psychic landscape,' the kaffar said, fleshless lips pulling themselves back in a hideous mockery of a smile. 'I must say, Lady Ressa, this is an entirely new experience for me. I did feel a pinprick of an attempt to invade my consciousness a week ago, when my assault began, but I dismissed it as easily as you would a servant.'

'It's not too late, you know? You could stop this madness, leave my friends alone and go on with your life.'

Hate and icy cold spewed out of the kaffar's psychic form. They became visible flames of black that streamed from his body. 'Oh, you would like that, wouldn't you? It is *you* who should leave this place, return to your body and spend your last pitiful moments on this world screaming along with your friends. A new day is coming, dark and magnificent, bathed in the glory of Varl Dressera, Mother of Darkness,' he said cackling, face craned towards the heavens.

'That day will never come to pass. As long as my father draws breath along with the people of Estria, you will not win!' She spat at him, startling herself with her own fierceness.

'Your father, eh? Interesting that you—'

Bellina cut the kaffar off by sending a sharp spike of sand at him. He turned himself into a large raven and flew into the sky. Bellina was stunned by it — this was no cognopathic technique she had ever seen or heard of. Pushing her amazement to one side, she began to mould the black sand into the form of the giant she had used to defeat Alcastus.

*

'What the fuck have you done?' Cirona screamed at the deranged cognopath. She grabbed him by his shirt and pulled him towards her.

'Some gratitude this is. Just set off the explosives, is all. Bring this place down around 'em,' Torkwill said, a look of complete bewilderment on his face.

'Why in the name of the gods would you blow up a fucking mountain?' she hissed at him.

'Strategic, innit? Last line o' defence, the colonel said. Laid the 'splosives so that if the Burkeshis attacked we could seal off this way into Chenta. But it has a higher purpose now, oh aye, t' send these devils back,' he said, gesticulating wildly.

There was another blast, the ground shook and dust fell from the ceiling. Cirona looked at the limp form of Bellina. *What the fuck do we do now?* 'How long do we have before the whole place comes down?'

"Bout fifteen minutes, give or take. Why're ye so worried, woman? Got plenty of time to escape, long as we leave the wee lass and that sand-fucker,' he said, shrugging his shoulders.

'Major, we have a problem here!' Elvgren shouted, panic clear in his voice.

She turned back towards the tunnel entrance. Ten of the nekrolytes had made their way into the room. One had Dargo pinned on his back, the young boy trying to deliver a blow to its skull, while Holger was trying to haul the corpse off. Another three had Elvgren retreating towards the wall, the rest were making for Bellina.

Cirona let go of Torkwill who stood observing the scene with casual indifference. She jumped onto the back of a nekrolyte and sent a knife through its skull. Two of those heading towards Bellina, peeled away and grabbed for the major. Cirona desperately tried to push them off, but she lost her footing and went tumbling to the floor.

'What are ye doing woman? Should be running down there, is what we should be. Ach! Come on Betsy, there's work to be done,' Torkwill said then walloped his blade into the head of one of the nekrolytes on top of her.

'No, you fucking madman! Stop them from getting to the girl!' she cried. Cirona watched helplessly from the floor as the group of nekrolytes pressed in on Bellina.

*

Bellina levitated and sat on the crown of the giant's head. She swung her creation's arms out trying to pluck the kaffar from the sky. His raven form wheeled and flitted to and fro, skilfully eluding her grasp.

'You will need greater skill than that. Better make it quick too, I fear your friends don't have much longer,' the kaffar cawed at her.

Bellina turned the whole of her sand giant into a massive wave. She flung its full force at the kaffar-raven, feeling great satisfaction when she saw the bird ensnared. Bending the sand with her mind, compacting it into a ball, she squeezed with all the strength she could muster but something was wrong. The ball exploded, the sand morphing into molten glass that whirled past her in a blur. Bellina stared at the kaffar floating in front of her. The sand behind him rose, turning into the head of a leoguar. Before she could respond, it lunged, catching her in its jaws. Darkness pressed in around her, only a plunging sensation in her stomach alerting her that she was being drawn downwards. The sand encased her body, smothering her, she bent every atom of her being towards it, willing herself upwards. It fought against her but she forced herself out into the open.

'You certainly are a fierce one. I am wasting a lot of my strength on this endeavour, but now it ends.'

Bellina could see sweat pouring from his face. The sand renewed its smothering grip, crushing her mercilessly. She struggled for breath, but it wouldn't come. The kaffar flew towards her.

'Ha! To think the mighty Lord Chancellor pinned all his hopes on you,' the kaffar said, his face inches from her own. 'One girl against all that we have been planning. The arrogance of your empire will be its undoing. Oh, we shall relish the look on the old *gavish*'s face when we tell him how you died.'

*

The whole room vibrated from the latest blast, the acrid smell of smoke wafted to Cirona. *Fuck, this is bad,* she thought. She watched the nekrolytes grab for Bellina while Reveeker scuttled away. 'Rev! Do something. They are going to kill her!' she screamed.

Just then, Torkwill delivered another blow from Betsy into the skull of the corpse pinning her down. Free at last, Cirona leapt to her feet, hacking and slashing wildly at the gang of dead soldiers. Suddenly, a scream of fury came from Reveeker. He leapt to his feet and set upon the nekrolytes, insanity etched on his face. Cirona watched him slice the tops off the heads of the corpses who had hold of Bellina. He fought them off her, black blood spilling from them and covering him. Cirona resumed her attack along with Torkwill and they soon cleared the nekrolytes away. She looked behind her to see that the others had successfully overcome their attackers as well. 'Get here, now!' she shouted at them and the three young men ran over. 'Right, this place is about to blow. Rev, welcome back to the land of the sane, grab Bellina and—'

A booming sound like thunder exploded from the tunnel just ahead. The blast sent a wave of stone crashing into the nekrolytes in the tunnel. At least twenty were blown into the room. Cirona watched in horror as they clambered to their feet, dismembered limbs coming forward with a will of their own.

*

A churning heat rose from the pit of her stomach. The strength of her fury was so great it almost swallowed her consciousness. The air around her and the kaffar began to shimmer and pop in tiny balls of flame whilst the sand holding her disintegrated into nothingness. Bellina turned the white heat of her anger towards the kaffar. He clawed at his neck, an invisible pressure crushing his larynx. 'You talk too much, fuckwit! Now I am going to tear your mind apart. I am going to rip your consciousness from you. Once I have finished, you will wish you were one of those corpse soldiers,' Bellina said, her voice carrying like thunder. To her surprise, he began to smile.

'We... will... burn... you...' the kaffar said, eyes bulging.

Bellina searched for his psychic core, commanding it to show itself to her. The kaffar's heart began to glow a purple-black in his chest. She pulled at it with her mind and the organ shot through the air towards her outstretched hand. She held it out so that the terrified kaffar could see what she had done. Bellina dug her nails into the pulsating heart, crushing it with all her strength. The secrets of the kaffar's mind were there, she could sense them. She tried to pry at them but she was repelled, a vision of twelve pairs of glowing eyes flickered before her. Who did they belong to? Whoever they were, they protected kaffar's mind from her. Bellina pulled back, frightened by the eyes. She would end this now. An onyx dagger appeared in her hand and she drove it into the heart. She watched his silent scream with grim satisfaction. His form spun apart, shredded like meat from a spit. Then he was gone.

Bellina knew she didn't have much time now. She had to escape back to her body before the psychic landscape collapsed. She tried to move but she couldn't. The dark blood that had oozed from the heart of the kaffar covered her hands. It trailed along her limbs, moving, writhing, alive. She tried to fight against it but it swarmed over her body and penetrated her mouth and nose. Her mind ricocheted in blind panic. Bellina could feel the blood working into her body. She frantically tried to sever the connection but nothing happened. She was paralysed, trapped in silent terror. Then there was nothing.

*

The nekrolytes paused in their tracks, looking around like they had just heard someone calling to them. Cirona watched as they collapsed to the floor in revolting spasms, twitching for one last, violent time.

'She did it! She did it!' Dargo exclaimed.

'Why hasn't she opened her eyes?' Holger said, looking down at Bellina's motionless form.

'No time, let's go!' Cirona yelled at the group.

Reveeker swung Bellina quickly onto his back and they all raced to follow Torkwill down the secret tunnel.

Another explosion, louder now, closer, seemed to shake the very foundations of the mountain. Still, Cirona and the group rushed onwards, fistfuls of stone showering down on their heads, dust choking their lungs.

'Not much further ye mad bastards!' Torkwill cried out.

Cirona could see that he was right, the mouth of the tunnel yawned before them. There was a blinding flash of light and she smashed into the rock wall. The air burst from her chest. She forced herself to her feet, ears ringing, a trickle of blood running down her face. The others were strewn in the rubble. Rev was pulling himself up, checking to see if Bellina was still breathing. He nodded his head to her with a look of relief on his face. Torkwill was on his feet further ahead, he seemed to have escaped the worst of the blast. Holger was offering his hand to Elvgren who refused it and pushed a pile of rubble from his torso. Cirona looked around frantically. *Where the fuck is Dargo?* The boy was nowhere to be seen.

Then she heard a thin moan coming through the wisps of smoke left by the explosion. She rushed towards it and saw him. Dargo's leg was pinned beneath a massive chunk of stone. He whimpered softly and pulled at his trapped limb, gazing at her with pleading eyes. She looked at the size of the rock — they would never be able to move it. Her stomach dropped and tears trickled from her eyes. 'I'm sorry Dar... I'm so, so, sorry,' she whispered, running her hand down the boy's face.

'Please Major... help...'

'I can't... you're stuck... there's no time... we have to go,' Cirona said, her voice cracking. Suddenly, she was pushed aside.

Elvgren raised his sword and brought it down with furious strength, cutting into the boy's leg, just below the knee. Dargo screamed in agony. 'We are not leaving him!' roared the young lord, delivering another blow that severed the bottom half of the boy's leg.

Cirona looked at Elvgren. She didn't know whether to kiss him or punch him in the face. Dargo had passed out from the pain, there was blood everywhere. He wouldn't last long at this rate. She tore a strip from her sleeve and bound it tightly around his leg to stem the flow of blood, an act she had performed too many times on the field of battle. 'Pick him up. Run,' she said. Elvgren gripped the boy firmly and lifted him free. Pushing him in front of her, she watched him set off running.

Cirona saw the others looking back at her, from the tunnel exit. She flung her arms forward, gesturing for them to run. They did. She sped after them, expecting another blast any second. It was there, the exit, not much further. She watched, vision bobbing madly, as the others went, one by one, out into the night air. She was but an arm's reach from the mouth of the tunnel now. Her heart gave a flutter of relief.

She was briefly aware of her body being blown forward before the world went black.

38

Elvgren watched Cirona's body cartwheel through the air. She slammed into the wide stone ledge with a sickening crack, then skidded a few feet. Elvgren shook his head, trying his best to get rid of the dream-like fog he was viewing the world through. The agony of his arm brought him back to reality. In his desperation to free Dargo, he had forgotten the pain. Now though it was back, enhanced by the dead weight of the unconscious boy. He saw Reveeker, from the corner of his eye, gently place Bellina on the ground before he bounded over to the major to check her breathing. The Burkeshi looked towards Elvgren and nodded. She was alright. The young lord exhaled and realised that he had been holding his breath.

Elvgren slid Dargo down from his shoulder and placed him on the floor. He cast the gaze of his good eye about him. The group was on a wide shelf of rock, not too far away stood the wrought iron cage of the lift. Holger had gone over to Bellina's side and was holding her hand. Elvgren felt a flush of anger run through him but he chose to focus it on the person who had caused all this madness. Torkwill was crouched, rifling through a kit bag that Holger had put down. Elvgren shot across the distance towards him and pulled him up by his shirt.

'What the fuck are you doing, you raving madman?' he screamed into Torkwill's face.

'Getting me grub. Got ye lot outta there, which I have had no thanks for, by the way, and I'm claiming my reward,' the cognopath replied, a look of indignant bewilderment on his face.

'Reward? Reward! I should slit you throat and string you up like a hog! That boy has lost his leg, Bellina is unconscious and the major was almost blown to the Void. All because you set off those charges. What in the twelve hells were you thinking, man?'

'I were fixing those devils, weren't I? They had us surrounded, couldn't take the chance on the wee lass winning against that shitstain Burkeshi wizard. Now let go o' me. If I hadn't thrown you that rope, those fucking hounds would 'ave been shitting you out by now!'

Elvgren released his grip on the man. His rage subsided as he thought on the truth of the words. He did owe Torkwill his life, but the man was a damned liability. *Better keep my eye on this one*, he thought, regretting that he only had one to accomplish the task with.

Reveeker had placed the major in a more comfortable position and walked over to him. Another surge of anger flared in him. 'Ah, the mighty Burkeshi gladiator! Managing to move without soiling your britches?'

'I am sorry. What more can I say? If I could take back the last hour of my life I would try to do differently. I fear though the outcome would be the same. You did not grow up with tales of the nekrolytes like I did, hearing the stories of Varl Farakstar and his army of the dead. You have your Mage War; we have Farakstar to scar the minds of our children.'

Elvgren listened to the man's words and wondered what he would do if he was confronted with a mage. The thought made him shudder.

Holger joined them, accompanied by the sound of Torkwill's frustrated grunts as he searched through the kitbag. 'Belle's still breathing, cold as ice though. How about the major?'

'She will be fine. Thankfully, she was just knocked unconscious,' Reveeker said. 'What are we going to do now? And what the hells do we do about the renegade cognopath?'

Elvgren noticed that they had both turned to him, a look of expectation on their faces. 'Why are you looking at me chaps? I don't know what to do,' he said, not enjoying the weight of responsibility their looks placed on him. *How does the major bear it?* he wondered.

'You have a keen wit Lord Elvgren; it is perhaps the only talent I will begrudgingly admire in you,' Reveeker replied.

Try as he might he couldn't stop the warm rush of pleasure at the Burkeshi's faint praise. He felt angry at himself when he realised how much he cared what these people thought of him. 'Alright. First things first, let's get the mad mind-melter over here and work out if he knows what the next step was to be, if the outpost hadn't been overrun by the undead. Torkwill? Torkwill? I say man, come here.'

Torkwill stuck his head out of the kitbag like a dog caught rooting through a bin and slunk towards them.

'Right old chap, where do we go from here? Did you know the plan?' Elvgren asked.

'Not so keen to be killing ol' Torkwill now, eh? Think he might be useful, after all? Well fuck you. I ain't telling!'

Elvgren ran his hand over his face in exasperation. He wondered whether the cognopath's brothers in arms had exiled him to the mountain caves out of frustration long before they'd become the undead.

'You stinking little shit, you will tell us now or—' Reveeker started to say.

Elvgren cut him off with a raised hand. 'Alright old boy, we're sorry. You got us out of a rum spot there and we are grateful. Now, if you know anything about our mission, you will know it is of the utmost importance. Any help rendered to us will be thought very kindly of by the top brass. Feasts and banquets held in your honour. How do you like the sound of that, eh?' Elvgren said, forcing himself to use a horribly sweet tone.

'Grub, eh? Top grub too, I'd wager. Not the shit they give us here,' Torkwill scratched at his mad nest of beard. 'Fair enough, I'll tell ye what I know.'

'Thank you,' Elvgren said.

'Not too sure on all the little details, but I know the main thrust. You lot were s'posed to cross the desert with a few guards, that's not gonna be happening now though.'

'How are we supposed to cross a flaming desert?' Holger said.

'Won't be on foot. No, no, no. Got ways of getting across the Desolation. Not ways I would choose but ne'er mind. It should be a pretty straight run from what I've heard and you got your own sand-shagger to help.'

Elvgren saw a vein pulse in Reveeker's forehead.

'Once you got to the Burkeshi capital, Kurgobad, you were to meet some intelligence man called Everett Gilroy. He was to sort ye out from there.'

'That's a lot of information, more than just the main thrust. How did you come to know all this?' Reveeker asked.

'I am a fucking mind reader you dolt. Plucked it outta the colonel's mind, silent as a mouse. Knew quite a bit about the miserable prig, like how he was helping supply the Hetong in Krangoon with shafi leaf. That his payment you got in your bag lad? Ha, don't answer, I know.'

'How did you ... Are you reading our minds? Where the hells is your control conduit?' Elvgren asked, feeling a sudden sting of fear towards the deranged cognopath.

'Wahoo! Dinnae shit yourself boy. Lost me power controls with the body of the colonel. Ye can come and search me if you want. Promise not to bite!' Torkwill said in a sing-song voice.

'That won't be necessary,' Elvgren replied, having no desire to get that close to the man's stench. There was a pause as they all took in the information. He didn't know quite how they were going to do it, but they would have to struggle on. His immediate concerns were the unconscious state of three of their party and Dargo's leg and his arm's need of medical treatment. 'Right, I think we have the necessary information. Reveeker, do you think you can carry the major?'

'I believe so.'

'Good, you take her over to the lift. Holger, you take Bellina. I will take Dargo. Torkwill go ahead and get the lift prepared, don't want to be hanging around up here any longer than necessary.' He felt a brief thrill at the power of command as he watched the men carry out his orders. It was different from how he used to feel when he threw his weight around at the military academy; it was more whole and satisfying somehow.

With each of the men bearing their loads, they made their way over to the lift where Torkwill had just finished pulling the levers and oiling the gears.

Elvgren looked at the iron cage gently swaying in the night breeze. He was not convinced. A single, thick cable sprouted from its roof and snaked towards a winch attached to the mountainside. *Can't lose face now*, he thought.

They all clambered in. Torkwill threw a lever and the lift lurched downwards with a stomach-churning jolt. A few heart-stopping minutes later and they were on the ground.

Elvgren stepped out of the lift and took in the moonlit scene. Stretched out in front of him was a vast nothingness of sand. A few pathetic tufts of grass and trees littered the near distance before the vast, barren desert overwhelmed any signs of plant life. Here and there he could make out rocky outcrops, forlornly reaching towards the heavens. The whole landscape was a collection of inky blues and pools of darkness beneath the night sky. Elvgren could hear the sand being whipped up by a slight breeze; it seemed to be laughing at him, throwing scorn on his pitiful idea of crossing the Desolation. He turned away from its taunts and saw a large, flat-roofed, wooden building, it looked like a stable of some kind with living quarters attached. The noises coming from it were not the gentle neighs of horses though.

'Ah! They got our scent. Not been fed for a while, eh, you stinking brutes?' Torkwill said, picking up a lantern and making his way towards the stable.

Elvgren and the others shuffled their way over too. Cautiously, he peeked his head into the gloom and a thin streak of pink shot at his head faster than his eye could comprehend. He felt a sticky wetness on his face. When he flapped his hand, the pink thing retreated. As his eye adjusted to the gloom of the stable interior he could make out where it had come from. It belonged to a giant lizard of some kind. A tiny dot of an eye peered back at him, encased in a circular, scaly divot. Fanning out from the side of its skull were magnificent crests and horns, scaled and multi-coloured. It was easily as long and wide as a horse but had none of the height. A low belly bowed down towards the ground, the middle of it just stroking the sand. From its trunk, immense, muscular legs splayed. At the end of each leg were huge, flat feet with wide, webbed toes. Elvgren had never seen something as beautiful or hilarious in his life.

'What the hells do you call these?' he asked Torkwill, a slight chuckle escaping with his words.

'Giant gaweldons. Best creature to cross the desert with, according to the Imperial Army. Fastest aye, but take a lot of looking after. Camels may be surly but they don't require as much food or drink.'

'I have not seen one of these since I was a child!' Reveeker exclaimed, going into the stable and running a hand over the gaweldon's scaly head.

'Dinnae get too close. They may be tame but they'll be fierce hungry. Let's get into the living quarters and sort ourselves out. Then we'll see to them. Gotta be some grub in there,' Torkwill said, disappearing through a side door.

Dargo will love these, Elvgren thought. His mind shifted back to the young boy, unconscious over his shoulder. He knew only too well the horror of losing part of yourself. If anyone could bounce back from it though, it would be Dargo. His resilience was just one of many things that Elvgren admired about the boy.

He followed the cognopath through the door into a small, rectangular room. Torkwill was crouched at the far end getting a fire going in the hearth. A small Gortrix stove sat next to it, the device's dark metal belly jutting out proudly. There were three cots against the wall and shelves filled with provisions. As gently as he could manage, he laid Dargo on one of the beds. Elvgren cast his eye down at the bloody stump of the boy's lower left leg. A shard of bone poked from the ruined mess of muscle and flesh, like a mole sticking its nose out of the ground. Holger and Reveeker passed him and placed their loads on the other beds.

'Are there any medical supplies in here?' Elvgren asked Torkwill who was holding a large metal poker in the fire.

'Yeah, bandages and all sorts on that shelf o'er there,' he said, jerking a thumb over his shoulder without turning round.

A quick search of the shelf yielded bandages, alcohol, ointments and ingredients for poultices. He gathered it all up and went back to Dargo's side. The boy's eyes flickered open, wide and darting, his face covered in a sheen of sweat. His breath became ragged and he began to howl in pain.

'It hurts Gren. Fuck me, does it hurt!' Dargo cried, between shuddering gasps for air.

'Don't worry, Dar, I've got some stuff here. We'll sort you out chap, don't worry.'

'That's not gonna do the trick, One Eye,' Torkwill said, walking towards them with a small hacksaw.

Dargo's eyes fell on it and he tried to pull away. An effort that only induced a blast of agony from his lips.

'Sorry laddie, but this is gonna get worse before it gets better. One Eye, go and get that bottle of luadonite. Sand-shit, come and pin his shoulders down. You lad, go and get the poker.'

The three men complied. Elvgren helped pour some of the opiate down Dargo's throat.

'Fucking hells, Gren. Didn't figure this into my idea of an adventure. Gonna be as ugly as you now!' the boy said with a half-hearted attempt at a smile.

Elvgren looked at him and felt an immense pride; even now, he could still give his lip.

'Bite down on this lad. And pray to whatever god ye like,' Torkwill said, placing a wooden bit between Dargo's teeth.

Torkwill set about his work. Elvgren knew the agony he witnessed on the boy's face would haunt him to his dying day.

39

A smell of damp emanated from the cave and the torches that lit the walls flickered from a gentle breeze. The sound of moaning reached Cirona, just before she saw them. The dead shuffled towards her on ungainly feet. Lifeless eyes searched around, looking for her. She recognised many of the faces: friends, comrades, even enemies and the one face she wanted to be there least of all. Trafford's hands stretched before him, clutching and pulling at the air. He led the horde as they advanced on her. His hand reached out and brushed past her face. For a moment his touch was gentle, then his finger's slid round Cirona's throat and began to squeeze. She stared into eyes that couldn't see and a tear rolled down her cheek. The grip went slack and the dead fell to the ground. Bellina walked through the middle of the collapsed bodies, cradling something in her arms. As the young woman drew closer, Cirona could see that Bellina held her bodyguard's child.

Stopping in front of her, the girl looked down at the baby in her arms before slowly raising her eyes. 'Are you ready to do what you must to get her back?' the vision of Bellina asked.

'Yes,' was all she could whisper in reply. The girl extended her hand and Cirona took it, skin so cold it was painful to touch.

*

Her eyes slowly opened, her vision focused and the real world came into view. The smell of baking bread drifted to her, drawing an angry growl from her stomach.

'Finally awake, eh?' Reveeker said, stepping into her field of vision.

'Seems so. How long was I out?'

'About two days. Here, take this,' he said, pressing a steaming metal mug into her hands.

She took a sip and the bitter tang of strong, thick coffee exploded in her mouth. Cirona felt instantly better for it. For a moment, it could have been an ordinary domestic scene. Was this what a normal life was like? A husband bringing you coffee in bed, bread baking in the oven?

The moment slipped away. She recalled their harrowing escape from the caves. Dargo, Bellina. 'How... how is everyone?'

'As well as can be expected. Dargo has survived, he's trying to carry on as normal but there is a little less light in his eyes. Though he wouldn't be here at all if it wasn't for the cognopath. I'll say one thing for that madman, Torkwill, he can fix up a wound.'

'What of Bellina?'

'The same, I am afraid to say. Nothing we have tried has reached her and she seems to grow colder by the hour.'

'Then we've got to reach some kind of civilisation as soon as possible. Got to be a medificer somewhere out there. What's the travel plan?'

'We have gaweldons. If they get up a head of steam and we stay true to our course, we should reach Kurgobad in a little under a week.'

'Good, we leave in an hour,' she said flatly, sitting up and thrusting her legs onto the floor.

'Are you sure you're alright?' he asked.

She looked at Reveeker with eyes that dared him to ask her again.

He threw up his hands in surrender. 'I'll start packing up in here. The others are outside tending to the lizards.'

Cirona cinched her belt in tight, realising how much weight she had lost on their journey. If only the ladies of Estria knew the best way to lose inches round their middles was to embark on a mission of national importance.

She saw the group standing by one of the giant lizards. Dargo was peppering Holger and Elvgren with insults and advice as they tried to hook a wagon onto a harness at the gaweldon's rear. The creature didn't seem too happy about it and was constantly shifting its sagging gut. Torkwill was laughing. Cirona saw, with a twinge in her stomach, the wooden stump that was strapped to Dargo's leg. Reveeker was right: the cognopath *had* done a good job, leaving the boy with an even stump that would fit an automaton limb easily. It was small comfort in the middle of the desert though.

'Ah, yer up, eh? Wondered how long you were gonna keep snoring for,' Torkwill said when he caught sight of her.

The others turned to look and Dargo's eyes were almost too much to bear.

'Morning, gents. Well, I *hope* it's morning anyway,' she said, nothing else coming to mind.

'Not too much of it left now, Major. Damned good to see you up,' Elvgren said nodding at her.

'Alright Major! Know anything about hitching wagons to uncooperative lizards?' Holger called out.

'Afraid not lads. Get it sorted as quick as you can, want to leave in the hour,' she said, command returning easily to her.

Holger and Elvgren nodded and resumed their battle with the gaweldon. She walked to Dargo's side and tapped him on the shoulder. 'A quick word,' she said with a smile. The boy returned it, but it didn't reach his eyes. They walked over to a corner of the stable, Cirona wincing with every faltering step Dargo took.

'How you feeling?' she asked.

'Leg's sore as all fuck. Get these weird sensations like it's still there sometimes. Does that happen to people when they lose bits?'

'Yeah, I've heard of it,' Cirona said, thinking to herself that you got that feeling when you lost anything important. 'For the little that it's worth Dar, I'm sorry.'

'Well, I won't tell ye I'm happy 'bout how it all went down back there. Thought you was quick to make up your mind on leaving me. Almost smothered ye with a pillow when you were out,' Dargo said with a laugh but his eyes betrayed the truth of it. 'I tried to think what I would've done in your shoes. Probably would've been the same, is what I realised in the end. So, I guess I forgive you. Just don't let yourself get caught in a situation that compromises the mission, dunno what I would do then,' he said with a genuine smile this time.

He extended his hand to her. She pulled him close to her and wrapped her arms around him. 'I'm glad you're alive, Dargo,' she said into the mass of his black curls.

In quick time, the group were packed and ready to leave. Cirona looked down at the lifeless form of Bellina. She was nestled in the back of the wagon, as comfortable as the group could make her. Cirona's mind flickered back to the question the vision of the girl had asked, *Are you ready to do what you must to get her back?* In her dream state, she had said 'yes', but in the stark light of reality it was not such an easy decision. How could she follow through on the mission when she had witnessed the strain put on the young woman by using her power? Did her father realise the toll it took on her body? Did he care? She banished the thought, remembering the familial tenderness he had displayed at their parting. Still, what he had asked Cirona to oversee would push Bellina to her limits, if they had not already been reached.

She took a deep breath, trying to cleanse herself of doubts, and strode to the head of the line. Three gaweldons would be their beasts of burden, each carrying two of the group. Reveeker was sat atop the lead lizard waiting for her arrival. Cirona swung herself into the saddle and patted the top of the creature's skull between its two, large, flared crests. 'Alright people, off we go!' she said, gently digging the heels of her boots into the lizard's side. She felt the gaweldon's muscles bulging beneath her, its splayed limbs plodding into motion.

The beasts padded forward and they began their crossing of the vast desert.

*

Hour upon tedious hour passed beneath the baking sun. Elvgren wiped the sweat from his brow, then cleared it from beneath his eyepatch where the beads were tickling at his scar. He was pleased to see that his arm was healing up nicely, with no hint of infection. *Would't do to be losing any more parts of myself.* A dull, rhythmical thump from Dargo's wooden leg accompanied the movement of the gaweldon. Elvgren thought how he hadn't been the only one to lose something on their trip and wondered how much more would disappear before the end. 'Gets easier, you know!' he called over his shoulder.

'What's that, Gren?' Dargo asked, as if he had been pulled back from a dream.

'Took me a while to get used to just the one eye. Soon enough starts to feel like it's always been that way,' he said, feeling the bitter truth of his words.

'Oh, me leg? S'pose I'll get used to it. Got used to a lot of shitty things in my life,' the boy said.

Elvgren wondered at a life that left you with such grim resolution at the age of fourteen. At Dargo's age all he had to worry about was whether the cut of his clothes was in the latest style. Now many miles, not merely the passage of time, separated Elvgren from the memory. The pair lapsed back into silence as the lizard strode on.

The sun stared down unrelentingly from the sky. Elvgren imagined that there were once two suns and Mother Darkness extinguished one out of spite, leaving the heavens, like his own face, with just one eye to look out with. *Damned heat's making me think funny as well now*, he thought, surprised by his theological musings.

*

The group had come to a stop. The gaweldons had nestled themselves comfortably into the scorching sand whilst Torkwill and Reveeker tended to the beasts, giving them food and a little water. The Burkeshi had told them that the lizards needed meat more than they needed to drink, since the lizards' massive drooping stomachs contained stored water rather than fat.

Elvgren helped the others erect a shelter so they could take refuge from the sun. The thin canvas strip offered a tiny respite from the heat. Elvgren took a sip from his water container which had just been filled from the group's main supply. He had to fight the urge to gulp it down, instead he followed the major's advice to drink it slowly.

Cirona stirred from her spot. 'I'll go check on Bellina,' she said, stretching like a cat.

'I'll go, Major. You went last time,' Elvgren found himself saying, not quite sure why.

Bouchard shrugged her shoulders. 'Make sure you drip the water into her mouth slowly, from the rag,' she instructed before settling herself back down.

Elvgren stood up and walked out from under the canvas. The sun's rays struck him after the shade of the shelter. He worked his way over to the wagon, nodding at Rev and Torkwill who were still checking on the Gaweldons. He clambered in and felt the relief from the shade offered by its canopy. He was not looking forward to getting back on the gaweldon, to being exposed and battling with the heat once again. Elvgren stared down at Bellina. He pressed his hand against her brow, pulling back, startled by the intense cold. Her breathing came in long drawn out pulls, and sometimes her eyelids flickered, dreaming. Wherever her mind had taken her, he hoped it was pleasant. He realised how much he wanted her to wake up, to shout at him and look at him with that peculiar fire in her eyes.

Elvgren picked up the water cloth from beside her head and ran a little liquid onto it from his own canteen. He squeezed it gently just above her dark, red lips and watched the beads of moisture slide over them. As he looked closer at her he could see how dark the blood seemed in her pronounced veins. He felt the urge to kiss her, see if that would wake her up like in the old stories.

What am I doing? Where have all these bloody feelings come from? She doesn't even have a decent set of tits. Must be too long since I had a woman, he thought to himself, before angrily clambering out of the wagon.

*

After five more hours of travel, with only a few rocky outcrops to mark their advancing progress in the otherwise featureless landscape, the group came to rest for the evening. As Elvgren lay beneath the canvas roof he came to understand why they had packed so many blankets. The night in the desert was as cold as the day was hot and he shivered violently. A thirst gripped him. He listened to make sure he could hear the monotonous snores of his companions before stealing out of his bed. The major had put all their supplies under strict rations but he was sure a tiny sip would not be missed. He crept away from the sleeping party and then looked back. Holger was out of his bed, Elvgren had an idea where he might have gone. The water forgotten, he covered the small distance to the parked wagon, moving silently on the balls of his feet. He pushed his ear to the side of the wagon and listened.

'Come back to me, Belle. Come back. I... love you. Not just like me sister, I need to hear your voice. Please, please, come back?' Holger whispered, his voice choked with emotion.

A surge of anger flared inside Elvgren. He stormed to the wagon's opening. 'This what you do in the middle of the night, eh? Sneak around stealing time with other men's women!' he hissed.

'What are you doing here?' Holger replied angrily, wiping the tears from his eyes.

'Pissing,' he lied. 'You can never have her. Why doesn't that penetrate your thick skull? She has been promised to me, someone of equal rank,' Elvgren said.

A glint of anger sizzled in the depths of Holger's eyes. He started towards Elvgren who couldn't help but step back. Holger stood an inch from his face and Elvgren appreciated for the first time how well built the Narvglander was.

'She deserves better than you,' he spat. Then he turned away and walked back to the shelter.

Elvgren was left by the wagon desiring a drink much stronger than water.

*

Two more days passed in the vast desert. The group had stopped for the fourth time that day. Cirona sat by Bellina's side wiping her brow. The freezing cold of her skin had been replaced by a burning fever. This however, was not the most alarming change in the young woman. Sticky black stuff had started to ooze from Bellina's mouth and nose. The veins over her body stood thick and raised, the blood in them also showing black.

Cirona felt powerless. After all she had done in her life, the obstacles she had overcome to rise to her position, why was she always left helpless to act when she was needed the most? The thought dragged up images of the moments that haunted her dreams. The bright and sunny morning when they came to take her daughter away, a scene played out as if she were not a part of it, merely an observer. The cold, impassive men following protocol: the tie that bound them all. Trafford's hand placed on her shoulder as he told her it was their duty. Then another image of Trafford. This time diving in front of the Emperor, the tiny bullet, so small a thing to make such an impact on her life, piercing his heart. His gurgled words that she couldn't hear while she watched him die in her arms. And here she was again, watching Bellina drift away.

None of them had the first clue what the illness was. Reveeker supposed it must be some darkness brought back from her battle with the kaffar but that was merely a guess and of no practical use.

'Major, a man has appeared on the next sand dune!' Holger called in to her, breaking her reverie.

Cirona ran a hand over her face, pinching at the bridge of her nose and feeling her jaw muscles tighten. *What the fuck is it now?* she thought. She hopped out of the wagon and walked over to where the others were standing. The man was about a hundred paces away, sitting atop a camel. Loose black robes covered his body, a headdress, also in black but held in place with a gold cord, protected his head from the sun.

'What do you make of it Rev? Think it's bandits?'

'I would think not. Their advantage is surprise, or numbers. He has neither.'

Then, as if the man had heard and taken it for an insult, at least another fifty camel riders appeared on the crest of the dune.

'Ah, for fucks sake!' cried Dargo. 'Can't we even cross a poxy desert in peace?'

'I say we rush 'em! That'll put the shits up the sand-fuckers, wit' their dust and hair. An' all them little bits in-between,' Torkwill said, rattling Betsy and making no sense whatsoever.

Before Cirona had time to even begin to formulate a plan, the man with the gold band called down to them in Burkeshi.

'*Gaeed dal samoon kaffar!*' he shouted.

Her stomach turned to a pit of snakes at the final word. 'What exactly did he say, Rev?' she managed to call out.

'It is an old language — most Burkeshis speak the common tongue now. I think he said the kaffar wants to see us.'

40

The gaweldons rushed forward at breakneck speed under the expert handling of the camel riders. None of them spoke the common tongue with anything close to fluency but Reveeker said they wanted to help them.

Elvgren thought they were in no position to argue, whatever their intentions. He and Dargo sat huddled together behind one of the Burkeshi nomads, who was leaning forward and whispering words of encouragement into the lizard's ear. Behind them, Reveeker and Torkwill were being driven by another rider, the cognopath's whoops and cheers ringing out across the desert. In front of Elvgren was the wagon that contained Bellina, Holger and Cirona. They were flanked by an escort of camel riders who were whipping the poor beasts into a frenzy in order to keep up.

Dunes and rocky outcrops flew past and a speck in the distance grew into the unmistakable outline of a camp. Many small, pyramid-shaped tents, all brightly coloured, surrounded a huge, circular one, like rays falling away from the sun. Before too long, the tent dominated Elvgren's view.

Clusters of men and women thronged around them as they came to a halt in the centre of the campsite. Women clutched babies to their chests, small children wailed; they all pressed in, speaking at a speed Elvgren felt would surely dislocate their jaws if it was kept up. The nomad with the gold headband dismounted the gaweldon harnessed to the wagon. He passed the reins to a young boy who hurried to take the lizard away. A fierce looking woman came up to him and spoke, arms gesticulating wildly.

Elvgren and the others dismounted and grouped themselves together. The noise of the crowd grew, though their anger seemed directed at the camel riders.

'*Camnature!*' a voice bellowed out.

The tone was old and frail but the force behind it made Elvgren's ears ring. The crowd fell into a reverent silence and parted. Through the gap, Elvgren saw the owner of the voice appear. A small, wizened, old man shuffled towards them. His skin, brown as a nut, stretched over his skeletal frame. A small, round face with sunken cheeks and eye sockets smeared black, stared at them, searching. He began to move forward as quickly as his age would allow, placing his weight on a staff carved at the top to resemble a voluptuous female figure. His cape of raven's feathers rustled and large bangles on his wrists and ankles jangled an otherworldly symphony.

'What do you want with us? Who the hells are you?' the major asked, on her guard.

'I am the kaffar who sent for you,' he replied in the common tongue. 'I realise you have had an encounter that may lead you to distrust me, but none here mean you any harm. I will answer your questions later but, for now, you must bring the girl. Follow me, quickly, she has little time.' He then turned towards the central tent and started towards it.

The major swung Bellina over her shoulder and caught up to the old man. The rest of the group hurried after her. Two guards pulled back the flaps to the tent's entrance for Cirona and the old kaffar. As Elvgren and the others advanced, the entrance closed, their way barred.

'What's the bloody idea, gents? That's my betrothed in there,' Elvgren said.

One of the men looked impassively at him. 'You wait. Too dangerous. Whatever happens next, you stay here.'

*

A small fire blazed in the centre of the tent, smoke rising merrily up and out of a small hole in the tent's roof. A camel lay to the side of the fire, its face painted with a thick black substance.

'Put her here, please,' the kaffar said, gesturing towards a raised wooden platform.

Cirona complied. The old man began an inspection of Bellina's body. Cirona's heart was in her mouth. She had no idea what to do and, in the still, oppressive darkness of the tent, her head began to swim. Why were these Burkeshis helping them? If that was indeed what they were trying to do. Reveeker had said they had offered aid but it was her job to ask questions, to keep them safe.

'What... what are you doing?' she managed to ask.

The kaffar had his head cocked and was leaning in close, listening to Bellina's heart. 'Trying to save her, if that is still possible,' he replied then shouted out an order in Burkeshi. A small girl stepped forward. She clasped a bowl in her hands and the old man dipped his fingers in it. They came out dripping with a black liquid. He raised his staff and hands above his head and began to jerk and twitch. He circled Bellina's body; clucks, whistles and all manner of strange sounds emanated from his throat.

The sounds turned into words and his voice reverberated in Cirona's bones. The flames of the fire turned blue and shot upwards. Bellina's body began to writhe.

*

A white dot. A voice. Words she didn't understand. What were these things? Why had they come? She wanted them to go away so she didn't have to feel. Feel she did, though. First, as cold as a glacier's kiss, then warmer than the inside of an oven. Visions swam before her, visions of a world beyond the blackness that now enveloped her. People, faces, and pain. The white dot grew, taking on the form of an old man. He was so bright it hurt; around him the darkness fled. He reached out his hand towards her but she didn't want to take it.

*

The rest of the group sat outside the tent. Elvgren's heart hammered as inhuman sounds and cries echoed from within. A blue light spilled forth when the tent flaps billowed outwards. It felt to him like the structure was pulling him towards it. There was a scream and the whole tent shook violently. He jumped up and tried to get in.

One of the men pushed him back firmly, but not unkindly. 'No. If you want to do something, pray, like them,' he said pointing over Elvgren's shoulder.

He turned round to see what must have been the entire population of the camp surrounding the tent. Men, women and children on their knees, hands clasped together, rocking back and forth, looking to the sky and wailing. Elvgren fell to his own knees and, for the first time since he was a child, offered up a sincere prayer to Father Light.

*

Cirona watched in horror as Bellina's body contorted on the wooden platform. Her back arched wildly, her stomach rising towards the roof. Round and round the kaffar paced, his voice growing impossibly loud. Her vision blurred and she felt an immense weight pressing down on her body. The air in the room rushed around her with a whirring sound. She fell to the floor and a thin trickle of blood slithered down her face. Cirona could feel the warmth of her tears, cascading from her eyes. She wanted it to stop, wanted Bellina back with her.

'Bellina! Come back!' she screamed, unable to stop herself.

*

She heard the voice. Recollections of a woman's face. What was her name? Why was she shouting *Bellina*? That name belonged to someone else, someone with ties and bonds, responsibilities. A person filled with anger and pain. She wanted nothing to do with that person, or her world. She wanted to go back to the nothingness. Why couldn't they understand? The figure of light stepped towards her. The darkness spat and hissed at him, writhing around him like a wall of snakes.

Look at me, the man said.

The darkness told her not to, whispered to her of the world he wanted to take her back to, the pain and suffering that waited. He took another step and the anger welled up inside her. *Leave me alone!* she screamed in a voice that sounded like two people talking at once. The darkness pounced on the man, eating into the light with ravenous jaws.

*

A breeze had picked up outside the tent, hot and gritty. It began to whirl around Elvgren. Sand was pulled from the ground as it gathered pace. Faster and faster it spun till he had to shut his eyes to stop the stinging. He felt the sand tear at his clothes and skin, particles like teeth nipping and nibbling. Clenching his jaw, teeth aching, he ground down. He dredged the prayers from deep inside. Words he hadn't used since he was a small boy filling his head. *Father of light show us the way. Lead us with your brightness from the grasp of the dark...*

*

The light had shrunk down to a flickering sliver between two slabs of black. It called out to her again.

Look at me girl! There is still time, but you must see now!

She fought against the darkness, intrigued, if nothing else, by the man's persistence. The dark howled at her to not listen, lies were all the man spoke. The voice of the blackness seemed different now, alien, remote, commanding. Why should she listen to what it had to say? She focused on the point of light and features began to appear. A man. Father — her father — his sad eyes, so sad, beseeching her. More feelings rushed into her; happiness, warmth, security, love. The sliver burst into life once more. Powerful, irresistible, it forced back the darkness. The figure of the old man returned, flickering invitingly in the brightness.

Leave her now Faisook, her choice is made. She will not be your vessel! he called out.

The darkness that was wrapped tight around her, howled in anguish. The old man reached out his hand and clenched his fingers into a fist. Wrenched from her body, agonising pain knifing through her, the darkness took on a form. A quivering hound of black flames twitched and snarled at her feet.

Look what you have become. A thing more beast than man. Love stayed my hand once but not again, the old man said. He walked forward and placed his hand on the hound. *Be gone now. Find peace in the Mother's embrace.*

The creature snapped and crackled. Tendrils of black shot outwards then recoiled. Churning and spinning the hound collapsed inwards shrinking to a speck before, with a pop, it was gone.

The old man reached out his hand again. And this time she took it.

*

Bellina's body flailed wildly like she was drowning. Cirona had to fight to keep her head up and her eyes focused. The kaffar stood still by the young woman's head now. Bellina's mouth yawned wide as black liquid poured forth. The old man beckoned with his fingers, coaxing it out. More and more of it streamed from the young woman. It formed a ball of black, hovering above her pulsing and bubbling, viscous spikes shooting out randomly. The kaffar whirled his hands and continued to chant then, with a sudden jerk, he thrust his staff towards the camel.

The black gloop shot towards the fretful beast, working its way in through the camel's flared nostrils. The beast moaned, its legs bucking. The fire burned with a fury that Cirona could feel against her skin. The kaffar held a small blade in its molten core. She saw the knife glow, white hot. He removed it and walked over to the beast. His chanting died to a hoarse whisper as he ran the blade along the neck of the poor creature. Its eyes rolled and it thrashed, blood pouring from the wound. Before too long, the camel grew still while the old man whispered soothing sounds into its ears. The weight that had been pressing down on her, fled. Her head still spun but Cirona forced herself to stand. She made her way to Bellina's side.

The young woman's eyes fluttered open. 'Major? You look an absolute state,' she said with a smile.

Cirona laughed and wiped away the tears from her eyes. Bellina's eyes closed once more and Cirona felt panic flood through her. 'What's happening? Is she alright?' she called to the kaffar.

He turned from the animal and walked to her side. 'She has come back to us. Now she needs rest but she is well.' He placed a hand on Cirona's trembling arm. 'We will talk later but, for now, go tell your friends the good news. I will tend to the girl.' He pushed her gently towards the exit.

Cirona felt lighter than air as she pushed back the heavy tent flaps. Sitting just outside the entrance was Elvgren; he was kneeling, buried up to his waist in sand. His hands were clasped in prayer, lips moving, mumbling the words to the Acquiescence of Light. Cirona was astounded, realising how much they had come to feel for each other. She knelt down and placed a hand on his shoulder. His eyes snapped open and looked into hers.

'She's going to be fine,' Cirona said smiling broadly.

41

The leg of meat rotated slowly on the spit. Flames hissed and leapt as fat dripped into the fire. Elvgren's stomach rumbled in anticipation and he wondered when the last time he had eaten fresh meat had been. There was a time when another version of himself would have turned its nose up at the nomad's simple fare. The Elvgren by the fire, though, was grateful and content. After the kaffar had finished with Bellina, he had come forth to the people and spoken to them. They had broken out in song, danced and embraced, not just each other, but the visiting group of strangers as well. Food was brought and a feast arranged. Tall, silver coffee pots were filled and their contents distributed. In fact, Elvgren had a small, steaming clay bowl of the drink now. He took the contents in one gulp, with some encouragement from the Burkeshis. The thick, brown liquid scalded his mouth and throat, causing him to cough and splutter. The men gathered round him whooped and cheered, whacking him on the back companionably.

Elvgren looked around the fire. Reveeker sat in deep conversation with the head of the tribe, a long thin pipe passed back and forth between them. Dargo was schooling some Burkeshis in the fine art of card sharking, cackling as he pulled a pile of winnings towards him. Torkwill had found the tribe's stash of wine and was dancing in a circle of nomads with enough carry on to wake the Twelve Terrors. Holger sat, looking mournfully towards the tent where the kaffar and Bellina were now. *It would seem my chat with him hasn't had the desired effect*, he thought. Finally, his eyes came to rest on Cirona. The major sat, legs stretched before her, looking serenely up at the stars. She looked older to Elvgren Lines and wrinkles, that had not adorned her face at the beginning of their journey, traced rugged furrows over her countenance.

The flaps of the tent flew open and, much to his surprise, Bellina walked out alongside the kaffar. She seemed even frailer than usual, swamped in a massive blanket which was covered in intricate geometric patterns. The pair walked towards the fire and, when the old man called something in Burkeshi, the nomads began to disperse.

'Eh! Whassa meaning o' this?' Torkwill cried as his dance partners melted away.

'I need to speak with you people alone. Much of what I have to say is old news to this tribe,' the kaffar said, placing himself by the fire. He warmed his hands appreciably as the others gathered round him. Once everyone was settled, including Dargo who now sported a fine gold bangle, the man began. 'I am sure you have many questions for me. I will try to answer as many as I can before these old lungs run out of air,' he said opening his hands out towards them.

Before any of them could start, Cirona spoke to Bellina. 'How do you feel, my lady?'

'Like I've just lost a fight with a leoguar but Varl Yevad assures me I'll live,' Bellina replied with a small laugh, pointing towards the kaffar.

'She will be fine,' Yevad chimed in. 'I would have liked to let her rest a while longer but she deserves answers as much as anyone else.'

Elvgren's mind raced; there were so many things he would like to ask the kaffar that the words all got jumbled in his head. 'Skin peel faces!' was what he finally managed to come out with. The group turned to him, their expressions showing that they thought he may have had too much time in the sun. 'What I meant to say was, we were attacked by kaffars who had taken on the faces of other men. How is this possible?' he said in more coherent form.

The old man stroked his chin. 'Hmm, interesting ... I doubt they were kaffars though.'

'But what else could explain it?' Bellina said.

'There are many dark things at work in this country, I am afraid. What you encountered was indeed kaffar magic but, more than likely, not practised by one.'

'Not to sound rude, but could you make a little more sense, old chap?' Elvgren said, his brows knitting in confusion.

'The power to assume other forms is practised by kaffars. But to take the form of another person is a dark thing. You must kill and eat the heart of the creature you wish to turn into. We use this skill to commune with the spirits and we can perform it endlessly with animals. On humans though, the magic is unstable and ravages the user's mind and body. Only threetimes can it be performed in a lifetime. No true kaffar I know would use the skill in this way.'

'Who would do this then?' Cirona asked.

'The naffir. Men and women who have consumed yaksit and been granted the temporary powers of a true kaffar.'

'What the fuck, sorry, hells, is yaksit when it's at home?' Dargo said.

'I will show you,' Yevad said. He hollered behind him and a small girl came towards them carrying a bowl. The old man took it from her and placed it on the ground.

Elvgren craned his neck to look at the bowl's contents. It was the same black liquid that had poured out of the shape-shifters' bodies, the faresks, and what had started to leak from Bellina. He felt himself shudder, noticing he wasn't the only one.

'To be a kaffar is a blessing and a curse,' the old man said, his hand hovering above the bowl. 'Revered yes, respected yes, but feared also. Every year all children will come before a bowl of yaksit. If it reacts to the child, he or she has the power of a kaffar. They are taken from their family to train and study with an older varl.'

Elvgren heard himself gasp as the black liquid rose up and began to twirl around the kaffar's fingers.

'It is said that we have received the blessing of Varl Dressera — the Mother of Darkness, in the common tongue. Bringer of life, bringer of death.' Yevad continued, watching the tendrils of darkness snake around his hand.

'How has it come to be that yaksit is being consumed? I have never heard of it being used in this way, honoured father,' Reveeker said with the pipe still resting in his hand.

'Marmossa. That is how. He harvests it from the ground. You can see for yourself if your travels take you past the town of Drevelle.'

At these words, Reveeker started forward, eyes wide. 'That is my home town! Honoured father what has become of it?'

'Ah. Then it is a sight I would not recommend to you. The whole place has been turned over to the mining of yaksit.'

Reveeker settled himself back taking a long drag from the pipe.

Silence descended before being broken by the major. 'Who the hells is Marmossa, anyway? I mean, who is he really, not just the stuff that's widely known?'

The old man thought for a moment. 'He claims he is a kaffar but, until twenty years ago, he was not known to the rest of us. According to him, he had studied our arts in the mountains. He arrived in the small multanate of Kurkar and brought the rains with him.'

'I remember the day. People danced in the streets as the heavens opened,' Reveeker said.

'Yes, and that was the start. I watched the young multan, Kurkeshi, take Marmossa to his side. Watched them swallow up the lands around them. Watched as the old ways died before my very eyes.' The kaffar was close to tears.

'Did no one question their actions or try to stop them?' Bellina asked.

'Us old ones did. We spoke out but the lure of water and power drew many to them. Soon our voices were lost on the breeze, our concerns ignored as the caution of tired old men. The young kaffars flocked to Marmossa. He promised shortcuts to power. Why spend a lifetime in discomfort and prayer when they could have it all now? Why live the life of a hermit when you can be honoured and rule? All this he promised them and they leapt at the chance. He used the yaksit and they grew strong, unconcerned for the repercussions. Then he began to give it to the new priests of his Mother Darkness cult and they gained the false powers of the naffir.'

'Why have they turned their attention to Estria?' Torkwill said, now looking remarkably sober.

'I cannot say for sure. I can only suppose they want to conquer everything in their path. Why? Who knows? But then some men are never satisfied.'

'How... how did you know where to find us?' Bellina asked.

'Aha! Here I can be more enlightening. The kaffar who you battled with, young lady, was a pupil of mine — Faisook. He was once part of this tribe but his head was turned by Marmossa. He consumed yaksit, knowing full well that it was forbidden, not caring about the ramifications, the imbalance it would cause in the Void or the years it would steal from his life. He craved power.

'I cared for him deeply, I had raised him since he was a child. I did not stop him when I should have. I kept track of his darkness, aided by his tribe who saw it as a matter of honour to stop whatever malevolence he planned. Alas, we were too late to stop him from creating the nekrolytes. How the horror of that action screamed out to me! I sensed the battle you engaged him in, you brave, young soul,' he said, looking at Bellina. 'After your victory, I could tell that he had latched his consciousness onto you and we made our way towards your group as fast as we could. It was a miracle you survived as long as you did. Another day and you would have been gone.'

A long silence stretched over the group like a blanket. Elvgren wondered to himself what the hells they had got into. Naffirs? Kaffars? Yaksit? The foreign words loaded with menace spun round in his brain. How could they go up against this? How had Estria's information on the situation in Burkesh been so sketchy? It was true that Estrians didn't pay much attention to other countries' customs and cultures, they were generally too focused on profit margins. Surely though, some of this information should have trickled through to them. The importance of the mission they had been sent on reared up and swallowed him. Panic flooded his body. Becoming Lord Chancellor, gaining power, achieving honour; all these things paled in comparison to what was at stake. Elvgren's dark musings were suddenly broken.

'Stone the fucking crows. I'm finding another bottle o' this and passing out!' Torkwill said, stumbling to his feet.

'I will finish here too, for I grow tired,' Yevad said. 'The battle to free you, my lady, has taken its toll on this old body but I will say one thing more. Darkness is coming. A night of infinite black and, for once in my long life — I am afraid.'

With that the old kaffar hauled himself to his feet and left Elvgren shivering in the wake of his words.

*

Bellina sat with the women of the tribe, helping them make bread — or trying to. The other ladies found her efforts funny and offered her instruction but her dough still would not achieve the right consistency. She didn't mind though, being quite content to sit with them and listen to their chatter. The nomads had been the perfect hosts. In the three days that had passed since Yevad had healed her, they had been fed, watered and each provided with a set of billowing robes made from the softest cotton. The friendly, humorous Burkeshis were a far cry from the baby-eating monsters she had been expecting. Bellina began to knead her dough again, the peaceful monotony of the task allowing her mind to stray. She wondered if anyone else had discovered the horrors of the military outpost yet. Had word reached her father? She shuddered to think he may, again, be of the opinion she was dead.

That was why, as relaxing as their stay with the tribe of nomads was, they would have to press on and locate this Everett Gilroy who Torkwill said they were supposed to meet. She watched the others assisting in menial tasks. Dargo and Holger were helping to tend to the camels and gaweldons, the young boy getting more and more nimble on his peg leg every day. Cirona and Reveeker were sitting close together, showing a tribesman a better way to store the nomads' balliskets and shot. Bellina could see how much Rev and the major enjoyed each other's company and wondered if anything more than friendship was in the air. Elvgren was helping — gods save us all — the Burkeshis manoeuvre the huge water containers that the tribe had to refill as they made their way from waterhole to waterhole. She watched him for a while, thinking how she much preferred his face now that it looked lived in and not just a reflection of his inner vanity. Torkwill was nowhere to be seen. Since the group's arrival he had been rather taken with a buxom widow and would follow her around, flirting.

'Ah! You have it!' Mateera, a woman who spoke a little of the common tongue, called out.

Bellina looked down at the dough and realised she had something that vaguely resembled what the other women had made. 'It seems I have,' she replied beaming from ear-to-ear.

'Here, let me take and put in the oven,' Mateerea said.

Bellina watched her carry off her creation with a great deal of satisfaction. Then she felt something, like there was a person just past the corner of her eye. She turned her head but no one was there.

'I think it's time we had a private chat lass,' the voice of Torkwill whispered in her ear.

She gave a start and looked round to see him standing where previously there was no one. 'How the hells did you... I'm not going anywhere with you when you go creeping around like that!'

'Ach, come on! I got lots to tell ye, bet ye wanna know how I did that, eh?' he said, eyes twinkling.

Now the initial shock had worn off, it was true that she was quite curious. 'Alright, but I'm telling the major where we're going,' she said.

'You wound me, my lady! Dinnae trust old Torkwill, eh? Go on then, run to yer oversized nanny,' he said.

Bellina didn't rise to the bait and went to the major before she accompanied her fellow cognopath. Torkwill led her just a short distance from the camp. Somewhere along the way he had helped himself to a wineskin. He sat down sucking it as happily as a babe on a tit.

'Must you? It's barely mid-morning.'

'Gotta be drinks o'clock somewhere, lassie. Anyway I didnae bring ye out here to discuss my drinking habits. I came to see what you can do.'

'What do you mean?'

'I mean what skills that pompous old queen, Alcastus, schooled you in,' he said.

'Well... he taught me to infiltrate minds, create a psychic landscape, move things with cognokenesis. Is that not the regular training one would receive?'

'Yes and no. He trained ye up for the big stuff, oh aye, but then he was always a one for a show.'

'How well did you know Alcastus?' she found herself asking.

'About as well as he knew himself. We were one of the last cognopaths to be born and raised outside of the School of Cognometry. Grew up together, became masters at the same time...'

'Hang on! You're a master?'

'Well, I was. Me and that goatshit fell out. I was put out to pasture at that fucking outpost, stripped of me right to wear my own control conduit. Rectified that now, though,' he said sliding back the sleeve of his robe and revealing not just his power restraint but the controls as well.

Bellina was shocked, she shuddered to think what the rest of the group would make of a cognopath running around unfettered. Especially one like Torkwill. 'How did you...?'

'Once it all started to go to shit at the outpost, I stole it off the colonel's corpse. Seemed a waste. Lied about it back at the outpost, I did'nae wanna alarm anyone.'

Bellina found it strange that Torkwill didn't think blowing up a mountain would alarm them but knowing he had his control conduit would. But then she knew for herself the reaction it would get if she were to have hers.

'Dinnae shit yerself! I'll tell the major, gonna have to if we're to train,' he said.

Bellina wondered what the lunatic could possibly teach her. 'I should hope you would. Although, if you had your controls why didn't you help me battle with the kaffar? Or destroy the nekrolytes, like I did,' she said, as he took another slug of wine.

'For one: psychic battle is not my particular area of expertise. Secondly, I am powerful, oh yes, but compared to ye I may as well be an ant fighting a leoguar,' Torkwill said with a crooked smile.

Bellina felt a flush of pride at his words then pushed the feeling back, not allowing herself to be flattered as well as flustered. 'I... I knew I was strong, but Alcastus never said...'

'Course he didn't! He was an arrogant arse, that's why his brains are now jelly. Gods save us all if that restraint o' yours was ever to come off,' he said.

She looked down at the ground, ashamed.

'Ach! Dinnae feel bad for him lass. He was a bully and a self-satisfied shit. I shudder to think how he must have trained you in those early days. He was not a subtle man, not like me, oh no. Which brings me back to myself. Now, I may not be the strongest psychic battler, but I am a master of defence and deception.'

'Defence? Deception? What do you mean?'

'Oh, for fucks sake! We really are starting from scratch, eh? Dinnae worry, with your power you'll pick it up easy. Ye heard of shedding? The look on yer face says no. Shedding is... well, I'll show ye. Now focus on me.'

Bellina stared intently at him. He vanished, though she was aware of a vague presence somewhere in front of her. She twisted her head left and right looking for Torkwill before he finally reappeared in front of her.

'That was shedding. Called that 'cos you shed all sense o' yourself, see? Tricks people's brains into thinking you're not there.'

'That's... that's incredible!'

'That's just the first of the three S's of cognopathic defence. The second is shrouding. Concentrate on me again and watch.'

Bellina focused her attention on Torkwill. The air around him seemed to shimmer and bulge. The next thing she knew, there was an old woman sitting in front of her.

'What do ye think o' that, lass?' the old woman said, in a high creaky voice.

'I... how...?'

The air shimmered again and Torkwill reappeared. 'Shrouding, projecting an image of someone else. Gotta really know the details of the image though, or you'll be found out soon enough. Ready for the third?'

She nodded her head, mind racing at the new world of possibilities he was showing her.

'Shielding. Here we go,' he said, throwing the wineskin to Bellina. 'Now I want ye to throw that at me as hard as you can. Come on now, don't be shy.'

Bellina hurled it at him with all her might. Instead of smacking him square on the jaw, the container bounced away harmlessly, a trickle of wine ran down an invisible barrier.

'And that is shielding. You imagine a wall in front of you and anything coming at you will bounce. Simple as that. Once stopped a ballistol shot with it, for a bet. Now you're gonna need to learn all this lass if you are to succeed in this mission. After what that old kaffar said the other night, this is fucking important.'

Bellina sat stunned by her ignorance of what her cognopathic powers could achieve. 'But my training... it was so inadequate. How can I learn all of this? Why wasn't I told about these other skills?'

'Firstly, you'll learn this quicker than a babe learns to shit. If you can take down kaffars and pop the skulls of the undead, this will be easy. As for why ye weren't told, I can only speculate. Maybe your father did'nae want ye being able to use your powers to find things out … you know, things you weren't s'posed to know, creep in places you shouldn't be.'

Bellina took in what Torkwill had said. It was certainly possible, given her temperament, that the Lord Chancellor had decided it was best his daughter didn't know how to turn herself invisible. It smarted to think he had considered her in that way but then she realised he would have been right; she would have used the ability for something reckless.

'If cognopaths like us are so powerful, why are we not used more? Why not send us into Burkesh under shrouding to infiltrate the enemy?'

'Partly fear. People are afraid of us. In the public's eyes we are only one step away from the mages. Don't want too many of us out and about at any one time. Another reason is there aren't that many of us. You've never seen the school, have you? There are probably only two hundred cognopaths there at any given time, maximum. Then you gotta think, out o' that two hundred, how many have the latent power and ability to pull off these skills. I said you will take to this easy and you will but you are a damned exceptional talent. I can feel the power coming off ye.'

'Why are you telling me all this? With your powers, you could easily escape going back into the army lead a better, safer life.'

'Can't exactly run away in a desert now, can I? In all seriousness, ye lot found me in a sorry state. I... I have turns ye see, lose the plot like. Now though, that brown wizard's words have scared me back to me senses. Plus, I wanna see how you come on. You remind me of someone,' he said, his eyes misting over. 'Anyway, you get yourself back to the major and tell her to switch off your constraints. We begin training at once.'

Bellina stood up and looked at him. Torkwill took another deep draught from the wineskin. She turned and walked back to the campsite, her mind spinning.

42

It was with a heavy heart that Cirona climbed back on to one of the gaweldons. After a week of enjoying the nomads' hospitality, the time to move on had come. The tribe had embraced them and placed a kiss upon all of their foreheads, a traditional Burkeshi gesture of goodbye. She stared at the faces she had come to know and respect. They had gifted them food and water and were now presenting Bellina with a small gold talisman to ward off evil spirits. Cirona hoped it worked. Then Varl Yevad came up to her. He cocked his head to one side and fixed her with a penetrating stare.

'Well Major, I wish you safe travels. The road you must walk is long and I cannot see the light at the end. I do not know all of your plans but, if you can help us avoid the calamity that haunts my dreams, you will allow an old man to sleep easier.'

'I will try, honoured father,' she said, slightly embarrassed. Cirona felt as if she had stepped into a legend, one of the heroic tales that had thrilled her in her youth.

'The people of this land do not crave war. Like anyone, anywhere, they want to sleep securely in their beds at night, live well and protect their children. But Kurkeshi and Marmossa plan evil and they draw more support to them every day. I hope it is not too late.'

'What will you do now?' Cirona asked.

'Me? I shall continue to lead the life of the wandering kaffar. I have little Disraa to teach as well,' he said pointing to the small girl who had held the bowl of yaksit. 'I feel in my bones that she will be my last apprentice. Ah! But enough of an old man's troubles, you have your own,' he said with a nod of his head.

He gave a small wave then shuffled away, leaving Cirona with the worries he had spoken of.

The nomads' camp faded into the distance and Cirona's mind drifted as her body rocked side to side under the motion of the gaweldon's movement. Behind her, she could hear Dargo laughing and cheering at Bellina's new skills. *Probably turning herself into a Burkeshi again*, she thought. She had not been best pleased to find out Torkwill had the controls to his power restraints. There had been a heated argument between her and the man which had ended when he asked her to take the controls from him, if she thought she could. Cirona knew that was not going to happen and a compromise was reached. Bellina said if she was allowed constant low level access to her powers she would be able to monitor anything Torkwill might get up too. The rest of the group settled for this. *If nothing else, the girl has earned our trust,* Cirona thought.

Though, it was disconcerting to turn around expecting to see Bellina and having a different face, or nothing at all, meet your eye. The more she thought on the matter the more she could see the strategic advantage of the powers Torkwill and Bellina now had at their disposal. The man had even said that they would be able to extend the reach of the techniques to the whole group. That would be more than handy if they were going to be sneaking around in the enemy's backyard. Enemy. Cirona dwelt on the word. Her brain was having a hard time reconciling the term with the people she had just met. She had fought and killed Burkeshis before under the banner of civilising the barbarians. She had never paid any mind to the cultures and customs of the people she had fought against. To her it seemed like a good trade: you give us rights and privileges for our merchants and we'll dig you a well or build you some roads. Not the highly intricate machinery, automatons or sortilenergy — wouldn't do for the great unwashed to have access to Estria's trump cards — but your goods for our engineering knowledge, what more could you ask? During the campaigns and battles she had fought to secure those rights for the Empire, she had not stopped to think that the barbarians had been getting on just fine without the Estrians for thousands of years.

It was a thorny subject. Some in the Empire argued for adapting to local cultures, others for their destruction. In the end, a halfway house was accepted — leave the countries alone for the most part but intervene when it was perceived that the Empire's interests were under threat. Sometimes that meant war, other times it meant a hard-headed leader, who couldn't see the value in the Estrian marvels, being made to disappear. Who was right? Who was wrong? *This is why soldiers just follow orders and don't fraternise with the enemy. Can't have us going soft on them.*

'So Rev, you sure about taking this route?' Cirona asked, desperate to get away from the turgid spiral of her thoughts.

'Yes. I need to see for myself what has become of my home,' he replied from his seat behind her.

'Sounds like masochism to me, but if you're sure.'

'Would you not be concerned for the welfare of your birth place?'

'Never had anywhere I thought of in that way, really. Orphanage, army, Imperial Guard — in that order. Nowhere to call my own or feel particularly attached to.'

'Then why did you fight for your country?'

'I... don't really know. Other than it was the only thing people thought I was good at,' she said, realising that she had never really thought about it before.

'Sorry Rona, I don't mean to get into some philosophical debate. Your reasons are your own. But for me, it was to protect the town I loved, the people I cared for and who cared for me. That's why I must see what has happened.'

The pair fell back into silence. A feeling of sadness came over her with the force of a storm-driven wave crashing against rocks. A home town to love, people to care for her and her for them. None of that had ever driven her, just the urge to do her duty. Here in the desert, it felt like a very poor reason to do anything.

*

Bellina felt the air around her shimmer. Dargo let out another cheer as she dropped the psychic image she had been shrouding herself with.

'Ha ha! Do it again Belle. Actually ... turn Gren into something,' he said.

She closed her eyes and focused on an image of a little old lady with a giant wart on her face — it was a woman who had scrubbed the dishes at her family residence. Hearing Dargo's unrestrained laughter she turned round to see if her experiment with her powers had been a success There, on the front of the following gaweldon, sat the image of the woman.

'Turn me back immediately!' said Elvgren.

His voice coming from the old woman's mouth made the whole scene even more hilarious. Bellina dispelled the image from her mind and Elvgren popped back into view. Holger, who had also turned to look at the scene, let out a short laugh of his own.

'And what do you think is so funny, fuckwit?' Elvgren spat with fury in his eyes.

'Just thought the old lady look was an improvement, One Eye,'

Holger replied.

'How fucking dare you! Get off that lizard now and let's settle this like men. Or should I tell Bellina about your midnight vigils?'

'Shut your mouth!'

'Make me, you jumped-up little shit!'

Bellina marvelled at how quickly the situation had got out of hand. At that moment, the air around Holger shimmered and he became a wizened old crone.

'There,' said Torkwill from his seat on the wagon. 'Laugh it up your lordship. We're all even now, eh?'

Elvgren didn't laugh but Torkwill's intervention seemed to placate him.

'Right lass, no more shenanigans. Won't do for us to be at each other's throats,' Torkwill said, before he lay back, swigging from one of the wineskins that the nomads had gifted them.

Since her initial meeting with the man, Bellina had been amazed at the transformation in her fellow cognopath. She wondered to herself if drinking somehow worked in reverse for him — the more he consumed, the more sensible he became.

'What did Elvgren mean about midnight vigils?' she asked Holger. She watched his face do a bizarre jig before settling into a nervous smile.

'Oh, nothing. You know what he's like, always trying to stir the shit. I... one night he heard me praying for you... that's all.' Holger's cheeks flushed and his eyes looked downwards.

Bellina thought how easy it would be for her to reach into his mind and see the truth of it but that was something she knew she would never do. She thought back to how violated she had felt when Alcastus had poked around in her mind — the memory made her shudder. She had to admit though, that she was enjoying having access to her powers, even at low levels. Bellina had progressed quickly in the more flamboyantarts of the cognopath, just as Torkwill said she would. In fact, if it hadn't been for the major's intervention, they would have progressed to attempting to stop ballistol shots already. In retrospect, she was quite glad Cirona had stepped in. She was having a hard enough time blocking stones, the small bruises covering her arms were evidence of that.

Another day of riding passed before Bellina began to see the sandstone walls of Drevelle on the horizon. She sincerely hoped for

Reveeker that it wouldn't be as bad as Yevad had said it was. The group pulled up a safe distance from the towers which flanked the main gate.

'Right then,' Cirona said. 'Bellina, Torkwill, you're on. Make us look like Burkeshis.'

Bellina cast her eyes towards Rev who was looking intently at the town walls.

'I think that would be best,' he said. 'The gates to Drevelle have been heavily fortified and those watchtowers are new. Whatever's going on here is being heavily guarded.'

'Lass, you focus on yourself and the Narvglander. I'll fix the rest,' Torkwill said.

Bellina nodded and concentrated, focusing her mind on the image of a young man and woman who she knew from the tribe of nomads. She saw the air shift and looked with satisfaction at the shroud she had managed to throw over Holger. Looking down, she saw that her own appearance had changed just as convincingly.

'Ha! This is amazing!' Dargo called out, inspecting his own hand.

'Try to contain yourself Dar. This is serious,' Elvgren hissed at him.

'Alright, alright!' the boy replied, rolling his pale blue Burkeshi eyes.

'Shall I shroud you too, big man?' Torkwill asked Reveeker.

'No. I will go as myself. I fear there will be no one to recognise me anyway.' Reveeker replied.

'Fair enough. We can't keep this facade up indefinitely though. Got about two hours tops to get through the town before the strain is too much. No one do anything to draw too much attention either, otherwise the shroud will be blown.'

'Right, you heard the man,' Cirona said. 'No stupid shit. Dargo, I'm looking at you. We keep our heads down and get through as quick as we can. Everyone set?'

The group nodded or voiced their assent. As they drew closer to the gates of Drevelle, Bellina could see that the watchtowers were indeed manned. There were two men with balliskets trained on them, as well as two further guards barring the door. Bellina's heart was in her mouth when they stopped before them.

'State your business,' one of the guards said flatly.

'We are traders on our way to Kurgobad. We seek passage through the town,' Reveeker replied.

'Do you have papers to vouch for you?'

'Papers? Where the hells are we? Estria?' replied Rev, feigning indignation. 'We wish to pass through, that is all.'

'No papers, no pass. You'll have to go around.'

'But that will add two days to our journey! What happened to the famous hospitality of Drevelle? Where is Elder Dalgeer?'

'You know the Elder?'

Bellina watched a look of contemplation pass over the guard's face.

'Wait here, I will fetch him. We'll see if what you say is true.' He said slipping through a small side door.

A few heart-stopping minutes passed for Bellina and the group. Finally, a short man of advanced years came out accompanied by the guard. A huge turban topped off a head that also claimed ownership of a particularly fine, white beard. His clothes looked as if they had once been very grand. Flesh hung loose from his forearms, his cheeks were sunken. The overall impression was of a wealthy man who had fallen on hard times. His eyes fixed on Reveeker who had climbed down from the gaweldon's back. For a brief moment, Bellina feared for how the whole thing was going to play out.

The Elder suddenly grabbed Reveeker in a tight embrace and tears fell from his eyes.

'You know this man?' the guard asked, surprised.

'Of course I do, you dolt. This is one of my oldest friends, returned after many years. Allow him and his friends access at once,' Dalgeer said with the tone of a man who was used to being obeyed.

'You may know him, but they still do not have the off—'

'Don't you dare start with that bureaucratic *kifet*! For what it's worth, I am still the Elder of Drevelle. I'll be damned if I'll be told that my friends are not allowed to pass freely through my town. They don't look like Estrian soldiers, do they? You bring shame on your family young man. How far will you turn from the old ways, eh?' Dalgeer said.

The guard looked ashamed of himself. 'Forgive me, honoured grandfather. Please accept my apologies. You may pass.' He banged his hand on the large doors, signalling for them to be opened.

When they began to make their way through the gate, one of the guards looked straight at Bellina. She could feel beads of sweat running down her forehead, the strain of the shrouding technique taking its toll. For a second, her focus wavered and the air around Bellina and Holger fluctuated. She swore at herself and regained her composure. The guard looked at her with a baffled expression on his face, he still wore the same expression as the town gates closed again.

'Elder Dalgeer, thank the Mother you are still alive! Thank—'

'We shall save our talk for somewhere more private,' said the old man. 'I feel I will need a pull from my shafi pipe to hear the tale of how a man I thought dead can appear before me.'

The Elder led them through the town of Drevelle. Bellina looked at the desolate place. Row upon row of abandoned houses stared back at her with eyes boarded shut. A few people wandered the streets aimlessly, looking at the group from sunken sockets filled with hunger. Before too long they were heading up the driveway of what had once been a grand home. Unlike most of the dwellings in the town, the large first floor was topped by a second. A stable was attached to the side. Like the rest of the building, its once brightly coloured plaster was cracked and falling from its walls. They stabled their beasts and were led into a large living room. A moth-eaten Varashi rug lay at its centre atop a mosaic of intricate geometric patterns. Ornately carved, arched doorways led off into other rooms. The old man walked into the middle of the rug and sat on a well-used cushion.

'Come, sit, all of you,' Dalgeer said, lighting a shafi pipe.

'When did you start smoking that?' Reveeker asked, eyebrow raised sharply.

'When this town went to *kifet*, old friend. Please sit, you dishonour me,' he said, looking at the group and patting the ground.

Bellina could feel her concentration wavering. There was a small pop and the effect of the shroud was lost.

'By the Mother! What devilry is this?' Dalgeer shouted, the pipe dropping from his lip.

'May as well all drop the act now, eh?' Torkwill said, allowing the rest of the group to resume their usual appearance.

'Honoured grandfather, we mean you no harm,' added Cirona, quickly. 'We are friends of Reveeker.'

'Is this true Rev? You are travelling with... Estrians?' the old man said, spitting the last word like a dart.

'It is true, Dalgeer. It is also true that without these Estrians I would not be standing before you today. I owe them my life and my freedom,' Reveeker said.

The old man took another pull on his pipe, eyebrows furrowed in thought. 'In that case, friends of Reveeker are friends of mine, however curious they may be. Come, all of you sit and be welcome. What is mine is yours. If only you had been guests when that meant I had anything to give,' Dalgeer said as they all settled themselves on the cushions he passed to them. 'Now tell me your tale Reveeker. The last time I saw you was on the day you were taken away in chains, branded a traitor. By the Mother, how the people of this town shook with rage. Never has this country been blessed with a more devoted son!'

'Thank you for your kind words, Dalgeer. Where to start?' Reveeker said, before launching into his tale.

The others filled in gaps where necessary, while Dargo added overenthusiastic embellishment.

With the tales of their woes complete, the old man sank back in his cushion, his hand clasped to his brow. 'How you are here at all is a miracle. Nekrolytes? Of the all the dark things I thought Marmossa's young kaffars capable of, I never believed they would stoop so low!'

'Unfortunately, it's true old boy,' said Elvgren. 'Hard to doubt when trying to stop one from biting your face off.'

'You have heard our tale, now please tell us yours, Dalgeer,' asked Reveeker. 'What has happened to the town I love? Where are the date groves? The people?'

'Gone. All of it gone. The town felt the shame of not being able to help you Reveeker, but that was the least of the indignities we have had to bear.' Dalgeer cast his eyes to the floor. 'It started when the rains stopped. No water, no dates to harvest, no produce, no money. The people, they left looking for work, for money to put food in the bellies of their children. They went to Kurgobad along with so many others from towns and villages like ours. The rains only fall upon the capital now.'

'Did you not try to stop them?' Reveeker asked.

'How could I ask that of them? There was nothing here. Still though, some remained. And we tried to carry on with our lives. That changed when the Arch Vizier paid a visit.'

'Marmossa came here?' Cirona said.

'Yes, and what an auspicious day we thought it would be too. Ah! The fools we were. Nothing but misery lies in the wake of that man, though many would disagree. We thought he had come to offer support, money, something. Instead he had come to claim the town. He came looking for yaksit, and he found it. As you have seen, the town was placed under guard. The last of us inhabitants were put under curfew with strict instructions to stay away from the harvesting site, under pain of death. Prisoners in our own home. Even the traders and travelling merchants stopped coming, put off by the excessive paperwork needed to gain entry. The only way I can get anything, even meagre amounts of food for the people, is by shaming the guards into it as I did today. Though you should not tarry long here and test their kindness.'

Bellina felt her heart stir at the plight of the people of Drevelle. All this misery to get some liquid from the ground. And for what possible purpose? To turn every Burkeshi into a naffir?

'We need to get into the harvesting site,' Cirona said, giving voice to the thought that was beginning to form in Bellina's own mind.

'You mustn't, for all our sakes! If you are caught, and the fact you have been here — that I have been harbouring Estrians — gets back to the guards, they will finish us for good,' the old man implored.

'Good sir, I can understand you fear,' said Bellina, 'but it is our mission to discover what is going on here. You must trust us. We are trying to avert a war that could destroy us all.'

'You will find none in Burkesh who desire war, not even with Estria, despite the lurid stories Marmossa and his followers spread. But how would you gain access to the site? Even if you can appear like Burkeshis — Mother give me strength to understand how — you cannot get within six paces of the place without being shot!' Dalgeer said, arms gesticulating wildly.

'Don't worry, we got our ways,' Torkwill said, with a twinkle in his eye.

43

The cold of the ballistol sent a shiver through Cirona's body. She let the tremor flicker through her with a sigh, then double checked the weapon was secure inside the waistband of her trousers. This, along with a pair of daggers and her short sword, made her feel she was ready for anything. 'Torkwill? Rev? We set here?' she asked the two men who were accompanying her to the harvesting site.

'Aye.'

'Ready Rona.'

She turned to look at the rest of the group. Bellina sat with a petulant twist to her mouth, angry at not being allowed to go too. Cirona knew it was risky to leave her, that she was supposed to keep the young woman safe. In her mind, the original parameters of the mission had shifted though. *Something big is going on here*, she thought, *and we may be the only ones who can find out what it is.*

'Right you lot, any hint of trouble make your way to Kurgobad,' she told the group. 'Find this Gilroy bloke and carry on from there. Elvgren, you're in charge of getting everyone there if something should happen.'

A look of surprise, followed by satisfaction, passed across Elvgren's face.

'Why's he get to be in charge?' Holger asked.

Cirona was taken aback by such a show of forthrightness from the usually placid young man. 'For one, he has military experience. Two, 'cos he thinks on his feet. And three, because I fucking said so. Anyone else got any problems?'

They all shook their heads.

'Honoured grandfather, please keep an eye on this lot. Make sure they play nice.'

'Do not worry yourself Major, I shall keep them like my own.'

'Thanks. We should be back in a couple of hours at most. Bellina, keep yourself alert in case we need to communicate with you. Let's go men.'

*

Cirona, Reveeker and Torkwill strode from Dalgeer's home, following the small map he had drawn for them. The trio made their way through the silent streets. Despite it being only a little after sundown, the small remnants of the town's population were already indoors. They passed a house with a dim light flickering from one window, it looked like the eye of a wounded man waiting for the end to come. The only other people they met on their journey were a handful of guards making a lazy circuit of the town. One pair of soldiers came straight down the dusty street towards them. The effect of Torkwill's shedding made it possible for them to see each other, so Cirona gestured to the others to press themselves against the nearest wall. The two guards sauntered past chatting amiably, she wondered if they would have even noticed them without the cognopath's help.

They continued on their way through the wide streets. The houses gradually thinned out amidst evidence of recent demolition. Finally, they reached their destination. A massive, mud-brick wall rose in front of them, easily five townhouses tall. Around the wall was a barren waste where the ghost-like traces of houses stained the ground. Black smoke rose from the other side of the wall, mingling sinuously with the darkness of the sky. Below, in the centre of the wall, were double doors wide enough for two carts to pass through. A pair of guards flanked the doors. It seemed to Cirona that they had no worries about anyone trying anything. The three spies crouched down as close as they dared get to the guards. Torkwill's voice rang in Cirona's head.

Right yous two. Got about an hour and a half to get this over with. No talking out loud, anything we need to say we can communicate mind to mind.

How do we get in? came Reveeker's voice.

We wait till someone comes out and we slip in. Can't open the door without the guards noticing, Cirona said.

Fifteen tense minutes passed in the shadow of the wall. Cirona prayed that someone would actually come out of the doors.

Ach! We could be waiting for fucking hours at this rate, I'm gonna— Torkwill started to say.

Hang on, something's up, Cirona said.

There was a banging from the other side of the door. The two guards stretched and slid the large wooden bar from across the entrance. With visible strain, the pair grabbed the brass handles and pulled the doors apart. A large horse-drawn wagon came forward and stopped in the doorway. The driver looked down at the guards and began to chat with them.

Cirona gestured towards the opening and they set off. Her heart hammered in her chest whilst she inched round the side of the wagon. Torkwill evidently had more faith in his abilities and stormed ahead beckoning her with his hand. As Cirona passed the back of the wagon, the glint of something shiny caught her eye. She peered in at the contents. Stored neatly, were row upon row of cylindrical iron kegs. She noticed the unmistakable trail of black yaksit ooze on the rim of the closest keg to her. It snaked a path down the container, smearing its way through the Burkeshi flag — three white stars, the point of the middle one extending down into a blade. *Must be how they're transporting the shit,* Cirona voiced to the others.

Fantastic Major, but get your peepers round this! Torkwill replied.

*

'Well this is bloody boring,' Dargo said, with a theatrical slumping of his body.

Elvgren was inclined to agree. Roughly an hour had passed since the major, Reveeker and Torkwill's departure, and the time had been spent in tense silence. Dargo yawned next to him and reclined back into the large, soft cushion. Holger paced up and down the room, while Dalgeer had taken himself of into a corner with his shafi pipe and was now floating in worlds of his own construction. Bellina sat alert, eyes narrowed, listening out for any news from Cirona. Elvgren's eyes fixed on her. He noticed the way she bit on her bottom lip when she concentrated, the rise and fall of her chest, her green eyes shining faintly in the candlelight.

'Oh, for the love of... why don't you go and talk to her instead of just staring?' Dargo hissed at him, the sound snapping him back to reality.

'What do you mean? I... I was looking out the window,' he replied.

'Yeah alright and I'm the King of Varash. If you ain't gonna do nothing, s'pose ol' Dargo will have to step in.'

'No Dar! Wait!' Elvgren whispered sharply.

The boy strode into the middle of the carpet and cleared his throat. 'Ladies and gents, the time ain't gonna pass no quicker with us all moping. Who fancies a little game?'

'Be nice to have something else to occupy my mind,' Holger said with a shrug.

'Belle 'ow 'bout you?' Dargo asked.

Bellina gave her head a gentle shake and turned her attention towards him. 'What's that, Dar?'

'Fancy a game, is what I said. You in?' Dargo replied, eyebrows raised.

'I suppose a small distraction wouldn't be unwelcome,' she said.

'Alright then, I think I've got the perfect game to get us a bit more lively. It's called Pass the Apple.'

'Oh, how very complicated! That should take all of thirty seconds,' Elvgren said, wondering how this was supposed to help him.

'That's where you're wrong, my one-eyed friend. Can't use your hands or arms, see. Can use any other part of your body though,' Dargo said with a wink.

'Sounds a bit risqué to me,' Elvgren replied.

'Oh Elvgren, don't be such a boring old fart. Let's do it,' Bellina said.

'Alright, alright!' he replied.

Dargo quickly set off to their supplies and returned with a bright red apple. 'Right, spread out in a square. That's it. I'll start. When you pass the apple over you have to nominate who that person gives it to. All clear?' As the group assented, Dargo tucked the apple under his chin and clasped his hands behind his back. He made his way slowly over to Bellina, peg leg thumping dully on the carpet.

Bellina laughed as she struggled to get the apple from under Dargo's chin, their heads and bodies brushing close.

Elvgren could now see what the brilliant little bugger had in mind. Eventually, after much laughing from the pair, Bellina managed to secure the apple.

'I nominate Gren,' the boy said.

Elvgren felt like kissing the boy and kicking him at the same time. He watched, heart banging in his chest, as Bellina closed the distance to him. She flicked her raven hair behind her shoulder, leaning her head and body towards his own. He inclined his head towards her to try and get hold of the apple. He felt the stubble from his cheek brush her face. The warmth of her breath on his lips. Then he felt Holger's weight steam into his side.

*

Above the orphanage dining room there was a painting depicting one of the twelve hells. Cirona used to stare at the picture with fear in her heart — the ground torn asunder, black smoke pouring into the sky, flames licking at the bodies of helpless people who had turned from Father Light and got lost when they tried to pass through the Weeping Veil. It was an image not too dissimilar from the one that confronted her now. Scatterings of hastily constructed buildings spread across the cracked and bruised ground. A huge pyramid of criss-crossing iron beams rose to a point from which a fire blazed, clouds of black smoke billowing away in the breeze. Dangling below this fire was a massive, spiked, metal needle. Winches and cogs whirred noisily as it was raised and then sent smashing into the ground below it. A dozen or so men swarmed about its base like ants. *What the fuck is that?* she called out.

I have no idea, Torkwill replied. *Let's get closer for a better peep.*

They made their way across to the machine till they stood within arm's reach of the busy workers. After each plunge of the needle the ground haemorrhaged thick, black yaksit. The men would hurry forward with long, canvas pipes and place them into the ooze. The pipes led back to large mechanised pumps which then sucked up the liquid.

This machinery... it's so advanced, said Cirona. *How are these things powered? Even a hundred illegal vorotorium cells wouldn't be enough to fuel this.*

Reveeker pointed to the base of one of the pumps. *There, look... they're using the yaksit!*

Cirona saw with horror that he was right. A tharg engine connected to a vorotorium generator throbbed below the machine. Brass gears, cogs and pistons, spun in perfect unison. At the heart of the generator, where she should have been able to see the familiar pulsating blues and purples of the captured sortilenergy, was a churning blackness. It bubbled and contracted as it was consumed at the heart of the generator, quivering and spiking out like it was in pain. Cirona reeled back in shock. *This* is what they were doing with all that yaksit. It wasn't just for creating naffirs, the Burkeshis were using it to mechanise. Fleets of iron clad Burkeshi ships floated through her mind, armies of automatons marching off to war. How far had they come? How had they acquired this level of engineering skill?

Calm down woman! Said Torkwill. *It's put the shits up all of us, but your thoughts are strong enough to break the shroud.*

Cirona drew a deep breath and tried to compose herself. She

watched the men begin to fill up kegs like the ones she had seen on the wagon. These were then hauled over to a moving belt that disappeared into one of the buildings. Gesturing for the men to follow her, she made her way to what she assumed must be a storehouse. However, when she peered inside, she was stunned by the interior of the building. Galvanic light bulbs shone from lamps attached to walls which were covered in murals. A procession of men and women marched across the floor towards the central image on the back wall. There, a woman's face hovered, a cape billowing out behind her, stars hanging in the darkness. Below this image, the moving belt carried the kegs through the room. A beautiful girl, of about sixteen, stood upon a raised dais formed from black marble. Her hands hovered over each open container in a blessing, the yaksit rising to meet her fingers. Cirona's mind was snapped out of its stupor as something moved in the corner of her eye. Reveeker, tears streaming silently down his face, was walking towards the girl. *Rev? What the hells are you doing?*

He didn't stop, he didn't even turn around. Instead, he spoke aloud. 'That's my daughter.'

44

Elvgren's stomach lurched as he rolled across the floor entangled with Holger. He lashed out wildly trying to connect any part of him with the man. Holger temporarily gained the advantage on him, sitting atop his chest and aiming a punch at his face. Elvgren punched him in the side and was about to pounce when there was a shout.

'Stop it! The pair of you!' Bellina cried.

Elvgren knelt on one knee. He was aware of Dalgeer giving a little start. Misted eyes stared out from heavy lids for a brief moment before closing, returning to drug-fuelled sleep. The young lord looked over at Bellina, her face a picture of fury. Brows scrunched, her hands trembled with rage at her side. Dargo placed himself between Elvgren and Holger. The boy let out a sigh and moved his jaw thoughtfully.

'Well this wasn't exactly how I intended it, but we're here now,' he said. 'Belle, which one of these two do you want? This crap ain't gonna end till one of 'em gives up.'

Elvgren's insides cringed. *This is ridiculous there's no choice here*, he thought, *she is mine, promised to me*. He studied Bellina's eyes, seeing them register shock before she cast them downwards.

'I... I have no idea what you mean Dargo,' she said, her sharp tongue absent for once.

'Don't gimme that shit. This was always gonna happen. One of 'em stalks your shadow and has travelled halfway round the world to stay near ye. The other is too pig-headed to admit how he feels, Estrian reserve and all that. So, sorry but you're gonna have to sort it out,' the boy said holding out his hands.

'I am betrothed to Lord Elvgren, my... my heart belongs to him,' Bellina said.

Her eyes, her eyes though. Elvgren watched how they lingered on Holger. His anger and wounded pride combusted. He pulled himself to his feet, every fibre of his body trembling with rage. 'Him? HIM? Don't even dare deny it, I see now. Fancy a bit of rough, do you my lady? Grubby little Narvglander with dirt under his nails to keep you warm in all the right places. You're fucking filth, you vile wretched witch. You should be honoured that I even deign to look at you, let alone want to stick my co—' Elvgren was cut off as stars filled his eyes and he fell to the floor. He shook his head to focus his vision, Holger was standing over him rubbing the knuckles of his right hand.

'That's enough,' he said.

*

Get back here, you fucking idiot!

Torkwill's voice bellowed in her mind. Cirona's nerves pinged with panic. 'Stop him!' she shouted out loud, cringing at her stupidity. The girl raised her eyes as the air shimmered around Cirona and Reveeker, exposing them to her gaze.

'Father?' the girl said languidly, showing no hint of shock, 'I see you have been making friends amongst our enemies.' There was a hint of boredom in her voice.

'Nisseen!' Reveeker cried.

Cirona watched him run towards her. Nisseen flicked her wrist and a wave of yaksit flew towards the major and Reveeker, clinging to their arms and legs, restraining them.

'Nisseen? My love, what are you doing? It's me, your father!' Reveeker said, tears still flowing freely from his eyes.

'I have no father now. Just a traitor, a spineless worm who could not do what must be done for the glory of Burkesh. Denvad has told me all about you, how you traded my mother's life for your own,' the girl hissed at her father, an inch from his face.

'Denvad? That bastard is the reason for all our misery. It was his orders—'

'Denvad is my husband. I am his third bride. He would not lie to me. If it was not for him, our glorious Grand Multan and the Arch Vizier, I would never have been able to accept the gifts of the Mother.'

'Hu... husband?' Reveeker said.

Cirona could only watch, heart rending, as the spark went out of Reveeker's soul. 'Show some fucking respect girl. That's you father! You have no idea what he has sacrificed for you!' she shouted at the girl, unable to contain herself.

'Do not speak to me, you filthy Estrian *durch*. You are the gutter *kifet* that warms him at night now, eh? I have heard enough from both of you.' Nisseen sent yaksit flying towards their mouths, silencing them.

'Denvad will know what to do with you. Move.'

Reveeker shuffled forward numbly. Cirona refused to move, shooting the girl a look of pure venom.

'Such eyes,' Nisseen said, walking towards her with Reveeker in tow. 'Such eyes you Estrians possess — the hate, the ignorance, the lust. I have no idea what you two are doing here but that is why we employ torturers.' She paused, stroking Cirona's face with the back of her hand before striking the mjor on the mouth. Cirona's eyes blurred and she tasted the tang of blood. She felt a flicker of hope. The girl had said 'two of us', so she couldn't have noticed Torkwill. As if in answer to her realisation, the cognopath's voice echoed in her head.

Major, I'm going back to Dalgeer's place. I could'nae hold the shed over ye two when ye started creating. I'm gonna take thethe lassie's power controls off yer wrist now while she ain't looking; gotta feeling we're gonna need them. Keep strong and your mind open. We'll get you outta this.

Thank you, Torkwill, she replied. In the time she had been communicating cognopathically with Torkwill, Nisseen had walked to the entrance of the building.

'Guards! Guards!' the girl screamed, drawing men pouring into the room. 'Take them to the capital, to my husband at the Multanial Palace. Let's see if a spell with the inquisitors can glean what treachery they have been brewing.'

*

Bellina stared down at Elvgren, tears forming in her eyes. How could he? Just when she was beginning to think he had changed. Why? Holger's broad back stood in front of her twitching with anger. And what the hells had come over him? She had already told him how it must be between them. Still though, she was touched by his defence of her. 'Holger, while I appreciate the sentiment I am still—'

'Yeah, yeah, yeah, betrothed to this prick,' he cut in, shaking with anger. 'But d'ya know what? You deserve better than him. I love you Belle. Not like my sister, I lied, I'm sorry. And I'm sorry about how I feel. But that's it, I've said it. It's yours to take or leave. Whatever you decide, I will be here for you, fuck the fucking protocol!'

Before she had time to form any kind of response a blast of cognopathic communication from Torkwill hit her like a tornado. *Lassie it's me. Shit has gone so far south it's come back on itself. The major and the*

Burkeshi have been captured. Get our stuff ready, we leave as soon as I get there. The message ended with the same suddenness with which it came. Her mind snapped into life.

'We've got to go. The major and Reveeker have been taken. This is not the time for us to fall apart. We are going to have to get on. I don't expect you two to ever see eye to eye but we need to pull ourselves the fuck together,' she said.

Holger's eyes looked back at her, set firm. Dargo looked at Elvgren with concern before nodding. Elvgren looked at Holger, malice glinting in his eye, but he too nodded at her.

'Let's get the gaweldons sorted for when Torkwill gets here,' she said flatly.

The others shuffled past her from the room. Bellina turned back to look at Elder Dalgeer. Soft, stupefied snores issued from his nose, rustling the white whiskers of his beard. She hoped with all her heart this turn of events wouldn't cause him and the town any more pain.

*

The group had just finished sorting the gaweldons when Bellina saw Torkwill come sprinting into the stables. The cognopath doubled over, panting for breath.

'Ye lot ready? What the fuck happened to One Eye?' Torkwill said, pointing to the darkening bruise on Elvgren's face.

'We can talk about that later,' Bellina said. 'Where are the major and Reveeker? What happened?'

'Turns out the Burkeshis are harvesting the yaksit to fuel tharg engines. Reveeker's daughter must be one o' them naffirs cos she was blessing the shit. Him and the major blew the shred — just managed to steal your controls from the major's wrist and get out of there before I lost complete control of it. They've loaded 'em up in a wagon and are taking them to the Multanial Palace in Kurgobad.'

'Shit,' Dargo said. 'What do we do now?'

'We get outta this town. If we can catch up to them, we try and get them back. If not we carry on to Kurgobad, meet Gilroy and wait for orders. I've got enough strength left to shed us. Lass, yer gonna have to use your powers for more blunt purposes...'

'What's that sound?' Elvgren said, pointing outside of the stables.

Bellina listened. Loud banging came from the front door.

'Elder Dalgeer? Elder Dalgeer, open this door! We have reason to believe you are harbouring enemies of the state!' A man's voice shouted.

'No response, Captain?' another voice said.

'*Vaksa!* Nothing. Check the stables, I'll get this door open,' the first man replied.

'Shit,' Torkwill hissed. 'Lass, cast the shedding on us now, I need to catch me breath.'

The air moved around the group, hiding them from sight just as the door to the stables opened. They all sat huddled together at the back of the room.

Bellina held her breath. She was finding it hard to maintain her concentration, yet she persevered, keeping her mind as blank as possible.

A young guard cautiously advanced along the line of stalls, sword drawn and flaming torch in hand. He poked around the gaweldons, inspecting the bag of supplies, sticking his head into their small wagon.

The guard came closer and closer to their position. Bellina could feel the sweat trickling across her brow. The air started to wobble in front of them, the strain of casting the shedding over so many people, taking its toll on her. The guard stared straight at them, his eyes narrowed and he licked his lips. Bellina's eyeballs throbbed as she forced herself not to blink, in case even that small action broke the illusion. Just whenn she thought she couldn't take anymore, a voice called from the front of the stable.

'Dalgeer's out cold on shafi and there's no sign of anyone else here. Any sign in there?'

The young guard hesitated for a brief moment then shook his head like waking from a dream.

'Nah, they must have left in a hurry. I've got their gaweldons and supplies here.'

'Alright then. I'll send some men over to collect the stuff. Let's get back to the search. They can't have got far.'

The young guard turned and walked out of the stable. Relief flooded through Bellina. The shedding fell away from them with a faint pop just as the stable doors closed.

*

The gaweldons sped through Drevelle almost as quick as galloping horses. The road to Kurgobad, was just beyond the gate that was closing in front of them. They raced past startled guards who shouted and made grabs at thin air.

Torkwill sat in front of Bellina, controlling the gaweldon, his body tense with the concentration of keeping up the shed. 'Right lass,' he called back to her. 'You're gonna have to push that gate open with your mind. I'm giving ye full access to your cognokinetic powers.'

'Torkwill... that gate is huge! I've never moved anything close to *that* big!'

'Gonna have to now, girlie. It's that or an adjoining cell with the major in the palace dungeons. Just focus yerself, ye can do this.'

They were closing in fast on the gate. Bellina focused her mind on it and imagined a giant hand pushing it open. She could feel the wooden doors straining against her mind. In the distance, the doors moved ever so slightly, just enough to alert the guards, who primed and lowered their balliskets.

'Torkwill, they're gonna fucking shoot us!' Holger called.

'I'll fix that. Come on lass, move that fucking door!'

'I... I can't. It's—' Her words were cut off by the sound of the balliskets being fired. She closed her eyes and screamed over the sound of wood snapping, like a huge tree being felled, and two faint pings.

'Ach! Fuck, fuck, fuck... that bloody hurts!' Torkwill cried. He had managed to deflect the bullets, but the shed had been lost.

Oaths and amazed cries rang around them as the guards realised that they were pursuing Estrians.

'Good work on the door lass!' Torkwill said.

Bellina had been too distracted to notice the havoc she had wrought on the gate. It had exploded outwards in a million splinters, one plank left swinging mournfully from a post like a drunk leaning against a wall to puke. *I did that*, she thought, stunned.

The gaweldons pressed on, seemingly undeterred by the turn of events. They rushed past the guards, who dived clear of the galloping lizards, and out on to the road to the capital. There were faint traces of hoof prints and wheels marks in the sand that had blown across the stone road — the group hurried after them, urging the giant lizards faster.

The town of Drevelle had grown small in the distance when Bellina first heard the sound of horses in pursuit.

'They're on us!' Elvgren called out.

'Shit on it all and send it to the Void!' Torkwill bellowed.

''Bout five of 'em coming up fast,' Holger said.

Bellina could feel the gaweldon tiring beneath her, the landscape no longer passing by as quickly. The horsemen were gaining on them, their shouts and hollers carrying on the night air. One of the riders caught up to her and Torkwill — he lowered a ballistol at them and fired. She had just enough time to throw up her cognopathic shield. The impact of the bullet ricocheted in her mind, her head snapped back and the world spun. As she fell from the wagon, the deflected bullet flew in the other direction.

*

Elvgren watched Bellina falling from her seat on the gaweldon. She hit the sand with a wince-inducing thump and rolled to a halt. He pulled the reins on the lizard that he and Dargo were riding and headed after her. Two of the pursuing riders were converging on the same destination so he willed the gaweldon onwards. A man was bearing down on Bellina's prone body — he was within arm's reach of Elvgren and Dargo but he paid them no mind. Knowing he had to do something, Elvgren stood on top of the lizard and launched himself.

The rider was just lowering his sword to stab Bellina in the gut when he caught sight of Elvgren flying through the air towards him. Elvgren registered the look of shock and fear on the man's face a second before he smashed into his shoulder. They pirouetted together through the air before landing hard on the sand. The horseman took the full force of the impact and his head snapped back with a sickening crack. Elvgren pulled himself up from the corpse and turned around. He could see Dargo leaning over Bellina a few paces away, listening to her heart.

Coming up on them was another rider, his face contorted in a snarl, sword raised high.

'Behind you!' Elvgren called, helpless to intervene.

There was the sound of a shot. The man's face exploded in a mess of blood and bone as he tumbled from his horse. Holger appeared, ballistol still smoking in his hand, riding to Bellina and Dargo.

Elvgren rushed over, legs heavy from the jealous grip of the sand. He watched with eyes that burned with anger from seeing Holger gently lift Bellina's head in his arms.

'She's alive but unconscious,' the Narvglander said without looking up.

'Get your fucking hands off her!' Elvgren shouted, trembling with rage.

'Make me,' Holger replied flatly.

'Aright you two, sort this out later,' said Dargo, 'Ballistols at dawn or something. Hey, where's the old mind-melter?'

'He was leading the other three off down the road last time I saw him,' Holger said.

'What should we do now?' Dargo asked, looking first at Elvgren and then Holger.

'We sit tight and wait for Torkwill,' decided Lovitz. 'If he can ditch those riders he'll be able to contact us cognopathically and let us know where he is. The gaweldons look like they've had it for the time being.'

'Much as I hate to admit it, I think he's right,' said Holger. 'Let's hunker down and keep a lookout. Dargo, get me a blanket from the lizard. I'll try and make Belle more comfortable.'

'You don't get to give orders. The major put *me* in charge!' Elvgren said.

'Oh, for fucks sake... Fine. You tell Dargo to get a blanket, I really don't care!'

'Dargo, get a blanket.'

The boy wandered off shaking his head in disbelief.

The minutes stretched by in a silence that bordered on reverence, Elvgren's good eye strained for any sign of movement in the gathering gloom. He looked across at Holger who sat next to the still unconscious Bellina and he felt his gut twist. His hate for the man writhed inside him, compacting, hardening into a cold weight at the bottom of his soul. He was determined to get revenge on Holger. The thought wasn't charged with anger, just a cold assessment of his intent.

One Eye, Rat Boy and Lovesick, can ye hear me? Torkwill's voice echoed in Elvgren's head. Holger didn't seem to respond but, by the looks of it, Dargo had heard him too.

Who you calling Rat Boy? Dargo said.

Ah, ye are there. Listen, I've ditched the sand-fuckers. Where are you and how's the wee lass?

We're just off the road where they first attacked us. Bellina's fine, but out of it at the moment, Elvgren said.

Right ye are. Stay put and I'll make my way back to ye.

A half hour passed before Torkwill and his gaweldon came slowly towards them. The cognopath brought the lizard to a halt and slid off. Elvgren saw that he was bleeding from a vicious gash on his forehead. The beginnings of what would become an exemplar black eye was visible too. *We'll be twins*, Elvgren thought with grim humour, rubbing at the bruise under his own eye socket.

'How'd you ditch 'em?' Dargo asked, looking curiously at the dried blood on the cognopath's face.

'They set upon me like the Terrors, knocked me off the lizard. Set about me with their swords, one of 'em scratched me,' he said, pointing at the cut just below his hairline. 'Had enough strength left to use me powers to stay their arms while I introduced 'em to old Betsy.'

'See the wagon with the major, old boy?' Elvgren asked.

'Nah, long gone. Driver's probably sitting down with a nice pipe next to the fire by now. Best thing we can do is get some rest, set out fresh in the morning.'

'We better take turns keeping watch,' Elvgren said. 'I'll go first if you like.'

'Good on ye, One Eye! I'm fit to drop!' Torkwill replied.

He and the others sorted out the rest of the blankets. Dargo came over and handed one to him as Torkwill and Holger settled down.

'Here ye go, Gren. Keep ye warm.'

'Thanks, Dargo.'

'Look, I'm sorry 'bout how the game turned out. I thought it would give ye a chance to... I dunno... didn't think old lover boy would come flying in like that. Gimme the word and I'll piss in his water bottle. He ain't got no right to treat you like that. Ye'r betrothed to her, he's gotta come to terms with it.' Dargo paused for a second, looking at him quizzically. 'But then you shouldn't have said those things to Belle.'

'I know, it just makes my blood boil. People like him, they sweep my hall, they clean my fucking privy. He has no right to talk to me, let alone strike me.'

'People like me as well then, I suppose?' Dargo said, eyebrows raised.

'No, no... Don't be stupid. You're... you're a damn good friend.'

'I ain't got no blue blood in me either, though. What happens when we get back? Ye gonna drop me like a sack o' hot shit?'

'Never. What would I do without you?'

'Hah! You'd probably manage to stagger on for an afternoon before you collapsed,' Dargo said, reminding Elvgren of a conversation with Benkins from back when the world made sense. 'Anyway, you ain't getting off that easy. I expect some kinda title for all me heroics and a nice bit of change in me pocket. Sure your folks will be grateful to have ye back, even if you've declined in the looks department.'

'I'm sure they'll be thrilled,' he said, forcing a smile and trying not to let his tone sound bitter.

'Night then mate. Gimme a shout when it's my watch.'

Elvgren sat staring into the darkness, gentle snoring the only sound. He imagined his brother laughing at him with his parents. *All that training only to get knocked over by some ship's boy!* they said. Their voices taunting him, their faces and words spinning round and round making him feel nauseous. They laughed at his missing eye, the company he kept. *They* would have killed the dirty little Narvglander. He pushed himself to his feet and walked towards the sleeping form of Holger. He silently drew his sword from his belt.

Elvgren stared down at the young man, the point of the blade dangling above his throat. *Do it!* the voice of his mother said. *Your brother would have.* He clenched his jaw, muscles so taut his face shook. Tears streamed from his eye and he collapsed to the ground, sword dropping harmlessly on to the sand. *No Mother. I'm not like my brother... I'm not like him at all.*

45

Bellina awoke from dreams of home with the heat of the sun warming her face. Her eyelids pulled themselves apart reluctantly as she hauled herself to a sitting position and took in the scene. Torkwill sat with a wineskin dangling above his head, smacking its bottom, trying to force out the last few drops. Dargo and Elvgren were together, sharing a husk of bread. Holger was checking the gaweldons' saddles, giving each beast a friendly pat.

The events of the previous night danced their way through her mind like drunken regrets. The major and Reveeker, captured. Dargo's game with the apple. The fight between Elvgren and Holger. Their dramatic departure from Drevelle. A bullet spinning away from her.

Bellina's gaze drifted back to Holger. She tried to dig out her feelings for him and found they were meshed together with so much else: she treasured his friendship, respected his honesty and, after all the adventures they had shared, a deep affection had formed. Was it love though? Or was it what love was born from? She couldn't work it out. It certainly wasn't the kind of love found in all the sappy books the young, female nobles of Estria gobbled up. She felt it would be hard to swoon into the arms of someone she'd slept next to on the bare floorboards of a ship, whose unwashed scent had mingled with her own as the still air of the jungle drew the sweat from their bodies.

Then there was Elvgren. She had always sworn to herself and her father that she would marry for her own reasons. But, in the end, Bellina had gone along with her father's request to alleviate some of the burden from his shoulders. She hadn't desired it, but once she agreed she had intended to follow it through. Her feelings for Elvgren weren't quite as muddled as they were towards Holger. For one, she certainly didn't enjoy his company, though sometimes he had flashes of brilliance. Bellina wondered if that was his true self coming through, a momentary slip, the mask descending just a little before being hastily rearranged. It seemed to her that he was punishing himself for something, not allowing himself to be free. Bellina stopped her train of thought and decided she was giving him too much credit.

What was it to be? One or the other? Neither? What did *she* want? Bellina had always thought she understood herself but, in that moment, her identity floated intangibly in front of her, teasing her with formless desires. Bellina suddenly felt ludicrously self-absorbed, her thoughts returning to the fate of Cirona, captured and hauled off. Visions of tools of torture filled her head, drawn from a book she had read about the Escambrian Purges — all the small and large devices of displeasure that the Estrian Empire's most devout country used to weed out heretics. She was saved from her morbid meanderings by a small loaf of bread bouncing off her head.

'Quit daydreaming, lass. Eat up. We've got a lot more to get through yet. Oh, and I thought ye might want this,' Torkwill said, as something round and shiny shot from his hand.

Bellina plucked it from the air and looked down. 'My control conduit?'

'Yeah. I think you've earned it. Now hurry up, the capital is still a few hours' ride away.'

'What happened? After I was shot at, I mean.'

'We're alive, the major and the sand-shagger are still captured. What more d'ya need to know?' he said with a shrug.

*

The hours on the grand road to Kurgobad passed by. Holger sat in front of Bellina, guiding the gaweldon. Elvgren kept shooting dark looks at them but they both ignored him.

Bellina felt she needed to confront what Holger had said to her the night before. 'Holger, about what you said yesterday...'

'I meant what I said. It's sappy as all shit, I know, but I couldn't think of another way to put it. I promise not to unleash any more sentimental bollocks on you but promise me you'll think on it. You're amazing Belle and you deserve someone who appreciates that.'

'Thanks Holger,' she said, feeling better for addressing the matter. 'It was pretty cringy though!' They both laughed.

'Hey watch it! Those were my best lines. I think I might have nicked them from a play I saw, but still!' he said turning his head to flash her a smile.

They fell into silence again, the varying sizes of the sand dunes the only things to mark their progress.

'Belle... If this is too intrusive let me know, but I am curious. How did the people around you react when they found out you were a cognopath?'

Bellina thought for a moment. It certainly hadn't been the best time in her life. 'My father took it pretty well, not much flusters him though. When the news got out to the other nobles, there was a bit of a furore. Father decided it would be best to confront it head on, not hide what I am. A large part of the nobility wanted me sent to the cognopath compound but my father fought hard to keep me with him. He is... he is a great man,' she said, tears filling her eyes. Bellina drew a deep breath composing herself. 'Why do you ask? In fact, you have been more interested than anyone ever has in the initial discovery of my powers.' *And how I feel about it*, she added to herself.

'Well... I suppose you should kno—' Holger began.

'Look at the size of that!' Dargo called out.

Bellina looked past Holger and saw the gates of the Burkeshi capital rising in front of them, large and imposing. The walls of the city were a pulsating turquoise blue. Depictions of grand kings being offered gifts from prostrated peasants, walked across it. Up close, she realised it was a mosaic made up of tiny fragments of jagged tile. Torkwill shrouded them and the group passed through the gates unhindered, mingling with the traders' wagons. They pressed a few coppers into a lad's hand to stable their gaweldons and continued on foot.

Kurgobad lay stretched out before Bellina like a lion in the sun. Despite Estria's fears and the knowledge she had gleaned on their journey, it did not look like a place preparing itself for war. Thousands of people crushed in around them. Children played barefoot in the street. Women in long silk shawls haggled with grinning stallholders. Men in white turbans chatted passionately in the shade of awnings, sipping coffee and standing in groups. Donkeys laden with brightly coloured cloths were harried along by disinterested handlers. It was a bustling, thriving place. With a pang of homesickness, Bellina thought that if she merely changed the people's attire she could be in Victory.

They worked their way through streets made narrow by the insistent pressing of stucco buildings that stood at least three stories high. Geometric mosaics and frescoes cut the structures in half, creating colourful bands, glinting cheerfully in the sun. Evidence of the city's expansion was all around them. Workmen hoisted mud bricks up on their shoulders or loaded them onto wooden pallets to be pulled up by pulleys. In the near distance, a massive, half finished, tower of black marble pointed accusingly at the sky. Rising above all of this was what had to be the Multanial Palace. Three massive domes sat atop a long rectangular building, each one pinched at the peak into a little bulge of gold that was crowned with three metal stars.

'So how do we find our man?' Elvgren called out to Torkwill.

'Should be waiting by the fountain at the centre of the city. He was to wait there at noon every day wearing a white feather.'

'And how, pray tell, are we to locate a piddling little fountain?' Elvgren asked.

'From what I've heard we shouldn't be able to miss it.'

By the Gods, he's right! Bellina thought, the clustered buildings thinning out into a large square.

Four rectangles of water, as large as lakes, stretched before them. Spouts of water issued from the middle of each, here and there crossing over into the other pools, leaving little rainbows hanging in the air while children ran beneath, laughing.

'S'pose the question now is not where the fountain is but what fucking part he's gonna be standing by,' Dargo said.

'Or how large his feather is,' Holger said, pointing to the left.

There, sat on the fountain wall, was a man wearing a turban that sported the most ridiculously oversized feather Bellina had ever seen in her life. She shuddered to think of how a bird of that magnitude took to losing it.

'Right lass, before we make contact we'll check his mind over. If you've seen these sand-fuckers change their faces, we gotta be sure that's him,' Torkwill said.

Bellina focused her attention on the man and reached out to him with her mind. She only touched its surface, listening out for the first thoughts in his head. This turned out to be a particularly bawdy Estrian drinking song. She looked at Torkwill who was grinning from ear-to-ear.

'A man after me own heart, eh? Reckon he's sound,' he said as Bellina nodded her head in agreement. The group made their way over to him.

Elvgren walked up to the man. 'Excuse me good sir, would you happen to be Everett Gilroy?'

'Yes. I must say you're incredibly well spoken,' came Gilroy's baffled reply.

'We're the group you have been expecting. We're using a cognopathic technique to disguise ourselves,' Bellina added as the look of confusion deepened on Everett's face.

'Prove it,' he said.

Bellina flashed an image of their true appearance across his mind.

He rocked back startled, puffing his cheeks out in a stunned whistle. 'Fair enough. Follow me,' Gilroy said, setting off at pace.

*

A scream echoed through the stone corridors and into Cirona's cell. She was hanging from the wall by her arms, wrists chafed and raw from her futile struggling. After hours of torture she was unsure of anything else. A bag had been thrown over their heads as soon as they had been loaded into the wagon. She thought it must be for dramatic effect because they knew exactly where they were going.

A key turned, the door screeched open slowly. *More dramatic effect*, she thought. Cirona had never been captured before *or* been interrogated but her Imperial Guard training meant she was prepared for what to expect — roughly, anyway. Through the bag's weave she could see the flickering of a torch. It drew closer until the bag was ripped from her head. The flames stung her eyes as her vision righted itself.

A man stood before her. He was tall with broad shoulders and a handsome face, he wore his black hair slicked back. When he smiled, he showed the warmth of a man who had never hurt anyone in his life. She had not been expecting this.

'Major. I am Colonel Denvad. Delighted to finally meet you. Oh, how rude of me! How can you reply with that muck on your face?' he said. With a click of his fingers the yaksit fell from her mouth.

'How the fuck do you know who I am? Where's Rev?' she spat at him, mouth dry.

'Patience Major, patience. One thing at a time. We know who you are, of course we do. We know so much about you Estrians. We've been infiltrating you for years, though your own pride and self-absorption prevented you from seeing it. One of my fellow naffirs had taken the form of... what was his name? Kraster? Keester? Ah, no matter, we knew of your plans. But I must say, your little group has proved rather elusive. By the time we reached Tavarar you had disappeared. The young lord and the Lord Chancellor's daughter gone as well. We hid the ship and paid off the Varashi's, though their hate for Estria meant their silence didn't cost much.'

'How did you get them thinking we had been shipwrecked at Timboko? You couldn't have paid off the whole country.' Cirona said, unable to contain her questions.

'My, my, Major. You have no respect for interrogation etiquette, do you? I suppose you can have a few answers before the fun starts,' Denvad said, brimming with arrogance. 'Illusion is one of the many powers of the kaffars and, through the gift of the Mother, the naffirs as well. Though, for it to work, we need some of it to be real. We gathered up a few pieces of your ship and conjured up an illusion of it sinking off the coast of Timboko … in front of lots of witnesses, of course.'

Cirona couldn't believe her ears. The power of the kaffars and naffirs was terrifying. How did Estria stand a chance against them? Why hadn't they extended their policy of enslaving people of magical capabilities across the world, she thought bitterly.

'Don't look so down, Major, you have led us a merry dance! Gulgarno wouldn't part with you. We could have used force but the fat bastard is the son of a Carthanian senator. Instead, we had one of our men in Tavarar, a Mister Faultwright, assist Lord Elvgren in freeing you. We had eyes on you till the bloated idiot Gulgarno tried to recapture you in Dronkor — you can imagine our astonishment when you sprouted wings and flew away,' he said, placing his hands together and fluttering them like birds' wings.

'Why did you do all this? Why not just capture us?'

'Ah! A fine question. Even with all the intelligence we have gathered, we had one mysterious roadblock. The Lord Chancellor, Culvin Ressa. Try as we might we could never glean any insight into the man. We wanted to see what orders he would give you once you re-established contact. That he told you to carry on, even with his daughter in peril, made us realise what a desperate and callous man he is. We assumed you would make for the pass at Chenta, though we dispatched kaffars and naffirs to any feasible crossing point. But there again you surprised us. The Lady Ressa is certainly a woman to be feared — to take down a true kaffar is no mean feat. That's where we lost you; that treacherous bastard, Yevad, screened you from our view. How happy we were then when you walked right into our hands in Drevelle, bringing an old friend with you as well.' He finished with a smile.

'What do you want with us if you know so fucking much?' she spat.

'The rest of your little crew still eludes us. We are hoping they will come to retrieve you. Also, we believe a man of such cunning as the Lord Chancellor would not send his treasured daughter here to merely read the minds of a few low-ranking officials. We wish to know his intentions, how far he will go.'

'You can do what you like to me, I will tell you nothing!' she said, cringing at how pathetic her claim was.

'We hope it doesn't come to that. Though we wondered how you would respond to seeing *another* at our mercy.' He clicked his fingers and Reveeker was dragged into the room by two guards. 'Now this should prove entertaining.'

46

Once the group were safely inside Everett's quarters, Bellina and Torkwill dropped the shrouding. It was a great relief, the strain had started to make Bellina feel lightheaded.

'Lady Bellina, it is truly an honour,' he said bowing low. 'Lord Elvgren, young sirs and former Master Burns, you are all welcome to my little corner of Estria in this forsaken cesspit,' he said with a broad smile.

Bellina looked around the room which was fashioned like an Estrian study. Bookshelves lined the wall and a large witch oak desk was placed before the narrow window. Everett retrieved a pipe from the table. The smell of tobacco filled the room, reminding her painfully of her father.

'Now, tell me your tale and what you have learned,' he said, smoke escaping from the corner of his mouth.

Bellina launched into their tale, everyone assisting with the details. She tried her best to be brief but it still took some time, by the end her mouth was parched.

Gilroy rubbed his chin thoughtfully, his face having gone through a range of emotions that would have put an actor to shame. 'I'll be dammed to the Void. I'm loathe to admit it but you have uncovered more in a few months in Burkesh than all our entire intelligence network has managed in years. Though, to be honest, that primarily consists of me, and has for the last ten years. I always warned we should take the Burkeshis more seriously,' he said, throwing his hands up dramatically. 'But I digress. The major and this Burkeshi, both captured, this is a disturbing development. I shall contact your father immediately for further instructions.' He walked over to a bookcase and pulled one of the tomes halfway out. There was a click like a key turning, then the whirring of gears. The case slid aside to reveal a small room. Inside was a vorotorium cell connected to a scribograph. He sat down at it and began to write. He looked up, catching the look of concern on Bellina's face. 'Don't worry,' he said, 'this is a secure line.'

It took Everett an hour to transmit the information to Estria, after which the group sat, awaiting news from the Lord Chancellor. Finally, the mechanical hand sprang to life and started to pen the response in his flowing script.

'What does it say?' Elvgren asked.

Everett's face turned white. 'I don't quite know how to say this but... We are to attempt to rescue the major. If that is not possible, she is to be dispatched by the Lady Bellina, cognopathically,' he said.

Bellina felt sick to her stomach.

'Don't expect much, does he?' Dargo said.

'That is not all. We are to attempt to gain information about the twelve kaffar councillors. The Lord Chancellor states that in consideration of your new abilities, we should be able to gain access to the palace. Then I am to follow the pre-existing extraction plan to get us out of the country. Oh, and he sends his love and apologies to his daughter and the rest.'

'Well, that makes it all fine then!' Elvgren exclaimed.

Bellina didn't know what to make of it all. She had no intentions of leaving Cirona behind but to try and push their luck and get to the kaffar councillors as well? *It's just like Father to expect so much*, she thought, the weight of his expectations bearing down on her from half a world away.

'Right then man, what can ye tell us? You've been here ten years: how do we go about this?' Torkwill asked.

'Hold on a damn minute!' Elvgren said, 'You haven't asked the rest of us what we want to do.'

'Can't leave Rona and Rev. They wouldn't do that to us,' Holger said, jaw set firm.

'Too fucking right, Gren!' added Dargo. 'Come on, what's one more suicide mission? We got her out of Gulgarno's didn't we?'

Elvgren's good eye darted about the room as if looking for an escape. He chewed at the inside of his mouth. 'Fine,' he finally replied. 'I'll hear you out, but I make no promises.'

'Maybe you have some of your brother in you after all, Lord Elvgren,' Gilroy said.

Brother? Bellina thought, *I didn't know he had a brother.* She saw how Elvgren's face pricked up at the word, like a dog who's heard the gate swing.

'You... knew him?' he asked.

'A long time ago. He was a fine man, and a great loss to the Empire.'

'Tell me something I don't know,' Elvgren muttered darkly.

'Alright, come on. Let's hear what you've got,' Torkwill said.

Gilroy dashed over to his desk and began rummaging through the paraphernalia that cluttered its top. He found what he was looking for and beckoned them over to him. Everett spread out a crude floor plan. '*This* is the Multanial Palace,' he said, arms spread wide as if he expected applause.

'Looks like a six-year-old drew it,' Dargo said.

'He is eight, actually,' Gilroy replied with a sniff, 'and an excellent source of information.'

Elvgren was staring at the map intently. 'So, where are the major and Reveeker likely to be? Oh, and the kaffars?'

'Prisoners would be beyond the kitchen. Out past the service entrance there is a courtyard that leads to the multanial dungeons. The kaffars are located here, adjacent to the throne room.'

'How many guards are we talking about? Patterns, shifts?'

'A guard of around two hundred men. They work in shifts that changeevery four hours, constantly patrolling the grounds in groups of two. The entrances to the throne room and the kaffars are constantly guarded. Servants, like my boy, are not allowed in — it's said the kaffar councillors haven't left that room since they entered it, five years ago.'

There was a pause and Bellina watched Elvgren's brow furrow in concentration.

'We'll need to split into two groups. Enter as the shift changeover takes place at sundown, when there will be the most movement and confusion. I suggest myself, Torkwill and... him,' he said, pointing at Holger, 'head towards the dungeons. If there is need for force it will most likely be there. Bellina, Dargo and you, Gilroy, will attempt to gain access to the kaffars. Dargo here is an excellent cut purse and should be able to secure the keys. A less subtle approach may be needed in the dungeons.'

'Seems you have a flair for this my lord,' Everett said.

'What? Oh... it's just a rough plan, you know...' he replied, trailing off.

'Then all we have to do now is wait till sundown, I suppose?' Bellina said, her stomach tightening.

*

The minutes and hours crept by. Bellina watched the sun descend.

At last, the glowing disc sat just above the horizon.

'We all set?' Gilroy asked.

Bellina nodded but felt like she was just about to stick her head into the mouth of a lion.

Gilroy led them through the streets of the capital, with the sun now almost completely set. Finally, they stood at the end of a wide boulevard.

'Right then,' Torkwill said. 'Me and the wee lass will cast the shedding. From this point on we only communicate with thought. I'm gonna set up a cognopathic network between us, using me as the hub to relay messages. Just *think* if you wanna speak and we all should hear ye. Good luck to us all and peace be.'

'Peace be,' Bellina heard herself mumble with the rest. They would certainly need divine intervention to pull this off.

They stole up to the gates of the palace. Two tall towers reared from the sides, atop a thick wall. An arched enclave receded, huge doors and two guards at its centre.

What do we do? Should we wait? Gilroy said.

Suppose we'll have to, Elvgren replied.

Ach! Bugger this! Torkwill crept towards the doors.

He slipped between the two guards as Bellina held her breath. He banged on them three times, then jumped back. The confused guards looked at each other. They shrugged and began to pull the doors open. Torkwill beckoned to them. Bellina and the rest hurried over and through the doorway. She heard the guards mutter to each other before the doors closed again.

They rushed down a tiled hallway lined with torches. Gilroy had taken the lead and was about to dart into the corridor at the end when he came skidding to a halt, arms outstretched to stop the rest of them.

Guards!

Bellina tried desperately to halt her progress. She came to a stop just behind Gilroy's hand. There was a bang behind her and she turned to see that Dargo had fallen over The small piece of cloth he had tied round the bottom of his peg leg to muffle it's sound, had slipped on the smooth surface.

'Shit!' Dargo said out loud and for a split second he popped into view.

At that moment, the two guards came past the mouth of the hallway. Bellina watched as one of the men passed inches in front of her. He turned his head to the side in a yawn and had a fraction of a second to glimpse Dargo being re-covered by the shedding.

'By the Mother!' he said, looking down the hall.

'What's wrong now?' his companion replied.

'I... I saw someone down there!' He pointed to where Dargo had fallen.

'What?' asked the second guard, peering down the hall.

Bellina's heart hammered against her chest.

'*Silem daloo!* There's nothing there, man. You're probably just tired. Now come, we've got this one last patrol before the night shift comes on.'

The first guard took one last look down the hall before shaking his head and following. '*Vaksa!* This place is haunted I tell you!'

'Oh, be quiet and move your sorry *parool*!'

Bellina listened to them bickering as they continued their patrol.

Sorry, Dargo said, looking sheepish.

Nae worries, wee man, Torkwill replied. *It's you who'd 'ave been keeping the dungeons occupied, not us.*

Gilroy turned to the group. *From here we split up. Lord Elvgren, do you recall the route to the kitchens?*

Got it down pat, old chap!

Right then. Good luck.

Bellina watched Holger, Elvgren and Torkwill split away. Holger turned back and looked at her. He gave a small smile and a nod of his head, then turned back to the others and crept out of sight down the left hallway.

*

The route Elvgren led Holger and Torkwill down was lined with thin columns and supporting arches, each offering a fleeting glimpse of an opulent room beyond. He had committed the crude map, as best he could, to his memory. He just hoped that, whoever this child was, they knew their way around.

The two guards who had almost discovered Dargo were now chatting with a serving girl. She carried a silver platter of exotic fruits and was blushing at whatever was being said. Elvgren and the others paused with their backs to the wall, watching. The chat soon ended and the girl set off towards where the kitchen should be. Elvgren decided to follow her.

He was soon glad that he did. The palace obviously had secret passageways for the servants to pass through without disturbing their betters. The girl pulled at the bottom of a light sconce and a seemingly solid stone wall slid to the side. Elvgren held up his hand to the others, gesturing them to wait. He let a few minutes pass before he moved forward and touched the light fitting the same way as the girl. Again, the door slid open.

The trio scurried inside and found themselves in a stone corridor with only enough room for one person to walk abreast at a time. They shuffled along it, Elvgren fervently praying that no one came the other way. When they exited the corridor, he let his breath out in a sigh of relief, straight into the ear of a passing cook who waved his hand at Elvgren as if batting a fly. The man's large digits slapped him squarely on the nose. Elvgren popped into view to the astonishment of the cook.

'What the *vaksa* is this?' the cook bellowed. All eyes in the kitchen turned towards him.

Elvgren stood stunned. Then he began wailing. 'Please! Please don't take me to the dungeons. I've done nothing wrong!' he said, turning back to Holger and Torkwill. He threw the cognopath a meaningful look and saw the man grasp his idea. The air shimmered and he found himself looking back at the image of the two guards they had previously passed. The Holger guard gave him a shove that Elvgren thought a tad excessive and the newly disguised pair stepped into the kitchen.

'Ah! Another Estrian, eh?' the cook said, jerking his thumb towards a doorway at the back of the room. 'Get him through as quickly as possible, don't want him upsetting the rest of the staff. They feel sorry for 'em for some reason.'

Elvgren held his hands behind his back to pretend they were bound and they strode through the kitchen with purpose. A few of the kitchen staff did look his way. The serving girl from the hall stood staring at him, tears welling in her eyes. *Well, I certainly do have a way with women*, he thought.

They pushed through the servants' entrance and found themselves in a courtyard covered in gravel. Some thirty paces away, a squat, turreted building loomed, a yawning opening with a portcullis for teeth at its centre.

Holger and Torkwill marched Elvgren across the courtyard, gravel crunching noisily. Another pair of guards stood watch on this gate and he tried his best to appear terrified, which wasn't too hard to fake at that point.

Torkwill nodded at one of the guards and jerked his thumb at the gate.

'Alright, Captain, alright. A please wouldn't go amiss,' one of the guards said, pulling a lever and opening the way for them.

Torkwill held Elvgren by the neck and pushed him forward.

'Don't forget you still owe me five denser, Captain!' the guard called after them.

Torkwill replied with a grunt.

They walked down a short, stone passage that led to a winding staircase which they followed all the way down. Elvgren swallowed hard when they stepped out onto the dungeon level. A vast hallway disappeared into the distance. On a stool at the bottom of the staircase, sat a fat turnkey, the means to open the hundreds of cell doors hanging in a great bunch from his waist. There was no one else in sight.

'Fresh meat, eh? Denvad will be hap—'

Torkwill cut the man off by pointing Betsy at his jowly neck, the shroud vanishing.

'What in the name of—' the turnkey started.

'Say one more fucking word without prompt and I'll slit yer stinking throat.'

'I'm afraid he means it, old boy,' said Elvgren. 'Quite unhinged this one. Now be a good chap and tell us where you have my fellow Estrian locked up.'

'Cell... cell fifteen,' he stammered, locating the key on his belt and handing it to Elvgren.

'I must say you've been most accommodating! Don't hit him too hard, Master Burns.'

In reply, Torkwill brought the butt of his sword smartly down on top of the gaoler's head. The man flopped to the floor with a fleshy thump, out cold.

Don't worry Major, we're coming, Elvgren thought as he and the others raced down the hallway. They soon reached cell fifteen. Elvgren fitted the key into the lock and slowly turned it.

47

The smell of charred flesh made Cirona gag. She stared at the bloodied and beaten form of Reveeker as Denvad lifted the brand from him. He whistled a little tune. The man had been carrying out his business for an hour now, taunting Rev with how he took his daughter, telling him of every part of her being he had violated.

'Anything to say yet, Major?' Denvad asked her.

She tried to spit at him but the paltry liquid from her dry mouth merely trickled down her chin pathetically.

'Ah, perhaps another finger then.' Denvad picked up a butcher's cleaver and one of the guards pulled Reveeker's arm in front of him across a table. The stumps of his already missing digits on his right hand quivered and bled. The blade descended with a wet smack and Reveeker's thumb spun across the table.

Cirona bit down on her lip to stop from screaming.

'You know Major, I am growing quite tired. Last chance, tell me your plans by the count of three or I kill him plain and simple. One.'

'I've already told you, you know as much as I do!' she screamed at him.

'Two.'

'Listen, you've had your fun, you twisted little fuck. Leave him be.'

Reveeker's eyes looked at her imploringly. *I'm sorry Rev, I can't*, she thought.

'Three.' Denvad brought the butchers cleaver down in the centre of Reveeker's head. She watched Rev's eyeballs roll back in his skull whilst his body convulsed violently, his jaw moved but he was unable to scream due to the yaksit still covering his mouth.

'You stinking cunt!' she screamed.

'Such language! But I'm afraid you have now run out of options, and it's your turn to join the party.' Denvad walked towards her. Cirona's body heaved with silent sobs. The naffir ran a finger gently across her breasts. 'I never had an Estrian woman. Don't think any of my men have either, probably gonna have them forming a—'

Denvad was cut off by the key turning in the lock and the door flying open.

'What in the name of *vaksa* do you think you're doing? I said I was not to be interrupted!' He screamed in a high-pitched whine.

Two guards stood in the door, looking rather sheepish.

'We are very sorry Colonel, but the Arch Vizier has requested the prisoner be brought down to him in the throne room. He wishes to conduct her interrogation himself,' the guard said.

Denvad's eyes bulged in his skull. He took a deep, shuddering breath, ran his hands through his hair and composed himself. 'Very well. It would seem, Major, I will have to wait until later to enjoy your company.'

*

Bellina and Dargo followed Gilroy as he walked along a corridor, which led them into a foyer. In its centre, sat on the checked, tile floor, was a silver globe of the world. Water trickled slowly over it with a laughing tinkle and pooled in a small square at its base. Hypnotic mosaic patterns flitted across the walls, sometimes forming into swirling text. In the middle of the far wall sat a ludicrously complicated looking door. Concentric circles of glistening bronze, spun inwards. Letters and symbols were etched into the metal shining out in a blaze of aquamarine. In its centre was a small circle with the imprint of a hand pressed into it. Two guards stood in front of it, impassive.

Don't think I'm gonna be nicking the key for this door, Dargo said.

Doesn't look like it, Dar, Bellina said, sighing inwardly. *Do you know anything about getting past this, Gilroy?*

I'm afraid not... hang on a minute... it looks like it's opening!

Bellina saw that he was right. The circles spun and whirled then slid back into the wall on each side. A guard came out carrying what looked like oversized babie's bottles.

Now's our chance. Move, Gilroy said.

The small group crossed the foyer as quickly as they dared, sidestepping around the guards and into the room beyond.

Bellina drew her breath in sharply and forced herself not to cry out. In front of her sat the twelve kaffars. They were seated in a circle around a gigantic engine. The spherical device rose up between them. A window in the sphere allowed Bellina to see a massive deposit of yaksit, the liquid bubbling, broiling and forming strange shapes. Sitting atop the vast engine were two metal prongs, forks of blue light shot between them in a state of great agitation. The kaffars wore robes of black with hundreds of silver stars stitched into them. Attached to their heads were wires that led back to the machine. Bellina looked into their faces. Their eyes were open but misted over and white like those of a blind man. Other than this, the room was empty.

'By the gods, what the hells is that?' Gilroy cried aloud.

The shedding broke around him and Bellina held her breath. Nothing happened. The kaffars didn't move a single muscle. She allowed the shedding to fall from them all, grateful for a brief respite.

'I don't like this, Belle. It all seems a bit too easy to me,' Dargo said, scanning the room.

'Never look a gift horse in the mouth, lad. Lady Ressa, see what you can learn from them.'

Bellina closed her eyes and focused on the kaffars. She was about to try to enter one of their minds when something caught her attention. She studied the kaffars with her cognopathic vision. They, like the one she had done battle with, appeared to her as the same disgusting, poisonous yellow. But what really drew her attention was the hundreds of thin purple lines spooling out from the metal prongs. She attached her mental self to one and followed it. Her mind raced away from the palace, from Burkesh, across the desert to another blistering yellow smear. She let go of the connection in case she alerted the kaffar to her presence and her mind flew back to her body.

'In the name of all that is holy!' she said in a stunned whisper. 'They're connected to every kaffar and naffir in operation.'

'You can stop hiding in there, my little mouse.' A voice called to her from the other room.

Her blood ran cold in her veins as double doors in the wall to her left flew open. She stared into the multanial throne room. Another small fountain trickled in the centre of the room. Behind this, underneath a broad wooden canopy, was a long, low couch. Stretched across it, in a state of perfect ease, was a massive man. He wore billowing trousers of purple silk and atop his head was a large turban with a giant ruby set in the middle of it. To his side, stood a tall, skeletal old man. She had once seen a mummified corpse that one of her father's archaeologists had recovered; its skin was dried and stuck to the bones in a similar fashion to the person she was looking at now. The top of his face was covered in black, his mouth cracked in a terrifying grimace of a smile.

He wore a cloak of ravens' feathers and he clasped a knobbly wooden staff in his hand.

'It certainly is nice to meet you, Lady Ressa. Don't be shy now, come in. The major will be joining us soon,' the old man said.

Damn it all, she thought. Elvgren and the others were down there, in the dungeon. Did they know where the major was? Had they already found her? She focused the image of Elvgren in her mind. *Elvgren, the major may not be in the dungeon. She is being brought to the throne ro—*

*

The cognopathic message shot into Elvgren's mind just as he was pushing the cell door open. Shit. He stumbled into the room. Elvgren felt his body crash into something solid and muscular. There was a pop and he became visible. The guard who he had fallen into turned towards him, the look of bafflement was chased off his face by fury. Behind the guard there was a man of clear Estrian descent chained to the wall.

'Sorry old boy, wrong room!' Elvgren said, he scrambled back out the door and pulled it shut.

'Throne room. Cirona. Go, now!' he called to Torkwill and Holger.

The air around them shimmered and popped and they too became visible as they sprinted back to the stairs.

He raced to catch up with them. Behind him, the door flew open and he heard feet chasing after them. Elvgren didn't even dare to look. He fixed his eye on the spiral stairs and chased after Holger's back. He took the stairs two at a time, hearing Torkwill engaging the guards at the entrance. He was just about to set foot on the landing when his foot slipped. 'Help!' he called out. Holger turned towards him. The last thing Elvgren saw before he fell was the man's hand stretched towards him.

48

'That's quite enough of that!' the old man said. He reached out his hand and the control conduit tore from Bellina's wrist and went spinning through the air towards him. At the same time there was a bang and a concealed door opened: Cirona was marched into the room, a ballistol aimed at her head.

Bellina ran into the throne room, Dargo and Gilroy just behind her. She tried to make her way to Cirona but her body froze.

'Tut, tut! Not so fast young lady. We have been most anxious to meet you all and I'm sure the rest of your little party will find its way here soon enough. Now allow me to introduce myself. I am Arch Vizier Marmossa and this is His Glorious Majesty, the Grand Multan Kurkeshi.'

The man on the couch nodded his head lazily.

'I hope the colonel wasn't too rough with you or former Captain Reveeker?' Marmossa said.

'Fuck you.' Cirona spat back at him.

'My dear Major! How unrefined.' Marmossa said stretching out his left hand.

Bellina watched the major grab at her throat. It appeared as if she was grappling with an unseen hand. Cirona was lifted into the air and floated towards the Arch Vizier where she was dumped on the floor before him.

'Now, Major Bouchard, I believe your interrogation was not quite complete.'

*

Elvgren felt his head bounce off one of the stone steps and he saw stars. His body rolled and tumbled awkwardly backwards, each step playing a symphony of pain on his bones. He felt his body smash into the two guards who had been chasing him and they fell back in a tangle of limbs. He hit the stone floor hard and groaned. Pulling himself to his feet, he begged the world to stop spinning. *That fucking Narvglander tried to kill me*, he thought. Anger like none he had ever known before burst up from his gut. He drew his sword from his side and stuck it into the neck of one of the guards lying prone on the floor. The skull of the other lay smashed open, dark blood forming a macabre puddle. He flew up the stairs faster than he thought possible. Rushing past the gate, he saw that Torkwill had dispatched the two guards there. He sprinted across the gravel courtyard and burst into the kitchen, hollering and whooping, waving his sword above his head. A blur of animalistic rage filled his mind as he rushed past the kitchen staff who had to scramble to get out of his way.

He banged into the walls of the secret corridor, trying to speed along it. Pulling a lever at the side of the concealed door, it slid open. He rushed forward, feet slipping on the smooth tiles, and fell to his knees with a crash. Up ahead, he saw two Burkeshi guards turn into Torkwill and Holger. The younger man stared back at him with terror in his eyes.

'Bet you didn't think you'd see me again, did you, you fucking peasant!' he screamed. Two real guards rushed him from the side. From his position on the floor, he slashed at their shins and they both fell to the floor.

'You told me he fell to his death!' Torkwill said to Holger.

There was no time to respond. His eyes were fixed on Elvgren as the young lord came rushing towards him. Holger sidestepped at the last second and tried to grab his assailant. Elvgren slipped free from his grasp and stood ready in a fighting stance.

'Listen to me! I—' Holger began.

'Enough of your lies! You pushed me!' Elvgren screamed.

A look of confusion passed across Holger's face. 'No! I tried to grab you but I couldn't reach. I would never do something like that, even though I hate your fucking guts!'

Holger wore a look of complete sincerity on his face. Elvgren didn't know what to make of it. All he had seen was the arm thrust towards him and he had assumed the worst. He hesitated.

'Torkwill can you read his mind, see if he speaks the truth?'

'Aye, do ye agree lad?' Torkwill said, looking at Holger.

'Of course,' he replied.

The cognopath focused his gaze on Holger. His look went from concentration to confusion before finally settling on surprise. 'I... cannae do it. I can't read his thoughts,' he said, fixing a steely glare on

Holger.

'Why the hells not?'

Torkwill slowly turned his head towards Elvgren. 'There is only one explanation but I think it will keep for another time. We need to get to that throne room. Even though I can't read his mind, I believe him. We need to stay together here!'

Elvgren reluctantly nodded and they set off.

*

Cirona stared up at the walking corpse that was Arch Vizier Marmossa. He stared back. It seemed like his gaze bore into her very soul. 'I've got nothing to say to you. I'm no traitor,' she said.

'How unfortunate. Your daughter is such a pretty, young thing. It would be a shame if something were to happen to her,' Marmossa said.

'You... what are you saying?'

'Your daughter. The one that was taken from you. We know where she is. A life is such a fragile thing, like a flame,' Marmossa said. He clicked his fingers and a blob of yaksit caught fire on his fingertip. 'One moment there, the next...' He waved his other hand over it snuffing out the flame.

'You're lying, you know nothing!'

'Oh really?'

His eyes flashed. Then before her she saw a young girl with Trafford's eyes and Cirona's nose. She was running through a garden. A man came into view, looming ominously behind the vision of her daughter.

'Are you ready to speak now?' Marmossa asked softly.

She closed her eyes and felt tears streaming down her cheeks. Cirona thought of Rev's face when the cleaver bit into his skull. She thought of Trafford lying in her arms a trickle of blood running from a dot above his heart. She thought of Bellina and the pain the words she was about to speak would cause her.

'The... the...'

'Yes, out with it woman. What did the Lord Chancellor really send you here to do.'

'What do you mean? Leave my father out of this,' Bellina screamed.

'He's not your father,' Cirona said flatly, her eyes staring at the tiled floor.

'Wha... what are you saying, Major?'

'He's not you father. You were brought to him from the School of Cognometry. He... My lady, I would never have let this come to pass but they have my daughter. Your father instructed me to get you an audience with Kurkeshi and this *thing*. He managed to get the key to your power restraints from the Emperor and told me to use it once we were in range..'

'By the gods. A lass as powerful as this one!' cried Torkwill from the back of the room. 'If ye took her restraints off she could die, taking everyone for miles with her!'

Cirona turned her head to see Torkwill, Elvgren and Holger panting in the doorway. She dared a look at Bellina and felt her heart break. The girl was slumped to her knees on the floor. Tears cascaded down her cheeks, her lips slightly parted.

'Ho ho,' said Marmossa, 'I see now what kind of man I am dealing with. He is cut from a cloth like myself. Sacrifice the girl he's loved and raised as his daughter, just to be rid of the threat from us. And where is the key to her restraint now, Major?'

'It's in my pocket.'

One of the guards who had brought Cirona in removed the key from her person. Suddenly, he let out a startled cry and she saw the key fly through the air into Torkwill's hands.

'Get him, you fools!' Marmossa hissed.

The guards rushed across the room. Elvgren dived at them and sent them colliding into Torkwill. The key leapt from his hand and landed on the tiles spinning towards Bellina.

*

The girl sat on the floor dimly aware of the tiny shining thing spinning towards her. She stretched her hand out and picked it up. She realised it was a key.

'Stop everybody! Girl, put the key down.'

The voice of the Arch Vizier seemed to call to her from another world. Bellina's mind was focused on the words she had just heard — her father wasn't her father. He had sent her here to die. Anger and pain shot through her. What should she do? In her hand, she held the key to ending the Burkeshi ambitions. *Gods, I don't want to die*, she thought.

At that moment, her mind slipped away. She didn't think of her home or the man she had called father. She didn't think of the Estrian people, their children laughing and playing in the streets. Instead she thought of her favourite place in the whole world. The little garden she had tended at the back of the grounds of her home. Bellina saw it all before her as if she was really there. The hedgerows, the roses, the daffodils and tulips. The little stream that ran through it, a wooden bridge spanning a gap you could jump across. Then she thought of the boots of Burkeshi soldiers violating that haven. Trampling it underfoot, that and everything else she loved in the world. She knew what she had to do.

Bellina moved the key towards the small lock on her power restraints. She heard Marmossa hiss and a force battled against her hand. Willing herself against it, she pushed the key into the lock. A tear rolled down her cheek as she turned it.

The restraint fell from her wrist with a gentle tinkle, then pain rushed through her body, greater than any she had ever known before. The thoughts of all the people for miles around burst through her mind. Bellina screamed and prayed for it to end. It felt like every atom in her body was trying to pull free. Every nerve of her body was on fire with agony. There was a sound like thunder.

Then nothing.

*

Cirona's eyes blinked open. A white light filled her vision, distorted, like looking through a rain streaked window. *Am I dead? Is this the Veil?* Then the ceiling of the multanial throne room came into focus. *I'm alive. By the gods, I'm alive!*

She pulled herself to her feet and looked around. The guards lay at her feet, a bloody, pink substance oozing from their ears. Marmossa and Kurkeshi lay in front of her in a similar state. Cirona turned and saw Bellina lying on the floor. A surge of emotion coursed through her body which prompted her to rush across the floor to the girl, stumbling over her feet. She crouched down beside Bellina's lifeless form — she looked so frail and cold. Tears fell again from Cirona's eyes and onto the girl's face. The major closed her eyes and let the sobs come.

'It's unbefitting for an officer of the Estrian Empire to cry.'

Cirona looked down and saw Bellina staring up at her. She wrapped her arms around the girl and held her tightly.

'Fuck me, it worked.'

Torkwill's voice came from behind her. Cirona turned her head and saw the cognopath coming towards her; Elvgren was helping Dargo to a sitting position, and Gilroy was being assisted by Holger.

'How did you...?' Bellina struggled to say.

'Dinnae say another word lass. Ye were brilliant. You'd have made your mother proud.'

'My mother?'

'We'll talk more about it later, but I've got a few suspicions about who you really are.' Torkwill said as Bellina's head lapsed back again.

'What did you do, Torkwill?' Cirona asked.

'It was a close thing but when she took off her restraint I threw up a shield around us and tried to suppress her power. I damn near shit me pants with the effort but I managed to knock her out before she killed us all. Get that restraint back on her wrist sharpish though, I'm still trying to suppress her now, even though she's virtually staring into the Void.'

Cirona picked up the ornate power restraint and clipped it gently back onto the young woman's arm.

'I think we should leave.' Gilroy called to them.

Cirona scooped Bellina into her arms and lifted her gently from the floor.

*

It felt like her body belonged to another person. Bellina floated along in the arms of the major. She saw Elvgren helping Dargo limp out of the room, Torkwill smiling at her side. Gilroy looked as if he'd soiled himself and was clinging to Holger for support. She was carried through the room with the twelve kaffars and saw that their brains were trickling from their ears. *My father will be happy*, she thought, and then realised her mistake.

They walked through the palace and out into the street, every person they passed was dead. Men, women, children. Bellina turned her face into Cirona's bosom, not wanting to see, feeling sick to her stomach. *I did this*, she thought. *He raised me to do this.*

'What do we do now?' Cirona asked her.

'We go and see my father' Bellina replied.

Epilogue

The multanial throne room stood silent, the bodies of the dead nothing but black puddles. The only two living people slid into view, seated on the couch.

Grand Multan Kurkeshi stood up in agitation and strode into the room containing the kaffars. Marmossa's voice reached him from the throne room.

'My, my, she certainly is a powerful little thing, isn't she?'

'Yes. It would seem the entire kaffar twelve have their brains oozing from their ears. Was this whole pantomime worth it, Marmossa?' Kurkeshi said, striding back into the throne room.

'Oh yes. Quite,' the old man replied with a smile.

'Damn it all, Marmossa. Thousands could be dead!'

'Yes, but now every Burkeshi will scream for vengeance. These people will be the sacrifice that glues this nation together like nothing before. I think it may be time to speed up our plans. Once the Estrian relic is in my hands, I will be able to summon rain for the whole of Burkesh. Thousands dead, yes, but to save millions. And as for the twelve, they can be replaced.' Marmossa strode across the room and grabbed the Grand Multan's arms. 'How much have we already sacrificed? Do not falter now.'

Kurkeshi paused, taking in his advisor's words. 'Very well. But why let the girl and her friends live?'

'Ah, my naive lord. You're still the little boy I met all those years ago, aren't you? I let them live because today we have created a terrible and subtle weapon. We have set the most powerful cognopath in history after the most powerful man in the Estrian Empire. A weapon with intimate knowledge of the Lord Chancellor.' Marmossa stopped and turned his eyes to the heavens. 'We have set another cog turning in the Machine of Infinity. Who knows what mayhem it will reap?' The old man finished with his arms outstretched.

Kurkeshi looked at him with a face full of reverence. 'As always your perception and forethought astound me.'

'You flatter me, my lord. But I am merely an interpreter for Mother

Darkness, the one who gave birth to all. Glory be to Her!'

'Glory be. Glory be indeed,' agreed Kurkeshi. 'Glory be to Her.'

Lightning Source UK Ltd.
Milton Keynes UK
UKOW08f2218020617
302550UK00002B/433/P